MW00721406

# FIREBRAND

# Mary Walz

**RCN Media Publishing**

# Firebrand by Mary Walz © 2022 by RCN Media

**First Edition: April 2022**

RCN Media was founded in 2015 by Colton Nelson. It is a publishing company for adult, young adult and children's books. The RCN Media logo is © 2015 by Colton Nelson & RCN Media. If you require bulk orders of an issue with an RCN Media contact, feel free to contact them with the info below. Special discounts are available on quantity purchases by corporations, associations, and others. For details, contact the publisher at the email address below.

Artwork created and adapted by Rowan Smith & Colton Nelson.

Map image © 2022 by RCN Media, all rights reserved. Map created by Rowan Smith.

Colton Nelson is the promoter for this book. For any comments or to contact the author, you can reach them through him (contact below), or you can contact RCN Media.

Contact:
www.rcn.media
(250) 206 0356
nelsoncolton16@gmail.com (subject: "Firebrand")

Also available as an eBook & Audiobook

1   3   5   7   9   0   2   4   6   8

ISBN Paperback: 978-1-989898-87-1

In loving memory of my grandfather, Ted Powell, who loved reading my stories but passed on before he could finish this one. Thank you for teaching me to love big words. I miss you.

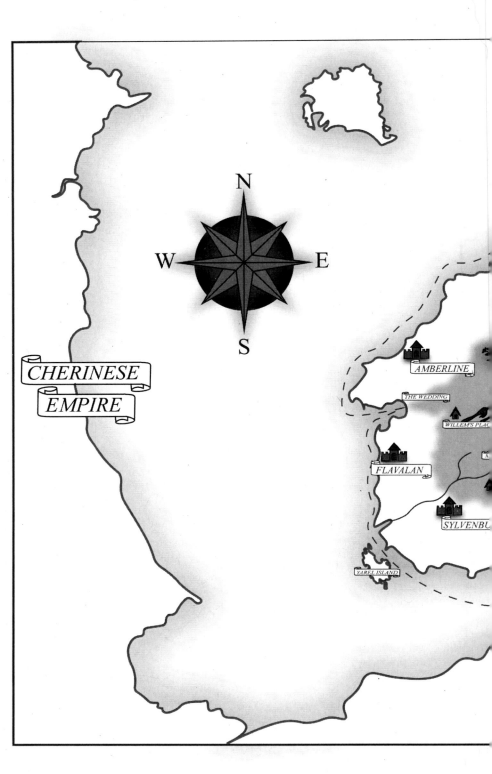

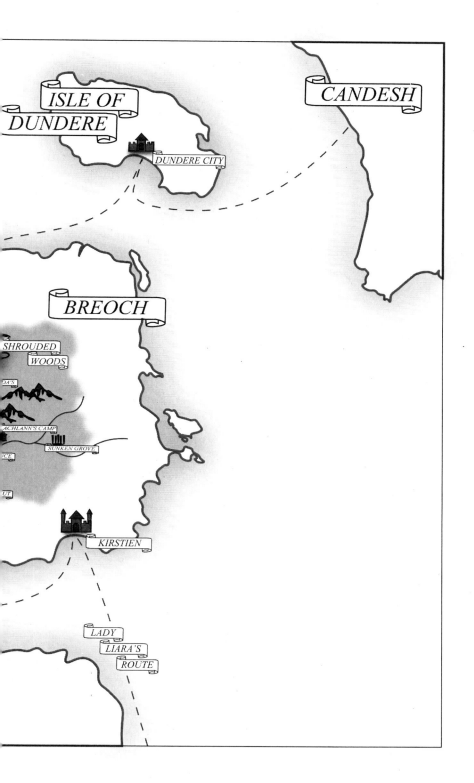

# Chapter One

**BANISHING DAY WAS** my least favourite day of the year.

I might have liked it more if I was living at home with my family—if I *had* a family, that is. Growing up, I'd always heard stories of families spending their Banishing Day visiting the country or the seaside, holding extravagant tea parties at their homes, or exchanging gifts at large get-togethers. And those things sounded nice to me.

Here at Sylvenburgh Academy, though, Banishing Day traditions followed a certain sequence of events, most of which I hated. That morning, as always, I'd been sorted into a team of kids who didn't like me, and as always, we'd spent the day engaged in silly physical competitions—tug of war and ball toss and archery and three-legged races. And as always, I'd been the weak link on my team, my gangly limbs and clumsy feet slowing us down, and the others in my group resented me even more than usual by the time the activities were done.

The one good thing about Banishing Day was the food, and now I sat in the dining hall at one end of a long table, dressed in clean, though uncomfortable, clothes. My dress was too small; the sleeves rode partway up my wrists, and folds of the stiff blue fabric pressed into my armpits and waist, as if demanding that I shrink back to my younger self. But Banishing Day dinner traditions demanded my best clothing, so I would wear the dress for the remainder of the day. Neither Trina nor I had taken the time to style our hair or put on makeup, though; Trina was unable to, and I couldn't be bothered to preen and fuss like most of the girls my age. So we'd beaten the rest of the students to the dining hall and secured some of the best seats at our table.

Trina shifted next to me, leaning her head back and inhaling the aroma of cooking food, her hair falling in perfect black waves around her shoulders. "Tell me about the colours, Saray," she said.

I looked around our enormous, high-ceilinged dining hall, which would later tonight become a dance hall. "Well, there's paper lanterns hanging from the ceiling; most of them are red this year, same as the tablecloths. And they've hung purple and gold fabric on the walls."

"Mmm," she said wistfully. "I miss purple. It was my favourite."

"You tell me that every time I mention it."

"Because it's true." She sighed. "The decorations sound lovely. I'm sure the dancing will be splendid too. I wish I could go."

"No one's stopping you," I replied, knowing exactly what her response would be.

"No one would want to dance with the blind girl," she answered. "I'd fall all over the place and make a fool of myself. It'd be a disaster." Her shoulders drooped, a faint blush colouring her tawny skin. Then she straightened up and grinned at me. "You could go to the dance, though. You *should* go to the dance. You shouldn't be spending all your time with a thirteen-year-old kid." Her voice had a bossy tone to it.

I snorted. "You know I'm not welcome. And I don't think the clumsy orphaned bookworm is any more likely to get dances than the blind girl."

She shrugged. "The others might be friendly to you if you spent more time with them, you know. They were nice enough to Carrie, and she was an orphan like us."

"They were only nice to Carrie because she was pretty," I argued. "I mean, the girl could walk into class five minutes after getting out of bed and still look like a princess. You should have seen her at her graduation last year; I swear the boys' eyes were falling out of their heads. Whereas me…" I grimaced and tugged at a strand of unruly red hair. "Sometimes I think the only reason you stick with me is because you can't see me."

"That's not true, and you know it," she huffed. "I'm sure you're lovely. At least you can look in a mirror and decide to do something about how you look."

"I can only do so much," I argued. "But it doesn't matter; I don't want to go to the dance anyway. I'd rather stay in our room and read." I glanced down at the book in my lap. "Books are better than people. Well, most people."

The students were beginning to trickle into the dining hall now, disturbing our quiet. The girls moved in packs, giggling, their hair done up in curls and jewels sparkling on their throats and ears. Several boys marched into the room, yelling and cheering, and I recognized them as members of Team Kirstein, this year's winners of the Banishing Day Games. Our table filled up slowly with the rest of Team Flavalan; like Team Kirstein, we were named after one of Breoch's major ports. The teachers randomly picked the teams every Banishing Day, we were told, but somehow each team always had an equal assortment of ages represented, from the giggly, pimple-faced kids a year below Trina to eighteen-year-old boys who already shaved. Our team captain, Jack, was one of those boys, and he met everyone at the table with a wide, obviously forced smile. No one was thrilled to be part of Team Flavalan today. A few of the kids threw glares in my direction, no doubt recalling my fall on the obstacle course and the fact that I hadn't been able to figure out how to nock an arrow during the archery competition. The two seats next to me were taken by girls in my grade, Lizzie and Becky. They sneered at me; I returned the gesture.

On the large stage that overlooked the dining hall, Miss Cockle, the school principal, was arranging her papers. I glanced at her and then leaned over to Trina. "Miss Cockle is wearing a really ugly brown dress, with a matching ugly brown hat," I whispered. "She looks like a giant mushroom." We both giggled at my description, and Lizzie and Becky rolled their eyes at us. I clamped my mouth shut just as Miss Cockle straightened up, giving Trina a nudge with my elbow to signify she should do the same. The dining hall fell silent; we all knew that in order to partake in the coming feast, we first needed to sit through the annual Banishing Day Storytelling. Miss Cockle looked over the tables of students with her sharp grey eyes and began to speak.

3

"Students and staff of Sylvenburgh Academy," she said in her shrill voice, "welcome to the annual Banishing Day feast! Before we eat and exchange gifts, we will pause to remember the events of the first Banishing Day forty-eight years ago, when our great nation of Breoch was freed from the tyranny of magic."

She began to talk at length about the significance of the holiday and how lucky we children were to be living in the current day and age. I squirmed in my seat and toyed with the fabric of my dress, trying to ignore the hollow feeling in my stomach and the tantalizing aroma of roasting meat and garlic. I sighed with relief when she finished her monologue by saying that this year, our vice principal Mr. Jeffries would be telling the story of the Banishing. Mr. Jeffries would make it concise, I knew, instead of turning it into one of the long-winded diatribes that Miss Cockle was renowned for.

I watched as Mr. Jeffries made his way up to the podium. Unlike Miss Cockle, he was dressed simply, in his classic black top hat and crisp white shirt. His brown mustache was impeccably waxed, and as he took the podium, he surveyed the room with a pair of keen, deep-set brown eyes. Mr. Jeffries was my history teacher as well as the school's vice principal, and even though he was just as strict as Miss Cockle, everyone knew he was one of the better storytellers at Sylvenburgh Academy. A group of girls at the Kirstein table began giggling; Mr. Jeffries silenced them with an all-too-familiar glare before beginning to speak.

I felt my mind begin to wander as Mr. Jeffries started telling us the familiar story of the events leading up to the Banishing, the punishment for those who did not comply, and its outcome. *Everyone knows this story; I don't see why they feel the need to retell it every year.* My stomach was beginning to rumble audibly as Miss Cockle took the podium once again to make a few closing remarks. I noticed that her mushroom-cap hat had gone slightly askew, and I giggled and informed Trina of what I saw.

It felt like another hour before she stepped off the stage to polite, forced applause from the student body, and the kitchen workers began to circulate the room with carts of food. Team Kirstein was served first, followed by the second- and third-placed teams. We would be served second last, in accordance with our placement in the games. We would also be second-to-last when it came to picking our first dance partners later that evening; I'm fairly certain this was the reason Lizzie and Becky had been throwing disgusted looks my way ever since we'd sat down.

The food finally arrived, and I dug in eagerly, securing plates for Trina and me before the rest of the team could devour everything. I filled our plates with roast beef, potato pancakes, meat pies, and vegetables in a spicy bean sauce. Then I handed Trina her plate and began to eat as the others served themselves. I grinned as I noticed a chubby blond boy from the year below me stuffing rolls into the pockets of his trousers.

"Hey! Where'd all the bread go?" a boy demanded as the blond boy pocketed another roll.

"Fredrick's taking them!" another boy said, pointing at him.

Frederick blushed, planting his arms firmly against his sides to cover his bulging pockets. "Am not."

"Well then maybe you're making them disappear by magic," the first boy suggested. "Are you a witch, Freddie? Do we need to turn you into a krossemage?" He grabbed his dinner knife and brandished it, grinning. "Seems like a fitting thing to do on Banishing Day." I glanced around nervously, looking for a teacher to come end the teasing.

"Do it, Mickey!" the second boy chimed in, his mouth full of potatoes.

A boy in my grade named Albert let out a nervous laugh. "Keep it down you two, or you'll end up bringing the wrath of The Mustache down on our table." A group of younger kids snickered at his nickname for Mr. Jeffries.

"Oh, I'm sure The Mustache would want to know if we had a hildakin at our table," Mickey's friend retorted.

Beside me, Becky gasped. "A what?" asked one of the younger kids.

"A hildakin. An elfieblood. A *witch*." Mickey's friend smirked. "All the things that Fredrick is." He turned back to Frederick. "Once Mickey's done with you, you can go clean the school with Walter! You'd like that, wouldn't you?" Next to me, Becky and Lizzie began to laugh, clearly enjoying the show. I glanced at Jack; he rolled his eyes at the younger boys and ignored their theatrics, turning instead to flirt with the blond girl on his right.

"Hey, stop it!" I exclaimed, jumping to my feet. "This isn't funny anymore!"

Everyone ignored me. I watched in horror as the first boy—Mickey—stood up and moved towards Frederick. Grabbing Frederick's right hand, he pinned it to the table and let his knife hover over his wrist. I spotted Mr. Jeffries standing up a few tables away, but before I could call him over, Frederick let out a panicked screech that made the dining room go quiet. Mr. Jeffries whirled around; his dark eyes set on our table.

"What exactly is happening over here?" he demanded, striding over.

Mickey let go of Frederick, whose eyes were brimming with tears. "They…they were saying I'm a witch," Frederick told Mr. Jeffries, emptying his pockets of several squished rolls as he spoke. "He was going to turn me into a krossemage."

"I was joking!" Mickey protested. "You can't *actually* cut off someone's hand—or cut out their tongue for that matter—with a knife like this." He gestured to his dinner knife.

Mr. Jeffries' eyes narrowed. "Even so, you'll be coming with me," he said sternly. "You know better than to joke about such things."

The other boy who'd been bullying Frederick stuck out his tongue at him as Mickey was led away. "We should've cut your tongue out first so you couldn't tattle."

Dinner continued without any more incidents, and when dessert was served, it was accompanied by a basket for each child containing brightly wrapped gifts. The students at my table hollered and cheered as they opened up their packages to find expensive toys and goodies from their parents. Trina's and my baskets were provided by Lacey, our dorm mother, who was getting quite good at buying us presents. My basket contained new boots—which I was sorely in need of—as well as a fiction book and some candy. Trina's also had clothing and candy, along with a small pipe flute. On my other side, Lizzie examined the pair of designer earrings in her basket. "These are lovely," she exclaimed to Becky. "It's so nice of our *parents* to send us these things, don't you think?" I didn't miss the glance she threw at Trina and me.

"Oh, yes," Becky agreed, grinning wickedly. "Did you know that my parents are taking me to the seaside next week? We're so lucky to have such generous families! Don't you think, Trina?"

"Don't you bring her into this!" I snapped, my face flushing hot.

Lizzie turned to face me. "All right then, Saray. Don't *you* think our parents are lovely for giving us these gifts?"

I glared at her. "I doubt your parents would even get you presents if they knew what a snobby little brat you can be," I muttered.

Lizzie's eyes popped at my choice of words. "Did you hear what she just called me?" she said, looking around the table. The boys, minus Frederick, all nodded gleefully. "I could get you detention for talking to me that way."

"Go ahead, tell a teacher," I challenged her. "Tell all the teachers. Tell them that you were picking on the orphans over things they can't control!" My voice rose, and students at several nearby tables were watching us. I felt familiar heat on my hands, and I balled them into fists and shoved them under my legs, my anger suddenly mingled with fear. *No. Not now.*

"Saray." Trina put her hand on my arm. "It's all right. Let's just get our things and leave."

I stood up in a huff, fists still balled. "This," I said to Trina, "is why books are better than people." I tossed the table full of students one last glare and then gathered my gifts and stormed out of the dining room, Trina in tow.

As soon as I cleared the doors, I broke away from Trina and began to run. I flew down the long, high-ceilinged halls, hot tears brimming in my eyes. By the time I reached the grand entry hall, with its curved staircases and massive chandelier, I could barely see through my tears. And perhaps that's why I collided with Walter.

I hit him head-on and then stumbled backwards, my books and boots and candy flying from my basket and landing all over the polished wood floor. I stared at the mess, momentarily dazed, and then looked at Walter.

Walter had dropped his broom when I ran into him, but he was ignoring it in favour of picking up my fallen books, placing them in the crook of his maimed arm, his sleeve hanging loosely where the stump of his right forearm ended. I grabbed my basket and began scrambling around on the floor, collecting pieces of candy, my cheeks burning.

"What happened?" Trina had just arrived in the foyer; her pace somewhat slowed by having to navigate the halls using only her cane. Now she was standing in the doorway, head cocked.

"It's fine. I just ran into Walter and dropped my basket," I mumbled. The door to Mr. Jeffries' office was open, and I threw a nervous glance in its direction, wondering if I was going to earn a lecture for leaving dinner early.

"Oh." Trina turned and stared vaguely in the direction of where Walter was working. "Hi Walter," she chirped. Trina was one of the only students who was always kind to our janitor.

Walter let out his strange, throaty chuckle, the only way he could communicate with Trina, and I tried not to cringe. He'd collected all my books and my boots and was standing over me. I finished picking up my candy, got to my feet and took my gifts from him. "Thanks," I muttered.

Walter nodded and picked up his broom and then turned back to me and cocked his head. I didn't miss the concern in his dark eyes, but any true gratitude I might have felt was overshadowed by a darker emotion as I looked at the rest of his face. Walter couldn't have been much older than Mr. Jeffries; his hair was still dark, save for a few glints of grey in his beard, but his face was prematurely lined from years of hardship, his cheeks oddly sunken, his shoulders bent.

Removal of the right hand and tongue and a lifetime of hard labour was the sentence given to offending magic users, Mr. Jeffries had reminded us in his speech. The amputations kept them from casting, though I only partially understood how this worked. The second part of their sentence, hard labour, was a source of confusion for me. Rumour had it that most krossemages were sold to the wealthy as slaves, but I'd never heard any talk from my rich classmates about their families owning one. Walter, for whatever reason, had been bought by the school and had been a fixture here for as long as I could remember. *Krossemage*, I'd learned in history class, meant *shattered mage* in Cherinese. It was a fitting description.

Now looking up at him, my stomach knotted, and I tried not to shudder. "I'm fine," I told him, annoyance creeping into my voice. "Thanks for helping me, I should go." Then I turned and fled the entryway, trying not to think about Walter's sad eyes or the things that had happened to make him who he was.

*          *

My stomach was still in knots two hours later. After we'd reached our room, Trina spent the rest of the evening amusing herself with her pipe, and I'd crawled into bed and tried, and failed, to read my new book. My mind roiled with questions, the same questions that I'd had since I learned six years ago that my parents weren't likely actually dead. True orphans were rare at our school, Carrie had told me; most of us were actually unwanted children whose parents had had the decency and wealth to leave us somewhere we'd be well cared for, instead of abandoning us to the streets or to one of the city's overcrowded orphanages. Most of the other kids knew this too, she explained, and this was why they were so cruel to us.

Trina's breathing had begun to even out, and I stared at the flickering candles, then at my hands, remembering how hard I'd had to fight the burning on my palms earlier. *I need to get this under control.* And the only way to do that, I figured, was through practice.

My gaze returned to the candles. "*Flamina finita,*" I whispered the familiar string of syllables as I willed the candles in the room to go out. All obeyed without hesitation. I glanced over to make sure Trina was definitely asleep and then spoke another phrase. "*Nalalae rainarae flamina.*" I watched as a small, fist-sized ball of flame appeared in front of me. I turned it over and over in the air, caused it to grow and shrink a few times, then extinguished it with the first set of words I'd used.

This, of course, was the other reason I hated Banishing Day.

I lay back down, my thoughts returning to my parents once again. *Maybe they abandoned me because they* knew. My talents hadn't shown up until I was eleven, but I had to wonder if perhaps they had looked down at their infant daughter and somehow seen what she would become, a freak who could control flame.

Maybe I was dangerous, and that was the real reason I was an orphan.

# Chapter Two

**THE NEXT DAY** was exceptionally warm for late spring. I spent most of the morning absorbed in my book, and after lunch and chores, Trina and I decided to visit our hideout—the flat, terraced rooftop of a tower in a rarely used wing of the school. We settled against the stone walls, enjoying the sun on our faces and the absence of other students. After a few minutes, a robin landed between us and began to wander towards Trina. It tottered onto the hem of her dress, and she reached down and stroked its feathers. I grinned as I watched; I'd never quite understood why animals liked Trina so much. The robin flew away after a minute or two, and she let out a sigh and lay back on the stonework, her hands behind her head. "I'm glad we found this place. It's so *quiet*."

I chuckled. "Me too. I like having a place where none of *them* can find us." I stood up and looked over the low stone walls that surrounded us; this place had a wonderful view of Sylvenburgh. Ours was the second largest city in the small island kingdom of Breoch, and it stretched out on all sides of the school, mostly little stone houses and shops, and, out past the city walls, farmers' fields. An occasional spire or tall building stood out among the houses—the mayor's house, another school, a stately row of mansions. The city centre, which sat a little north of us, was the only exception; its few blocks were crammed with apartment homes stacked above busy shops and bustling taverns. Far beyond the city to the south, barely visible from this vantage point, was the ocean; to the north sat the impossibly tall trees of the Shrouded Woods. Life at Sylvenburgh Academy rarely allowed for its students to venture outside its walls, save for small trips to the bakery down the road to buy warm bread and cookies and a yearly organized trip to the fair, when it came to town. In all my years here, I'd only been through downtown three times and had never been outside the city walls or to the ocean. Sylvenburgh Academy aimed to protect its students from the hardships of city life, but most days this place felt like a prison, not a sanctuary. One day, I promised myself, I would break free.

I gazed at the cluster of mansions and the familiar ache returned, the thought that was always just under the surface of my conscious mind working its way to the forefront. "I wonder if my parents live in one of those mansions," I mused. "I mean, they'd have to be rich to send me here, right?"

"Maybe you could go look for them, once you've finished school," Trina suggested.

I snorted. "How, exactly? Am I supposed to wander the streets, asking if there's someone out there with the last name McAllister who gave up a child?"

Trina shrugged. "There can't be many McAllisters in those mansions you're talking about."

"Maybe not. But even so…" I sighed and trailed off.

"What, you don't want to find them?" She looked directly at me with her wide brown eyes as she spoke, an ability of hers that sometimes caught me off guard. "I'd give the world to see my mother again."

"Yes, but you actually remember her," I countered. "And you've told me that she sent you here for a good reason. I don't know why I'm here. I mean, if my parents didn't care enough to keep me, why would I go looking for them?" I grimaced, trying to ignore the hollow ache in my chest.

The screech of a bird distracted me from my woes, and I glanced up to see a large white-tailed hawk fly over us, unusually low. "That's a massive hawk," I observed, staring at it.

"I heard it, it sounds close," Trina said.

I watched as the hawk alighted in a tree near the edge of the school property. A large cloud of smoke in the same area caught my eye. "Looks like they're having a bonfire today," I informed Trina.

"Figures," she replied, sitting up. Bonfires were common on holiday weekends; they were always lively events, with teachers and occasionally older students telling stories and sharing songs and performances. "I love bonfires," Trina went on. "Can we go?"

I watched the slow trickle of students making their way toward the fire pit. In honesty, I was perfectly happy up here in the tower, with the sunshine and my book for company. But I knew Trina wouldn't be able to make it to the bonfire unaccompanied. "Give me half an hour," I said. "I just want to read a chapter or two. Then we can go."

"All right," she replied, lying back down. I smiled, sat down with my back against the tower wall, and cracked open my book.

The bonfire was already in full swing when we arrived. Mr. Shaar, a tall, bespectacled teacher with perpetually rosy cheeks, was standing in front of the assembled students, talking. *No doubt about his time in the Shrouded Woods.* Mr. Shaar had been chased into the woods by bullies as a youth and had spent nearly three days lost in their depths. He was known among the student body for his Shrouded Woods tales.

"I was exhausted from my earlier encounter with the bear," Mr. Shaar was saying as Trina and I sat down. "But I forced myself to keep going, until I found shelter in a little cave near a stream. I settled down in there, and I was nearly asleep when I heard footsteps.

"I got up and peered out of my cave to see five men dressed in strange clothes. I called to them for help, and they turned to me, and that's when I realized that they might not be friendly. They were all armed, and their faces were hard.

"I was terrified, but I managed to tell them that I was lost and was trying to find my way out of the woods. One of them stepped forward and looked down at me with cold blue eyes. 'A city boy,' he snickered as he pulled out a knife." Mr. Shaar paused and looked over the assembled students. "And I think that's enough for today."

The group let out a collective breath, and a few students groaned and begged him to continue. He smiled and gave us a small bow, then took a seat as another pair of performers stood. I made a face. *It's Lizzie.* The young man with her, a newer student whose name I didn't know, was holding a drum and was presumably going to be providing music for her.

I watched as they made their way to the centre of the circle. The young man seated himself on a log and put the drum between his knees and began to pound out a steady rhythm. Lizzie started to dance slowly, swaying her hips in a manner that had all the older boys gawking and some of the girls glaring. She lifted an arm above her head, twirled slowly, and returned to the hip maneuvers. I giggled and described the scene to Trina. *What a show-off.* I rolled my eyes as I watched Lizzie move back and forth, close to the fire, then away from it, then back again.

Up in the trees, the hawk let out a shriek, causing me, and all the other students, including Lizzie, to look up.

And that's when her skirt caught fire.

How exactly it happened—whether the hawk was responsible for it or not—I wasn't quite certain. All I knew was that suddenly her skirt was ablaze, and she was screaming. A few of the teachers ran towards her. "Drop to the ground!" someone yelled from behind me.

"What's happening?" Trina asked.

"Lizzie's skirt is on fire!" I jumped to my feet and stared, frozen, as the orange and yellow flames moved closer and closer to her body.

Then, without my consent, my right arm lifted and words formed in the back of my throat. *"Flamina finita,"* I found myself whispering.

The fire went out.

Lizzie collapsed, sobbing, the burnt shards of her skirt falling apart and revealing bare, reddened legs. A ripple of relief spread through the crowd, followed almost immediately by a wave of confusion. I sank back to my seat as people began to glance around uncertainly, attempting to figure out what had just happened.

"It's witchery!" someone in the crowd exclaimed, causing people to look around even more fervently. I joined in the looking, turning my head from side to side as if trying to find the culprit.

"It might have been." Mr. Shaar was making his way to the center of the circle now. He glanced at Lizzie's crumpled, sobbing form, then looked up at the students. "And if it was, we will deal with that later. What matters now, though, is that Lizzie is safe." Becky jumped from her seat and offered Lizzie her long coat for cover, and Mr. Shaar instructed her to take Lizzie to the infirmary. I watched as Lizzie got to her feet, shakily wrapped the jacket around herself, and slowly walked out onto the field, escorted by Becky. They disappeared around a corner, and I breathed a quiet sigh of relief. The fire was out, no one was hurt, and no one had realized that I was the one who had been using magic.

At least that's what I hoped.

The following day was a school day, so Trina and I rose early. I picked my crumpled navy blue school uniform off the floor and dressed myself, then pulled Trina's uniform—hung up neatly in the closet, of course—and passed it to her. Trina was quieter than normal this morning, talking only when she was spoken to directly. When I finally asked her if she was all right, she frowned, and I saw fear in her eyes. "I'm worried."

"Why?" I asked.

"I'm scared you're going to get caught."

"Get caught for?…" I suddenly understood, and my body went cold.

"I heard you," she confessed. "I hear better than most people, remember? It was you who put out the fire yesterday."

I couldn't reply for a moment; my heart was caught in my throat. "You…won't tell anyone?" My words came out as a squeak.

"Of course not." There was a hint of exasperation in Trina's voice. "If I was going to, I wouldn't be talking to you about it, silly. But everyone knows that *someone* used magic yesterday, and I'm scared they'll figure out it was you."

I exhaled slowly, my heart still pounding despite her reassurances. "So you don't think I'm a monster for being able to use magic?"

"Nah." Trina shook her head. "I don't actually think magic is evil. I've heard stories about people using magic to heal people and do other good things. So it can't be all bad."

I stared at her. "I didn't know you thought that."

"Why would I tell anyone? They might think *I'm* a magic user." She grinned.

We talked about my abilities as we finished getting ready, Trina peppering me with questions about how my magic worked. By the time we headed off to breakfast, I was significantly less anxious than I'd been earlier. My best friend had just learned my darkest secret, and she clearly wasn't about to abandon me or turn me over to the authorities.

Now I just had to hope that anyone else who had figured out what happened yesterday would react in the same way.

Classes after a holiday weekend were always full of restless students, and today was no exception. During math, my first class, a group of boys decided to use their slingshots—newly acquired Banishing Day gifts from obviously ignorant parents—to throw spitballs at the teacher, and the entire group got sent to Miss Cckle's office together. With those boys gone, things were definitely a bit calmer in English, my next class. Mr. Shaar seemed distracted today, though; he kept confusing words, going off on tangents while he taught, and throwing strange, anxious glances at the class. History, my favourite subject, followed English. Today Mr. Jeffries was teaching us about the wars that Breoch had gone through to gain its independence from the large, wealthy Cherinese Empire and the installment of our first king, Patrick, a decade or so before the Banishing. Mr. Jeffries seemed to be lacking in patience today; by the end of the class, he'd given detention to two students and threatened the entire class with extra homework. So, when he asked me to stay back when class was dismissed, a knot formed in my stomach. *What is it this time?* I got good grades, but it seemed like he was always scolding me for something. In this last month alone I'd been reprimanded for undone homework, illegible handwriting, and whispering in class. *At least he doesn't lecture me for slouching, like Miss Cockle likes to.*

I sat at my desk, feigning nonchalance, as all the other students filed out. When it was just me and Mr. Jeffries in the room, I approached his desk nervously. "What is it, Mr. Jeffries? Am I in trouble again?"

He looked up at me, and I saw something I didn't quite understand in his deep brown eyes. "No," he replied. "Well, actually, yes. More precisely, you're in danger."

My eyes narrowed. "Danger?"

He nodded. "Yesterday, when Lizzie's skirt caught fire, Mr. Shaar saw you jump to your feet and raise your hand. The fire went out seconds after." He eyed me. "He doesn't think it was a coincidence."

I stiffened at his words. Tears began to well in my eyes.

"Oh, don't start crying now," Mr. Jeffries muttered. "I'm not going to hurt you. I don't hate magic users."

"But you told us the story of the Banishing..." I protested, my voice squeaking.

"Because it's part of my job. Now we need to figure out what to do with you. Mr. Shaar reported you to Miss Cockle, and a few of us were dragged into a meeting this morning. She's alerted the authorities, and the Breoch Guard will be coming by tomorrow morning to collect you."

"Breoch Guard," I echoed. All my childhood I'd heard stories about the mysterious, uniformed men who showed up at people's homes to collect magic users. I felt the blood drain from my face. "I don't want them to turn me into a krossemage! I need to get out of here, I..." My voice had risen several octaves, and I looked around frantically.

"Oh, calm down." Mr. Jeffries huffed. "I'm not telling you this just to scare you, Saray. I'm telling you because I intend to help you."

"How?"

"I'm going to get you out of here, that's how." He stood up. "Meet me in my office at five tomorrow morning. Dress warmly and bring a few changes of clothes and anything you'll need for the road. You may have a long journey ahead of you."

"Where are you sending me?"

"Probably to the Isle of Dundere, for now at least." He gestured to the map on the wall, pointing at the small island that sat several miles northeast of Breoch. "You'll be safe there. Now go, before the next class shows up."

I nodded and stumbled out of his classroom, my mind reeling.

I drifted through my remaining classes, barely concentrating on the lessons. My stomach was in knots, and I found myself looking out of the corners of my eyes at fellow students, wondering if they suspected that I was the culprit.

After class, I walked silently back to my room. Alone, I pulled out my sparse collection of dresses and selected three that were plain and good for travel and bundled them into a bag. My head spun. *This doesn't feel real.* It felt like packing for a small weekend trip, not preparing to run away from the only home I'd ever known.

Trina came into the room while I was closing up the bag. She shut the door behind her, leaned her cane against the wall, and paused. "Saray?"

"I'm here," I said to her. "I'm packing."

"Packing?"

I filled her in on my earlier conversation with Mr. Jeffries. "He's sending me to the Isle of Dundere, where I'll be safe," I concluded, my voice sounding hollow in my own ears. Saying the words aloud didn't make them feel any more real.

Trina inhaled sharply. "Dundere," she muttered. Her eyes were wide. "If that's where you're going, then I'm coming too."

I stared at her. "No, you aren't," I replied. "Trina, I can't bring you along! You're a kid, and you're blind, and this is going to be dangerous."

"I want to come *because* I'm blind." Trina replied. "Remember how I said that magic can be used to heal people? The governor of Dundere is a healer. My mother told me about her right before she left me here. She said that when I got older, I should try to get to Dundere and have the governor fix my eyes. I've wanted to go there my entire life." Her voice wavered. "Please, let me come with you, Saray."

I gave Trina a long look and then sighed. "Fine. I suppose it makes sense."

Trina's face broke into a grin, and she clapped her hands. "Thank you," she whispered. "I'll try to keep up, I promise."

"I'm sure you'll manage," I said. "And I won't mind the company. But you'd best get packing—I'm leaving at five tomorrow morning, whether you're ready or not."

# Chapter Three

SYLVENBURGH ACADEMY WAS still shrouded in complete darkness when Trina and I left our room the following morning, my pack firmly secured to my back. Neither of us had slept much, and I fought off a yawn as we made our way down the shadowy dorm hall.

We reached the heavy door that separated the girls' dorms from the common area, and I pulled on it, only to meet resistance. "Wonderful," I muttered.

"What?" asked Trina.

"The main door is locked at night," I told her. "I forgot. Mr. Jeffries must have..." I gasped as a definite *click* sounded on the other side of the door. When it swung open, I found myself staring at Walter. He put a finger to his lips and motioned that we should follow him. I frowned; I hadn't expected Walter to be a part of our escape.

We made our way across the grand, richly carpeted common area. "Did Mr. Jeffries ask you to help us?" I whispered to Walter when we'd safely reached the staircase.

He glanced back at me and nodded.

"Did he...tell you why I'm running away?"

He nodded again. I didn't miss the concern in his eyes.

"So you know that I'm like you." For once, I felt a sense of kinship with Walter, rather than the usual revulsion. "Want to see what I can do?" I grinned as I whispered the familiar words; this was the first time I'd intentionally shown off my gift.

Walter smiled at my fire as well. He pointed at it, then at himself. My eyes widened. "You used to be able to make fire?"

He nodded, and I felt a surge of pity. "I…I'm sorry," I managed.

"You should come with us," Trina piped up. "We're going to see a healer in Dundere."

But Walter shook his head and motioned towards the stairs.

When we reached the first floor, I breathed a sigh of relief. Mr. Jeffries' office door was open, the room lit by what appeared to be only a single candle. I quickened my pace, taking Trina's arm and pulling her along until we were through the doorway, and found myself staring up at a very disgruntled Mr. Jeffries. "What's *she* doing here?" he hissed, motioning at Trina.

"She…wanted to come along," I muttered, suddenly nervous about my decision.

"Absolutely not." His eyes narrowed. "Do you have any idea how dangerous this is, Saray? You have no right to drag one of your friends into it—especially one who is younger than you and blind!"

"That's why she brought me," Trina spoke up, her voice calm. She repeated to Mr. Jeffries the things she'd told me earlier about the governor of Dundere. The end of her story was punctuated by a meow as Whiskers, the cat who lived in the offices, jumped down from his perch and began to wind around her legs. Trina crouched down and petted him.

Mr. Jeffries stared down at her for a long moment. Then he sighed. "I suppose it makes sense. I just hope you'll be able to make the journey safely." He glanced at Walter. "You should head to my carriage." Walter nodded and ducked from the room.

"Is Walter coming with us?" I asked.

"Partway," Mr. Jeffries replied. "I asked him to help you two escape, on condition that I'd help him do the same. He has family in Sylvenburgh." He adjusted his hat. "Now, if this venture of ours is going to succeed, I'll need you girls to trust me. There are some things that will happen in the next few minutes that will be strange, but I want no questions until we're out of the city. Is that clear?"

Several new questions popped into my head, but I clamped my mouth shut and nodded.

"Good." He looked us over. "You two should probably join hands."

I frowned at his instruction but took Trina's hand in mine, and he reached out and touched my shoulder. *"Dominae araknae invida,"* I heard him whisper. My eyes narrowed. *Did he just cast a spell?*

Nothing seemed to immediately change; I felt the same as I had seconds ago. When he touched Trina's shoulder and muttered the same words, though, I gasped as she disappeared from sight. Looking down at my hands, I realized that I too had been rendered invisible. I stared down in awe at where my body should have been, gawked at Mr. Jeffries for a moment, and then informed Trina in a whisper about what had been done to us. I heard her giggle in response, her laugh seeming to come out of nowhere.

"Follow me, you two," Mr. Jeffries whispered. "Don't fall behind."

We followed Mr. Jeffries out of his office and down the darkened hall, then out of the main entrance to the school. An open carriage and horse waited just outside the gates; Walter was sitting in the driver's seat. "Everybody here?" asked Mr. Jeffries.

"We're both here," I told him.

"Good." He motioned at the carriage. "Climb in, then. There are blankets on the back seat; they'll become invisible once they're around you."

I giggled, doing my best to help Trina into the coach. Then I seated myself and wrapped one of the thick wool blankets around my shoulders; as promised, it disappeared as soon as I was wearing it. Mr. Jeffries climbed into the seat next to Walter. I stared at him as the carriage began to move. "How did you?..."

"Shhh," he interrupted, turning and raising a finger to his lips. "No questions, remember?"

*Right.* I sighed and turned to look at the neat rows of small houses that we passed. The carriage bumped up and down on the cobbled road, and candlelight flickered in the streetlamps. The streets appeared to be deserted at this time of morning.

The small homes gave way to taller structures as we made our way into Sylvenburgh's downtown area. I stared up at the buildings that loomed on either side of me. Some were as many as four stories tall, many of them topped by elegant metal work or spires. Most of the buildings appeared to be shops or taverns at ground level, their windows darkened for the night, but the occasional window in the apartments above was lit up, undoubtedly early risers headed to work. A window above one of the taverns opened, and a woman stuck her head out, giving a yell before dumping a pan of something onto the street below. My nose wrinkled when I realized what had almost certainly been the contents of the pan.

We cleared the downtown area and made our way towards the city limits. The carriage stopped just short of the gates, and I watched as Walter climbed out of the driver's seat. He gave us a wave and a grin and then turned and disappeared into the night.

Mr. Jeffries climbed into the drivers' seat, and we resumed our journey. We drove through the tall gates flanked by statues of lions, the cobbled road beneath us turning to a dirt one. Once we had been travelling for another minute or so, Mr. Jeffries spoke. "Grab onto me, both of you."

I obeyed, and I assume Trina did as well, because a moment later, he mumbled the words, *"Invida finita,"* and I could see her again.

I grinned at Mr. Jeffries. "I can't believe you're a magic user."

"Yes, well, it's not exactly something I advertise," he grunted, but he was smiling.

Trina shook her head. "It must be hard for you, telling us the story of Banishing Day."

He shrugged. "I'm used to it by now. It comes with the job."

"Am I the first magic user you've helped escape the school?" I asked.

Mr. Jeffries nodded. "I've given stern warnings to several children whom I've caught using magic over the years. But you're the only one I've had to help escape. Most kids don't make mistakes that are quite as public as yours was." He shook his head and glanced back at me. "So tell me, how long have you been using magic, Saray?"

I bit my lip. "I think I was eleven when it started," I told him. "I used to be afraid of fire, and I remember walking down the hall one night, holding a candle. I noticed that the flame seemed to be angled away from me, like I was willing it to stay as far from me as possible. That happened a few more times,

21

and then just before I turned thirteen, the hem of my dress caught on fire, just like Lizzie's did. Suddenly I found myself saying these unfamiliar words."

"Casting words," he said, nodding.

"And my dress, it just stopped burning," I went on. "That was when I knew for certain that I could use magic. I mean, I knew it was forbidden and all, but I thought that being able to start and stop fires could be useful. So I started practicing when I was alone." I eyed him, deciding against telling him about all the times when anger or fear had made my hands begin to smolder.

Mr. Jeffries nodded again. "I was about the same age," he told me. "Though I somewhat expected it. My father was a vanisher like me; he figured at least one of the children would inherit his gift."

I frowned. "So magic is something you inherit?"

"Absolutely," he replied. I frowned. *Were my parents magic users?* "My parents didn't stop me from experimenting with my abilities; they simply advised I be careful," he continued. "Though my parents were a bit unconventional." He glanced to his left. "Speaking of which, there's my home."

The carriage made a turn into a driveway, and we drove down a narrow lane towards a small farmhouse, its windows lit up. "We're going to your house?" Trina asked.

"Just for a moment," Mr. Jeffries replied. "I need to grab a few things. You two stay in the carriage; if I bring you inside, my mother will start fussing over you and trying to feed you, and we don't have time for that."

Mr. Jeffries parked the carriage and disappeared into the house, and I looked around curiously. The farm was fairly small; I didn't see massive fields of grain or large pastures, just a stable and chicken coop and a few other outbuildings behind the main house. A large, well-maintained vegetable garden sat nearby, and I watched as a rooster strutted back and forth near it, his bright plumes barely visible in the early morning light. Beside me, Trina inhaled deeply. "The air smells lovely out here," she murmured. I breathed in; the air was clean and smelled of hay and grass and livestock.

Mr. Jeffries returned several minutes later carrying a bundle, a long knife and an axe, and a large, covered plate. He placed the bag in the back of the carriage and passed the plate to me; it was warm. "Breakfast for you girls. Mother insisted." He shook his head and grinned.

I pulled the cloth off the plate; it held warm scones with jam and butter and several sausages. My mouth began to water. "That smells amazing," Trina commented.

"It *is* amazing," Mr. Jeffries assured us, turning the carriage around. "My mother is an incredible cook. She packed you some food for the road as well; it's in the pack."

"So why do you live with your mother?" Trina asked, biting into a scone.

He eyed her. "Well, first of all, my father passed away several years back, and it didn't seem fair to leave her alone with the farm. And second, it's a convenient arrangement for everyone involved. My twin brother lives here too, though his work has him away from home a lot. Mother gets to keep the farm that she loves, and my brother and I help her out when we can and get to enjoy her cooking." He pulled the carriage back onto the dirt road, and we continued northward.

"You have a twin?" I bit into my own scone as I spoke; it was warm and sweet and dotted with some sort of berries. "Are you identical?"

Mr. Jeffries laughed. "Technically yes, but we look nothing alike. Lachlann and I chose very different paths in life." He let out a sigh. "I wish he was at home right now; if he was, I'd simply hand you two off to him. He knows the Shrouded Woods well; you'd be safe traveling with him."

I almost choked on my scone. "The Shrouded Woods?" I squeaked. "You're sending us in *there*? I thought we were going to Dundere!"

He nodded, keeping his eyes on the road ahead. "Going through the woods is the fastest way to reach the north coast, where you'll find a ship to Dundere. And you might find that the Shrouded Woods aren't as terrifying as you imagine. In fact, you might even like them. It's where most of the magic users live."

Really?" Trina's eyes widened. "I thought most of the magic users had left Breoch."

"That's the story we're meant to tell you," he answered. "You girls know that when the Banishing was announced, King Patrick gave all the magic users six months to either stop practicing or leave Breoch."

I nodded; he had said those very words two days before during the Banishing Day festivities.

"But what you haven't been told is that many magic users chose to do neither," Mr. Jeffries continued. "Instead, they retreated deep into the Shrouded Woods and began a new life. Nowadays there's an entire society in there, made up mostly of magic users in hiding." He glanced back at me. "The ways of the woods-folk are strange when you're not used to them, but they're mostly good people."

I shook my head, still uncertain about the prospect of venturing into the Shrouded Woods. "What do we do once we get to Dundere?" Trina asked.

"Well, it sounds like you plan to go see the governor, which is what I'd tell you to do even if you weren't looking to be healed," he told her. "You'll need to talk to her about seeking asylum."

Trina frowned. "You mean we'll have to stay there forever?"

Mr. Jeffries shook his head. "Doubtful. Dundere is safer for now, but once a few months have gone by, you could return to Breoch and live safely enough within the Shrouded Woods, if you wished."

"But we're just kids," I protested. "And we don't know the way. You can't expect us to make the journey through the woods on our own. And who will take care of us when we reach Dundere?"

"I'm sure that the governor will be able to find you a place to stay in Dundere," he replied. "As for your journey there, there's a woman named Kirilee living in the woods, a friend of my brother's, who should be able to help you reach your destination or find someone who can."

"How will we find her?" Trina asked.

"She'll find you, trust me," he replied. "She's gifted that way. She can sense people in need in the woods, and she seeks them out." He looked back at us and smiled. "There are some who call her the queen of the Shrouded Woods."

"Queen?" I repeated.

"You'll understand when you meet her. She's something special. In fact, I'm convinced that Lachlann is in love with her, and that's why he takes shortcuts through the woods when delivering his wares." He shook his head.

"I'll take you partway into the woods myself this morning, but after that you'll be on your own until Kirilee finds you. I doubt she'll be long, though."

There was a pause, and then Trina spoke. "Are you going to get in trouble with the Breoch Guard? Helping us escape like this?"

Mr. Jeffries shrugged. "Not so long as they don't know I was the one who helped you. And so long as I make it back to the school in time for the morning staff meeting, no one should suspect me. They might suspect Walter, but they have no idea where he's gone."

"Do we need to worry about the Breoch Guard tracking us in the woods?"

He laughed. "That's part of the reason I'm sending you through the woods instead of the cities. Most folks—Breoch Guard included—are too terrified of the woods to track anything through there." He shook his head. "Trust me, you'll be safer in the woods than anywhere else."

We were quiet after that; my stomach had worked its way into a knot again at the prospect of venturing into the woods. The clouds had turned several shades of pink from the impending sunrise, and the farmers' fields were becoming smaller and sparser as we drove. Soon I was staring at nothing but rolling green hills, some topped by small clusters of trees, their grasses unkempt and knee high. The road was bumpier now; the carriage jolted as it ran over ruts and rocks in the dirt path. A wall of green was steadily approaching, and when we finally stopped moving, I found myself staring up in awe.

The trees of the Shrouded Woods stood directly in front of us, towering green behemoths with massive trunks. They were huddled close together, and I wasn't sure if their presence was inviting or terrifying. Beside me, Trina inhaled again, no doubt taking in the cool, sharp scent of the trees.

"This is as far as we can go by horse," Mr. Jeffries informed us. He shouldered the bundle he was carrying. "Your cane won't be much use in the woods on its own, Trina; you'll need to hang on to Saray or myself."

We made our way into the woods slowly, dodging tangled vines and low-hanging branches. Mr. Jeffries walked at a steady pace, and I held Trina's left arm while she used her cane to feel out the terrain with her right. The air in here was cool and moist and smelled of growing things, and the trees formed a canopy over us, only letting in patches of early morning light. *I can see why they call it the Shrouded Woods*. I could hear birds singing morning songs in the branches high above us, and the ground beneath my feet felt soft and spongy; glancing down I saw that it was carpeted in moss. The trees themselves were a mix of the impossibly tall, thick-trunked giants that I'd seen from outside the woods and smaller trees with twisting trunks and branches and teardrop-shaped leaves.

Mr. Jeffries turned to a patch of tall grass and plucked a strand. "This is called hangman's grass, and it's edible," he told me, handing me the stalk of grass with its heart-shaped leaves. "And there are small, bright purple berries on vines that are edible too." He plucked another piece and handed it to Trina, and I nibbled at mine curiously. It tasted fresh and crisp, much like lettuce.

Mr. Jeffries removed the food bundle from his back, then moved so that he was behind me and attached it to my pack. Then he handed me a long knife and an axe. "You might need these for gathering firewood."

I smiled weakly. "Are you leaving us now?"

He nodded. "I need to get to work. There's likely to be quite a ruckus today, with two students having gone missing and all." He chuckled. "Keep following the trail until you reach a clearing next to a stream. That's a good place for you to camp until Kirilee finds you."

He bid us one last farewell and then turned and disappeared into the forest. I looked down at Trina and took her arm again. "I guess we're on our own now."

We made our way deeper into the forest, taking in the new sights, sounds, and smells of the Shrouded Woods. More varieties of trees appeared: squat trees with reddish bark and sprawling, thick branches that looked perfect for climbing; trees with long, yellow-flowered branches that nearly touched the ground; and delicate, white-barked trees covered in large clusters of pink and purple blooms. I caught the occasional glimpse of large, bright birds high in the branches, and squirrel-like creatures scuttled through the trees every now and then, intent on finding food. I quickly learned that leading a blind person through forest was much more difficult than school hallways; Trina found most of the tree roots and loose rocks with her cane, but there were several overhanging branches I forgot to point out that she nearly ran into. Trina, thankfully, was a better sport than me about running into things, but by the time we reached the clearing Mr. Jeffries had mentioned, my cheeks were burning from embarrassment. Trina inhaled deeply. "It smells so…green in here."

"It does," I agreed, looking out over the clearing. A brook ran along the edge of the glade; I led Trina over to it, and we shed our packs, dropped to our knees and drank in the cold, sweet water. When we were finished, I took her over to a fallen log so she could sit and then began digging around in the pack for food. I found some more scones and some homemade bread and cheese, which we shared, and then I watched as Trina leaned back against the log and closed her eyes, listening to the chirping birds and gurgling stream. I glanced around the clearing, too nervous to relax, and remembered that when Mr. Shaar had spent time in the woods, he had made himself a shelter out of tree branches.

I selected a tree with several low, angled limbs as my base and began dragging large branches over to it, forming them into a crude lean-to. Then I began filling in the gaps with smaller branches and moss from the ground. Mental pictures from the stories Mr. Shaar had told us began to dance in my mind as I worked—images of waking up to bears attacking us; coming across strange, black-clad robbers; running into the Breoch Guard. *What if Mr. Jeffries was wrong about them being afraid to track us in here?* I tried to shut the images out, to stay in the present and focus only on patching up the small holes in our shelter.

I was just about finished when I heard a laugh from Trina. I glanced over at her, and my eyes widened. A large swarm of brightly coloured butterflies had made its way into the clearing at some point, and they fluttered wildly around her in a flurry of motion and colour, several of them perching on her clothing and skin. "Trina," I gasped, "you're covered in butterflies!"

"I know," she giggled as one landed on her cheek. "It's lovely."

I wasn't sure how a blind girl could be aware of such things, but I let that thought slip away and watched her, smiling at the strange turn of events.

The swarm of butterflies left after some time, and I returned to building our shelter. Once I was finished, I glanced over at Trina, only to find that she had dozed off. My eyes narrowed. *How is she so relaxed?* I shrugged off what felt like irritation at her as I began collecting scrap wood. I fetched a few large rocks and formed them into a fire ring and then arranged the wood in the centre and lit the fire. My stomach was beginning to rumble, and I noticed that the sun was not shining quite as brightly in the glade anymore. *Must be getting close to dinner time.* I walked over to the pack, pulled out more food, and then went to wake Trina.

"What now?" Trina asked me while we ate. "Do we just stay here and wait for this Kirilee person to show up?"

"Apparently," I replied. "I like this place, but I have a feeling I'll get bored now that I've finished setting up camp. I wish I'd brought a book."

"At least you have things you can do. I'm no use out here."

"Don't say that. There's plenty you can do out here." I frowned, chewing on a piece of bread. "Did you bring your pipe? You could play us some music."

She brightened at my suggestion. "Actually, yes." She tossed away her apple core and then pulled the slender instrument out of her pack and raised it to her lips. The sounds were halting, given that she was new at the instrument, but after a while they became smoother, and I found myself relaxing and enjoying her obvious talent. The fire crackled and leapt in front of me, and I amused myself by making the flames dance higher than they needed to.

"I'm curious, Trina," I said when she'd finished a song, "is getting your eyes healed the only reason you wanted to come with me?"

Trina paused for a moment and then nodded. "It was the main one," she said. "But maybe not the only one."

"What were your other reasons, then?"

"Well, first of all, everyone else at school ignores me. It's funny, I'm the blind one, but the other kids act like they can't see me, if you know what I mean. Like I'm invisible."

"Right." I nodded knowingly. "I think I'm more of a nuisance to the other kids than someone to be overlooked. But you're quieter than me."

"Exactly. So, you can imagine how things would go for me if you left without me."

"I suppose so." My shoulders hunched. "What were you planning on doing when I graduated, Trina?"

"I don't know." Her voice was pained. "I've worried about that. I suppose I'd just be miserable for three years."

"So you came with me because you didn't want to be left alone," I concluded.

"That, and I didn't want to leave *you* alone."

I frowned. "You think you need to take care of me?"

"In some ways." She fiddled with a leaf she'd plucked earlier. "Saray, you're a wonderful person and my best friend. But you can be a little...hotheaded. You say things that get you in trouble sometimes. Like that whole scene at the Banishing Day dinner. Me, well, yes, I'm quiet, and most people think I'm this shy, weak little girl, but I know how to stay calm. When people get in fights, I can sometimes see both sides. It's not always a good thing, being like me, but I think we balance each other a bit."

I stared at her. Trina wasn't usually this direct. "I, uh, you're probably right about all that."

"There's one more reason I wanted to come," she said.

"What's that?"

"Well, Mr. Jeffries said earlier we might need to see if we can stay in Dundere," she said. "And when I think about it, that might actually be best for me. Because my mother told me to go there and get healed, so I figure if I stay there, maybe one day Mother will come looking for me."

"You really want to see her again, don't you?"

"I do. I don't quite understand why Mother gave me up. I think it was something to do with whatever it was that made me go blind. But I remember her crying and hugging me before she left, telling me she loved me. So I know I want to find her."

"Lucky you, having those memories." The words came out more bitter than I'd intended.

"Not really. Maybe you were given up because your parents knew they couldn't love you in the way you deserved to be loved. Maybe you're better off growing up how you did. Me, I know that I'm missing out on my mother's love. I just don't know why." Her voice wobbled, and she let out a sigh. "We should go to sleep. This is hard to talk about."

I extinguished the fire, and we lay down under my makeshift shelter, huddled together for warmth under the blanket Mr. Jeffries had given us. And only now, in the darkness and quiet, did my earlier anxiety return, accompanied by a strange pang of something that I could only describe as *homesickness.*

For years I'd fantasized about escaping the prison that was Sylvenburgh Academy, sneaking out at night or scaling the walls, never to return. But now, lying here in the cold on the rocky ground, it was hard not to want everything to go back to exactly how it had been two days before. Next to the looming uncertainty of these woods, my old life seemed like a safe haven.

Nothing was predictable now, and it was hard not to be afraid of what might become of us.

I was awoken early the next morning by a scuffling sound. I groaned and rolled over on the hard ground, not entirely aware of my surroundings. I opened my eyes ever so slightly and stared blankly at the dimly lit glade.

And then I bolted upright, my heart pounding.

There were two men. One of them was staring down at our shelter; another was attempting to light a fire in my ring on the other side of the clearing. The one who was nearby gave me a smile. "Hi. We were just borrowing your fire ring. Need to cook breakfast, y'know." His voice, I noticed, had an odd lilt to it.

I stared at him for a moment, debating his trustworthiness, and then nodded. "All right, sure. Just don't borrow any of our food; it's all we have."

Trina was sitting up now, rubbing her eyes, and I explained to her what was happening. We stumbled over to the fire, half awake, to see the men cooking some type of sausages. The men were odd looking, I thought as I stared at them. One had close-cropped hair, the other had hair past his shoulders, and they both had strange, whirling patterns etched into their arms with some sort of ink. The one who'd spoken to me earlier—the nearly bald one—wore no shirt, save for a vest that looked to be made of animal skin. The other wore dark blue armour and a necklace that might have been carved from bones or wood. The bald one offered Trina and me each a sausage while telling me their names—the other one was Rich, and he was Fergus. "So, what are two city girls doing out in the middle of the Shrouded Woods, ai?" he asked.

"Running away," I replied. "We were in danger back home."

"And you don't think you'd be in danger here?"

"Well, hopefully less danger," I said, taking a bite of my food. "We're looking for someone named Kirilee, do you know her?"

Rich laughed. "Everyone knows Kirilee. We've had a few run-ins with her, though I've not seen her for months."

My heart sank a little. *Maybe Mr. Jeffries was wrong about her being in the area.*

The men finished their breakfast silently and collected their belongings. "We'd best be off," Fergus said, standing up, "And we'll be taking those." He gestured at our bags.

*Wait, what?* I started to protest, but my words froze in my mouth.

"*Nalalae eroknae sangnatae,*" Rich mumbled, and suddenly I was stuck in place, unable to move or speak. Out of the corner of my eye, I could see that Trina was in a similar state. My heart began to pound. *We've been tricked!*

31

# Chapter Four

**FERGUS WAS GRINNING** at us as he shouldered our food bag. "That was easy. Only had to offer you a few scraps of food."

I struggled against my invisible bonds, screaming inside. *Let us go!*

Fergus glanced at Rich. "You sure the spell will hold until we leave?"

Rich grinned and nodded. "I don't see how they'll get out, unless one of them can summon the Breoch Guard with their mind."

"Mmm." Fergus stroked his chin. "Y'think we should we just leave 'em, then? They any use to us?"

Rich frowned. "Could always use one for a life transfer, bring back Josephine."

Fergus snorted. "You know how to do a life transfer, Rich?" He chuckled. "Didn't think so. And you can only do those with a fresh corpse. Jo's been in the ground for a month now. I know you loved her, but you'd best accept that she's gone and find yourself a new girlfriend." He stared at his friend for a moment and then leered at us. "We've got two fine girls right here, y'know. The dark-haired one's 'specially pretty." Fergus stepped towards Trina and ran a finger down her cheek.

Anger mixed with horror surged up in me. I squeezed my eyes shut, and then they flew open when I heard a yelp. Looking over at Trina, I saw that Fergus's hand was engulfed in flame. He slapped at it, his eyes wide.

"One of them's a firebrand!" I heard Rich exclaim. His eyes narrowed. "By the Fae, how'd they manage to…" He was cut off as a large hawk flew into the clearing. It let out a shriek and dove at the men. Rich screamed and swatted at the bird. "He bit me!"

"Run!" Fergus shouted, and the two men sprinted into the woods, the bird giving chase. Rich's spell dropped when they'd disappeared, and Trina and I both collapsed, gasping.

I took several deep breaths, fighting back tears, and looked over at Trina. "Are you all right?"

Trina's gasps had turned into sobs, but she nodded.

I reached over and put my arms around her, and she buried her face in my shoulder. "I should go after them," I mumbled, my stomach tightening. "I should set both of them on fire."

Trina pulled away from me and shook her head. "No, you shouldn't," she said, her voice wobbling. "It wouldn't make anything better. We should probably find somewhere new to camp tonight, though."

I nodded, the rage in my gut beginning to subside. "And find more food. They took our bags."

Trina frowned. "Did they take my cane?"

"I think so." I sighed and then glanced up at the sky and shook my head. "That was strange, that bird attacking them. I wonder if it knew we needed help."

Trina shrugged. "Maybe. I bet some of the animals in these woods are magical."

"I swear that was the same bird we saw right before the bonfire at the school too," I mumbled, gathering up the few small loaves of bread that had fallen out of the pack when the bandits fled.

We ate a meager breakfast, and then we gathered up our blanket, the only belonging of ours that Rich and Fergus had left us, and set out to try to find something to replace the food we'd lost.

We found plenty of hangman's grass to eat, and halfway through the day I stumbled upon a bush full of the bright purple berries that Mr. Jeffries had mentioned, which had a sweet yet tart sort of flavour. I did notice that I was getting better at leading Trina through the woods; I kept my eye out for both low-hanging branches and tree roots, and she only tripped once. Trina seemed to be in her own little world again, humming to herself, apparently unbothered by our lack of food. I tried to ignore the strange pangs of resentment I felt towards her as we walked.

Eventually, we settled in a new glade at sundown with the few coat pockets' full of plants and berries we'd gathered—nothing even closely resembling a good dinner. We ate them anyway, and afterwards Trina pulled out her pipe again while I built us another shelter. I was just putting the finishing touches on it when I realized that I hadn't emptied my bladder for most of the day.

I told Trina that I'd be back in a few minutes and made my way into the forest. Something bright caught my eye as I squatted down in the bushes, and when I was finished, I walked over to it cautiously, wondering if I was about to encounter more humans. Then my eyes widened. The lights were not signs of human life, I realized, but were coming from the plants nearby—specifically the pink and purple hanging flowers that I'd noticed on our way into the woods.

"This is interesting," I murmured, plucking a flower off the vine and studying it. I'd heard stories about plants that glowed in the dark, but this was my first time encountering one. The flower's petals were a bright, luminous white-pink. I giggled and impulsively picked more of the flowers, then made my way back into the glade. "I wish you could see this!" I said to Trina as I walked back towards the campfire.

"That sounds lovely," she responded after I described the flowers to her. "Once my eyes are healed, we'll have to come back here so I can actually see all these things!"

"Absolutely," I agreed.

We were quiet for a moment after, and then she spoke up again. "Saray?"

"Yes?"

She gave me an amused glance. "You realize that you didn't have to wander off into the forest to…well, you know. I can't exactly see what you're doing."

The truth of her statement, for some reason, struck me as immensely funny, and I found myself throwing back my head and letting out a guffaw. We laughed together for a good ten minutes, some of my earlier tension fading away. Then we settled down, our amusement over the situation making me care just a bit less about the hard ground and my empty belly.

My sleep that night was troubled, punctuated by long periods of lying awake listening for bandits or wild animals or Breoch Guardsmen. When I finally fully awoke the next morning, my stomach was rumbling, and my head spun. "This isn't fair," I grumbled, struggling to my feet. "I'm stuck in the middle of nowhere, and I'm starving, and I can't sleep, all because of stupid Lizzie and her dancing."

"You can't sleep, huh?" Trina said. "I slept just fine."

"Really?" I frowned. "Aren't you worried about getting attacked again?"

"A little bit," she replied. "But I also feel safer out here."

"*Safer?*" I huffed. "What's gotten into you, Trina? You've been acting like you're in some dream world ever since we got out into the woods!"

She shrugged. "I just…like it out here. It's hard to explain. Never mind. We should go try to find some food."

We set off on our search for food, our pace lethargic, going a different direction today to see what this part of the woods held. "If only I knew which plants were safe to eat," I lamented as we trudged along, collecting hangman's grass and berries wherever we found them.

The hours dragged by, and a bank of heavy clouds obscured the sun as morning turned to afternoon, bringing damp air and the threat of rain. It was nearing mid-afternoon when I heard a screech above us. I looked up and then ducked as a large form swooped down towards us. Instinctively, I pulled Trina down with me.

When I looked up again, a hawk was perched on the branch of a nearby tree, at eye level with me. It let out a strange chirp and began to fly, much lower this time. My eyes narrowed. "That's…the same bird who attacked those bandits," I said, scratching my head.

Trina nodded, seeming unsurprised. "I think it wants us to follow it."

"I think you're right."

The hawk had landed in a tree a little further away, and we approached it cautiously. It took off again, flying low, and we followed it. We continued like this for what felt like a good hour, the hawk occasionally pausing to let us catch up with it, until we stumbled into a clearing.

And I found myself staring at a house.

It wasn't a house like the ones in Sylvenburgh; it certainly wasn't crafted of brick and roof tiles. It was more of a hut, made of roughly woven-together sticks and bark and moss, like a much more efficient version of our lean-to. The hawk perched on the roof of the house, clearly inviting us inside. "Trina," I gasped, "you're not going to believe this. The hawk led us to a *house!*"

Trina nodded, seeming completely unsurprised by this information.

I crept forward with Trina in tow, every sense on edge, wondering if the hut was inhabited. As we got closer, I saw what looked to be a vegetable garden and a fire pit outside of it. *Someone definitely lives here.* I took a deep breath, then strode towards the doorway and peeked in.

The dimly lit hut was unoccupied at the moment, but it was clearly someone's home. It held little furniture other than a table of sorts and a hammock that was strung up in a corner. The kitchen area seemed well developed though; there was a fireplace and wooden counters and a wash basin, and the counters housed various pots and knives and other sorts of cookware. But it was the far counter that interested me the most; on it were several loaves of bread and wedges of cheese, slabs of dried meat and various types of vegetables. More meat and vegetables hung in bunches from the ceiling. My stomach growled, and I made a lunge for the counter.

Instinctively I grabbed a loaf of bread, tore it in half, passed half to Trina and started wolfing it down. I let out an audible groan of relief as the hunger pangs began to abate.

"Do you think we should be stealing food?" Trina asked.

"I don't care," I replied, my mouth full of bread.

Once my loaf was finished, I quickly fashioned our blanket into a makeshift bag and started stuffing food into it. I was so preoccupied with my task that I didn't hear the rustling in the doorway. It wasn't until someone cleared their throat that I looked up—and promptly dropped my blanket, the food spilling all over the dirt and straw floor.

There was a young man standing in the doorway of the hut, dressed in a plain, slightly tattered brown shirt and matching breeches. Next to him stood a large, shaggy black dog. The young man was holding a bow with an arrow nocked, and it was pointed directly at me.

# Chapter Five

**I STARED AT** the young man in horror. "What do you think you're doing, ai?" he demanded.

Before I could answer, though, the dog let out a low growl that somehow turned into a whimper. Then he burst forward and jumped onto Trina, knocking her backwards. "Hey!" I protested, but looking down I saw that the dog was licking Trina's face, not attacking her.

"Bailey, get back!" the young man ordered. Dropping his bow, he lunged forward and reached out to grab Bailey by the scruff of the neck.

Then he stopped short. He hovered over Trina, staring down at her. "By the Fae," he mumbled. "Who are you?" His voice was tinged with confusion.

"My name's Trina," she replied, her voice devoid of fear. "Who are you?"

"I'm Kip," he said slowly, his angry demeanour seeming to subside. "And this is Bailey. Though it seems you've met him." His voice had the same lilt to it that I'd noticed in Rich and Fergus's speech.

Trina nodded and scratched the dog behind the ears, then got to her feet. "Come closer," she said to Kip. He hesitated, then obeyed, and flinched as she reached out to touch his face. "I'm blind," she explained. "This is my way of seeing you."

"Ah." His shoulders relaxed ever so slightly.

Trina paused as her fingers cupped his chin. "You're young," she said softly. "Your face is still smooth. How old are you?"

"I'm…uh, I'm seventeen," he told her. He glanced at me with a pair of wide eyes that were an icy blue-grey colour, and as I looked him over, I could see that he was, indeed, younger than I'd first thought. He was tall enough to be an adult, and his voice was nearly deep enough, but there was a hint of childish softness in his thin face, and his shoulders were not quite broad enough to be those of a grown man. His light brown hair was long and pulled back using a leather strap. *He's kind of cute,* I found myself thinking. "How old are you two?" he asked.

"I'm thirteen, and Saray is sixteen," Trina told him.

"Saray," he repeated, glancing at me.

"You're a bit young to be living out here," Trina commented. "Are you an orphan, like us?"

"You two are orphans?" He looked us over. "Ran away from the cities, ai?"

Trina nodded. "It wasn't safe for us there. And we had food, but we got attacked by bandits yesterday. They cast a spell on us and took our packs. We haven't eaten much at all since then."

"Sorry for trying to take your food," I added, gesturing at the blanket on the floor. "This will sound odd, but a hawk led us here, so we figured this food must be for us. We'll be on our way now."

Kip glanced down and then sighed. "I can't let you take all that, but I'm not about to let you starve, either. Why don't you stay for dinner?"

I hesitated, uncertain whether to trust him.

"Really?" His eyes narrowed. "You're hungry enough to steal my food but won't take it when it's offered? You city folks make no sense."

I shrugged. "The last people who offered us food ended up threatening us with magic and taking our belongings."

"Right." He chuckled. "Well, you needn't worry about that. I'm no witch, and by the looks of it you've got next to no belongings for me to take." He glanced back at the burlap bag that he'd been carrying when he walked in, which was sitting in the doorway. "Come on, stay for dinner, ai? I just caught a goose; there should be plenty."

"We'll stay," Trina said before I had a chance to respond. "At least, I will." She looked over at me. "Saray?"

I let out a sigh and allowed my rumbling stomach to make my decision.

"So, you never told us whether you're an orphan," Trina said to Kip two hours later as we sat down to a stew of goose meat, root vegetables, and herbs.

Kip shrugged. "Might as well be. My father's dead, and my mother's gone crazy. I ran away from home for the same sorts of reasons you girls left your school—it wasn't safe anymore."

"And how long ago was that?" she asked.

"Seven years," he replied nonchalantly, taking a bite of his food.

"Seven years?" I repeated, my eyes narrowing. "You've been on your own since you were *ten?*" I took a bite of my own stew; it was warm and savoury and provided even more relief to my growling stomach.

Kip frowned. "I s'pose so. Though there were a few older woods-folk who used to look out for me. And I wasn't on my own for the first few months, y'know. My little brother came with me, but he got sick when winter set in and..." He trailed off and looked away.

"I...I'm sorry," I offered.

He shrugged.

"Do you like to talk about your brother?" Trina asked. "Because if you want to tell us about him, we'll listen."

Kip stared at her for a moment, his eyes wide. Then he blushed and looked away. "Thanks," he mumbled. "But no."

We returned to eating, tense silence reigning in the room. I picked at my food and searched for something to say. "Do you know a woman named Kirilee?"

Kip let out a short laugh. "Course I do. She comes by here once a month or so, and we exchange wares. Why?"

"We're supposed to find her," I told him. "She's hopefully going to take us to the Isle of Dundere."

"And why are you going there, ai?"

I bit my lip. "We know people there who might be able to help us," I said evasively.

"You may not need to go that far, y'know. Whatever you're looking for in Dundere, you can likely find here. There's all sorts of trade going on in these woods—weapons, food, clothing, medicines, and nearly every type of witchery you can think of." There was a scornful edge to his tone, and he glanced towards the doorway. "These woods are full of strange things. It's why I stay close to home. Whenever Kirilee comes by, she tells me I should come along on one of her adventures, but I don't think I'm cut out for running with elfiebloods."

I nodded slowly, feigning nonchalance.

"Why don't you like magic?" Trina asked.

"It's not safe," he replied. "People with special powers running around, doing whatever they want with them—it's bound to cause trouble, y'know? I figure you can see that yourself, after what happened with those bandits."

I looked down at my food, my heart sinking a little. Clearly, I'd have to hide my ability so long as we were in Kip's company.

A thunderclap shook the hut then, followed by the sound of heavy raindrops pelting the roof. Kip looked out the window and sighed. "Well, I'm not going to send you out into that. Might as well get comfortable—looks like you'll be staying the night." He glanced at his straw-covered floors. "Hope you don't mind sleeping on the ground."

I reddened at the thought of sleeping in the same room as a boy, especially a cute one. But Trina answered before I could protest. "We'd be sleeping on the ground if we were out there, but we'd be cold and wet," she said to him. "Thank you for your hospitality."

After dinner, I helped Kip clean up while Trina settled in a corner and pulled out her pipe. Bailey wandered over to her, and after a few songs the music ceased. Glancing over at her, I saw that she was asleep, curled up against the dog. I walked over and covered her with our blanket, then settled down at the table, suddenly feeling nervous. I was, essentially, alone with Kip now, and it was hard not to notice the way his ice-blue eyes seemed to follow my every move. I stared at my hands for a moment before speaking. "Trina...um...seems really attached to your dog." I finally managed to say.

"She does," he agreed. He sat down beside me, seeming not to notice my discomfort. "And Bailey's hardly listened to me since she got here. She always do this to animals?"

"Trina's always liked animals, a lot," I said, trying to keep my voice neutral. I shifted awkwardly; I was extremely aware of the very few inches of space between us and uncertain whether I wanted to pull away from him or move closer. "And they seem to like her too. But this is new." I glanced at my sleeping friend again. "So, where will Trina and I go tomorrow?"

"There's a path that'll lead you to where Kirilee normally spends her time," he told me. "She comes and goes a lot, but I figure she'll be there eventually. I'll send some food with you and show you a few plants that you can eat."

"Thank you," I said. "We city folk don't know much about the plants in the Shrouded Woods. Back at the boarding school, they made it sound like everything in these woods was out to kill you, plant life included." I let out a nervous giggle.

He nodded. "They probably don't want students wandering off into these woods, so they make them sound as frightening as they can, y'know?" His eyes narrowed. "So, did you live in a boarding school or an orphanage back in Sylvenburgh? Thought you said you were orphans."

"It's a boarding school," I told him. "There are a few students, though, who are orphans or whose parents couldn't keep them, who live at the school."

"And which are you two?"

"Trina was left here by her mother," I replied. "She has some memories of her parents—though I think her father's dead—and she remembers arriving at the school when she was about six."

"And you?"

I felt my face flushing. "I don't know," I admitted. "I have no memories of my parents." I tried to keep sadness from creeping into my tone, but I could tell by Kip's face that I'd failed miserably.

"You like your school?" he asked, obviously trying to change the subject.

I frowned at his question. "You know, it's funny. For years I wanted to run away. The kids there were terrible to Trina and me, just because we're orphans."

"But now you want to go back?"

My shoulders hunched. "I probably wouldn't actually be happy there. But at least I'd be safe, unlike out here."

"Doesn't sound very safe to me," Kip replied. "Having to live every day with kids who hate you sounds awful. I'd much rather live in the woods." He stifled a yawn. "I figure it's time to sleep. Do you want the hammock or the floor?"

We decided that I would sleep on the floor near Trina, but Kip insisted on giving me the only blanket in the hut, which he normally slept under. It was faded, but the material was soft and slightly shiny, and I could tell by looking at it that it was once something luxurious. I settled onto the floor under the blanket; as I did, I couldn't help throwing glances at Kip as he arranged himself in the hammock in the near-dark. Then I shook my head and closed my eyes. Awkward as I might feel around him, I had to be thankful for our newfound friend. It seemed, for now at least, that our fortunes had taken a turn for the better.

We awoke early the next day and had a breakfast of bread and cheese, neither of which, Kip told us, had been made by him. "These woods have a sort of trade system going," he explained. "Folks find something they're good at, a service or something they can make, and they trade for other things they want."

"What do you do?" Trina asked.

"I hunt," he said, motioning to the bow and quiver of arrows that sat in a corner. "I'm a better hunter than most people too, y'know. So I hunt down game and smoke the meat and sell it."

We finished breakfast, and Kip took a burlap bag and put in several portions of bread, meat and cheese for our journey. "You need to store this up in a tree at night," he told me. "The animals won't bother you if they can't get to your food."

We headed outside after that, and Kip walked over to his garden and began pulling up vegetables and adding them to our bag of food. He was halfway through pulling out a large carrot when we heard the screech of a bird overhead. Kip cocked his head, then smiled and stood up. "I'll be back," he said, then darted into the forest.

I could hear the sound of his return less than five minutes later. "You won't have to go looking for Kirilee," Kip called out as broke through the forest. "She's found us!"

# Chapter Six

**I'M NOT SURE** what I was expecting the queen of the forest to look like, but the woman who followed Kip out of the woods was certainly a surprise. She looked younger than I expected, and I couldn't help but notice her lack of clothing. She was clad in a green top that tied behind her neck, leaving her shoulders bare, and a patched brown skirt that barely reached her knees. Her feet were bare, and her dark hair was woven into a strange style, with some sections hanging loose and others intricately braided together. Like Kip, her skin was bronzed from exposure to the sun, and like Rich and Fergus, she had patterns inked into her skin and wore jewelry that could have been made of bone or shell. Her bright blue-green eyes, I noticed, were nearly the same colour as my own—though hers were ringed with dark makeup. Most surprising of all was the large, now-familiar hawk perched on her shoulder. Bailey stared up at the hawk, letting out a whimper.

Kip made introductions, and Trina moved forward to greet Kirilee in her usual way. Kirilee remained still as Trina touched her face, not asking for an explanation for Trina's behaviour. "What can I do for you girls?" she asked with the lilting accent that I was beginning to associate with the Shrouded Woods. "You're not from around here, ai?"

"We're looking to travel to the Isle of Dundere," I informed her. "One of our teachers told us that you might be able to escort us there. We're from Sylvenburgh, and we don't know the way, and we're a bit young to be travelling alone."

"I see that." She looked me over, her eyes lingering on my dirt-smudged dress. "I can see you partway there, though I can't take you the whole way. But I do have a friend who's planning to go to Dundere soon; he might let you accompany him on his journey. And I think I know where he'll be tonight."

"We'll come with you, then," Trina said. I nodded.

We went into the hut to fetch our belongings. Returning outside, I turned to Kip. "Thank you for your generosity." I felt my heart flutter slightly; a part of me wished that he was coming as well. Then I shook my head at my own thoughts. *Since when did you become so silly around boys, Saray?*

He gave us a quick nod and a smile. I took Trina's arm, and we began to follow Kirilee down the path. A few strides into our journey I heard a whimper. I glanced back and saw that Bailey was following us at a distance, throwing glances back at Kip. "Bailey, no," Kip said in a sharp voice. "You stay here."

Bailey whimpered more and continued to follow us. Kirilee gave the dog a curious glance. "He's obsessed with Trina," I explained.

"He likes your bird," Trina added. "And he wants to come with us."

Kirilee chuckled. "Then why doesn't he?" she asked. "And you as well?" She glanced back at Kip.

"Me?" Kip frowned. "Why?"

"Because, clearly, your dog wants you to," she replied, grinning.

Kip frowned. "Y'know I don't like going far from home."

"Oh, come on." Kirilee's voice held a teasing note. "Just this once, ai? We could use a hunter."

Kip stared at Bailey for a moment and then let out a sigh. "Fine," he relented. "Let me get my things."

I found myself smiling slightly as he retreated into the hut; I hadn't expected my unspoken wish to come true. Then I turned to Kirilee and stared at the hawk on her shoulder. "We've met your bird before," I told her. Trina nodded.

"Oh, really?" Kirilee cocked her head. "And when was that?"

"It led us here, to Kip's place," Trina said. "It's like it wanted us to find him."

"And he led me here as well this morning," Kirilee said. "Seems the Fae wanted all of us to meet for some reason."

"That wasn't the first time we met your bird, though," I put in and told her about our run-in with the bandits.

"By the Fae," she said, shaking her head. "I know those two, and they're fools. They wouldn't have actually harmed you, but they love to scare people, especially city folk. I'll have words with them if we come across them, don't you worry." She reached up and patted the bird's talons. "I'm glad Persius was able to help."

Kip was walking out of his hut now, wearing an animal-skin vest over his shirt, a bag slung over his shoulder and a bow and quiver of arrows on his back. Bailey's tail began to wag at the sight of Kip coming to join us. "Why'd you need a hunter?" he asked Kirilee as we began to move forward. "You not know how?"

"I do, but I don't own a bow," she replied. "I like to carry as little as possible."

"How do you eat meat then?" Trina piped up.

"Sometimes I get Persius to hunt for me," she said. "Though I doubt his catches could feed all four of us. Other times I'll trade my wares for meat, or not eat it at all. You can live off of only roots and vegetables if you know the right ones to eat, y'know."

"Really?" Trina turned towards her. "Could you teach me how to do that?"

"I s'pose I could," Kirilee told her. "You don't like meat?"

She shrugged. "I don't mind how it tastes but...well, it's complicated."

"What do you sell?" I asked Kirilee.

"I collect herbs and plants and make them into healing potions and salves and all sorts of things," Kirilee answered. She bent down and reached into a bush; when she stood up, she was holding a large cluster of yellow-green blossoms. "These are yarel blooms. If they're dried and made into a tea, they can do wonders for a person with a cold." She slid her pack off her shoulder and placed the blossoms inside. Then she touched a bright orange flower nearby. "This is a skunkflower, and it can be used as a weapon," she went on, rooting around in her pack. When she withdrew her hand, she was holding what looked like a small clay ball. "This is filled with powdered skunkflower," she informed us. "If I throw one of these at someone and it breaks open, it'll release a dust that'll blind them temporarily. They can be useful in confrontations with bandits." She smiled wryly, picked a few of the orange flowers, and stowed them in her bag.

We made our way deeper into the forest and were soon surrounded by plants I hadn't seen before—large ferns with blue-green fronds, small leafy trees no taller than me, and showy red flowers with bulbs protruding from their centres. Kirilee stopped every now and then to pull a plant from the ground and dust off its root or climb a tree and emerge with a handful of leaves, always telling us what the plant was called and what it was useful for. By the time we stopped for lunch, my mind was spinning with new information, most of which I doubted I'd be able to remember.

After lunch was very much the same as before, and after several hours of walking, my legs began to ache. It was at about that time that Kip suddenly shushed us, pulled his bow off his back and nocked an arrow. I watched, transfixed. He stood perfectly still, muscles rigid as he looked up into the trees, his eyes set on a creature that I couldn't see from my vantage point.

Then he let an arrow fly, and a large, brightly coloured bird plummeted to the ground moments later. He looked down at it and then at us. "Care for some dinner?"

"Ew," Trina replied, cringing.

"What?" Kip asked.

"It's just…I heard that bird squawk when you shot it." She shuddered.

Kip raised an eyebrow. "I s'pose you city folk don't think much about where your meat comes from, ai?"

"I suppose not," Trina agreed. "Maybe we should think about it more."

Kirilee disappeared into the forest while Kip prepared the bird. I walked around the area, collecting the necessary items to build a fire and creating a ring on the mossy ground. "Y'know how to light it?" Kip asked me as he plucked the feathers from the bird.

"I, uh…" I looked away and trailed off, unwilling to truthfully answer his question. "I can try."

He nodded. "There's a flint and steel in my pack."

I retrieved the flint and steel and crouched by the fire pit, hitting them together and trying to create a spark. My efforts got me nowhere, and I was about to attempt to use magic without Kip noticing when a voice behind me spoke, startling me. "Here, let me."

I glanced up at Kirilee, who had returned, her arms full of roots. She set them down, took the flint and steel from me, and created a flame within seconds. Then she reached over to where Kip was preparing the bird, took a brightly coloured feather, and cleaned off its end with a leaf. She tucked it behind my ear, grinning. Persius flew by with something in his beak, and Bailey got up and trotted over to where the bird had landed. A second later there was a flurry of barks and shrieks, causing both Kip and Kirilee to look up and begin sharply calling off their respective animals. Trina stood up calmly and walked towards them both, and my eyes widened as Bailey slunk off and Persius returned to his dinner. *How did she do that?*

Some time later, we sat down to a dinner of roast bird, along with Kirilee's tubers cooked in the fire's embers and spiced with some of her dried herbs. Kirilee assured Trina that she would do just fine eating only the tubers for dinner, and Trina ignored the meat in favour of them. I wolfed down my own food, thankful that today we were eating well. "So, where do you live, exactly?" I asked Kirilee. "I assume we're heading to your home for the night?"

She exchanged a glance with Kip. "Where *don't* I live is a better question." She gestured to the forest around her. "All of Firenholme is my home; where I make camp in it varies from night to night."

My eyes narrowed. "So you're homeless then?"

"Homeless?" she scoffed. "Absolutely not. Any place with food and herbs to gather and good friends nearby—that place is home." She eyed me; it was hard to tell from her expression whether she was amused or irritated. "As for tonight, if my friend is where I think he is, then he'll likely invite us to stay in his camp. If not, then we'll find somewhere with good cover. There's nothing wrong with sleeping in the woods, y'know."

"Trina and I slept in the woods for the first two nights of our journey," I told her. "The first night we were attacked. It doesn't feel very safe to me."

"Right. But bandits aren't so likely to attack a group of four."

"What was that name you used?" Trina asked. "Firholme?"

"Firenholme. It's an old Cherinese name for the Shrouded Woods. It can mean either 'home of the fairies' or 'kingdom of fire,' depending on how it's interpreted."

"Why would 'kingdom of fire' be a good name for a forest?" I asked.

"Because once, a long time ago, some angry people set these woods on fire. But the magic in these woods kept them from being burned down." She glanced up at the sky, barely visible through the canopy of trees. "We should move, ai? It'll be another hour on foot before we reach my friend."

We cleaned up our area and set off. The sky began to darken as we walked; Persius flew into the trees to find a perch for the night, and the luminescent flowers started to glow all around us. After a long while I saw firelight flickering beyond the trees; the sounds of laughter and what might have been drums grew louder. A few more minutes of walking brought us to a large patch of open space, with trees towering on every side. There were probably thirty people present, most of them seated around a large bonfire that crackled in the centre of the clearing. A man stood up. "Kirilee!" he bellowed out. "What lovely new friends have you found us today?"

Kirilee laughed, telling the man each of our names. The man's expression changed as we moved closer. "You brought city folk to a Moon Dance?" he said, his voice turning cold.

"City *children* under my care, Ronin," Kirilee replied evenly. "And y'know full well that all are welcome at our celebrations."

Another man stood up on the far side of the circle, his form mostly obscured by shadow. "If you hate city folk so much, why haven't you kicked me out yet?" His voice was oddly familiar.

Kirilee grinned. "Exactly who I was looking for," she said. "You three wait here."

I watched as Kirilee walked towards the fire. The man named Ronin gave us a long, suspicious glance and then returned to pounding out a rhythm on a large drum.

I took a seat on a log and pulled Trina down next to me. A few of those present had begun dancing with partners, twirling merrily around the fire to the beat of the drum. Some of the women danced with other women here, I saw, and a few of the men danced with men as well. One girl who was wearing a lot of jewels was dancing on her own, shaking her hips in a way that reminded me of Lizzie from the school. Several of the people present wore jewelry and had inked skin similar to Kirilee's. I shook my head. *These people are strange.* They seemed to think we were equally strange; they all kept their distance from our log, many of them throwing occasional glances our way. *They don't trust us.*

A light a few feet away from me caught my attention, and I watched as a young man dressed in only a pair of breeches held a small ball of fire in each hand and then began twirling them around rhythmically, creating patterns with the flame. Someone else must have cast some other sort of magic on the bonfire itself; now it danced with varying shades of blue and green and purple, and a halo of pebbles was suspended above the fire, spinning in time with the music. I whispered to Trina about the strange things I was seeing and then threw a glance at Kip. He was still standing, rooted to the ground with crossed arms, a wary expression on his face. *Dangerous,* he was probably thinking.

Kirilee reappeared out of the shadows, the man with the familiar voice in tow, but instead of returning to us, the two of them joined the group of dancing couples, laughing and whirling together. After a few minutes of dancing, they broke from the crowd and approached us. When the man came close enough for me to see his features, I found myself staring.

"This is my friend, Lachlann," Kirilee said to us. "He's agreed to take you to Dundere."

It was, without any doubt, Mr. Jeffries' twin brother. There was no mistaking the deep-set brown eyes, the broad shoulders, the familiar smile. I could see why Mr. Jeffries claimed they looked nothing alike, though; Lachlann was considerably more muscular than his brother, his skin tanned far darker. He had a neatly trimmed beard instead of the familiar mustache, and his hair, which fell to his shoulders, had a blond tinge to it. He wore plain, dark-coloured clothes topped by a suit of intricately detailed black leather armour, and a sword hung from his belt. "It's a pleasure to meet you all," he said to us in a voice that was nearly identical to his brother's, but somehow a bit friendlier.

Trina cocked her head at the voice. "What are you doing out here, Mr. Jeffries?" she asked, clearly having missed his name.

He raised a questioning eyebrow at Kirilee. "How does your friend know my last name?"

I laughed. "It's not the Mr. Jeffries you think, Trina." I turned to him. "We know your twin brother," I explained. "We used to live at Sylvenburgh Academy. He was the one who sent us on this journey."

"Is that so?" he replied, his eyes widening. "My brother is sending children into the woods now?"

"We were in danger," I explained. "He was helping us escape."

He exchanged a look with Kirilee that I didn't quite understand and then turned his gaze to us. "Well, if Tomlin sent you, I'm all the more willing to take you to Dundere." He grinned. "Though our journey will have to wait a week or so; I have a delivery I need to make first and a wagon to take back home. You're all welcome to stay at my camp until I return, if you'd like."

Another song was starting up, and Lachlann gave us all a nod and took Kirilee's arm. I watched them curiously as they walked back towards the fire, recalling Mr. Jeffries' comment about Lachlann being in love with Kirilee. I wondered whether or not she might feel the same about him.

A boy was approaching our log now, a stocky young man in bright-coloured clothing who appeared perhaps a year older than me. A creature that looked like a large lizard was perched on his shoulder. The boy flashed me a grin as he walked up. "Would you dance with me?" His voice was smooth and confident; he was clearly unafraid of us city folk.

"I…uh…" I stammered, heat creeping up my neck. "Would you show me how? I don't know any of the steps."

He waved away my concern. "There are no steps, don't worry. Come on, ai?" He extended a hand to me, and then he was pulling me to my feet, dragging me towards the fire. "I'm Ambrose."

"Saray," I returned, giving him a nervous smile. I watched, fascinated, as the lizard creature flew away from his shoulder. *I've never seen a flying lizard before.*

He nodded. "Pleasure to meet you." He took my hands and pulled me into position and then lowered his voice. "Are you the girl who can cast with her mind?"

I frowned. "The...what?"

"There are stories going around 'bout a city girl who can cast spells with only her mind," he told me. "Rumour has it she set some men on fire when they tried to rob her."

My eyes widened at his words, but I shook my head. "That's not me," I lied, glancing in Kip's direction. "I can't cast."

"Too bad." Ambrose's smile faded. "I was hoping you were her. I've never met anyone who can cast with their mind before."

The song that had at first been a steady drumbeat turned into something quite unlike any other music I'd ever heard. There were pipers and a man who was playing something that looked like a violin, and the music was fast paced and lilting. The dancing, it seemed, was comprised mostly of fast spinning and long lines, and I almost tripped several times trying to keep up with Ambrose. He was solid enough that I didn't have to worry about falling, though; he kept me whirling and moving in time to the music, seemingly without effort. When the song was done, he grinned at me. "Another?"

The flying lizard had returned to his shoulder, and I recoiled as it let out an unexpected puff of flame. Then I gasped as I realized what this creature actually was. "Is that a *dragon* on your shoulder?"

"Just a baby dragon, ai." Ambrose's grin widened. "Adult dragons don't live in this part of the Shrouded Woods, lucky for us. His name is Spark."

"I'll dance with you again if you let me pet him," I said.

Ambrose leaned forward, and I ran my hand over the tiny dragon's scales. Then Ambrose grabbed my hands, and suddenly we were spinning about again. I threw my head back and laughed, allowing myself to relax, to abandon my reservations and move in time to the rhythm.

When Ambrose finally deposited me back on my log, I was breathless but grinning widely. I thanked him for the dances, and he sauntered off in search of a new target; I turned my attention to the others. Kirilee and Lachlann had returned, and Lachlann had secured two small hand drums and was teaching Trina how to use one. Kirilee was perched on the log a little way down from them, absorbed in a conversation with another woman. Two little girls—at least, I thought they were girls; it was hard to tell by their clothing—were sitting on Kirilee's lap, and one of them was toying with one of her braids. Kip stood apart from the group, Bailey by his side, surveying the area with a watchful eye. He caught me staring at him and frowned. "That wasn't so smart," he said.

"What?"

"Dancing with that boy."

"Why?"

"He could've been an elfieblood. Probably is one, in fact. Most normal folks don't keep pet dragons."

I shrugged. "So what if he was? I was just dancing with him."

Kip's frown deepened, and he moved towards me and crouched down. "You don't get it," he hissed. "If he was one of *them*, he'd just have to mumble a few words, and you'd be dead, y'know." He glanced around warily. "These people, they aren't safe."

I snorted, suddenly annoyed with him. "Kirilee's talking with one of them over there, and I don't see you lecturing her."

"Kirilee knows these woods," he replied, his tone softening slightly. "You're new here; you don't know what to look for." He paused and touched my shoulder lightly. "Just be careful, ai?" He backed away from me before I could reply, and I stared at the fire for a few minutes, conflicted. The way he'd spoken about magic users made my stomach turn, but I was still very aware of where he'd touched my shoulder, and a part of me wished that his hand had lingered for a few moments more.

I snorted at my own thoughts. *Who am I becoming?* Just last night I was blushing and giggling over Kip, and tonight I danced with another boy at the fire and enjoyed it fully. *I'm acting just like Lizzie and Becky and all those girls at the Academy.* I glowered at the flames, angry at myself for being so silly and vapid, for acting like *them.*

A movement to my right jerked me out of my reverie, and I glanced over as Kirilee sat down next to me. "Everything all right?"

I shook my head, not ready to fill her in on all my thoughts. "Kip's just…bothering me."

"How so?"

I repeated to her the things Kip had said to me, and she smiled and shook her head. "He means well," she told me. "Kip can be too serious for his own good sometimes. Don't let him stop you enjoying yourself, ai?"

"He's very afraid of magic," I observed.

"As are most people. Why, aren't you?" She grinned at me, amusement dancing in her blue-green eyes, and then got up and left before I could answer.

The dancing lasted another couple of hours, and I spent most of that time staring at the magic users. Strange as they all were, it was hard for me to ignore my desire to join them. The people at the fire seemed less wary of me after my dance with Ambrose; a woman came by soon after with treats— dates covered in sugar and some sort of spice—and I took several and ate them eagerly. A little while later, a bottle of something dark was passed around, but Kirilee intercepted it before it could get to me, stating that I was too young for such things before taking a swig herself and passing the bottle to Lachlann. After a while, Trina lay down on the ground in front of the log, and Bailey trotted over and curled up next to her. The moon shone down, full and bright, on our party, and I stared up at it and wondered what the significance of the Moon Dance was.

Eventually, the fire died down, and the musicians began to disperse. Lachlann suggested that we follow him to his camp. He scooped Trina up easily, not waking her, and set off, the rest of us trailing behind him.

Lachlann's camp was about a ten-minute walk from where the party had been, situated in a small break in the forest. The clearing contained a fire ring, a good-sized tent made from some sort of hide, and a large covered wagon. A horse was tethered to the wagon; it grazed contentedly on a nearby patch of grass. Lachlann ducked into his tent, still carrying Trina, and returned a moment later without her. "We'll let the girls take the tent tonight," he said.

"What's in the wagon?" I asked.

"Would you kids like to see?" was his response. I nodded eagerly, and he lit a torch and opened up the back, then climbed up inside. I followed him into the wagon, Kip close behind me, and looked around curiously.

One side held several swords on racks. Their blades were varied in size, each of their hilts unique. I stepped towards one and studied the intricate patterns that were engraved into the pommel. Hung on the other side of the wagon were several pieces of leather armour—a couple of breastplates, half a dozen sets of bracers, and a few belts with pouches strung along them. A single round shield rested on the ground below them. The far end of the wagon contained several boxes that appeared to hold pieces of unfinished leather and tools. I stared at the armour, then at Lachlann. "You made those?"

"I did," he said rather proudly. "I make and sell them for a living."

"Swords too?" Kip asked, a note of disbelief in his voice. "And the shield?"

Lachlann nodded. "I can't make the swords on the road, of course, but I have a forge back at the farm where I craft them. The shields I can make anywhere. Though they're best when made out of aiken wood, and I'm all out, which is why I'm headed to Dundere. Aiken trees don't grow here."

"You go all the way to another country to buy wood?" I asked.

Lachlann laughed. "Any excuse for an adventure, my dear."

Kip was running his fingers over the hilt of one of the longer swords. "These are amazing," he said softly. "You know how to use them all?"

"Of course I do," Lachlann replied matter-of-factly. He glanced at Kip. "Do you know the sword?"

Kip shook his head. "I hunt with a bow. I've never learned the sword."

"Well, I can teach you if you'd like, so long as you keep travelling with us," Lachlann offered.

Kip frowned. "I doubt I'll stay long enough to learn. Thanks, though."

"Well, the offer stands so long as you're with us." Lachlann turned to me. "And what about you?"

My eyes widened at his offer. "I'm...a bit clumsy," I admitted. "I doubt I'd be a good student." My gaze shifted to Kip; I certainly didn't want to make a fool out of myself in front of him.

Lachlann shrugged. "Suit yourself." He motioned to the door of the wagon. "Come on, let's get back to Kirilee."

We exited the wagon to find a fire going and Kirilee sitting by it. She had changed while we were in the wagon; now she wore a pair of breeches that looked like boys' clothes and a long brightly colored patchwork coat.

Ambrose had shown up at our campsite and was sitting with Kirilee, Spark perched on his shoulder.

"What do you think of Lachlann's trade?" Kirilee asked us. "Quite the craftsman, ai?

"He definitely is," I agreed. I stared at Lachlann. "How did you end up out here? Your brother is the vice principal of a school and you…travel through the woods and make swords and armour?"

He chuckled. "In case you've not figured it out yet, Tomlin and I aren't very similar." He sat down on the other side of Kirilee and looked up at me. "Tom was the smart one of the two of us. He excelled in school and excelled in magic as well. Me, I'm the dumb one."

"Stop saying that!" Kirilee scolded him, elbowing him in the ribs. "You're just as smart at Tomlin, and you know it."

"Perhaps that's true," he replied. "But the teachers at my school didn't see it that way. They told me once I finished school I should join the army, like they told every other big dumb boy to do. And so I did. I served for about seven years. And it was a good experience, mostly. I got to see a lot of places, make some wonderful friends, and gained some confidence and some new skills, like how to use those properly." He nodded at his wagon full of weapons. "But there were some very hard times. There generally are when you're expected to go into battle for a living. So, after a while, I decided I'd seen enough war. I left the army and spent another five years or so just travelling, working on ships and finding work in various ports. And it was in one of those ports that I found a job as a blacksmith's apprentice, and I discovered that I like making swords better than fighting with them.

"By that point, I was getting a little homesick. My father passed away shortly after I turned thirty, and I knew I'd be needed at home. So I went home and started helping with the farm, but I also built my own forge in the backyard. Tom told me he knew some folks in the Shrouded Woods who might be interested in buying my wares. So I began making trips into these woods. It was pretty soon after that I met Kirilee, and Ambrose a few years after." He grinned at them. "And it was an old woman here in the woods named Kallah who persuaded me to try leatherwork. So now I travel both through the woods and into the cities, selling my wares when I'm not needed at home. It's a good arrangement. I like it out here. It's more peaceful. And the company is infinitely more interesting. For example, you don't meet fellows with miniature dragons back in Sylvenburgh."

"Well, that's for certain," I chuckled and then stifled a yawn.

Ambrose caught my yawn; he gave us a grin and stood up. "I'll let you folks sleep. I'm only a few trees away, if you need me."

"Yes, it does seem like it's that time, for you two at least," Lachlann said, gesturing at Kip and me. "I'll stay up a bit later."

"And you?" I glanced at Kirilee. "I suppose you'll be sleeping in the tent with Trina and me?"

Kirilee exchanged an amused glance with Lachlann. "No need for that," she said. "I'll keep watch through the night. I don't sleep."

"You...don't sleep?" Kip repeated.

Kirilee shook her head. "I don't need to. Haven't for years."

I gaped at her. "Are you sure you aren't a magic user?"

"I'm not." She shook her head. "My not needing to sleep is thanks to a spell that was cast on me years ago. It's a long story."

"Do you not get tired?" I asked incredulously. "What do you do all night?"

She chuckled. "I do. At night I usually rest or meditate or commune with the fairies."

Lachlann caught my expression and laughed. "Don't let it worry you, Saray," he said. "Just go to bed, have a good night's rest, and be glad that none of you need to keep watch."

I stared at my travelling companions—the odd swordsman who was our teacher's brother, the magic-fearing archer boy who made me feel funny inside, and the strange woman with the inked skin and sparse clothing who befriended hawks and didn't sleep and apparently believed in fairies—and shook my head. *They seem just as odd as Rich and Fergus*, I thought, ducking into the tent. *But I suppose I'll have to trust them regardless.* Strange as they were, the three of them were our ticket to Dundere, to my safety and Trina's healing. And I wasn't about to try to navigate the Shrouded Woods on my own.

# Chapter Seven

**I AWOKE THE** next morning to the crackling of the campfire and Kirilee and Lachlann's voices talking outside. I attempted to smooth down my hair and then crawled out of the tent, squinting as I made my way into the morning light. Everyone else was up, gathered around a large boiling pot that was suspended over the fire. Kirilee greeted me by scooping porridge out of it with a ladle and into a bowl and handing the bowl to me. "Morning, Saray. Eat up."

"Where did you get this?"

"I brought it with me," Lachlann answered. "My mother knows how to make a good porridge. Fills you right up."

Kirilee and Lachlann discussed the plans for the day while they ate, deciding that Kirilee would take Trina and me plant-gathering with her this morning. "Trying to separate the boys from the girls?" I asked her.

She laughed. "Actually, yes. I figure it's a good time for us girls to visit the river."

I nodded and ran a hand through my tangled curls; I'd been so preoccupied with our adventures that the thought of bathing had simply not occurred to me.

"Can we go to another dance tonight?" Trina asked. "Last night was amazing. The music was like something from another world."

Kirilee grinned. "Those dances only happen on the full moon, sadly. But we can make some music of our own later, if you'd like."

We finished up breakfast, and Kirilee shouldered her pack and motioned that Trina and I should follow her. Trina said goodbye to Bailey, promising the dog that she'd return, and we left the camp. Persius glided down from a nearby tree as Kirilee walked and perched on her shoulder, occasionally staring at me with his beady black eyes. After about fifteen minutes of walking down narrow but well-established paths, we entered a glade and Kirilee stopped walking. She turned to Trina. "Do you want to help us gather?"

"I...well, do you think I can?" Trina replied.

"I know you can," Kirilee assured her. She took Trina's hand and sat her down in front of a large patch of mushrooms, then guided her hands towards them. "Pick as many of these as you can find by touch," she instructed. She removed her pack and moved one of Trina's hands so she was touching it. "Put them in here."

Trina began to pick the mushrooms, and Kirilee turned to me. "Remember the yarel blooms from yesterday?" She motioned at a cluster of bushes that I now recognized, then reached into her coat and extracted a small knife. "They're not easy to pick if you're not used to doing it, so use the knife to cut the branches out."

"How many do you want?" I asked.

Kirilee glanced at the three yarel bushes. "Maybe take as many blooms as you can from one bush?"

I noticed one of the trees that glowed at night nearby, and I walked over and picked a flower. "Are those good for anything?"

Kirilee took the bloom from me. "Vilettas? Nothing more than lighting up the forest at night and making things more beautiful." She reached down and put the flower behind Trina's ear.

Trina giggled and touched the flower. "What colour is it?"

"Your favourite," I told her.

She let out a wistful sigh. "I miss purple."

Kirilee grinned. "I know of a flower that smells like purple."

"Smells like purple?" Trina repeated incredulously. "Things can't smell like they're a colour."

"You won't think that after you smell this flower," she replied. "If I come across one, I'll show you. Now you'd best get picking." She handed me the knife and then shed her coat, Persius alighting from her shoulder. Then she reached up into one of the twisting trees and hoisted herself up.

I watched for a minute as Kirilee began to climb the tree, her feet finding sturdy branches with obvious ease. Then I turned my attention to the yarel blooms. I reached into the bush, seizing a clump of flowers near its base, and used the knife to cut it free. The branches were tough, but after picking several of them I found myself developing a technique for cutting them quickly and efficiently. I threw repeated glances up into the tree that Kirilee had climbed; she was nearly invisible now, though I could hear her humming to herself high in the branches. I was halfway through cutting a branch when a large clump of blue-violet berries fell from the trees and landed close to me, startling me. I let out a yelp as the blade nearly grazed my finger. "Everything all right?" I heard Kirilee ask from above.

I brought my hand out and examined it; thankfully, I was unscathed. "I'm fine," I called back up.

I went back to my work, only startling slightly when more clusters of berries hit the ground around me. When Kirilee jumped to the ground from a low branch a little while later, her fingers were stained purple. She looked with approval at my bag of yarel blooms and then glanced at Trina. "You done mushroom picking?"

Trina shrugged and looked up. "You tell me, am I?"

Kirilee chuckled and looked over the area. "I'd say you have enough. Let's move on."

"Where to now?" I asked.

"The river," Kirilee answered. "It's time for our baths."

The river was a short walk from the field, and I couldn't help but gape when we arrived. A massive waterfall tumbled and roared above us, coating our faces in a fine mist, and the water below it churned noisily over the rocks. Our bathing spot was a mostly enclosed pool off to one side of the river, safe from the foaming rapids nearby. "The water's about chest height for me at the deepest part," Kirilee told us. She touched Trina's shoulder. "You'll want to stay near the edge."

I watched as Kirilee removed her coat, along with her pack and the several belts that she used to hold her belongings to herself, and jumped in the water still wearing her clothes. She landed with a loud splash and disappeared under the surface. When she appeared again, she was grinning, her dark hair dripping wet. "What are you waiting for? Come on in, ai?"

I hesitated for a moment and then slowly removed my shoes and stockings. I loosened my dress, let it fall to the ground, and walked to the edge of the pool in only my undergarments. I tested the water with a bare toe and shivered.

"It's not so bad once you're used to it," Kirilee encouraged me. "Why don't you two jump in together?"

I nodded and turned to Trina, who was still dressed. "Let's do it."

She shuddered slightly but then nodded her assent and pulled off her dress. We walked to the edge together, hand in hand. "One," I counted us down, "two, three."

We threw ourselves off the edge, and I let out a shriek as the icy water enveloped me. It closed over my head for a moment, and then my feet found the bottom. A moment later I surfaced, gasping and sputtering. Beside me, Trina popped up, spitting out water. "This is cold!" she exclaimed.

"Give it a minute," Kirilee said. I saw that she had removed her clothes while in the water and was scrubbing them against a rock near the edge of the pool.

I shivered and hugged myself, trying to acclimatize to the temperature, and then paddled to the side and retrieved our dresses. I handed Trina her dress and explained what we were doing, and then I followed Kirilee's lead, soaking my dress and using the rocks to scrub out all the dirt. "You girls need some better clothes for these woods," Kirilee commented. "City dresses don't work so well out here. I'll make you some clothes like mine." She gestured to her top and skirt, which she'd arranged on a rock to dry.

I wrinkled my nose. "I don't know," I said. "I mean, I like to wear a little more than you do." I blushed as I imagined parading around the forest wearing so little, likely attracting the attention of every male in the vicinity. "You forest people dress strangely."

"We forest people dress how we please," Kirilee replied, raising her eyebrows. "Here in the woods, there's no one to tell us what to wear, or how to speak, or how to live. We live how we wish." As if to prove her point, she hoisted herself out of the water and sat on a rock, completely nude.

I stared at her for a moment and then looked away. "Aren't you worried the men are going to show up?" My stomach twisted at the thought.

She laughed. "Not at all. Lachlann knows where we're bathing; he's not disrespectful enough to show up without invitation. And Kip's too afraid of girls to even think about it. As for any others who might come this way, they can choose to look away if it bothers them."

I frowned as a thought from last night popped into my head. "Are you and Lachlann together?"

"Are we together?" Kirilee asked, sliding back into the water. "Why'd you think that?"

"Well, I saw how you were dancing yesterday, and you seem to really like each other..." I trailed off.

Kirilee eyed me and shook her head. "We're not," she said. "It wouldn't work."

"Why?" I asked. "Is he too old for you?"

"Why do *you* ask so many questions, ai?" Her voice had that irritated-yet-amused tone once again. "And no, it's nothing to do with something so superficial. I'm older than I look. It's far more complex than that." Her tone left no room for argument. I let out a huff and leaned back against the rocks.

We were quiet after that, listening to the sound of the churning river and the birds singing above it, waiting for our clothes to dry. I cast the occasional glance at Kirilee, afraid I'd earn another lecture for asking too many questions. *She's starting to sound like Mr. Jeffries.*

Eventually, we crawled out of the water, dressed, and resumed walking. We took a different route back to our camp; this one was more populated. We passed several people, Kirilee exchanging smiles and hellos with each of them. I noticed what looked to be houses nestled high up in the trees at one point, and when we passed through a meadow, I could see a few huts dotting the nearby hillside. "Is there a village anywhere in the Shrouded Woods?" I looked at Kirilee out of the corner of my eye, afraid that this question would earn more harsh words from her.

But she shook her head, seemingly unbothered. "Most of the people of Firenholme are too transient to form a village. Though we do have a few gathering places, like the clearing we went to for the Moon Dance." She paused for a moment and then reached up into a tree. When she withdrew her hand, she was holding a branch of bell-shaped flowers. She thrust them at Trina. "Here, smell these and tell me they don't smell like purple."

Trina took the branch, held it to her face and inhaled. When she lowered it, she was smiling. "You're right," she said slowly. "They do smell like purple. If purple had a smell, that is."

I took the flowers from her and breathed in their scent. It was rich and floral but also somewhat spicy, like wine or cinnamon. I looked up and shook my head; I couldn't argue with Kirilee's claim.

Kirilee reached into her pack and pulled out what looked like a small ornament made from woven sticks and twine. She put the sprig of purple-smelling flowers into its centre and hung it from the branch of a nearby tree. "A gift," she said. "For the fairies."

"You actually believe fairies exist?" Trina asked.

"I *know* they exist," Kirilee replied. "As do all the Seekers in these woods. In fact, most of us have seen them with our own eyes at the temple of the fairy priestess—though only a few of us know where that is."

"Seekers?" I repeated. "Are you...religious?" The word felt strange on my tongue. Religion was rare in the cities; it wasn't illegal, but most people associated it with magic and thus avoided it.

"We Seekers honour the fairy magic," she explained. "The magic that exists here in Breoch came from them, y'know. We do small things like leaving gifts and dancing every full moon, in hopes that one day they'll run free within Firenholme again." She sighed. "I'll explain more another time. We're nearly back at camp, and it's time for lunch."

After lunch, sunlight filled the clearing, and Kirilee laid out the plants she had gathered in the sun to dry. She had some other, previously dried plants in her pack, and those she began preparing further, removing leaves and flowers from stems and grinding them down to a fine powder using a mortar and pestle from her bag. Kip went off to hunt, and Lachlann began assembling a set of armour using a hammer and anvil and small metal rivets. Halfway into the afternoon, a young couple walked into the clearing. Kirilee looked up and smiled. "Terran, Lila—how are you?"

"We're well," the young man, Terran, replied. "Tomi told us you'd be here; we're looking to get some salve for an infected wound." He glanced over at Lachlann and grinned. "I see the city boy has returned to us, ai?"

"For a short while, yes," Lachlann said, standing and shaking the other man's hand. He eyed the sword on Terran's hip. "How's the blade treating you?"

"Wonderfully," Terran replied. "It's the best one I've ever had. Thank you again."

Kirilee stood and walked over to her pack and rummaged through it until she found a bottle. She returned to the couple and placed the bottle in Terran's hands. Lila, meanwhile, thrust a bundle at her. "For you, as payment." Kirilee nodded and thanked her.

The couple left, and Kirilee and Lachlann returned to their work. It was only an hour or so later that another person showed up, this one seeking leather bracers from Lachlann, then another who wanted Kirilee's sleep-inducing tea. The gifts they brought in exchange were varied—a new, hand-sewn shirt, a bundle of bread, a bottle of mead, a promise to fix Lachlann's boots next time they wore through—and by the time Kip returned with dinner, I was beginning to understand how the trade system of the Shrouded Woods worked.

We were just about to begin cooking when we heard footsteps approaching. Kirilee stood, looking intently into the bush, and when she looked back at us, she wore a mischievous grin. "This'll be fun," she said. "Saray, Trina, you two hide in the tent."

I gave her a bewildered look but crawled into the tent nonetheless, Trina following me. Then I stifled a gasp as our visitors walked into the clearing. It was none other than Rich and Fergus. Kirilee walked up to Fergus and greeted him by slapping him across the face. I covered my mouth, trying not to burst into giggles, and then whispered to Trina about what I was seeing.

"I hear you've been mistreating young women, ai?" Kirilee said sharply to him. "Stealing their goods, using spells on them, threatening to take advantage of them." Her gaze turned to Rich. "Talking about using them for a *life transfer*, of all things."

The two men sputtered and gasped, seemingly lost for words. "We…we weren't going to *actually* hurt them," Fergus finally protested, rubbing his cheek. "And besides, they were city girls." He said the words with disdain.

"This is how you treat city folk?" Lachlann got to his feet behind Kirilee, his hand resting on the pommel of his sword. "Well, if that's how you feel about us, perhaps I'll stop selling to you. You'll have to go elsewhere for your weapons."

"And for your medicine," Kirilee put in.

"But you're the only medicine woman for miles!" Rich whined.

Kirilee huffed. "Maybe I'll change my mind if you return what was taken." She turned and glanced at the tent. "Come on out, girls."

I couldn't help but smirk at the men as I crawled back out of the tent, Trina close behind me. The men gawked at us. "Well?" Kirilee prompted. "Their belongings?"

The two men exchanged a glance, and then Fergus began pawing through his massive sack, finally extracting my bag. "Some of the food is gone," he mumbled, tossing it in my direction. "But everything else is there."

Kirilee nodded her approval. "Very good. Now you'd best get going, don't you think?"

"But we never got to do business with you," Fergus argued. "We need some sleeping tea!"

"Sleeping tea?" Kirilee repeated. "If it was a real medical emergency, I might consider selling to you. But sleeping tea?" She huffed. "Get out of here. Perhaps a few nights of no sleep will teach you to treat children better!"

Fergus glared at her and stomped off into the woods, Rich following close behind. Kirilee rolled her eyes as they retreated. "Idiots," she scoffed. I nodded in agreement, trying not to laugh. Kirilee caught my expression and grinned at me. "That was enjoyable, ai? Come on, let's eat."

\*           \*

It was getting dark by the time we finished dinner, and I was exhausted, so I was all too happy to comply when Kirilee suggested we head to bed immediately after we'd cleaned up. I followed Trina into the tent and succumbed to sleep almost immediately, only to find myself awake again some time later. Firelight flickered outside, the flames that were visible through the tent's opening making dancing patterns on the walls around me. I could hear men talking nearby. "We know they're with you, sir," an unfamiliar male voice was saying. "Two young girls were reported to have left with your party after a dance last night." I sat up, my heartbeat picking up at the man's words.

There was a pause, and then Lachlann spoke. "And what do you want with our guests?"

Another male voice let out a sharp laugh. "They aren't your guests, sir; they're lost children who need to be returned to their home. And if you refuse to hand them over, I could have both of you charged with kidnapping."

"It's not kidnapping if the children come to you," Kirilee protested. "From what they told me, they were running away from some sort of danger. Perhaps you're the danger they are running from, ai?"

"Let us into the tent, lady." The man's voice was sterner now.

I heard the sound of a sword being drawn. A shadow fell over the tent's opening as Lachlann stepped between us and the men. "If you want to go into the tent," Lachlann said evenly, "you will have to go through me."

I heard the drawing of several more blades, and then the shadows outside began to move, accompanied by the clashing and shouting of fighting men. There were several yelps and cries of pain, and at one point someone began yelling about an archer in the trees. I sat rooted where I was, my heart thumping wildly in my chest. Beside me, Trina sat up. "What's happening?"

Before I had time to respond, something crashed through the opening of the tent, and a large uniformed man nearly fell on top of Trina. The man righted himself and stared at her and then wrapped a beefy hand around her arm. "Got you."

"Don't touch her!" I lunged forward in an attempt to yank his hand off of Trina. He howled in pain, and only then did I become aware of the flames dancing on my hands. He backed out of the tent, his sleeves engulfed in flame. "The redhead!" he screamed. "She set me on fire!"

*I suppose my secret is out now.* "Stay back," I hissed at Trina. Then I kicked off the blankets and poked my head through the tent's entrance. Looking out, I saw one man on the ground, unmoving, an arrow lodged in his chest; another was hunched over, clawing at his eyes and seemingly unable to fight. Two others were attacking Lachlann, their blades meeting his shield time after time as he fended them off. Kirilee was crouched a short distance away from him, her body tensed and her knife drawn. In her other hand was what looked like a skunkflower bomb. An arrow flew from the trees above and hit the man who was on fire, piercing his shoulder and making him scream all the more. All the men were clad in matching blue uniforms. *City guard,* I realized. *Not Breoch Guard, but still not good.*

One of the men who fought Lachlann turned then, and his eyes met mine. He let out a yell, broke away from Lachlann and began to run at me. My eyes widened as a jet of fire streaked towards him, hitting him square in the chest. Kirilee threw her bomb at the man as I cast; it landed on the ground near him and exploded, sending a cloud of dust into the air. A moment later, the dust ignited, and the man was suddenly engulfed in flame. When the fire ceased, there was only a crumpled, blackened corpse where he had been.

"Retreat!" yelled the man fighting Lachlann. The guard who'd attacked Trina and the one who'd been incapacitated by Kirilee's first bomb rose unsteadily to their feet, and the three of them turned and scurried into the woods, away from us. Then they were gone, and we were left staring at the two dead men and at one another. I noticed that Lachlann's shield was broken in two.

"You folks all right?" I turned to see Ambrose standing at the edge of our clearing, looking us over. "I woke up halfway through whatever just happened. Was going to send Spark over, but you folks seemed to have fire magic of your own." He eyed me, and I didn't miss his smirk.

"We're fine," Kirilee assured him. She glanced at me. "And you're right, we do seem to have a firebrand with us."

"A...firebrand?" I repeated, recalling that I'd heard the bandits use that same word.

"One who controls fire," she explained. "That's what they called your kind back before the Banishing." She frowned. "Did I see you set those men on fire without using any words or hand motions?"

I nodded. "I can cast with my mind." I snuck a look at Ambrose; he winked at me.

"By the Fae," she said softly.

Trina joined me at the edge of the tent, causing Bailey to jump up and trot over to her. "They're gone?" Her voice shook.

"They're gone," I assured her.

Kip was making his way out of the trees now, his quiver nearly falling off his back. He jumped from a low branch, landed on his feet near the bodies and looked down at them. "We should deal with these," he said in a low voice. His gaze turned to me, his blue-grey eyes cold. I felt the blood drain from my face. "And after that, I think Saray owes us an explanation."

An hour later our camp was cleaned up, and we sat around a freshly kindled fire, which I had started with magic while the adults buried the two guards. Trina hadn't stopped shaking since she'd emerged from the tent, and I'd ignored my knotted stomach and swirling thoughts in favour of comforting her. Now, though, with Kip, Lachlann and Kirilee all staring at me, their eyes full of questions and, in Kip's case, accusations, it was hard to dismiss the reality of what I'd done. "Well?" Kirilee prompted me. "Are you going to tell us your story, Saray?"

I took a deep breath and began to speak. I told them how I had learned about my abilities in my younger years, about the incident at school that had forced me to flee, and about how Lachlann's brother had taken me from the school and sent me here. I told them how Trina had come into the situation and about our true motivations for trying to reach the Isle of Dundere. "I hope you're still willing to help us find our way there," I concluded.

Kirilee, who had been staring intently at me for the duration of my monologue, frowned and glanced over at Trina. "I wish I knew a lifebringer in these woods I could take you to instead, Trina," she mused. "But healing magic is rare, and lifebringers are paid well in countries where their gifts are legal, so most leave Breoch." She shrugged. "But to answer your question, I'm sure Lachlann will still take you."

Lachlann nodded. "I figured either you or Trina was a magic user," he put in. "My brother doesn't send kids into the woods for fun, you know."

"Thank you," I said, letting out a sigh of relief.

"We'll need to delay our trip, though," Kirilee said. "I'll need to see that you receive some training before you leave Breoch. I have a friend named Willem who lives on a nearby mountain; he can likely help you. I'll head into the woods and do some gathering tonight so we can leave early tomorrow."

"You can count me out." Kip's voice was sullen. I had been avoiding looking at him while I told my story; now I saw that his arms were crossed, his eyes narrowed. "I'm not getting involved in any witchery—not any *more* of it, at least." He glared at me. "Why didn't you tell us before that you're a hildakin?"

"Enough." Kirilee's voice was firm. "You don't use that word around me, do you understand?"

"What does it mean?" asked Trina.

"It's a slur for the Seekers," she explained. "Though it's become common for folks to call all sorts of magic users that name."

Heat rose in my cheeks as I stared at Kip; I wasn't sure if I was angry or ashamed. "I didn't tell you before because I didn't want to be treated like *this*," I informed him. "All this time you've been kind to me, but as soon as you learn about my magic, you treat me like I'm some sort of scum? What's wrong with you, Kip?"

He let out a scoff in reply and looked away.

"Yes, would you care to explain yourself?" Lachlann put in. "What exactly is it about magic that has you acting so rudely?"

Kip snorted. "Hildaki—er, magic users, put everyone in danger," he answered. "You've lived in the cities; y'know why the laws exist."

"It's more than that," Kirilee said, turning to him. "I've sensed it for a while now—your hate for magic is personal. I think you should tell us what's really going on, ai?"

Kip looked at her out of the corner of his eye and then sighed. "My mother hated magic."

"But you said your mother was crazy," I protested. "She was so dangerous that you had to run away from home. Why would you hold on to her views?"

"Cuz before he died, my father told me why my mother was crazy," Kip replied, looking at his hands. "He said that my mother's little sister was killed by some witch who cast a spell in her sleep, and my mother saw it happen. Father told me that seeing her sister die hurt my mother's mind in a way that couldn't be fixed. If that hadn't happened, maybe I wouldn't have had to run away, y'know? And maybe my brother would be alive too, and maybe…" He trailed off, his voice laced with frustration

Kirilee was staring at Kip, a strange expression on her face. "Is your last name Burgess?" she asked, her tone suddenly cautious.

He shook his head. "Robinson," he said. "My mother's maiden name was Burgess, though."

She nodded, as if she'd known this. "And what was your mother's sister's name? The one who was killed?"

"Clarita," Kip answered. "Why?"

"By the Fae." Kirilee let out a long sigh. Her demeanour changed completely; she seemed to deflate as she stared into the fire.

"What's wrong?" Lachlann asked.

Kirilee looked at him, then at Kip, and I thought I saw tears in her eyes. "Kip," she said, her voice slightly unsteady, "the person responsible for your aunt's death is me."

Kip's head snapped up. He stared at her for several seconds before speaking. "That's impossible. This happened almost fifty years back. And you're no witch."

"I'm much older than you think," Kirilee answered him. "The same spell that prevents me from sleeping also keeps me young. And I'm not a magic user anymore, but at one time I could move things with my mind."

Kip was still staring at her dubiously; Trina was the next to speak up. "What happened?" she asked. "How did Kip's aunt die?"

Kirilee sighed again and looked into the fire. "I was a guest at your family's home the night before all this happened," she told Kip. "I had lots of nightmares in those days, including that night. When morning came, Mrs. Burgess—your grandmother—sent her girls to go wake the guests." Her eyes flickered to Kip. "When they came in to wake me, I was dreaming that I was being attacked. In the dream, a man came rushing at me, and I used magic to take his dagger and stab him through the heart. And then I woke to blood and screaming." Her voice shuddered, and she met Kip's eyes. "Like you said, I'd been casting in my sleep when the girls came into my room. When they got close, I picked up the quill pen that was lying on the night table and sent it through Clarita's chest." She said nothing for a moment, and when she finally spoke, her voice faltered. "I know an apology will mean nothing to you, but I've not lived a day since without deep regret for what I did."

We all stared at Kirilee for a few long minutes. I was having trouble believing that she was old enough to have been responsible for something that happened so many years ago. "But it was an accident," Trina spoke up. "You didn't mean to kill her."

"Of course not, but that doesn't change the fact that I did," Kirilee responded. "And I could've done better. I'd had troubles with sleep casting before, and I had friends who could've helped me. But I was too proud to ask."

Kip stared at her; I could see that he was beginning to believe her. "So most of what's gone wrong in my life—my mother's mind being damaged, my brother and me having to run away from home, and then my brother dying out in the woods from the cold—it's all because of you, ai?"

Kirilee looked away and nodded. "I'm afraid so."

He let out a long sigh. "All these years we've known each other, and you never had the guts to tell me that you're the witch who killed my *aunt?*" His voice had turned cold.

"I'd no idea she was your aunt," Kirilee replied. "I didn't put all this together 'til tonight."

Kip shook his head and stood up swiftly. "I'll be leaving in the morning," he said, his tone clipped. "I'm done with the lot of you." He stalked into the shadows before any of us could protest, and we were left staring at one another.

Lachlann moved so he was next to Kirilee and put an arm around her shoulders. Then he looked over at Trina and me. "You girls had best get back to sleep," he said. "We'll deal with Kip in the morning. There's no use talking to him while he's this angry."

Trina and I returned to our tent and lay down, Bailey following us. Trina was curled up against the dog and breathing evenly within minutes, but it took me what felt like ages to fall asleep, and when I did, my dreams were strange and vivid. Over and over in my mind's eye I saw the face and heard the screams of the man whom I'd set on fire, saw the bright red blood of the guard Kip had killed and the charred body of the one that Kirilee and I had taken down. After what felt like several hours of tossing and turning in a half-sleep, I found myself fully awake, staring at the opening of the tent and the fire crackling beyond. *I'm having nightmares,* I realized, my heart beginning to thud in my chest. *Am I going to end up hurting people, like Kirilee did?* A tear trickled down my face, and suddenly great heaving sobs were wracking my body. I buried my face in my knees and wept quietly, trying not to wake Trina.

"Saray?" I heard a male voice whisper from outside the tent. I heard rustling as the tent flap opened, and a moment later, I was looking at Lachlann's concerned face. He stared at me for a moment and then motioned that I should follow him outside. I got to my feet and crawled out of the tent, still crying.

Outside, Lachlann sat down by the fire and patted the log next to him. I sank down beside him and buried my head in my arms, sobbing. A moment later, I felt weight settle on my shoulders as Lachlann put his cloak around me. He put a hand on my shoulder, and I could feel his gaze on me as I cried. When my sobs had begun to subside, he gave my shoulder a squeeze. "Tonight was rough for you, wasn't it?"

I nodded. "I…I was having nightmares about what we did to those guards," I admitted, my voice trembling. "I don't want to have nightmares; I don't want to hurt someone like Kirilee did…" I trailed off, fresh tears streaming down my face.

Lachlann sat back. "Of course you were having nightmares," he said, shaking his head. "The first time a person kills someone else, they usually come out of it pretty shaken. I didn't sleep for days after my first kill."

I turned to look at him. "But it seemed like what happened tonight was nothing to you," I protested.

"A few years in the army taught me not to think too hard about it," Lachlann replied. "I still don't like killing, though. But sometimes it's the only way. Those men weren't going to stop until they had you and Trina, and we weren't about to let that happen."

I nodded. "I didn't mean to kill that guard," I said, swiping at my eyes. "I was just trying to protect myself, and Trina..." I gazed down at my hands, remembering the feel of flame on them. "Do you think I'm...dangerous, Lachlann?"

"Dangerous?" Lachlann eyed me. "Well, maybe a little, but not in a way that isn't easily remedied."

"What do you mean?"

"Your ability with fire, it's a tool," he explained. "And like all tools, you can use it for good or for harm. But you're more likely to cause harm if you don't know how to use it. You with your fire right now would be like Kip with a sword, or perhaps me with a gun."

"Gun?" I repeated.

"It's a weapon," he explained. "A new one, I've seen them but never used one. Though I don't doubt for a second that with proper training I could learn how, just like how you're going to learn how to control your fire. I'm sure Kirilee's friend Willem will be able to help you."

"What about the nightmares? You don't think I'm going to start casting in my sleep?"

Lachlann frowned. "I doubt it. But I'd talk to Kirilee about that if I were you. I don't know a lot about these things." He turned suddenly and looked up. "Speaking of which, I think that's her I hear now."

Kirilee emerged into the firelight a minute later, carrying a full bag on her back. She looked us over. "Everything all right?"

Lachlann nodded. "Saray's feeling a little overwhelmed by tonight, that's all."

Kirilee sat down on the other side of me. "She's probably feeling overwhelmed by a little more than tonight. These last few days have been hard for you, ai?"

I nodded, fighting the lump that was threatening to rise in my throat again.

"Having to run away from home, having all sorts of people find out you're a magic user, and now having men hunt you." She shook her head. "It'd be enough to make anyone cry." She gave me a smile and then stopped and inhaled sharply, her face contorting into a grimace.

"Are you all right?" I asked.

She nodded, letting out a long breath. "Just a cramp. I get them sometimes." She took a few deep breaths and then turned to Lachlann. "What were you saying that Saray should ask me about?"

I repeated to her my concerns about the nightmares, and she frowned. "Lachlann's right, it's likely just because you're overwhelmed," she said. "But if they get worse, or if you do ever cast in your sleep, let me know right away. I'll give you something to help you sleep better."

"I think I could use some of that tonight," I replied.

Kirilee nodded and picked up Trina's pipe, which was sitting by the log. "Well, then go back into the tent, and I'll play you a lullaby. I know a special song that lulls anyone who hears it to sleep. Except me, of course."

My eyes narrowed. "You play?"

"Obviously." She smirked.

"Won't your song wake the others?" I asked.

"If it does, they'll be lulled right back to sleep by it," she replied, smiling wryly.

"Right." I stood up, returned Lachlann's cloak to him, and retreated to the tent. The music started moments later, a low, mournful tune that sounded like it would be difficult to play. *She's really talented.*

I felt my eyes begin to drift closed halfway through the song, and I lay back and let the melody carry me away, hoping that this time my sleep would be dreamless.

# Chapter Eight

**KIP HAD RETURNED** to our camp when we woke up the next morning, though he ate his porridge sullenly, refusing to speak to any of us. When we were done eating, he packed his belongings in his bag, picked up his bow and shouldered his quiver. "I'll leave you the rest of the food," he said, his tone flat. "Let's go, Bailey."

Bailey, who had been sitting at Trina's feet, let out a whimper of protest.

"I said, let's *go,*" Kip repeated, his voice rising slightly.

The dog whimpered more, staying rooted where he was.

Kip let out a frustrated sigh and marched forward. He seized Bailey by the scruff of the neck and tried to pull him to his feet. Bailey remained planted and let out a low growl. Kip stared down at his dog and then looked up at Trina, his eyes blazing. "What witchery have you cast on my dog, girl?" he demanded.

"Leave her alone!" I jumped up, threw myself between Kip and Trina, and reached out and shoved him.

"Saray!" Trina protested. "Don't!"

Kip stumbled backwards, but his hands flew up and caught my wrists in an iron grip. He glared down at me. "Don't you touch me, you filthy little hildakin," he hissed.

I let out a shriek of protest, and suddenly fire was spewing from my hands, unbidden, burning the flesh on his arms. Kip yelped and let go of me. I didn't see his fist coming until it connected with my jaw. I let out a howl of pain and lunged at him, fresh fire dancing on my hands.

I never made it to him, though; a pair of arms grabbed me from behind, their grip stronger than I would have expected. Kirilee wrapped an arm around my waist; her other arm pinned my own arms back against my chest, forcing my hands towards my face. The flame extinguished automatically. I struggled and glared at Kip, who I saw had been restrained in a similar fashion by Lachlann. "Enough, both of you." His tone was familiar enough to make me stop struggling. *Lachlann sure sounds like his brother when he's mad.*

Kirilee released me; when I turned to face her, she was glaring at me. "That was beyond inappropriate."

I stared at her, then at Kip, who Lachlann had just released. "He was going to hurt Trina," I protested. "I couldn't let him…"

"I don't want to hear it," she snapped. "You've both behaved shamefully." She looked beyond me at Kip, whose arms were beginning to blister, and sighed. "Lachlann, you take Saray and go do your errands. I'll tend to Kip's arms." Lachlann nodded.

Kip snorted. "I don't want *your* help. Or to be left alone with you."

Kirilee shook her head. "You don't have to like me, Kip. But you need to let me help you. If I don't, you'll be in a lot of pain, and you might get an infection."

"And you won't be alone with her." Trina stood up, her voice calm. "Bailey and I are right here."

Kip huffed and then sank down next to Kirilee; my eyes widened as Trina sat down on his other side. "Trina, don't…"

"It's fine, Saray." Trina's voice remained calm. "He's not going to hurt me. If he did, his own dog would turn on him." I thought I saw her smirk.

"Right." I nodded and rubbed my throbbing jaw. I could taste blood in my mouth, and I could feel my lip beginning to swell.

"Still got all your teeth?" Lachlann asked me, concern etched on his face.

I moved my jaw around for a moment and nodded, satisfied that nothing had come loose.

"Well, you'll have a nice bruise tomorrow, but you'll survive. Come along." He moved towards his horse and began untying him.

I stared back at Kip for a moment. He met my gaze, his eyes narrowed. "I should've shot you when I had the chance," he mumbled.

My eyebrows shot up at his insult. "I shouldn't have agreed to stay for dinner," was the best reply I could manage.

"Enough, you two." Lachlann stepped in front of me, clearly concerned that I was going to attack Kip again. Then he sighed. "This way, Saray."

Lachlann was silent for the first few minutes of our journey, leading his horse carefully down the wooded trails. When he spoke, his voice was tired. "Remember what I said to you last night about your magic being a tool that you can use for good or harm? Well, today you certainly used it for the latter."

"But he called me a filthy little hildakin," I protested. "And he *punched* me."

"To be fair, he punched you after you tried to set him on fire," Lachlann said. "Kirilee's right, though, you both acted like bloody children today. I'll make sure he knows that too; I don't think Kip's likely to take correction from Kirilee right now."

"I didn't mean to burn him," I huffed. "It just…happened."

"You said that exact thing to me less than twelve hours ago," Lachlann observed. "You know, I'm surprised it took you this long to be discovered if your first instinct when you're angry or scared is to start burning things."

"It's been getting worse," I admitted, glancing down at my hands. "I mean, I've had a lot of reasons to be scared and angry lately."

"Right," he said, nodding. "You still need to learn to control yourself, though, especially since we'll be travelling aboard a wooden ship soon. I'm glad we're headed to Willem's—I'm definitely not willing to take you to Dundere until you have your gift under control." He shook his head. "What I wouldn't give for some Dundere style anti-magic right now."

I was about to ask him what he meant when we came upon a small wooden cottage nestled amongst some trees. To the right of the cottage the woods cleared away to form a meadow, where a few horses grazed contentedly. The door to the cottage swung open before Lachlann had the chance to knock, and I found myself staring at Ronin from the fire. He gave Lachlann a nod and then looked beyond him to his horse. "I see you brought Checkers for a visit."

Lachlann nodded. "For an extended visit, I was hoping. I need somewhere to keep him for a few days." He smiled at Ronin. "Perhaps you can come back to my camp with me and select something from my trailer as payment."

"I think that can be arranged. How long do you need me to keep him?"

"I think five days at the most," Lachlann replied, offering Ronin the reins. Ronin took them and led Checkers into the pasture. When he returned, we turned and headed back the way we'd come, Lachlann chatting with Ronin while they walked. It was clear that my earlier lecture from him was over.

When we were a short way from camp, Lachlann paused at the base of a tree. I followed his gaze upward; only now did I notice the house built into it. "Ambrose!" Lachlann called out. "You home?"

We were answered not by Ambrose but by Spark peering down at us. Lachlann ducked as the creature let out a puff of flame. A moment later, Ambrose appeared above us, shirtless and grinning. "Well, hello again."

"Want to earn yourself something from my trailer, boy?" Lachlann asked.

He crawled out of his treehouse and slid effortlessly down the tree. "Doing what?"

"I need someone to watch my camp for a few days," Lachlann told him.

"Ah! That should be fine. Let me pack my things, and I'll meet you there."

Trina and Kip were still sitting together when we reached camp; both of Kip's forearms were encased in bandages, and Bailey lay across both their feet. Kirilee, who was busy taking down the tent, gave Ronin a nod and a smile. Then she glanced at me. "You feeling a little calmer?"

I nodded and then stole a nervous glance at Kip. He caught my gaze and glared back, but he didn't say anything. Lachlann looked him over. "You're still coming along, then?"

Kip let out a sigh. "It's that or abandon Bailey," he muttered. "I don't have much choice."

Lachlann nodded. "Well, in that case, why don't we fit you with some armour? I think there's a good chance we'll have to fend off more guards or bandits, and I don't want you getting hurt." He glanced at me. "I'd offer you some as well, Saray, but I doubt I have anything small enough for you on hand."

"And you know my answer already," Kirilee put in.

"I know, it's too bulky, you don't want to carry it around." Lachlann chuckled. "Suit yourself. Come along, Kip."

Kip walked to where the other men were standing. Ambrose showed up just then, a bag on his back and Spark perched on his shoulder, and the four of them disappeared into the wagon. I sank down next to Trina. "Are you all right?" she asked.

I winced. "My jaw hurts," I admitted. "But I'll survive." I glanced at the trailer and lowered my voice. "Is *he* all right?"

She frowned. "I think he's hurt worse than you are. And he's angry. But he'll be okay." She sighed. "Saray, I know you want to protect me, but maybe don't do it like that again. There were plenty of other people here. I don't think Kip would've actually hurt me in front of all of them."

I huffed. "I don't know. He seemed pretty angry."

"Yes, he did," she countered. "But you made it worse."

I sighed and stood up, knowing she was right but not wanting to admit it. Kirilee looked up as I stalked across the camp. "Where are you off to?"

I shrugged and was about to respond when the wagon door opened, and the men began to climb out. Ambrose was carrying the shield that I'd seen last night, and Ronin held a massive sword with an intricately patterned hilt. Kip was clad in a dark green leather breastplate; the added layer made him look much broader. He carried a matching set of bracers that I assumed he couldn't wear until his arms healed. Lachlann glanced at Kirilee as he locked up his wagon. "The tent's all down, everything's packed?"

She nodded.

"Good." He smiled and shouldered his pack. "In that case, are you folks ready to begin our adventure?"

We bid farewell to Ambrose and Ronin and headed into the woods. Kirilee led the group, followed by Trina, who had stopped holding my arm when we walked in favour of holding onto Bailey—who did a good enough job of leading her that she no longer needed her cane, much to my surprise. I walked behind them, carrying most of the food on my back, and Kip followed me at a distance, always alert, his eyes scanning the trees for hidden dangers. Lachlann took the rear, carrying his weapons, the tent, and the cooking pot on his back, and Persius flew above us, letting out the occasional screech. I was calmer now than I'd been earlier, but tension still hung in the air; none of us spoke as we made our way through the forest.

After a good few hours of walking, the trail began to slope upward. My legs tired quickly, and I was relieved when Trina asked if we could take a break. We stopped near a stream, ate lunch from my pack, and drank the cool, clear water. Then we carried on.

The road became narrower and began to angle upwards; several sections were rocky and treacherous and had Kirilee guiding Trina up them slowly and carefully. The constant overhang of trees fell away, and the sun beat down on us, leaving me parched and weary. I forced myself to put one foot in front of the other, to ignore my burning muscles and to continue moving. A large stone shelf rose up on our left, and the land to our right was peppered with rocky fields and scattered bushes. After some time, Kirilee paused and looked back at us. "You should all enjoy this."

We followed her around a bend in the path, and when I turned the corner my jaw dropped. The land to our right fell away here, leaving us looking out high above a vast forest. Several lakes were visible from this vantage point, as well as a few green patches of meadow. "This is incredible," I breathed.

"It is indeed," Lachlann said, rounding the corner, chuckling. Kip nodded in agreement, though I could tell he was trying to appear nonchalant.

"There's a waterfall just up this way," Kirilee told us, indicating a path that branched away from the main one, cutting a wedge into the mountainside. "We can make camp here tonight. I think we've travelled enough for one day."

We followed Kirilee into the gap and found ourselves next to a small pool with a waterfall tumbling into it. "Kip and Saray, you two set up the tent," Kirilee said. "Lachlann, see what you can find in the way of firewood."

Kip's eyes narrowed. "Shouldn't I be hunting?"

Kirilee shook her head. "There aren't many animals in these parts; it's too barren. This pool has plenty of fish, though, and I can catch fish with my bare hands."

"Can't I go collect firewood?" I protested. "I don't want to work with *him*."

"Absolutely not." Kirilee's tone was even, but I didn't miss her glare. "You two don't have to be friends, but as long as we're all travelling together, you *will* work together as needed." She shook her head at me as she took off her coat and then turned away and waded into the pool.

"Come on, let's set up the tent." Kip's voice was flat.

I let out a huff and then began helping him assemble the long metal poles and drape the large, complex piece of fabric over top. Kip worked quickly and methodically, avoiding my gaze, while I sent the occasional glare in his direction. I wasn't sure whether I was more frustrated with him or with Kirilee.

Lachlann returned with an armful of wood, created a fire ring, and then walked over to where Kip and I were working. "I'll take over, Saray," he said. "You go start the fire."

I gave him a grateful smile and moved to the fire ring just as Kirilee threw a large fish onto the shore. "There," she said triumphantly, walking over to the flopping creature. "Haven't done that in a while." She pulled out a knife and stuck it in the fish's gills, causing Trina to squeal in disgust, and I turned away and started the fire.

"How much longer 'til we get to this place?" Trina asked as we ate dinner half an hour later. "Just one more day?"

"Yes," Kirilee assured her. "The terrain will be rough tomorrow, though, so we'd best all get to bed early."

We were quiet after that, concentrating on our food. Just as we finished eating, a large bank of clouds rolled in overhead, and thunder sounded above us. The rain came soon after, sheeting rain that worked its way into our little nook and left us drenched and shivering. I tried to use magic to keep the fire going despite the rain, but after five minutes of intense concentration, the fire fizzled into nothing. "I s'pose we'll all be staying in the tent tonight," Kirilee mused.

"You're not keeping watch?" Kip asked.

She shook her head. "No one will find us up here. But I'll be awake, so if anything does come our way, I'll hear it." She glanced at his arms. "I'd best change your bandages before we move into the tent."

Lachlann and I cleaned up dinner while Kirilee tended to Kip's arms, and then all six of us, including Bailey, crawled into the tent, shivering. We divided the blankets among ourselves, and Trina pressed herself against me for body heat. "Let me try something," I ventured.

I spoke my casting words, and a small ball of fire appeared in my palm. I moved it so that it hovered just above Trina and me, near enough to warm us and dry our clothes but not close enough to hurt us. Kirilee laughed and put her hands out, warming them in the fire. "Good idea, Saray." She gave me a smile; she didn't seem to be in a lecturing mood anymore. I caught Kip glowering at me and decided not to send the fireball in his direction.

Kirilee asked Trina for her pipe after that, and she played us a merry tune, Trina gaping at her while she played. "You're really good," Trina said when she was finished.

"I'm decent," Kirilee told her. "Want to hear another?"

She played us a few more tunes after that, and I grinned, my mood beginning to lighten somewhat, and made my ball of fire dance and crackle to her music. Then I extinguished it and simply listened. Eventually the music ceased, and I fell asleep to the sound of rain drumming on the top of the tent and the waterfall roaring nearby.

I was awakened some time later by the sound of sharp, heavy breathing. The rain still pounded on the tent, and I opened my eyes to see a single candle burning. I rolled over, and my eyes widened. Kirilee was hunched over, nearly curled into a ball, her breathing coming in shuddering gasps. Lachlann sat next to her, his hand on her back, staring down at her. "What's wrong?" I whispered.

Lachlann looked up. "She's not doing so well," he told me. "This happens sometimes." His eyebrows knitted.

I frowned. "Is there anything we can do?"

He shook his head. "It'll pass by morning. Just go back to sleep. It's best if some of us get a good night's rest, at least."

I nodded and lay back down, trying to ignore Kirilee's laboured breaths and hoping she'd recover from whatever was ailing her.

*       *

Sleep must have found me eventually because when my eyes opened next, it was light; the rain had stopped and both Kirilee and Lachlann were no longer in the tent. I sat up, rubbing my aching jaw and wondering how bruised it might be. I made my way outside to see Lachlann hunched over the fire ring, trying to light some damp wood. He glanced up. "Excellent timing, Saray. Would you mind?"

I formed a fireball in midair as I stepped towards the ring and then let it settle on the wood. The sticks and logs hissed and crackled, and steam rose from them, but after a minute or so, they caught. Kirilee walked over to join us; I gave her a concerned glance. "Are you...feeling better?"

"Mostly, yes," she replied. Her face looked tired, I noticed, and her eyes were ringed by dark circles. But her smile seemed genuine enough. "I'm worried about today's walk," she continued. "It's a tricky enough hike as it is, but the trails will be muddy today, and Trina'll likely slip. I'm thinking of getting Kip to take my pack and carrying her on my back. Do you think she'd mind?"

"Mind what?" Trina asked as she made her way out of the tent, rubbing her eyes. Bailey followed her out, pausing to stretch and let out a large yawn, and Kip followed after both of them.

Kirilee repeated her idea to Trina, and she nodded. "That's fine. I don't mind being carried as long as I'm not too heavy."

"I doubt that. I'm stronger than I look," Kirilee assured her.

"Are you sure you feel up for that?" Lachlann asked.

"I'll be fine," Kirilee replied. She leaned over the now-boiling pot of water and stirred in the porridge.

We ate a quick breakfast, packed up, and began our trek, Trina riding on Kirilee's back. Less than an hour of walking proved Kirilee right; the path was littered with sharp branches, slippery rocks, and ankle-deep holes of mud. I slipped several times, bashing my knee hard on a rock once. When another fall left me covered in mud and nearly crying, Kip walked up beside me and let out a sigh. "You need someone to teach you how to walk in this kind of country."

I glared at him as I stood up, face flaming, and wiped the mud off my own hands. "I don't want your help."

"You need it, though." His jaw tightened. "Having you falling all over the place is just going to slow us down, y'know."

"I don't need anything from…" I began to slip yet again. Kip's arm shot out, his hand closing around my bicep before I could fall.

I steadied myself and then stared at his hand. "Not afraid I'm going to set you on fire this time?" I managed to say.

He snorted. "I'm trying to help. If you set me on fire now, you're more of an elfieblooded idiot than I imagined. C'mon, let me show you how to walk."

"He's right, Saray," Kirilee said from in front of us. "Let him help you, ai?"

"Of course you'd take his side," I mumbled. I let out a huff and looked at him out of the corner of my eye. "Fine, show me what to do."

He looked down at my mud-covered boots. "First," he said, "when you're walking in mud, it's best to put your foot down heel-first."

We spent the next few hours walking close together, Kip telling me where to put my feet and what places to avoid. I nearly fell a few more times, but he caught my arm every time, righting me and pointing out my errors. His voice held no malice now, but I was painfully aware of his proximity to me, and I couldn't help but flinch every time he grabbed my arm. My aching jaw wouldn't let me forget what had happened yesterday. It was strange to think that only a day before that, I would have enjoyed this sort of contact with Kip.

The path levelled out after a long while, and trees—these ones not nearly as tall as the behemoths at the bottom of the mountain—began to enclose us once again. Kirilee put Trina down, and she returned to walking with Bailey. I noticed the sun beginning its slow slide towards the horizon and inquired about dinner. Kirilee shook her head. "We're nearly there," she said. "Willem always has extra food on hand; I don't think he'll mind feeding us."

"How do you know Willem?" I asked curiously.

"Ah." Kirilee glanced back at me. "I've known Willem for many years. When I was quite young, and still a magic user, I attended a school of magic that his father ran."

"A school of magic?" My eyes widened. "Those exist?"

"They used to," Kirilee said, "though I don't think any do now. I was very lucky to end up there."

"How did you end up there?" Trina asked.

"That's a bit of a story." Kirilee slowed down so that she was walking closer to Trina and me. "See, I'm an orphan like the two of you," she informed us, "but I grew up on the streets of Sylvenburgh. When I was a kid, I survived by begging and stealing."

"Really?" Trina's voice had a skeptical edge.

"Really," Kirilee replied. "I was about twelve when I first began to move things with my mind, and I quickly realized that my ability would help me steal. It's a lot easier to pick someone's pocket when you don't actually have to reach in and grab anything, y'know." She grinned, and Trina let out a giggle.

"When I was about fourteen, I went and pickpocketed a fellow magic user," she continued. "He felt my magic reaching into his bag. But instead of hurting me or turning me over to the police, he took me back to his house, gave me a meal and a place to sleep, and in the morning he told me that he wanted to take me somewhere I could learn to put my magic to better use. And the next day I met Ashlar, Willem's father, and I spent four wonderful years at his school."

She stopped talking as the terrain to the right of us dropped off again. We were skirting a ledge once more; large patches of forest were visible below us, and what appeared to be an unfamiliar city lay in the distance. "That's Flavalan," Lachlann informed us. I winced at the name, recalling the Banishing Day games I participated in the day before my life changed completely.

"Where's Persius?" Trina asked.

"He stopped following us around lunchtime," Kirilee answered. "A wild bird has no place in a home like Willem's. I'll be coming and going while Saray trains, though, so I'll get to see him."

"How did you know Persius was gone?" I asked her.

Trina's eyes widened, and then she grinned. "I notice sounds better than most sighted folk. I haven't heard him in a while."

"You must have some very keen ears, then," Kirilee replied. She paused and walked towards the rock face on our left, staring intently at a particular spot where the stone jutted back from the edge for a few feet, allowing a small patch of grass and a single viletta tree to grow in front of it. I followed her gaze and noticed that the grass leading up to where she was looking was worn; only now did I see the small door embedded in the rock face, hidden behind some of the viletta's branches. Kirilee raised her hand and knocked on the door in a pattern that I did not recognize.

There was a long pause, and then the door cracked open ever so slightly. Kirilee looked intently through the crack. "Hello, Willem."

# Chapter Nine

**"KIRILEE!" A MAN'S** voice exclaimed from inside. "I certainly wasn't expecting to see you today!" The door swung open. "You have friends with you?"

"I do," she replied. "I hope you don't mind us showing up like this, but we need your help." She turned back to us and motioned that we should come inside.

I followed the others through the door and found myself standing in a large, mostly bare room with rock walls lit by torches. I glanced around the room, then turned and looked at our host. Willem was tall and thin, with dark brown skin and a neatly trimmed beard. He appeared to be considerably older than either Kirilee or Lachlann; his face was lined and his curly black hair peppered with grey. He wore a long black robe with gold trim along its edges, and his dark eyes were keen as they looked us all over.

"You might remember Lachlann," Kirilee said, gesturing. "He's the one who sold you a sword a few years back."

"Of course." Willem stepped forward and shook Lachlann's hand. "Good to see you again." His gaze turned to us. "Now, who are the children? And the dog, for that matter?" His voice was deep and rich and oddly lacking in the Shrouded Woods lilt.

Kirilee introduced each of us. "The children are why we've come here," she told Willem. "One of them is in need of your help."

Willem looked us over, his eyes lingering longest on my muddy clothing. "Well, first of all, I think they need hot baths and a good meal," he said. "Then we can talk about what else they may need." His eyes narrowed as he looked at my jaw and at Kip's bandaged arms. "You folks get in a fight?"

There was an awkward pause. "We've had a few scraps," Kirilee said. "We're all fine, though."

"Right. Come along, then."

Willem led us down a long hallway dotted with torches, its walls carved out of the same stone as the entryway. We passed what looked to be a parlour and a kitchen and several closed doors, and when we reached the end of the hall, he gestured towards the final door. "Ladies first, of course," he said. "I'll show you gentlemen to your quarters while the ladies wash up."

He opened the door, and Kirilee, Trina and I stepped through. My eyes widened; the room contained what appeared to be a genuine waterfall, its waters tumbling noisily into a pool below. The air in the room was warm and damp. I walked towards the pool and tested the water with my toe. "It's warm!"

"Indeed it is," Willem said from the doorway.

I glanced back at him. "How?"

"Magic, obviously," he replied with a small smile. "There are towels in the cupboard to your left." He pointed at a pair of wooden doors nestled into a rock wall. "Once you're done, the room immediately to your left when you exit is where you girls will sleep."

Willem closed the door, and I stripped off my mud-soaked clothes and plunged into the pool without hesitation. The warm, churning water provided instant relief to my sore legs, and I let out a laugh. "I wonder how he warms the water up using magic," I mused.

"Ask him," Kirilee said, peeling off her clothes. "Willem knows more about magic than anyone I've ever met, except maybe his father." Kirilee lowered herself into the water and let out a sigh. She glanced back up at Trina, who was struggling to remove her dress. "You got that?"

Trina nodded and frowned as she attempted to unbutton herself. A moment later, the dress slid off, and she crouched and felt her way to the edge of the pool, then climbed in.

We lounged around in the pool for a good half hour, revelling in the warmth, and then washed up and climbed out. We wrapped ourselves in thick towels and headed to the room that Willem had pointed us to, our bags and dirty clothes in tow. The room we'd been given was small and simply furnished and lit by candles that burned with a dim purple flame. I smiled, watching the minerals embedded in the rock walls glint with violet light. *I wish Trina could see this.*

I looked through my bag until I found a dress that wasn't completely dirty, then changed into it and picked out a dress for Trina. "While we're here, I'll see if Willem can head into Flavalan and buy some fabric for me so I can make you those clothes I mentioned," Kirilee said. She gestured at the clothes she'd just changed into—a bright blue tunic that covered more than the one she'd been wearing for the last few days and a pair of breeches. "Would something like this be modest enough for your tastes, Saray?" I didn't miss the sarcastic note in her voice.

"I suppose so," I conceded, shrugging.

"Do you make your own clothes?" asked Trina.

"These, yes," Kirilee replied. "I know how to sew simple things. The coat was a gift from a friend, though; I don't have the skill to make that."

We finished dressing and walked out of the room to the smell of food cooking. "Need any help in there?" Kirilee called out to Willem as we passed the kitchen.

"Absolutely not," he called back. "Go take a seat in the dining room; dinner will be served as soon as the others are ready."

The dining room, in contrast to the entryway and our bedroom, was opulent. A large table was covered with a rich cloth and several place settings and flanked with high-backed chairs, a massive wrought-iron chandelier hung from the ceiling, and the rough stone walls were home to several elegant art pieces. Candles in stands around the room provided flickering light that danced on the walls. We seated ourselves in three of the large chairs, and Kip and Lachlann joined us soon after; it appeared that Lachlann had helped Kip change his bandages. Moments after they were seated, Willem came into the room with a large cart bearing our meal.

Willem, it turned out, was a fantastic cook. The dishes were varied and unusual, but each one was incredibly good—fish in some sort of berry sauce, spiced roasted vegetables, a thick soup whose taste I couldn't quite identify, a large roast that Lachlann told us was likely venison. Willem even brought out a small bowl of cut-up meat for Bailey, which he placed on the floor. "So, what exactly do you need my help with?" Willem asked.

Kirilee told him the story of how she'd met Trina and me, how my talents had revealed themselves, and her concerns for the remainder of the trip. "Having a firebrand with us is certainly useful," she said to Willem, "but Saray doesn't have the control she needs." She paused and levelled her gaze with Willem's. "I was hoping you could teach her."

Willem's expression changed from one of interest to surprise mixed with suspicion. "You want me to open up the school?"

Kirilee nodded.

Willem said nothing for a moment and then shook his head slowly. "The school's been closed for years, Kirilee, and for good reason. You know that."

"I do," she said, nodding, "but I also know that re-opening it for one student wouldn't be difficult for you. You have access to more magical knowledge than anyone I know. Would you at least think about it?"

"I think you're mistaking me for my father," he argued. "He was the teacher; I'm simply a scholar."

"But you *can* teach," Kirilee insisted. "And you do it well."

Willem sighed and sat back in his chair. "I'll consider it."

The adults made polite conversation for the remainder of the meal, and then Willem rose and told us he'd be back with dessert. When he returned, he was carrying a platter holding several tall glasses and smiling. Kirilee laughed when she saw what he was carrying. "Back to your old tricks, ai?"

I stared at the glasses and shook my head; they contained a fizzing substance that changed colour every few minutes. It faded slowly from pink to brown, then to blue, then orange. Willem placed one in front of me, and I eyed it. "What is it?"

Willem shrugged. "I don't have a name for it, but it's good. Try it."

I raised the cup to my lips tentatively and took a sip. The drink was cold and thick, which surprised me, and it crackled and popped in my mouth. Strangest of all was the flavour. It tasted like vanilla when I first began to drink, but halfway through the first gulp it tasted more like strawberry. I looked up at Willem with wide eyes. "How does it do that?"

"Again, magic," Willem said, grinning. "Obviously."

Kip stared at his drink suspiciously and slowly pushed it away without tasting it. "May I be excused?"

"You haven't even tried it!" Willem protested.

"I'm...I'm all right," Kip said hastily.

"Don't mind him," Lachlann chuckled. "He's just afraid of magic. Had to convince him the hot spring was safe before he'd go in too." Kirilee opened her mouth as if to argue with Lachlann, but Willem cut her off.

"Afraid of magic?" he repeated, his voice turning cold. He turned and stared at Kirilee. "You brought someone who is *afraid of magic* into my home?"

"Willem, I..." Kirilee began to protest.

But Willem was on his feet, staring down angrily at Kirilee. "You of all people know how my family has suffered because of magic fearers," he said, his voice rising. "And yet you thought it was a good idea to bring one of those people here, to show him where I live, to mention the *school* in front of him?" He shook his head incredulously. "What were you *thinking,* Kirilee?"

Kip was standing now too. He glared at Willem and then turned his gaze to Kirilee. "You see?" he said. "Told you I shouldn't have come. If *she* hadn't bewitched my dog," he paused and his eyes flickered to Trina, "I'd be safe at home, and none of this'd be happening!"

"But it *is* happening, and now something must be done about it." Willem glared at him and then turned back to Kirilee. "I'm going to have to wipe his memory, you know."

Kip's eyes narrowed. "You're going to *what?*"

"Make you forget how you got here." Willem's expression softened ever so slightly as he looked at Kip. "Oh, don't look at me like that; it's not going to hurt. But I can't have people like you running about, knowing where I live and all. Hold still, it'll just take a second."

He took a step towards Kip, and Kip backed away from the table, his eyes narrowed. "Keep away from me, you witch," he hissed.

"Willem, y'know this isn't necessary," Kirilee put in, standing up.

"*You* know that it absolutely is," Willem retorted. He took another step towards Kip. "I'm not trying to hurt you, boy," he said, his voice becoming gentler. "I just need to protect my home. Now, come on and let me do this. I swear it won't be painful." Bailey let out a growl and stepped in front of Willem. Willem responded by extending a hand towards the dog, and Bailey froze in his tracks, seemingly unable to move. I gaped. *He just did the same thing to Bailey that Rich did to Trina and me.* Beside me, Trina recoiled, seeming to be able to sense that something had been done to Bailey.

"Don't touch me," Kip growled. He was backing towards the entryway now, eyes on Willem, his fists clenched and every muscle in his body taut.

"I don't have to touch you," Willem responded. "I just have to do...this." I watched as his hand extended in Kip's direction.

"Stop!" Once again, I was moving before I could think, throwing myself into the gap between Willem and Kip, fire dancing on my hands. "Get away from him!" I demanded, glaring up at Willem.

Willem met my gaze, his lips parting in surprise. His eyes travelled to my hands. "*Flaminia finita,*" he whispered. Then he stared at me, his expression unreadable as the fire on my hands fizzled out. My heart thudded in my chest; I was suddenly very aware that I had crossed someone far more powerful than myself.

Then he shook his head. "Did you just cast with your *mind?*"

"You see why I brought her here." Kirilee was standing behind Willem now. She sighed and clapped him on the shoulder. "Come on, enough theatrics. You and I should talk in private."

Willem gave Kip one last glare, but he allowed Kirilee to drag him out of the room and into the kitchen.

A heavy silence descended on the room. I glanced back at Kip; his face was white, and I saw that his hands were shaking. He met my gaze. "Um...thanks for that, ai," he mumbled, looking away. Then he brushed past me and headed towards his room, leaving the rest of us staring after him.

Half an hour later, I sat in the parlour, which was decorated much like the dining room, tapping my foot restlessly and waiting for Kirilee and Willem to return. Lachlann stood nearby, studying one of the pieces of art on the wall, and Trina sat on the floor petting Bailey, who had turned into a whimpering mess as soon as Willem's spell broke. The awkward silence hadn't yet lifted;

Trina seemed more concerned with Bailey than anyone else, and Lachlann had thrown several concerned glances my way but appeared to be at a loss for words. I wasn't sure I could have put my racing thoughts into words if I'd tried.

Finally, Trina spoke up. "I don't like how he treated Bailey." She huffed. "I don't know if I like *him*."

"Me neither," I admitted.

"I mean, casting a spell to stop a human from attacking you, I understand," she went on. "But poor Bailey here was just trying to protect Kip. I don't care if he's a fancy wizard who knows all the spells, I don't think I like him."

Lachlann looked us both over; I could tell he was trying to figure out what to say in response. But Kirilee appeared in the doorway before he had the chance to speak. "It's been decided," she said. "Willem's not about to open the school with Kip here, so Kip will go with you," she gestured at Lachlann, "on your errands. While you're gone, Saray will learn magic. I don't know what will happen when you return."

Lachlann nodded. "Seems fair. I'm sure Kip won't mind a reason to leave this place."

"That's what I figure as well," Kirilee agreed.

"Is Willem actually going to wipe his memory?" Lachlann asked.

Kirilee shook her head. "I managed to talk him down from doing that. But he still won't teach with Kip around."

"I'm not sure that I want to learn from him," I said.

"Me neither," agreed Trina.

"You've no choice, Saray." Kirilee turned to me. "Neither Lachlann nor I is willing to take you further until you have better control. If you want to go to Dundere, you'll train with Willem."

I glanced at Lachlann, hoping he'd disagree with Kirilee's stance, but he was nodding solemnly. I shook my head as my gaze returned to Kirilee. "Why can't you train me? You said you used to be a magic user."

A wry smile worked its way onto Kirilee's face. "Aren't you full of surprises tonight? First you defend Kip, and now you're asking me to teach you, when you know full well I'm just as likely as Willem to snap at you."

I shrugged. "I just didn't think it was a fair fight. Kip wasn't even armed, and Willem had all that magic. And you might get mad at me if you were teaching me, but at least I know you can't kill me just by waving your hand."

Kirilee chuckled. "So you're scared of him. I s'pose I can't blame you, after what you just saw." She shook her head. "He's not as terrifying as you think. He's usually quite kind, but he has his irrational moments."

"He most certainly does," Trina agreed. "Who treats a dog like that?"

"Yes, what he did to Bailey back there was a little...dramatic." Kirilee sighed. "But Willem's the least of your worries, Saray. I'd rather you have to deal with his antics than with accidentally burning down Firenholme. Now, you two had better get to sleep, ai? You're likely exhausted from the journey, and your next few days will be very full."

# Chapter Ten

**WHEN I AWOKE** the next morning, Trina was still asleep. I crawled out of bed and walked drowsily down the long hallway, and soon enough I could hear voices coming from the kitchen. I poked my head into the doorway to see Kirilee and Willem sitting at the kitchen counter, eating eggs and bacon and toast and chatting animatedly; last night's tension seemed to have dissipated. "Morning, Saray," Willem greeted me. "Care for some breakfast?"

I frowned uncertainly for a moment, until Kirilee nodded and beckoned me in. I sat down next to her, and Willem took a clean plate from a nearby stack. He threw a slice of buttered bread and a few strips of raw bacon onto it. Then he cracked one egg onto the plate, then another. My eyes narrowed, and I was about to protest when he flicked his wrist and waved his hand over the food. I watched in awe as the bacon, eggs and bread all cooked perfectly within seconds. "There." He gave me a wry smile and presented the plate to me.

I gawked. "How'd you do that?"

He rolled his eyes. "Do you really need to ask?"

"I know it was magic," I replied, taking the plate from him, "but what kind? I didn't see any fire."

"It's simple heat magic," he told me. "Same as what I use to heat the bathing pool."

"But you didn't say any words."

"Most experienced magic users prefer hand motions over words," he told me. "It's simpler, quicker. I still use words on occasion so I don't forget them, but they're not necessary for me."

"Where are Kip and Lachlann?" I asked, taking a bite of my eggs.

"They left first thing this morning, with Bailey," Kirilee informed me.

"They managed to tear Bailey away from Trina?"

She nodded. "Not sure how, exactly."

Trina wandered into the room as I was finishing my food; I saw that she was using her cane again now that Bailey had left. She let out a huff when Willem greeted her but allowed him to make her a plate of breakfast similar to mine. "While I'm teaching Saray, perhaps you should help Trina develop her gift," Willem suggested to Kirilee as he handed Trina her plate.

Kirilee turned to him. "Which gift is this, ai?"

"Don't tell me you haven't realized that Trina has an ability of her own." He looked over at Trina, whose eyes were wide, her food not yet touched. "The girl can communicate with animals. Which is why she's none too happy with me for how I treated Kip's dog yesterday."

My mouth fell open.

Now Kirilee was chuckling. "I didn't want to give her away," she admitted.

I stared at Trina incredulously. "Is he telling the truth?"

Trina hesitated and then bit her lip and nodded. "I didn't want anyone to know," she said softly. "I've been able to talk to them for as long as I can remember." Her eyes narrowed, and she turned to Willem. "How did *you* know?"

"I'm observant," he replied. "And I'm trained to look for magical talent. I saw the way you were interacting with the dog last night, and it was pretty obvious to me."

"So that's why Bailey likes you so much!" I exclaimed. "And why you feel safe in the woods—you're surrounded by animals!"

She smiled slightly and nodded.

"Is that why you don't like eating meat?" Kirilee asked.

She nodded again. "I don't like hearing the animals die. I'll eat it if I have to, but I think I'd prefer not to."

"Well, I wish you'd told me that yesterday before I made you dinner," Willem said.

She shrugged. "I didn't want to be rude."

"You needn't worry about rudeness around me. I enjoy cooking, so I have no problem making food without meat for you."

Trina nodded slowly. "Thank you," she said, her tone uncertain.

"Does this mean that I can steal your bacon?" I asked Trina, grinning.

"Absolutely." She held her plate out to me, and I plucked the strips of bacon from it. She took a bite of her eggs and frowned. "You remember when Persius attacked those bandits, Saray? That was me. I heard him nearby and called for help."

"I know," Kirilee told her. "He told me. I knew you could speak with animals before I met you."

"You can talk to them too?" Trina frowned. "I thought you weren't a magic user."

"I can only speak to him," Kirilee said. "He was a gift from the priestess; she created a special bond between us using fairy magic. Everyone thinks I find people needing help in the woods by instinct; truth is I have a trained bird who spies for me." She grinned. "I'm convinced Persius can speak to the fairies as well, which is why I think the fairies brought us all together."

"How do you speak with them?" I asked Trina. "I mean, I thought animals used body language to communicate, and you can't see them."

"They're just...drawn to me, I suppose," she replied. "Once I can hear an animal nearby, I can usually get it to communicate with me. I can see their thoughts in my mind." Her eyes narrowed. "It's hard to explain."

Kirilee was nodding. "Animals don't really use words to speak, they use images and smells and memories of touch," she explained. "With Persius, I can see those memories and use images and thoughts of my own to respond."

Trina nodded. "That's exactly the same as me."

"It sounds like your gift is pretty well-developed already then," Kirilee said. "You probably won't need much training. But I'll work with you anyway."

"So if you can identify what the animals are showing you, Trina, then you must have been able to see at one point," Willem observed.

Trina nodded, her grudge with Willem at least temporarily forgotten. "I lost my vision when I was six, I think. I only have a few memories from before that. I remember both my parents, and I know my father died about a year before I went blind. I remember our old house, and that I had a purple bedroom." She sighed wistfully.

"But you don't know how you lost your sight?" Willem asked.

Trina shook her head. "I don't remember that part."

Kirilee smirked. "So, should we tell Kip you've been talking to his dog, ai?"

Trina shrugged. "Maybe one day."

"Speaking of Kip, were you the one who convinced Bailey to go with him?" I asked.

Trina nodded. "I told him that Kip feels a bit lonely and scared, that he needs Bailey right now. Also I don't think Bailey wants to be around here after what Willem did to him last night." Her voice grew acidic, and she let out a huff.

Willem sighed. "I didn't mean to upset Bailey, but I couldn't have him attacking me, Trina. Perhaps when you see him next you can give him my apologies, though."

She sighed. "All right. I'll do that. But promise you'll never do that to him again."

"I promise," Willem said. "In the future, if I need to keep a dog from hurting me, I'll use a sleeping spell rather than a freezing one. It's much less terrifying to be on the receiving end of."

She nodded and gave him the smallest hint of a smile. "Good."

"You said Kip was scared," I said to Trina. "What's he scared of?"

"Everything." Trina turned to me. "All this change, all this magic. *You*. You mean you can't tell?"

I shook my head slowly. "I just thought he was…mean."

"Sometimes people are mean *because* they're scared," Kirilee put in. "It's not at all uncommon." She gestured at Trina's untouched food. "You'd best eat up, Trina. We've a lot to do today."

\*　　　　\*

98

After we finished breakfast, I followed Willem through a door off of the home's entryway and down a short corridor, this one much wider than the one I was familiar with. Light flickered off the walls from candles sitting in stone sconces, and the doors in this hall were dusty with unuse. When we reached the end of the hall, Willem faced the wall in front of us, seeming to study it for a long moment. Then he placed his hand on it and muttered a phrase.

Slowly, the wall vanished into a vapor, revealing a dark tunnel beyond. Candles began to flicker in the tunnel, and as they came to life, I realized I was looking down an extension of the hallway we were in. Willem turned back and beckoned that I should follow him. I stepped forward cautiously; I still wasn't sure how I felt about training with Willem.

"My late father Ashlar once ran a school of magic," he told me. "This is where it was located. If you look into any of the doors along this hall, you'll find old classrooms."

I peeked into one of the rooms; sure enough it contained several old wooden desks, a lectern, and a few dusty bookshelves.

"The room at the end of the hall is my favourite," Willem told me. "Come, I'll show you."

I followed him to a pair of large double doors at the hall's end. They had intricate patterns engraved into their dark wood, similar to those on some of Lachlann's swords. Willem pushed one of the doors open and walked in; I followed. What must have been several dozen candles instantly lit up the darkness that surrounded us, and I found myself standing in the middle of a large, high-ceilinged octagonal room whose walls were almost entirely covered in bookshelves. Several desks and tables were scattered about the remainder of the room, and it was floored with brightly coloured tiles that created whirling patterns under our feet. I looked around the room in fascination. "Are all these books about magic?" I asked.

"Most of them," Willem replied. "Though there are some that are about science and math as well, and certain types of histories, and some fiction too."

"Fiction?"

He nodded. "Father had to allow his students to read for fun as well as for education. Most of these books contain information about magic though, some of it not very well known and most of it banned. There are a handful of men who would pay good money to anyone who could direct them here, which is why I'm so cautious about people knowing where I live."

I nodded; I knew this was an attempt to explain his actions from the night before. He walked over to a low table, sat down at it, and patted the chair next to his. "Sit with me, Saray. I think this is a good place for you to begin your lessons."

I sat where Willem directed, and he turned to face me. He paused for a long moment and then began to speak. "The first thing that you must understand," he said, "is that magic is simply the manipulation of the forces of nature that most people can't control. The average human cannot, for example, control fire, but a magic user—or *magikai*, as they were once called—can, with practice, learn to do just that.

"Magic is usually inherited," he went on, "but it can also be learned. It's much like any other talent. Anyone can learn to sing, but for some it comes quite naturally, while for others it would take years of practice even to carry a tune."

"So I could learn to do things other than control fire?" I asked. "I mean, like, go invisible? Or do all sorts of things like you do?"

He nodded. "Indeed you could, though you'll only end up like me if you're willing to dedicate the rest of your life to study. Those who are born magikai usually develop one ability—such as controlling fire—without ever having to learn it. All other forms they must learn, which takes years of effort and practice. One day you might learn to go invisible, but for now we'll just work with your innate talent."

"What's your innate talent?" I asked.

"I'll let you see if you can figure it out yourself."

I nodded. "So, where did the magic come from? Kirilee said something about it coming from the fairies?"

"That's the most popular theory," he responded, looking past me over the shelves of books. "There are a few others, one being that it's simply a part of the world we live in, available to whoever seeks it out. There's also a theory that Breoch was once populated by elves, who at one point left this place for another. Before they moved on, though, they left some of their magic in this world. Some also believe that the elves interbred with humans and that we born magikai are their descendants. Hence the term 'elfieblood.'" He sighed and stood up. "I think that's enough theory for one day, though. Show me what you can do with fire."

I stood up as well, took a deep breath and mumbled the casting words, and a small ball of fire appeared in my palm. I made it grow and then shrink, then tossed it in the air a few times, then extinguished it. Then I put out all the candles in the room and relit them.

"Very good," he said when I was finished. "Last night I saw you cast with your mind. I'd like to see that again."

I nodded and willed fire to dance on my hands, much like I had the night before.

"That's an extremely rare talent," Willem said. "I've been practicing magic for decades, and I know hundreds of spells, and I can't even do that."

"Really?"

He nodded. "Most magic users need either casting words or motions made by their dominant hand to cast—which, of course, is why krossemages have their right hands and tongues removed. I've only ever seen one or two people do what you just did." His eyes narrowed. "I wonder if you happened to have two parents who were both very powerful magikai and that's what made you able to do that? Or perhaps the magikai are evolving, becoming stronger?"

I frowned at his words, unsure what to think of them.

"But regardless, power without control can be dangerous," he went on. "Kirilee mentioned that last night wasn't the first time you cast without even thinking about it. That's normal the first time you cast—most magikai discover their gift this way. But it can be extremely unsafe, especially given your ability to cast with your mind and the fact that you're a firebrand. So I think that learning control will be the primary focus of our lessons." He gestured at the doors. "Come with me—we aren't going to do this here."

"What happens to left-handed magic users who are caught?" I asked Willem as we left the library and started down another long hall. "Do they have their left hand removed?"

"They do if the authorities are aware that they're left-handed," Willem replied. "But I imagine that many left-handed krossemages don't give up that information and use it to their advantage later, perhaps to help themselves escape. In fact, I know one woman who did just that many years ago. Ah, here we are." He pulled open a door, and we walked into a medium-sized, circular room. This room was completely bare and was lit by shining panels embedded in the ceiling that I was certain were fueled by magic. The walls and ceiling and floor were all covered in a strange, pearlescent material that was hard and cold to the touch, save for a hole in the ceiling that appeared to be a vent leading outside. "What is this place?" I asked.

"Practice room," Willem replied. "The material you see on the walls is resistant to magical effects. Your fire won't hurt it." He walked to the center of the room and turned to face me. "*Incantus ravenous bardeous,*" he mumbled, and I watched as a strange, iridescent bubble enveloped him. "Now your fire won't hurt me either."

I stared, fascinated by the protective bubble that he'd created. "Will that protect you from everything?"

He shook his head. "Just your fire. There's another, more powerful shield spell that exists, but if you try to cast or fight through it, the spell breaks down. Don't worry about that for today, though. For now, I'm going to throw several spells at you, and you need to try to defend yourself using fire."

I nodded and walked into the center of the room, facing him. My heartbeat picked up; I remembered how easily he'd deflected my fire last night. *I'm supposed to defend myself against someone like him?*

My eyes stayed on Willem as he paused and then waved his hand. I braced myself as a pair of sticks appeared out of nowhere and flew towards me. I nearly shouted my casting words, and fire consumed them immediately.

"Good," Willem said. "That seemed easy enough for you; now let's try some other things."

He hit me with a sour-smelling gas after that and then a pair of large predatory birds that he assured me were not actually real before I set them on fire. After that he went invisible, popping up to attack me from several different directions before returning to his normal form. Then he cast a spell that blinded me. I flailed in the dark for a moment, not sure what to do; then I had an idea. I cast my spell and drew the fire around me like a curtain, protecting myself from anything he might throw at me.

"Impressive," he said when he had ended the spell. "You have a sharp mind. A lot of people wouldn't figure out how to use fire to counter a blinding spell quite so fast. Now we're going to try something different. I'm going to throw more spells at you, though these ones will be different, and you have to try very hard *not* to respond with fire."

I frowned and nodded.

"I promise that I won't actually hurt you," he continued. "I have very good control over my spells. But I'll likely scare you—that's the point."

He faced me again, and then one of the large birds was back, circling above me. I looked up apprehensively as it cawed. Then it dove, its sharp beak pointed directly at my face.

Instinctively, my hands went up to my face. I felt words forming on my tongue; I tried to hold them back, but when the bird disappeared, its tail was engulfed in flame. I dropped my arms and sighed.

"Not bad," Willem said. "Not casting instinctively to protect yourself will take practice. Let's try again."

Willem went invisible after that, and a moment later, I felt something hard tap my side. I whirled and threw my hands out but bit down on my tongue to keep myself from casting the spell. My eyes widened when a ball of fire appeared regardless.

"You're casting with your mind again," he said. "It seems to be an instinct when you're scared. You're going to need to try to not let that happen."

"How?" I shook my head.

"Well, my understanding is that you have to control your thoughts. With mental casting, you decide in your head when to cast, and so you have to make a decision not to."

"All right, I'll try," I said uncertainly. "I'm not sure if I can do it, though."

"Try," Willem replied. As he spoke, I became aware of a white haze moving slowly towards me.

I stared at it. "What is…"

I trailed off as Willem raised a finger to his lips. "Wait and see," he replied. The mist enveloped me, and I felt my consciousness begin to slip away. I stumbled to the ground helplessly, trying to stay alert. After what felt like an eternity, something sharp stabbed at my ribs, jolting me awake.

I sat up quickly, my eyes flying open. I thought I saw a flicker of flame as I awoke but managed to rein it in before it got near Willem.

"Better." Willem nodded. "Now you're getting it. Let's try something new."

After that, he put me in situations where I had to assess danger before I cast. He made the room turn shadowy and put a hand on my shoulder; when I whirled around, he had taken on the form of a bear. The next time he touched me, he looked like Trina. Then he approached me as a heavily armoured man, only to lift the helmet's visor and reveal Lachlann's face. Then he had several birds fly at me, instructing me to only set a particular one on fire. All these exercises were significantly more difficult, and by the end of our session, Willem was eying me gravely. "You're very powerful, but you definitely struggle with control," he said. "You might be here a few weeks before it's safe for you to move on."

I nodded, my shoulders dropping.

"Let's go find the others and have some lunch," he went on. "I find that magic practice always makes me hungry."

I nodded again and followed him out of the room, trying to leave my feelings of discouragement behind.

We made our way outside, where I found Trina sitting on a ledge next to Kirilee. Several rabbits, a couple of squirrels, and a mountain goat of some type had congregated around the two of them, none of them seeming bothered by Persius's presence in the viletta above. "How's your training going?" Kirilee asked us.

"Pretty good for a first day," Willem answered. "Looks like Trina is doing well."

Trina smiled. "This is amazing. I knew that I could talk to animals, but Kirilee showed me that I can *command* them too. Watch." She mumbled a phrase under her breath, and several dozen birds rose from a nearby tree, did three loops in the sky, and settled back onto their respective perches.

"That could be useful if we're in a conflict, Trina," I pointed out. "Can you imagine how one of those guards might react if he was overrun by rats or raccoons?"

Trina giggled. "Very true. Though I don't want to practice any of those moves on any of you."

"I don't think we want that either," Willem agreed. "Come on, let's go have lunch."

We continued our lessons as the week progressed. Days were spent in the practice room, working with Willem to gain control of my fire, and evenings were spent sitting in the hot spring with Trina, spending time in the kitchen watching Willem use magic to cook extravagant dishes for us, listening to Kirilee and Trina play music with Trina's pipe, and walking around outside. Trina seemed to have mostly forgotten her quarrel with Willem now that he'd told her to apologize to Bailey for him, but she still seemed partial to Kirilee being the one to teach her. Occasionally in the evenings, I would sneak back into the school and wander the halls, poking my head into dusty, deserted classrooms and wondering why such a wonderful endeavour had been abandoned.

One day during training, about a week and a half after we'd arrived, I decided to broach my questions about the school to Willem. He frowned when I asked about what had happened to it. "I should have known that you'd ask about it eventually," he said. "Let's head outside and talk about it there."

Outside, we settled on the ledge overlooking the woods. Trina and Kirilee sat nearby working on their own lesson; I saw that Trina was now simultaneously commanding a flock of birds to swoop in a pattern and about a dozen squirrels to scale a particular tree. Kirilee glanced over at us. "What's happening?"

"I'm telling Saray what happened to the school," he said. "You and Trina can join us."

Kirilee nodded and called to Trina, and the two of them perched on the low-hanging branch of a tree near the cliff face. Willem stared off into space for a few moments after we sat and then began to speak. "The school was large and healthy when I was a child," he told me. "When the Banishing happened, there was an influx of magic users into these woods. Many magikai came to the school, eager to learn more magic. It was a safe haven for magikai in a world that was perilous for us."

"It sounds wonderful," I said.

"Indeed it was," he replied, nodding. "By the time I was a young man, the school's attendance had dwindled slightly—fewer people were interested in learning magic, and a lot of the magic users had ventured back out into the cities, hoping to hide their talents and live halfway normal lives. My family still lived here at the school, but the trade system that exists in the woods today wasn't quite so developed then, so trips into the cities were needed to buy goods. On one such trip, my mother was captured. Turned out a former student had leaked some information about the school to the authorities.

"Our family had a safeguard in place in case of this. When it happened, Mother cast a spell to seal off her voice, one that could only be broken by someone who knew the breaking words—so, Father or me. They tried to get information from Mother; they tortured her badly." He averted his gaze when he said these words, but his voice remained steady. "When they could get nothing from her, they decided to make her into a krossemage. They saw little reason to cut out her tongue, seeing as she was unable to speak, but they did cut off her right hand."

"Wow." I cringed. "That's awful."

He nodded. "But Father and I weren't about to let them keep her. We could use magic to detect her whereabouts from home, but we knew that getting her back wouldn't be easy. We tried several times to break into the compound where she was being held before we succeeded. It took a lot of very covertly used magic—invisibility spells and teleportation and false images and a knife that was able to magically cut through metal—for us to succeed, but we eventually got her out.

"When we finally got her back home, we knew we couldn't continue with the school. The risk of something similar happening again was too high. So we sent all the students home, wiping the knowledge of the school's location from their memories as they went, and sealed off the school. No one other than my parents and I have entered it since—until now, that is."

"Did your mother recover from what was done to her?" Trina asked.

"She never got her hand back," Willem replied. "But we found a way to deal with that. As for the emotional impact, well, she's a very strong woman. She seems to have recovered, though I can't be completely certain." He glanced back at the house. "You can see why I was hesitant to teach you."

"I can see why you didn't like Kip much too," I said cautiously.

Willem frowned. "I may have overreacted when I first learned about his fears," he admitted, glancing at Kirilee. "You were right; it wasn't fair to treat someone so young the way I did. But magic fearers have hurt my family badly."

"And Kip is afraid of magic because magic users have hurt *his* family," Trina pointed out. "Maybe you two have more in common than you think."

Willem opened his mouth to speak, but he was cut off by a familiar whimper. I turned around, and my eyes narrowed when I saw Bailey bounding up the trail towards us. *Where are Kip and Lachlann?* The dog ran past Willem and me and nearly collided with Trina. Trina frowned, put her head near Bailey's for a moment, and then stood up. "We need to follow Bailey. There's trouble." She grabbed onto his fur. "Take me to them, Bailey."

Willem, Kirilee and I got to our feet and followed Bailey and Trina into the forest. We'd been walking down the familiar rocky path for about ten minutes when Kirilee stopped short, causing me to nearly collide with her. I glanced over her shoulder at the scene before me.

Kip was hunched over on the ground, gasping. He was covered in dirt, and his hair was matted, long strands hanging in his eyes, and he had a good-sized bruise on his left cheek. But it was Lachlann, not Kip, who made my eyes go wide. Lachlann had been lashed to a makeshift sled using ropes; it appeared that Kip had been dragging him. One entire sleeve of his shirt was drenched in blood, and he was completely still. I swallowed the lump that was rising in my throat. "Is he... dead?"

# Chapter Eleven

**KIP LOOKED UP** and met my eyes, then looked at each of the others. "Thank the Fae you're here," he gasped. "I can't drag him any further; I'm too tired."

Kirilee moved towards Lachlann's still form, and she crouched down, looking him over. "He's not dead," she surmised, "but something's very wrong." She glanced at Kip. "What happened?"

"There were bandits on the mountain road last night," he said in a ragged voice, standing up. "They had an archer, and he shot at me. Lachlann saw it coming and shoved me out of the way, and the arrow went through his bracer. It must have been poisoned; Lachlann was like this an hour later. Figured it was best to bring him back here because you know medicine, and if you can't help him, well, maybe Willem knows another way." He gave Willem a wary look. "You should be glad that you didn't wipe my memory, y'know."

"Kirilee and I will take a look at him and see what we can do," Willem told Kip. He paused and took a deep breath. "You, uh, don't look so good, boy. Go back to the house, bathe and rest. I'll prepare some food for you when I get a chance. You've done what you can for Lachlann."

Kip eyed him. "You're going to let me back in your house, ai?"

Willem sighed. "Yes, I am. Perhaps you and I need to talk some things out later. But we have more pressing things to deal with right now." He glanced down at Lachlann.

Kip frowned. "All right, then. Uh, thank you." He turned and walked slowly towards the house.

Willem knelt in the dirt next to Kirilee. "Lachlann, can you hear me?" Lachlann let out a slight groan, and his eyes flickered open.

"Well, he's at least somewhat conscious," Willem said. "That's reassuring. Let's move him somewhere where we can get a better look at him." He touched Lachlann's head, and I gasped slightly when Lachlann disappeared. "He's in the house, on the dining room table," Willem told us. "Don't worry."

We headed back to the house and into the dining room; sure enough, Lachlann was laid out on the table, which had magically been stripped of all of its place settings and decor. His face was pale and covered by a fine sheen of sweat, I saw, and when I looked closely, he was shaking. Kirilee walked over and laid a hand on his head. "The fever is bad," she said. "Let's see his arm."

Willem gingerly rolled up Lachlann's sleeve. I couldn't help but recoil at the swollen, festering wound on his left forearm. Kirilee frowned and studied it. "It's certainly infected," she mused, "but I think Kip's right about the arrow being poisoned. An infection wouldn't have a person in this sort of shock so quickly." She extracted a small jar from her bag. "I'll put some of this on it and give him something for the fever, and we'll see how he is in an hour. I wish we knew what the arrow was poisoned with."

Kirilee cleaned the wound and gently applied her salve and then retreated into the kitchen. She returned several minutes later holding a tankard with steam rising from it. Willem held Lachlann's head up, and Kirilee inched the mug towards him. Lachlann's eyes fluttered open as the cup touched his lips, and he managed to swallow the liquid without choking, but when Willem laid him back down, his face went blank again.

"Now what?" My voice was tinged with anxiety.

"Now," Willem replied gravely, "we wait."

A few hours later, Kirilee and Willem hovered over Lachlann again. Kip had rejoined us, looking considerably better than before but clearly keeping Willem at a distance. "He hasn't improved at all," Kirilee said to Willem in a worried tone. "I'm not sure what else I can do for him without knowing what sort of poison was used."

"Well, then, I think this calls for my mother," Willem said. Kirilee nodded.

"What can your mother do?" Trina asked.

"My mother used to be a lifebringer," Willem explained. "She lost her healing powers in an incident when I was a child, but she retained certain abilities that are related to healing. One of those is being able to look into an injury or illness and see its cause. She also innately knows what's needed to heal a person naturally, if it's possible." He frowned. "If she can determine what sort of poison caused Lachlann's condition, as well the best course of action, then maybe we can help him. She lives nearby, in Flavalan, but it's easy enough to bring her here right now."

Willem strode into the parlour; the rest of us followed curiously. He reached into the neck of his robe and pulled out what appeared to be a pendant, then ran his fingers over the surface and mumbled a soft phrase.

Nothing happened for a good minute, and then the air next to Willem began to shimmer. The next moment, a flickering shadow appeared in the middle of the shimmering, and then the shadow materialized into a person. I stared, transfixed. The woman next to Willem was small and bent, clothed in a plain blue dress and a white bonnet. Her skin was the same dark brown tone as her son's, and her face was lined with age. Her dark eyes were alert and merry, though. She looked around the room curiously, her face breaking into a smile when she saw Kirilee. "So good to see you, darling!" she exclaimed, stepping forward and embracing her.

Kirilee returned the woman's embrace. "It's a pleasure to see you as well, Claudi."

Claudi pulled back, then turned and embraced Willem. "Who are our guests?" she asked. "And to what do I owe the honour of the visit?"

Willem introduced Kip, Trina, and me to his mother and then told her about Lachlann's condition. Claudi bobbed her head gravely when Willem explained his symptoms. "Take me to see him, then."

We walked into the dining room, and Claudi made her way to the table and looked Lachlann over, pulling back the blanket and staring at his wounded arm for a moment. "Mmm," she said, frowning. "He's very sick indeed. And you say this was caused by a poisoned arrow?"

"That's what I figure," Kip told her. "He was like this an hour after the attack, I don't think an infection would make him this sick, this fast."

"Well, let me see if I can find out," Claudi replied. Gingerly, she placed her hand over the wound and then closed her eyes and began to sing softly. I watched in awe. *She can cast spells by singing?*

"I see the attack," she said after a moment, opening her eyes. "As for the poison…" Here she closed her eyes again and concentrated for a moment. When she opened them, her face was grim. "It was a cursed arrow."

Kirilee's face went pale. "I was afraid of that."

"A what?" I asked.

"There are some magikai who know how to use magic for dark purposes on their weapons," Willem explained. "If you get wounded by one of these weapons, it brings fever and delirium, and it'll cause the flesh around the wound to rot slowly."

"So will it kill him?" I asked uncertainly.

"Eventually, if it's not treated. There's only one way to deal with this." He met Claudi's eyes as she spoke, and Claudi nodded. Kirilee nodded as well; she appeared to be blinking back tears. Claudi put a reassuring hand on her shoulder. "I have an idea," Willem continued, motioning to the parlour. "Come, let's sit."

We seated ourselves in the parlour, and Willem looked around the circle. "The only way to save Lachlann is to amputate his arm," he told us plainly. Trina let out a gasp at his statement, and I felt my stomach constrict. "If we do it soon, we should be able to amputate below the elbow. You need to understand, though, that losing his arm may not hinder Lachlann in the ways you'd expect." He exchanged a glance with his mother.

I frowned. "I don't understand."

"We've already had to deal with a lost limb in this family," Willem explained. He looked at Claudi again, who was slowly removing her right glove to reveal a hand that appeared to be made of metal. *Right.* In the middle of all the concern about Lachlann, I had all but forgotten the story Willem told me earlier.

Willem was repeating that same story now, telling the others about Claudi's imprisonment and loss of limb. I, meanwhile, stared at her metal hand in fascination. It appeared to work like a normal hand; she was removing her left glove with it as Willem spoke.

"Can I touch your hand?" Trina asked Claudi.

"Of course." Claudi reached over and took Trina's hand in her metal one, and Trina ran her fingers over it, eyes wide.

"When we'd made it safely home from rescuing my mother, I delved into my books, eager to see if there was some sort of magic I could use to restore her hand," Willem was telling us now. "And while I didn't find anything that could do that beyond the powers of a lifebringer, I did find something else— a guide to fashioning working limbs using magic and metal and a few drops of blood from the person the limb is intended for."

"Blood?" I wrinkled my nose.

"Indeed." He nodded. "Using blood in magic is a taboo among many magikai, and I hesitated to do it myself. But I figured my mother's well-being was a special enough circumstance for me to try it. Now, finding a blacksmith that was willing to help craft the limb, that took a few months. But I don't imagine I'll have any trouble this time." He looked in the direction of the dining room and smiled ruefully.

"You think he'll be able to work a forge with only one hand?" Kip asked.

"I don't doubt that he'll need some help," Willem replied. "But I'm more than willing to provide that, and I imagine most of you are too."

I nodded eagerly. "Who's going to amputate his arm?"

"We need to figure that out," Willem responded. "I would think that Kirilee knows medicine better than any of us, though she's likely never used it to cut off a limb before."

Kirilee nodded, her face still pale. "I've never performed an amputation or any sort of surgery," she admitted and let out a long sigh. "But I'm willing to do it if I'm the only one who can. I've a general idea how it's done."

"I could help, if you wanted me to," Kip volunteered, glancing warily at Willem.

Kirilee turned to him. "You know medicine?"

"No." He shook his head. "But I hunt, which means I also butcher. I'm used to cutting through flesh, and blood doesn't bother me at all, y'know.

You should probably do the amputation, since you know medicine, but I can be your assistant. I've some tools in my bag that might be useful too."

Kirilee nodded. "That'd be helpful. But I'm going to have Willem help with some spells, and I know how you feel about magic."

Kip raised an eyebrow and glanced at Willem again. "What sort of spells?"

"Most importantly, I'm going to have him keep Lachlann asleep so he doesn't feel any pain and doesn't struggle," Kirilee explained. "I was also thinking that Willem could put a heat spell on the knife that'll cauterize the flesh and help avoid infection." She glanced at Willem, who nodded, then looked back to Kip. "Do you think you can handle that?"

Kip took a deep breath and then nodded, to my surprise. "Yes. I think I can handle that."

"Is there anything I can do?" I asked.

Willem shook his head. "This will be an unpleasant endeavour, Saray, and I'd rather not include you or Trina in it. We'll likely need you to help forge the new arm, though." He frowned. "This will take a few hours to set up. Let's have some lunch, make our preparations, and meet back here in two hours."

Three hours later, I paced the length of Willem's library, my stomach in knots, waiting for news. We had reconvened an hour ago, as planned, and Willem had teleported Lachlann into a classroom in the school wing that they'd set up as an operating room. I'd offered to help once again, and Willem had once again refused to allow it. So I'd retreated here, to the library further down the hall, hoping to distract myself with books.

At the beginning of the hour, my plan had worked. Among the books I'd found a fascinating introduction to the history of magic, a book specifically on fire spells, and a novel about a group of children who'd fled their home to live in the woods. As the hour had passed, though, I'd become increasingly restless, and now I fought the urge to walk up to the classroom nearby and peek my head in, just to make sure everything was going smoothly.

I jumped when the doors swung open a few minutes later. Kip walked into the room. He had blood on his clothing, his hair was dishevelled, and his face looked tired. "It's done," he said.

"How is he?" I asked, picking up the books I'd found and walking over to him.

"He's asleep right now; Willem moved him to the parlour. We amputated the arm just fine, but we'll have to wait and see if his fever drops. Kirilee said it might be another day or two before we know."

"Where are the others?" I asked.

"Kirilee's gone to rest, and Willem is cleaning up," Kip replied. "Claudi and Trina are in the parlour, watching Lachlann. You can go see him if you'd like."

I stared at Kip curiously as we made our way up the hall. "What's happened to you?" I asked. "You don't seem as afraid of magic anymore."

Kip sighed. "I'm trying to look at witchery—er, magic, differently," he told me. "Lachlann decided to lecture me during our journey. He said that my problem is that I see magic as only bad, y'know, instead of being a tool that can be used for good as well. He spent the first few days pointing out situations that would've been easier if one of us used magic." He gave me a shy smile. "Like the first night, when it was pouring and neither of us could get the fire to light. I didn't want to admit it, but you would've been useful then."

I returned his smile, feeling the all-too-familiar flutter in my chest. We were at the entrance to the parlour now, and Lachlann was stretched out on one of the long couches, mostly covered in a blanket, his eyes closed. Claudi sat nearby, watching him, and Trina leaned against the couch with Bailey next to her, petting him absentmindedly.

"I was annoyed at him at first," Kip went on, "but then he went and took an arrow for me in the fight. And that made me realize that he seems to care about me, even though I haven't been the nicest lately. So I figure I owe it to him to give his friends, and his ideas about magic, a chance." He glanced at me out of the corner of his eye. "After that, when I had to start dragging him back here, I couldn't stop thinking how useful one of those—uh, teleport spells, I think they're called—would be. And I knew that magic might be useful in helping him get better. Seems like it has been too." He walked over and looked down at Lachlann's sleeping form. "I'm glad he didn't have to be awake while we cut off his arm."

"Me too," I agreed. I stole a glance at Kip, suddenly feeling awkward again. "How about your arms? Have you…healed up all right?"

He frowned. "Almost. Kirilee did a good job taking care of them." He glanced at me, and I thought I saw his face redden slightly. "Your jaw looks better than it did. I'm sorry for punching you, by the way. And I'm sorry for calling you what I did. I didn't mean it, y'know."

I shook my head. "I suppose I deserved to get punched; I did set you on fire." My shoulders hunched, and I looked at him out of the corner of my eye. "And I'm sorry too. I didn't actually mean to hurt you, it just happened."

"I know," Kip replied. "That's what worries me. Willem makes me nervous, but I'm glad you're learning from him."

I nodded. "Willem has his reasons for feeling how he does about magic fearers," I said to him cautiously. "I mean, you heard what happened to his mother. And I suppose you have your reasons to fear magic as well. Me, for example." I let out a nervous laugh.

He chuckled too. "Well, I'm trying to stop being so afraid. I still think magic can be used badly, y'know—look at what the cursed arrow did to Lachlann—but I s'pose swords and knives and bows can also be used badly."

"And fists," I put in, giving him a wry smile.

He raised his eyebrows and returned my grin. "Those too."

"And all this is exactly why magic being legalized would be a good thing," Willem said, striding into the room. "If it was legal, the government could regulate it; they could ban things like cursed arrows and employ it for useful things, like magical metal limbs."

"When do we start on that?" I asked.

"As soon as Lachlann is well enough," Willem answered. "Though he won't be able to wear it for several weeks yet; he needs to heal first. Looks like the lot of you won't be getting to Dundere quite as quickly as you'd hoped." He stifled a yawn. "I'm going to go rest; I'll see you all at dinner."

I walked over to Lachlann and looked him over. His face was peaceful now, his breathing even. "Do you think he's going to be all right?" Trina asked me.

I sighed and sat down beside her. "I *think* so," I said. "I mean, he definitely looks better. I suppose all we can do now is hope for the best."

# Chapter Twelve

"HOW IS HE?" I asked the following morning as I walked into the parlour to find everyone else awake and present.

"Much better," Kirilee replied, hovering over Lachlann's sleeping form. "The fever broke in the middle of the night." She glanced at Willem. "Now that we're all here, should we wake him?"

Willem nodded and walked over to where Kirilee stood and then waved a hand over Lachlann's face. A moment later, his eyes fluttered open, and he let out a groan.

"Welcome back," Kirilee said to him, reaching for his hand.

Lachlan stared at her for a moment, a confused expression on his face. Then he bolted upright. "Kip," he gasped. "Is he all right? Did the bandits…"

"I'm fine," Kip said, coming over to join Kirilee and Willem. "You're back at Willem's place, and everyone's all right. Except you, that is."

Lachlann let out a sigh of relief and looked around the room. "What happened to me?"

"The fellow who shot you put some sort of curse on his arrows," Kip replied. "You nearly died. We had to cut off your arm to save you, y'know."

Lachlann frowned and let go of Kirilee's hand. Then he pulled back the blanket, revealing the bandaged stump where his left forearm once was. He stared at it for a moment, shaking his head. "Well, damn," he said softly, "this'll make getting to Dundere a little more difficult."

Willem nodded. "Don't worry. We'll have you back to normal soon enough."

Lachlann frowned. "And how will you do that?"

"I'll explain once you're a little better," Willem reassured him. "Right now, you need rest."

He nodded and lay back down. "Why am I not in pain?"

"Would you like me to lift the spell that's keeping you pain free?" Willem asked.

Lachlann stared at him for a moment and then shook his head. "I think I like that spell."

"Figured as much." Willem gave him a wry smile. "How's your appetite? Care for some breakfast?"

"Breakfast would be wonderful," Lachlann replied.

"In that case, I'll go make some for you and for everyone else while I'm at it." Willem strode out of the room.

Lachlann turned to Kip. "How did we get away from the bandits? I don't remember anything after being shot."

"I put an arrow in the eye of the other archer about five seconds after he hit you," Kip told him. "After that, Persius appeared out of nowhere and dove at one of the others, and Bailey took a bite out of the third one." He grinned and glanced at Kirilee. "I'd no idea your bird was following us."

Lachlann shook his head. "I don't remember any of that. How in the king's name did we get back here? Don't tell me you carried me."

"No. Made a sled out of sticks and rope and dragged you back. Bailey helped me; I trained him to pull sleds years ago. I had to leave a lot of our gear behind though, including your armour." Kip frowned. "I'm sorry, but I know you can make more."

"You dragged me all the way back here, through that bloody mess of rocks and mud?" Lachlann's eyebrows arched. "I didn't think you liked me enough to do that."

Kip shrugged. "I wasn't just going to leave you to die, not after you likely saved my life, y'know? And you should be thanking Kirilee; you'd definitely be dead without her."

Lachlann's gaze turned to Kirilee. "I take it you did the honours?" he said, gesturing at his arm.

"Kip and Willem helped, but I did most of it." Kirilee gave him a sad smile. "I hope you'll forgive me."

"Well, seeing as I might be dead otherwise, I suppose chopping off a limb is a forgivable offense." Lachlann smiled at her and then looked down at his arm again, his smile fading slightly.

"Can someone help me bring in the breakfast?" Willem called out from the kitchen.

"I'll help," I called back. I got to my feet and sauntered off to the kitchen, eager to eat breakfast and happy that Lachlann was on the mend.

Lachlann slept through the rest of that day and most of the following one, but that evening at dinner he was awake and talkative again. We all ate in the parlour so he wouldn't be alone, and Willem filled him in on our plans for the metal hand. "I hope it works," he said when Willem was finished explaining. He glanced down at his stump. "I'm already starting to miss my hand."

Kirilee averted her eyes, moving slightly away from him on the couch, and he sighed. "Oh, come on, that wasn't directed at you, Kirilee. You did what you had to; I know that." He let out a short laugh. "If anything, I think you're brave. That couldn't have been easy for you, cutting off someone's arm. I mean, I'm assuming you've never done that before?"

Kirilee shook her head and gave Lachlann a smile that seemed almost shy. "It was terrifying," she admitted. "I was so scared I was going to kill you. I don't know what I would've done with myself if I had."

"I thought you weren't bothered by killing." Lachlann's voice had a teasing note to it.

Kirilee snorted. "It's a little different when it's someone you love. It's…" She trailed off suddenly, her eyes going wide.

Lachlann's expression changed too, and he turned and stared at her. "Am I hearing things," he said to her, "or did you just say that you *love* me?"

She met his gaze, and I saw a slight blush colour her cheeks. "I s'pose I did."

His eyes narrowed. "Did you mean it as a friend?"

"Well, yes, but…perhaps in another way as well." She gave him a shy smile, and suddenly she seemed small, vulnerable, not her usual fearless self.

Willem cleared his throat. "I think the kids and I should leave."

"Thank you," Lachlann nodded. Willem stood up and collected the plates. Kip headed towards the front door, Bailey following him, and Trina and I began to trail Willem towards the kitchen. Trina was walking slowly, I noticed, running her hand along the wall. When we reached the entrance to the dining room, she paused and grabbed my sleeve, smirking as she pointed at the dining room and cupped a hand to her ear. I chuckled as I realized what she wanted and then stole a look at Willem; he was walking into the kitchen, seemingly unaware of us. Trina giggled as we ducked into the dining room and crouched next to the doorway leading back into the parlour. I poked my head around the partition.

Kirilee and Lachlann hadn't moved from their respective spots, and they were staring at one another intently. "I don't understand," Lachlann said. We've talked about this before, and you've always said that we would never work. What's changed?"

She shook her head and sat straighter, seeming to regain her composure. "It still wouldn't work," she told him. "But when you were lying there nearly dead, and I had to try to save you, I found myself realizing that I wish it *could* work. I wish I could be with you."

Lachlann's eyes widened. "Well, perhaps we should establish why you think it wouldn't work. You've always been elusive about that."

"There are a few reasons." She shifted her body so she was facing Lachlann. "First of all, I'm far, far too old for you."

"How old, exactly?" He grinned. "Are you over one hundred?"

"No, not quite." She toyed with a braid and looked at her hands for a moment before responding. "I'm seventy-four. I haven't aged a day since I was twenty-five." I raised my eyebrows at her claim, and I heard Trina let out a quiet gasp.

"Seventy-four," Lachlann repeated, shaking his head. One corner of his mouth turned up. "You're exactly twice my age, did you know that?"

She let out a small laugh in response. "As I say, far too old for you."

"Well, what other problems are there? I might be able to overlook that one thing; I certainly don't *feel* like you're twice my age."

Kirilee gave him a sad smile. "The other thing is much more important," she told him. "The spell that keeps me young—and keeps me from sleeping— also prevents me from finding a home, from living in one place. It's why I wander so much."

Lachlann's eyes narrowed. "One day you're going to have to tell me how you got under this spell." I nodded in silent agreement.

"One day I will," she replied. "But right now I think we're having a different conversation." She sighed. "See, I know you believe in marriage, being from the cities and all, and you need to understand that I could never make a home with you, Lachlann. I'm doomed to wander for the rest of my years. I've had other lovers in the past, and none of them worked out for this exact reason. And I value your friendship too much to let it become another romance destined to end in heartbreak." She shook her head. "I'm sorry it's taken me so long to explain this to you."

Lachlann was silent for a few moments, staring at a pattern in the rug. Then he turned to her. "You know, I wish you'd told me this years ago," he finally said, "so I could tell you that what you believe about yourself is nonsense."

"Nonsense?" she repeated. "It's true, though, Lachlann. I could never be a good wife, or even a good partner, to you."

"That's absolutely not true," Lachlann insisted. "What you're trying to say is that you couldn't be a good *traditional* wife."

"What do you mean?"

"Most wives make a home for their family," he explained. "Most wives take care of the home, and bear children, and raise them together with their husband. And yes, it's true that you couldn't do these things. But do you really think that's what I *want?*" He shook his head. "Really, Kirilee, I've taken care of myself for years. I hardly live at home myself—I'm out travelling constantly. You know that. I haven't thought about the possibility of children—or having a house of my own or a job that keeps me at home—for ages. I may be from the cities, and yes, I do like the idea of being married.

121

But I'm not looking for a traditional wife, or a traditional life for that matter. You of all people should know that much."

Kirilee shook her head. "Even so," she said, "it wouldn't be an ideal relationship. If we did get married, I wouldn't even be able to live with you, y'know?"

"It wouldn't be ideal," he agreed. "But I'd rather have a non-ideal relationship with you than an ideal one with any other woman." He smiled and reached out to put his hand on top of hers. "Think about it, Kirilee. All these years you've been without a home, but maybe home doesn't have to be a place. Maybe *home* could be another person." I felt a strange, unexpected pang go through me at his words.

Kirilee blinked hard, and I watched as she slowly wound her fingers into his. "By the Fae," she said softly. "That sounds…wonderful." Her voice was ragged. A single tear worked its way down her cheek, and Lachlann let go of her hand, reached out and gently brushed it away, his fingers trailing down to her jawline and lingering there. They stared at one another for several long, tense moments. I held my breath.

"What's happening?" Trina whispered.

Kirilee jerked away from Lachlann and whirled towards us. My eyes widened, and I ducked behind the wall, but it was too late; she was already marching towards our hiding spot, her blue eyes blazing. "What exactly do you think you're doing, ai?" she demanded.

Heat flooded my face, and when I tried to reply, my words caught in my throat. Trina, meanwhile, began to giggle uncontrollably. "I…I'm sorry, Kirilee," she chortled. "But this is just so *romantic*…"

Kirilee huffed. "Romantic or not, eavesdropping on adult conversation is completely uncalled for."

"Go to bed, you two," Lachlann called out from the couch. "Give us a bit of privacy." Glancing at him, I saw that he was smiling wryly; he clearly found our antics more amusing than Kirilee did.

Trina and I ducked out of the dining room and made our way down the hall, into our room. As soon as the door shut, we both burst into giggles. "I think Kirilee's going to hate us forever now," I gasped between laughs.

"Nah, she won't." Trina shook her head and took a deep breath, trying to control her laughter. "Do you think they're going to get married?"

I shrugged. "I mean, Lachlann seems to like the idea. I'm not sure about Kirilee. I'm sure we'll find out soon enough, though." I felt the strange pang again as I crawled into bed, and my cheeks flushed. *I'm jealous, aren't I? I'm being a silly, shallow girl again. Just like the girls back at the Academy.*

"Weddings are lovely," Trina said sleepily from her own bed. "I hope they get married. And I hope I get to have a wedding someday."

"I hope you do too, Trina," I said, smiling. *And I'm glad I'm not the only one who's being a silly, shallow girl right now.*

The following morning, I walked into the parlour to find Kirilee and Lachlann sitting on the couch. Lachlann was leaning up against the couch's end, still half covered in the blankets he'd slept under, and Kirilee was wedged up against him, his good arm around her shoulders and his hand clasped in her own. Kirilee gave me a wry smile; she didn't seem to be angry anymore. "Morning, Saray."

"Morning, you two." I chuckled, eying them. "I take it the rest of your conversation went well last night."

"I'd say so," Lachlann replied, exchanging a grin with Kirilee. Claudi walked in from the kitchen, giving everyone a welcoming smile and settling into her chair.

"So, now what?" I asked, giving Kirilee and Lachlann a grin of my own. "I mean, you were talking about marriage last night."

"And you weren't supposed to hear that." Kirilee laughed. "But we figure we'll date for a little while, at least, before we make that decision. Lachlann managed to convince me we're both mature enough to stay friends if it doesn't work out."

"One would hope you're mature enough, you old woman," Lachlann teased her. Kirilee responded by jabbing him in the ribs with her elbow, and he laughed.

"Well isn't this adorable," Kip said, walking into the room behind me.

"Aren't they, though?" I turned to him and grinned. "You missed out on Trina and me listening in on them last night. I thought Kirilee was going to rip our ears off."

Lachlann chuckled. "A fear that isn't unfounded, given that she seems to have a knack for removing body parts. You two had better watch yourselves."

"I'll remember that," I said, feigning seriousness. Then I sighed and turned to Kirilee. "One thing you said last night got me curious."

"What's that?" Kirilee asked.

"You said you'd tell Lachlann your whole story one of these days. Would you be willing to tell the rest of us too?"

Kirilee's smile faded, and she exchanged a glance with Claudi. "Maybe," she said. "My story's not an easy one to tell. There's a reason I don't talk about it much."

"Would you be opposed to me telling the children?" Claudi asked. "I know most of your story quite well."

Kirilee frowned. "I s'pose you could."

Willem walked in from the kitchen then, carrying trays stacked high with pancakes. I gasped; pancakes were a very rare treat at Sylvenburgh Academy, and I hadn't eaten them in years. "Anyone know where Trina is?" asked Willem.

"She was sleeping when I left the room," I replied.

"I'll go wake her," Claudi said, standing up.

Claudi headed in the direction of the bedrooms, and I took my tray from Willem, sat down, and dug into my pancakes. Claudi returned a few minutes later, accompanied by Bailey and a very sleepy looking Trina. "Morning everyone," she mumbled as Claudi escorted her to a chair.

"There you are." Kip was staring at Bailey. His gaze turned to Trina. "Was the dog sleeping in your room last night?"

I snorted. "He was sleeping on Trina's *bed* last night," I informed him between bites of my meal.

"Huh." Kip reached down and petted Bailey. "Why're you so attached to Trina, boy?"

Trina flinched at Kip's words, and I exchanged a nervous glance with Willem. "I know why," Trina admitted after a long pause. "I'll tell you later, all right? I want to enjoy my breakfast; I haven't had pancakes in years."

"All right, tell me later," Kip conceded, and I relaxed slightly and turned my attention to the food. I wasn't sure how the conversation that would need to happen later would go, but for now, I would enjoy my meal.

The day got warmer as it progressed, and by lunchtime, Kip was talking about heading outdoors. After lunch I followed him outside, and we settled on the shelf overlooking the drop-off. The city of Flavalan lay in the distance and beyond that, the ocean. "Have you ever been to the ocean?" I asked Kip.

He shook his head.

"Me neither," I said to him. "I can't believe we're going to cross it. I wonder how long it'll take to get to Dundere?" I'd seen Dundere on the maps in Mr. Jeffries' classroom, but it was hard to tell from those drawings how far away the island was from us.

"Thought I'd find you out here." Trina was approaching us now, holding on to Bailey. The two of them settled on the ground nearby.

Kip eyed Trina. "So what were you going to tell me about you and Bailey?"

"Right." Trina cleared her throat and turned towards Kip. "Bailey likes me for a few reasons," she explained. "One of them is that I can talk to him."

Kip's eyes widened as she explained her gift to him. "I knew it," he said, shaking his head. "You *were* using witchery on my dog. I'm surrounded by magic users." He let out an exaggerated sigh, smiling slightly.

Trina ran her hand through Bailey's fur. "There's more, though," she said. "Bailey...he knows me, or at least he thinks he does. He seems to think that he knew me before Saray and I first met you." Her eyes narrowed. "That first day, when he jumped on me in your hut and started licking me...it was like he was thrilled to see me again. But I don't remember him."

"Odd," Kip said, frowning. "Maybe he's mistaken you for someone else."

"Maybe. The strange thing is, he seems to know me by another name. And it's the name I went by when I was very young, so I wonder if I knew him when I was little."

"Your real name isn't Trina?" Kip asked.

"It's my middle name," she replied. "My mother started calling me by it right before she took me to the orphanage; she told me not to tell anyone my real name." She frowned. "Though I did tell Saray once."

I nodded, recalling that conversation. "Anna," I said softly.

"Anna." Kip drew in a sharp breath, his eyes suddenly wide. "Your real name is Anna?"

"Yes," she replied, her head cocking slightly. "Anna Katrina, Trina for short. Why?"

"By the Fae." Kip was staring at Trina now; his face had gone white. "Come here."

Trina frowned but obeyed, and Kip took her face in his hands and stared at her. "You...you could be her, y'know," he said slowly.

"Kip, what's going on?" I asked. "Who's this person you think Trina might be?"

"How old are you again, Trina?" Kip asked, ignoring me.

"Thirteen," she said.

"And do y'know anything about your life before the school? You remember your old home, or your mother's name? Or your last name?"

She shook her head. "I remember my mother's face, but I forget her name. And my last name is Carmichael."

"Carmichael." He nodded. "That sounds right." He frowned and then looked at her again. "So you used to be able to see, ai?"

She nodded.

"Do you know how you went blind?"

"I don't remember what happened," she replied. "But maybe Claudi could tell you."

"What?"

"Remember how Claudi used magic to figure out what was wrong with Lachlann?" she asked. "Maybe she could do that for me."

"Go get her," Kip said, his tone turning impatient.

I stood and went inside to the parlour. Lachlann was asleep again, and the other adults were sitting huddled around an old-looking book that Willem was holding. I filled them in on what was happening, and Claudi chuckled at

Kip's request. "I suppose I can try to see into her wounds," she said. "It may be harder, given that they are very old, but I'll do my best." She rose to her feet with a slight groan and followed me out of the room. Looking back, I saw the others trailing her.

Outside, Claudi made her way over to where Trina was sitting. "So, you want me to look into your blindness?"

"*Kip* wants you to look into my blindness," Trina corrected.

"Wait, Kip is requesting that someone cast a spell?" Willem asked.

Trina nodded. "He thinks I'm...someone else."

Claudi gave her an amused look, then knelt on the ground and placed her hands on Trina's head, closed her eyes, and chanted the phrase I'd heard her use on Lachlann. She hummed to herself for a few minutes and then was silent, concentrating. After a couple of long moments, she began to speak. "I see a large room with vibrant wall hangings and expensive-looking furniture," she began. "There are two women and three children in it; you're the youngest of the three. And one of the women is very angry. She's shouting at the other woman, telling her to get out." Her eyes narrowed. "The angry woman has just grabbed a large vase, and she's beating you on the head with it. The second woman is screaming and trying to pry her off you, and the other children are backing towards the door, looking terrified. When the second woman finally gets the first one to stop, you're unconscious on the ground, bleeding from your head and barely alive. The angry woman goes and..."

"Stop," Kip interrupted, raising a hand. His face was pale again, and his jaw was clenched. "You've told me what I need to know."

Trina shook her head. "I...I don't remember any of that."

"You wouldn't." Claudi removed her hands. "That vase did damage to your brain. It should have killed you; it's a miracle that you only lost your sight. You likely lost some memories as well."

"But why was the first woman attacking me?" Trina asked.

"Because she was scared of you," Kip answered, his voice shaking. "She caught you talking to the dog, and she figured you were a witch and needed to be destroyed."

Trina shook her head. "How do you know?"

"Because the woman who attacked you was my mother," he explained. "The woman protecting you was your own mother, who was married to my father's brother, and the two children in the room were my brother and me. And the dog you were talking to was Bailey, of course." He took a deep, shaky breath, and when he spoke again, his voice wobbled. "Trina, you and I are cousins. And until today, I thought you were dead."

An hour later, we all sat in the parlour together. Lachlann was awake now, and Kip had told us the full story of the events that caused Trina's blindness: how his aunt and her young child had come to live with his family following the death of both Kip's and Trina's fathers in a pox outbreak and how his mother had disliked Trina—or Anna, as was her name then—from the start. He'd explained how young Anna had formed a strange attachment to the puppy that the family acquired shortly after her arrival, and how his mother's attack on Anna had been the event that caused him to take his brother and the puppy and flee the family home for the Shrouded Woods. "When I first met you, I thought I recognized you, y'know," he told Trina.

Trina's eyes narrowed. "How did you recognize me if you haven't seen me since I was six?"

"You look nearly exactly the same as your mother, that's how," he told her. "Your skin's a bit lighter than hers, and that makes sense because your father was light skinned. But your face is quite like hers." He sighed. "That's why I was kind to you and Saray, y'know. I didn't hurt you, even though you two broke into my house and tried to steal my food, because you made me think of the cousin I'd lost. But I never figured you'd actually *be* her, that you might have survived what my mother did to you." He shook his head. "Trina, I'm so, so sorry that I didn't help defend you. I've felt awful about it for years. I was young, and scared, and I...I thought you were dead because I did nothing..." His voice shuddered, and he trailed off and looked away.

"Don't worry." Trina placed her hand on his arm. "If your mother was as angry as Claudi said, you probably wouldn't have been able to stop her from hurting me. It's not your fault."

"But it is mine." Kirilee was staring at Trina, her expression grave. "It seems that what I did to Clarita affected you as well, ai?"

Trina shook her head. "I already told you, that was an accident. And even if it was partly your fault, it doesn't make sense to stay angry at someone else, or at yourself, for something that happened years and years ago." She turned towards Kip. "Right?"

Kip stared at her and then nodded slowly. "I s'pose it's best to leave the past where it belongs," he said in a shaky voice. He glanced at Kirilee. "For all our sakes."

Trina grinned and wrapped her arms around him in response. A few tears slid down Kip's face as he embraced his long-lost cousin. I bit my lip, feeling a pang inside me that was similar to how I'd felt last night. *Jealousy.* I shook my head at my own emotions.

"Well, now, this is wonderful!" Claudi exclaimed.

Kip looked up and nodded. "Thanks so much for helping us."

"Aren't you glad you stuck around, boy?" Willem grinned at Kip. "And that you're becoming less afraid of magic?"

Kip swiped at his eyes and gave him a sheepish nod. "I'm definitely starting to see how it can be useful."

"Indeed it can be," Willem agreed. "And in a few weeks' time, we're going to use more of it."

"How so?"

"Lachlann, Saray and I are going to start making Lachlann's new arm once he's a bit more healed up," he replied. He glanced at Kip. "You can come help us if you'd like."

"What will I be doing?" I asked.

"Well, I don't have a proper forge here, and you need a forge to fashion things from steel," he explained. "What I do have, though, is a room made specifically to handle stray magic effects, and a young firebrand. Before we can start, I'm going to need to teach you how to make your fire hotter."

I bit my lip. "Do you think I have enough control for that? I mean, I don't know if I'll be able to keep a flame going for as long as you'll need."

He nodded. "That's why we're going to train more before we start. Helping make a magical arm will certainly be a learning experience. You'd best get a good night's sleep tonight; the next few weeks will be busy for you."

# Chapter Thirteen

**TIME PASSED QUICKLY** after that. Lachlann stayed on the couch most of the time, with one or more of us keeping him company more often than not. He spent a lot of time sleeping, but when he was awake, he was talkative and alert, eager to begin working on Willem's plans for the metal limb. Kirilee tended to his arm often, changing the bandages and covering the stump with a salve that she claimed would quicken the healing process. Some mornings I'd come into the parlour to find Kirilee lying wedged up against Lachlann on the couch or sitting with his head in her lap while he slept. Watching them made me uncomfortable at first, but as the weeks passed, their affection began to feel more natural, and it became harder for me to ignore the subtle pangs of jealousy.

As the weeks passed, I spent more and more of my time training with Willem. As promised, he spent several days teaching me how to make my flame hotter and cooler using only concentration. He also began demanding that I keep my flame burning for long periods of time without adding fuel like wood or oil, an exercise that I found extremely difficult and frustrating. Kirilee left often to gather herbs, sometimes leaving us for days. One day she took Kip and me with her, and we spent the day climbing trees and pulling up roots. I returned to Willem's place exhausted but happy.

When I came into the parlour the following day, I found Lachlann stretched out on the couch with his sleeves rolled up. Kip was measuring both Lachlann's good arm and his stump and relaying the measurements to Willem, who was standing nearby recording them in a book.

Once the measurements were recorded, Lachlann and Willem hovered over the book, sketching. Claudi walked up to them, an amused expression on her face. "This might help," she said, extending her right hand to Lachlann. He took it uncertainly, then let out a yelp as it detached from her arm. Claudi giggled like a child and walked away, leaving her artificial hand with Lachlann and Willem.

"Can I see the drawing?" I asked.

"As soon as we're finished, we'll show all of you," Willem promised.

A few minutes later, Kirilee walked into the room carrying a tray of breakfast. I took a bowl of porridge and continued to watch the men work. Trina came into the room soon after, holding on to Bailey. After another ten minutes, Lachlann cleared his throat and announced to the group that he and Willem were ready to show us what they'd come up with. We all piled onto the couch, and Willem cast an enlarging spell on his book so we could all see his drawing clearly.

"The arm will have an outside made mostly of steel, with an interior made of ashlarite," Willem began, pointing to the image on the page. Kirilee let out an excited gasp at the unfamiliar word, and Claudi smiled as well.

"Of course, most of you are wondering what ashlarite is," he went on. "The answer to that question is that I don't know exactly. Before I was born, a meteorite fell from space and landed near this place, causing what many students thought was an earthquake. My father went to investigate and found a large piece of rock near the school. He and some students carted it back here and spent a good few months investigating it. A lot of the meteorite was made purely from rock, but they also found chunks of an unfamiliar metal in it. They extracted as much of the metal from the rock as they could and purified it. Then they began experimenting with it, and among other things, they learned that it's a good conductor of magic."

"Conductor?" Trina asked.

"Yes," Willem said. "You know how some materials, like metal, conduct heat, while others protect you from it? Well, ashlarite, as the students began calling it, conducts magic. It's what will allow Lachlann to be able to move the arm and hand at will, as if it is a part of his own body. Mother's hand has an ashlarite core too." He held up the hand and grinned.

"Now, ashlarite is too soft a metal to use on its own," he continued, "so we're going to make the core and the joints from ashlarite, and the exterior from an alloy made mostly of steel, with a small amount of ashlarite and a few drops of Lachlann's blood—which I collected when we performed the amputation."

Lachlann frowned. "Explain that part to me again—why do you need my blood?"

"Adding your blood to the metal is what will allow the arm to identify its owner," Willem explained. "If I do this," he put a few fingers into the socket of Claudi's artificial hand, "I have no natural ability to control what the hand does. If my mother puts it on, though," he continued, throwing the hand to Claudi, "well, watch."

We turned to look at Claudi as she did up the straps that attached the hand to her stump. Sure enough, once it was attached, the hand moved as if it were a normal limb. "The hand recognizes Mother because it contains her blood," Willem explained. "This arm will only work for you, Lachlann. It will be an extension of your body."

"It'll take some getting used to though," Claudi warned him. "You won't have feeling in your artificial hand, so picking things up with it will be hard at first. But once you're accustomed to it, you'll find that it doesn't act very differently than a normal arm and hand."

Kip shook his head slowly, staring at the drawing. "It's hard to believe this is possible."

"That's because you've spent the past several years being afraid of magic instead of entertaining the possibility that good things could be done with it," Willem said.

"You're never going to let me forget that, ai?"

"Maybe one day." Willem smirked at Kip. "Now we'd all better eat so we can get started."

"Get started?" I repeated. "Wait, we're going to start on this *today?*"

"Absolutely." Willem gave me a wry smile.

"But I…I'm not ready," I protested. "And you didn't warn me."

"Mainly because I didn't want you up all night worrying," Willem explained. "You'll do fine, Saray. I'm going to help you; you'll be borrowing some of my magic today."

"And how would I do that?"

"You'll see," Willem replied. "Eat up, we have lots of work to do."

Fifteen minutes later, Kip and I were following Willem down the familiar hall to the practice room. My eyes widened as we walked in; Willem had moved a good amount of equipment into the room. There were multiple hammers, a large anvil, a few massive sets of tongs, what looked like a big drinking cup made from a strange black material, a tray of wet sand with indentations pressed into it, and several bars of both a silver metal that appeared to be steel and an unfamiliar metal, darker than the steel but with a strange, iridescent sheen. A stone table sat in the very centre of the room; Lachlann sat next to the table on a small stool.

"Is that ashlarite?" Kip asked, pointing to the iridescent metal.

Willem nodded. "Thankfully, it's all been purified already, otherwise we'd have a lot more work to do. This process will take a little over a week, most likely." He picked up the object that looked like a cup and handed it to Lachlann. "Today we're going to be making the steel alloy for the exterior of the limb. This will be a good practice round for you, Saray, as it will require a very hot fire but not one that lasts all day."

I smiled weakly. "I'm still not sure about this."

"What did I tell you? We're going to do this together. Speaking of which, I need to cast a spell before we start. Take my hand."

I did, and he held it tight while saying a few words. I gasped as what felt like an electric shock surged through me. I thought I could hear thunder rumbling in the distance. "What was that?" I asked when he let go.

"Close your eyes," he replied, "and I'll show you."

I obeyed and was startled when an image appeared, clear and realistic, in my mind's eye. "You see two different-sized pools, with a small stream connecting them," Willem said, and I nodded at his explanation of the image. "The small pool represents your own magical energy—the amount of magic you can cast before becoming too exhausted to continue. The larger pool is my own. What I've done is created a channel between the two pools, a connection. Now watch what happens when the smaller pool is drained." I watched as a man came along with a large bucket and began taking water away from the smaller pool.

"When the small pool is drained, water from the larger pool trickles over," I said, opening my eyes.

"Exactly," Willem replied. "And when your magical energy is depleted, it will automatically refill itself from my own store. Since I'm more powerful and experienced than you, and thus my store of magical energy is far larger, it shouldn't hurt me. You'll still need to concentrate for the duration of the spell, though, which will be the hard part for you. The connection will last until I sever it—in this case, until this project is done." Willem glanced at me. "I trust that you won't take advantage of it."

I nodded and then frowned as I heard the strange rumbling once more. "Why do I hear thunder? And why does the room smell like...like a library?"

"You're sensing my magic," he explained. "You'll never notice your own, but when you're connected to another person's, you'll often sense theirs. I've been told that my magic sounds like a storm and smells like old books." He turned towards the table in the centre of the room. "Now to work. Let's see you cast the hottest flame you can muster up, right here." He pointed to the table, and I moved towards it, closed my eyes, and focused. When I opened my eyes, a large yellow flame that burned blue in the centre danced on top of the table.

Willem nodded his approval at my work. "Your job now is to keep that fire burning. Don't let it cool down or die unless I tell you to. If you start having trouble, let me know immediately." He glanced over at Lachlann. "Start when you're ready; let me know if you need help."

I watched as Lachlann reached for the steel bars that sat nearby. He put them into the cup, which he then took with the tongs and moved so it sat on the table in the middle of the fire. Then he stood back and watched the fire, waiting. When he removed the cup some time later, he peeked in and then turned to Willem. "It's ready."

Kip's eyes narrowed. "How'd you not melt the cup?"

"The crucible, you mean?" Lachlann asked. "Simple. The material it's made of has a higher melting temperature than the metal we're working with."

At Lachlann's instruction, Kip picked up a small bar of the black metal and put it into the crucible. Then Willem removed the vial of blood from his coat. The outside of it was fogged; Willem had clearly put some sort of cooling spell onto it. He poured the vial in, and the mixture sizzled. Willem waved his hand over the crucible and mumbled some words. "That's to ensure proper mixing," he told us. "One does not normally put human blood in an alloy."

I nodded but didn't say anything. My head was beginning to pound; despite access to Willem's magic, holding the spell for this long was getting hard.

Lachlann returned the crucible to the fire and waited for a moment. Then he turned to Kip. "Pass me those tongs?"

Kip nodded and reached for the tongs. As he did, though, he knocked another set off the table. They hit the floor with a metallic clang. My head snapped up in surprise, and a moment later, Lachlann let out a yelp. My gaze returned to the table; my fire had gone out, and Lachlann was staring at his hand. My eyes narrowed. "What happened?"

"You lost concentration when Kip dropped those tongs," Willem told me. "Your spell flared before it went out. Looks like you burned Lachlann." He walked over to Lachlann and examined his hand; I could see that it was beginning to blister.

I stared in horror. "I…I'm sorry…"

"You should get Kirilee to look at that," Kip said to Lachlann. He glanced at me for a moment; I saw no malice in his expression, but I felt my face begin to burn nonetheless. "I'll go fetch her."

Kip left the room, and Willem stood next to Lachlann. "Let me at least put a cooling spell on that."

Lachlann shook his head. "I need to finish this, before it solidifies." He glanced at me. "I need your fire again, Saray."

I bit my lip and then attempted to whisper the casting words, but they caught in my throat. "I…I can't do it," I said weakly.

Lachlann sighed. "Oh, come on, Saray," he said, frustration evident in his tone. "It's just a little burn. I need you to do this for me, all right?"

I shook my head, tears beginning to prick at my eyes. "I'm sorry, but I can't. I'll mess it up and hurt you again. I told you I wasn't ready to help, I don't have enough control..." I trailed off, my voice breaking and my breath coming in gasps.

"Saray." Willem began to move towards me, a look of concern on his face. "You can do this. I'll help you."

"I can't!" I shook my head vigorously and then gasped as a burst of flame flew from my hand towards Willem. He dodged it, and it disappeared harmlessly into the wall.

I ducked my head when Willem turned back to look at me, my face burning. *I need to get out of here before I hurt someone else.* I sprang to my feet and bolted out of the room and down the corridor, my vision blurred by tears. I passed Kip and Kirilee; both of them stared at me, and Kirilee called out my name, but I didn't stop. I burst through the front door, inhaling gulps of the fresh morning air, and settled on the ledge outside, trying to control my tears and my swirling thoughts. *I should have known I was going to mess this up. Even with Willem's training, I'm still dangerous.* I felt something wet nudge my elbow, and I looked over into Bailey's concerned eyes. Trina was standing above him. "What's wrong?"

"I...I accidentally..." The words caught in my throat; I just ended up sobbing harder. Trina lowered herself gingerly to the ledge and put an arm around me. We sat together, looking out over the Shrouded Woods, Trina holding onto me while I wept.

When I couldn't cry anymore, I stared over the ledge in a daze, Trina's arm still around me, uncertain what to do next. Eventually, I heard the front door open. "There you are." I heard Willem's voice behind me. I looked up and saw him staring down at me with concerned eyes. Lachlann followed him; I noticed that his hand was bandaged.

I looked away from them both, fresh tears pricking at my eyes, and for a moment I wondered if Willem was going to explode at me like he had at Kirilee on our first night here. "I'm sorry I messed up," I mumbled. "You shouldn't have asked me to help you. I'm still so new, I'm going to hurt someone again…"

"That's enough." Willem's voice was firm, but when I looked up at him, he was smiling. He offered me a hand. "Saray, everyone makes mistakes. You're right that you're still learning, but the only way you'll improve is if you practice and repeat and, yes, make mistakes. I made a mistake myself today; I should have thought to put a spell on all of us protecting us from your fire."

I shook my head as I took his hand and got to my feet. "My gift is so dangerous, though. I mean, look what I did to Lachlann! Look what I almost did to you!"

"You didn't do anything to me that I haven't done to myself." Lachlann said. "I'm a blacksmith by trade, Saray. I've burned myself hundreds of times. I can handle it."

I blinked back fresh tears. "But…you were mad at me…"

"I was frustrated, not mad," he replied. "And it wasn't because you burned me, either. It was because I just want to get this done." He let out a sigh and then met my eyes again. "Saray, you need to understand that this isn't easy for me. I came with the group because Kirilee trusts me to protect you kids and to get you safely to Dundere. But now I can't even hold a shield, much less take care of you three. It's bloody frustrating, needing help to do the simplest things."

Trina nodded and got to her feet. "It's no fun, is it?"

Lachlann chuckled. "I don't know how you handle it, Trina."

She shrugged. "It was scary at first. I don't remember much from before I lost my vision, but I remember coming to the Academy and being in this new place that I couldn't see and having to have someone lead me around all the time. Now I'm mostly used to needing help. But I'm glad it will be over soon."

"Me too." Lachlann smiled. "I'm a bit impatient to get this arm done and be back to our adventure." His gaze turned to me. "But I'm sorry for snapping at you, Saray. You didn't deserve that. And I agree with Willem, learning involves making mistakes. I hope you'll keep working with us."

I frowned. "Did you manage to finish without me?"

Willem nodded. "Remember, I know how to make fire too. But it's not my specialty, so I'd rather have you do it. We're done for today, but are you willing to keep working with us tomorrow if I place a spell on all of us protecting us from the flame?"

I hesitated and then nodded.

"We might get you doing more than just making fire," Lachlann put in. "Kirilee thinks I should take a few days off of forging so the worst of the burn can heal, which, of course, I'm not very enthusiastic about." He grinned. "Kip is fascinated by the process, though, so I'm willing to let him do some of the forging under my supervision. If you'd like, Willem can make fire one day so that you can try too."

I nodded. "I think I'd like that."

"Glad to hear it," Willem said. "Why don't you go wash up for lunch and find Kip and Kirilee?"

I nodded again and went inside to find the others. Today had been exhausting, and I was more than ready for lunch.

The next several days were busy. Lachlann first had Kip work with the ashlarite, then with the steel, heating and hammering the bars of both metals into the various shapes that were needed. The steel pieces were to be wrapped around the ashlarite, Lachlann explained, so the limb would have a strong outer shell and a magical core. On the fourth day, Willem made fire, as promised, and Lachlann walked me through my part of the process. The work was exhausting, and by the end of my day forging, I was sweaty and sore and had a newfound appreciation for Lachlann's work.

The following day Kirilee and Trina joined us, and Kirilee held Trina's hands in her own while Lachlann talked them through the process so that Trina could partake in the making of the limb. At the end of the day, he smiled and said that he was fairly certain he was ready to pick up the hammer on his own again—which was good, as the next part required precision.

The day after that, Lachlann told me that he'd need me to make a flame that was cooler than the ones we'd been working with. I focused on keeping the flame's temperature steady while he held various pieces in the flame for a few minutes, then pulled them out and moved them to the oil. It was slowly becoming easier to hold my fire at certain temperatures for long periods of time, I realized at the end of the day. Lachlann informed me that evening that my part of the job was finished, but that I was welcome to stay and watch the final parts of the process. Intrigued, I stuck around and watched Lachlann and Kip polish the pieces of the arm, using coarse rock and then sandpaper to take them from a rough texture to a smooth, shiny silver colour. Then they fitted the joints together, piecing together the arm, hand, and fingers, and lastly, Lachlann brought out his leather-working tools to fashion the socket that would connect the artificial limb to his body. Willem packed the inside of the socket with cotton and fabric, leaving bare a small disc of ashlarite in the centre that he explained would serve as the "nerve" of the arm—the connection point between Lachlann and the prosthesis. Then he cast a spell over the socket area that would prevent chafing and keep Lachlann comfortable.

Finally, Lachlann stood back, admiring his work, and announced that it was ready to try on. Kip went to fetch the others and returned soon with Kirilee, Trina, and Claudi in tow.

Claudi's face lit up when she saw the limb. Kirilee walked over to inspect it and began asking Willem about the magical aspects of it. Trina asked to hold it before it was fitted onto Lachlann. He passed it to her, and her eyes widened as she took it. "It's heavy."

"It should be about the weight of the part of the arm Lachlann lost," Willem explained. "I weighed the amputated part specifically for that reason before I got rid of it, and then we used a proportionate amount of metal to make the new limb."

Trina passed the arm back to Lachlann. "Are you going to put it on now?"

Lachlann nodded and rolled up his sleeve, and we all watched as he slid the leather socket over his stump. "It fits perfectly," he mused, tightening the straps. "As I'd hoped."

"Try moving it," Willem prompted.

Lachlann frowned and moved his elbow a few times. Then, ever so slowly, the wrist of the artificial limb began to move. Then the hand opened and closed, and the fingers moved individually. "This is incredible," he whispered.

"Isn't it, though?" Willem's voice had a proud note to it.

"Pass me that anvil," Lachlann said to Kip, gesturing at the table. "I want to see how I do picking things up."

Kip nodded and passed the anvil to Lachlann, who took it with his right hand. Then he reached over with his new hand and carefully closed his fingers around the anvil. He moved the arm up and down a few times, then grimaced as he nearly dropped the anvil, catching it with his right hand. "I've lost strength in this arm."

"Of course you have," Willem said. "Looks like Saray's not the only one who needs to train right now. You'll be back to your normal self in no time, though." He eyed Lachlann. "And speaking of training, if you want to get used to your sword again, I'm more than willing to spar with you."

"That would be wonderful." Lachlann grinned at him.

"You know," Willem said, "I think this calls for a celebration. I'll prepare a feast for tonight." He gave Kip a wry smile. "I think I'll be making my special drinks for dessert again. Given all the magic you've encountered over the past week or so, I don't suppose you'd be less afraid to try them? I have a feeling you'll like them."

Kip laughed and shook his head. "I s'pose," he conceded, "that there's only one way to find out."

Lachlann went gathering with Kirilee that afternoon, and about fifteen minutes after they'd left, Claudi appeared in the doorway of Trina's and my room. "Come to the parlour," she said to us. "I think this afternoon would be a good time for me to tell you kids the story that I promised you."

We followed her to the parlour, where Kip was already seated, and settled on the familiar plush couches. Claudi looked around the room with her keen dark eyes. "So, you want to know about Kirilee's curse."

We all nodded.

"Well, I don't know too much of her life before she came to the school, so I'll have to start telling the story there." She smiled at us and then sat back in her chair, folded her hands in her lap, and began to speak.

"I was working at Ashlar's school when Kirilee showed up," she told us. "I knew from her first day in our classes that we had a challenge on our hands.

She was very bright and clearly quite powerful, but she had no idea how to function off of the streets. She was wary and easily angered and very, very stubborn. That last part hasn't changed much." Claudi grinned. "As time went by, she calmed down; she learned how to behave and became less jumpy. She did have a persistent problem with nightmares, though, likely from spending so many years having to watch her back on the streets. And as her magical powers grew, she started having troubles with casting in her sleep. Ashlar gave her a potion to stop her from dreaming, and that seemed to help her."

"There are magic potions?" I asked.

Claudi nodded. "Ashlar was quite skilled with potions, but they're not Willem's preferred form of magic, so you probably won't see any while you're here." She smiled. "Anyway, I was a bit worried about what would become of Kirilee once she finished school. But every time she visited, she seemed to be doing well. Then one day, she showed up with a young man in tow. His name was Jacien, she told us, and they were in love. Jacien seemed like a nice enough boy, but it was apparent right away that he was quite well off. Ashlar and I weren't sure how Kirilee would do with someone who'd grown up in such a different world than she had.

"Kirilee visited us with Jacien several times after that," Claudi continued, "and then one day, she came alone and seemed a bit nervous. When we asked her what was wrong, she told us that she was pregnant."

"Kirilee? Pregnant?" Trina repeated.

Claudi nodded. "She told us that Jacien's family was pressuring them to marry, and that she'd agreed to it because she wanted a good life for their child. But I don't think she was completely happy about it." Claudi sighed. "We didn't hear from her for about a month after that, and then one day she used a summoning spell to call Ashlar and me to her location. And we discovered that she was in prison." She frowned. "The nightmares—and sleep casting—had come back following her engagement, but she'd been afraid to tell us about them. It was only a few days before this that some friends of Jacien's parents had thrown the two of them an engagement party. It was at a manor located a way out of town, so Kirilee and Jacien were invited to stay the night. I'm under the impression that you know the story of what happened during their stay?"

We all nodded solemnly. "The party's hosts must have been your grandparents, Kip," Trina put in.

Kip nodded. "Sounds right, from what I know of the story."

"So after all that happened, Kirilee was arrested for her crime and sentenced to death," Claudi went on.

"Death?" My eyes narrowed. "Why not make her a krossemage?"

"That practice didn't exist back then," she explained. "And the Burgess family was one of some significance, so death it was. They weren't going to execute Kirilee while she was pregnant, though, so she was held in a cell until the day she went into labour. I helped her give birth, on the dirt floor of her cell. Thankfully, it happened very fast." Claudi's face turned sad. "Poor girl only had an hour with her baby boy. She nursed him once, gave him a name, and then he was handed off to Jacien."

"What was his name?" Trina asked.

"Marcus," Claudi said softly. "He was a beautiful baby."

"Marcus," I repeated. "Do you know what happened to him?"

"I do, actually." Claudi smiled. "I didn't think much about Marcus—or Jacien for that matter—for a good twenty years. Then one day, a letter arrived at our home from Jacien. The letter said that Marcus had turned out to be much like Kirilee, a powerful telekinetic. He'd been discovered about five years before this, and the Breoch Guard had taken him away." She sighed. "Jacien had spent the last few years looking for him, and now he'd decided that it was time to move on. He had nothing left in Sylvenburgh, he said, so he was returning to Dundere, where his family was originally from. He asked Ashlar and me to keep our eyes open for Marcus. We brought Kirilee to the house, showed her the letter, and naturally passed the task on to her, even though we didn't expect anything to come of it."

"But something did?" Trina asked.

She nodded. "It was over fifteen years after that," she told us. "Kirilee showed up at our home looking very frazzled, with a man in tow, and told us that she'd found Marcus." Claudi chuckled. "One of her friends had found him in the woods, delirious from fever, and brought him to Kirilee for treatment. And, of course, she'd noticed that he was a krossemage and that he looked quite similar to Jacien, so she started asking questions and discovered that he was, in fact, her son."

I laughed. "That must have been a shock for both of them."

"I imagine so." Claudi nodded, chuckling. "Kirilee told us that he'd gotten into some sort of trouble with his master, so he'd run away from their home and was looking to travel to Dundere and find his father. He'd fallen ill while making his way through the woods in search of help. Kirilee wasn't sure how to help him get to Dundere, so she'd brought him to us. And so the four of us traveled to the outskirts of Flavalan. Ashlar put a vanishing spell on Marcus that would last for a full day and told him to make his way to the docks and find a ship heading to Dundere." She frowned. "That's the last any of us saw of him. I don't know if he made it to Dundere; I have no clue what became of him." She smiled sadly.

After a minute or so, Kip cleared his throat. "That's very interesting," he said. "But I'm still wondering how Kirilee got away from her death sentence."

"Right." Claudi chuckled. "I suppose that Kirilee's pregnancy was useful to Ashlar and me because it gave us time to figure out what could be done for her. We considered trying to break her out of prison, but she was under heavy guard, and neither of us was particularly talented in teleportation at that time. We decided that our best chance was to try to bring her back after she'd been executed."

"You can resurrect people?" Trina asked.

"At one time I could, though resurrection isn't as simple as most other healing magic," Claudi said. "There are three ways that a lifebringer can bring someone back from the dead. The first involves getting to the body before the brain has completely died, healing whatever killed them and then restarting the heart—but Ashlar and I doubted we could get to her that fast. The second is a life transfer, but of course, I wasn't about to do something so...troubling." She wrinkled her nose. "The third is something called soul magic, a type of fairy magic that calls the person's soul back from the next world. Ashlar and I studied soul magic for several months before deciding that it was the best option."

"But you'd have to steal her body to do that," I pointed out.

Claudi nodded. "Stealing a corpse is much easier than breaking out a prisoner; corpses aren't generally guarded very heavily." She paused, a faraway look in her eyes. "So the day after Marcus was born, they led Kirilee out to be hung. Ashlar and I were far enough away that we couldn't see much, and I looked away when she dropped, but I can only imagine how terrified she must have been, poor child." She shook her head. "When we got to her body a few hours later, she looked very much like I expected her to—all stiff and bloody and with her neck bent at an odd angle. It was kind of gruesome. But we snuck her out regardless, and I collected a few fairies on my way back home. Once we'd brought Kirilee home, we began the process of calling her soul back from the world beyond."

"Didn't you have to fix her broken neck first?" Kip asked.

Claudi nodded. "Mending her body was easy. Getting her soul back, now that was harder. We succeeded, of course, but at great personal expense." She frowned. "See, soul magic takes large amounts of energy and complex, deep fairy magic, which often demands something from the lifebringer as well as the one being brought back. Neither leaves the experience completely whole. I knew this going into it, but I didn't realize just how much I'd lose." Her frown deepened. "The truth is, my ability to heal was taken from me from that day. I know Kirilee feels bad for my loss, but I've never blamed her; it was my own choice to engage in soul magic. And I feel like the outcome of our magic was worse for her than for me."

"What happened to her?" I asked.

Claudi sighed. "There was a curse, I suppose you'd call it, that was placed on Kirilee. As her soul was being restored to her body, the fairies who were helping with the ritual sang a song over her, placing restrictions on her that none of us expected. Both she and I remember the song perfectly nearly fifty years later." She paused. "Would you like me to sing it for you?"

We all nodded, and Claudi leaned forward, closed her eyes and began to sing.

*Innocent blood has been shed by your hand*
*A family is left to mourn*
*To die was your sentence, and that you have paid*
*Now from Death's hand you've been torn*

*Called back to life, and yes, you shall return*
*Yet, not as the person you've been*
*Live, yes, you will, but a life that will make*
*Atonement for this most grave sin*

*Sleep you shall never, age you will not*
*Never shall you find a home*
*The pain of the slain you will carry always*
*These woods you shall endlessly roam*

*Restless and wild, you'll live out your days*
*'Til the one that you've maimed is made whole*
*'Til the one you've made hate learns instead how to love*
*'Til the orphan you've left finds true home*

*Your misdeeds you'll pay for, your wrongs you'll redeem*
*The blood that you've shed will run dry*
*And then, on the day that all of this has passed*
*You'll age, and then sleep, and then die*

The melody was a low, haunting tune that I recognized as one of the songs Kirilee had played on Trina's pipe. When Claudi was finished, we were all quiet for several moments. Kip spoke first. "Huh. That explains some things."

"It does," Claudi agreed, meeting his eyes. "The curse is the reason Kirilee doesn't age and doesn't sleep, and it's why she cannot make a home. It's why she doesn't stay here for more than a few days at a time, why she doesn't believe she can accompany you to Dundere, and why she was so convinced that she and Lachlann could never be together. It's also why she's in constant pain."

Trina's eyes narrowed. "Kirilee's in pain?"

"All the time." Claudi nodded. "Severe pain too, though she's learned to manage it over the years."

"What sort of pain?" I asked.

"From what she's told me, she lives with a sharp sort of burning feeling in the center of her chest," Claudi told us. "When it gets bad, it can spread further. We think that it's meant to mimic what Clarita felt when Kirilee sent the quill pen through her. Neither natural nor magical pain remedies do anything for it."

"I would never have guessed." I shook my head. "I mean, she mentioned having cramps, and I saw her in worse pain once, but I didn't know it was constant."

Claudi nodded. "She hides it well, and as I say, she's learned ways to handle it. She says it's worst at night, which is why she meditates and communes with the fairies; it helps distract her. Apparently music helps too, for some reason. Her first few years under the spell were awful, though." Claudi sighed. "Moments after we brought her back, she started screaming. And she was screaming and crying, on and off, for days after that. It took her months to be able to live normally on her own; Ashlar and I had to take care of her during that time. And once she could take care of herself, she was angry and scared and miserable. She didn't want to be alive. In fact, she tried to take her own life three times, three different ways."

Kip's eyebrows arched. "She tried three times and never succeeded? How'd she manage that?"

Claudi's shoulders hunched. "The first time she ate poisoned berries, which made her stomach pain about ten times worse for a day but didn't kill her. The second time she slit her own wrists, but she didn't bleed out like a person normally would. That's part of why she has the tattoos on her arms, she doesn't want the scars to be visible." She sighed. "And the third time, she jumped off a cliff. Broke dozens of bones, damaged some of her insides. She's very, very lucky that there were other lifebringers in the forest in those days; otherwise she'd be living life as a cripple after that incident. I think it was finally then that the reality of being unable to die set in for her. So she began looking for better ways to cope, and I think she's done quite well for someone who lives in her state."

"She...she can't die?" Trina asked.

"Not until the conditions of the spell have been fulfilled, at least," was Claudi's reply.

"I didn't quite understand that part," I said.

"*I* don't understand it, and neither does Kirilee," Claudi admitted. "We've both spent years trying to figure it out, and neither of us has any idea how to break the spell."

"Did Kirilee lose her magic when you brought her back from the dead?" Kip asked.

"Technically, yes, though it wasn't because of the soul magic," Claudi replied. "That was Ashlar's decision. He was concerned that she'd repeat her mistakes if we brought her back, so he found a way to separate her magic from the rest of her. After she'd been resurrected, he told her that he'd return her powers to her once he'd seen that she was mature enough to do better. It was only about five years later that he offered to restore her magic, but she refused, and she hasn't taken it back to this day." Claudi let out a sigh and sat back in her chair. "Well, there you have it. That's Kirilee's story."

"I can see why it'd be hard for her to tell," Kip said.

Claudi nodded. "Kirilee has become a very strong person. She manages her pain well, and she's learned to make the best of being forced to wander. She knows the plants and animals and people of the Shrouded Woods better than anyone else in Breoch, and there are some who call her the queen of these woods because of that. But I know it's hard for her, not having a place to call home."

"It must be lonely," Trina said, frowning.

Claudi nodded. "She's led an extremely lonely life. There have been many times when I've wondered if Ashlar and I made a grave mistake bringing her back. It seems like both she and I have suffered badly because of that choice." Claudi's shoulders hunched, and I felt an unexpected surge of pity for Kirilee and her strange plight. Then Claudi sat up straight. "But nothing can be done about that, of course. Now you kids had best run along; I need to help Willem with some tasks this afternoon."

We all nodded and left the parlour silently, our minds preoccupied by the gravity of the story we'd been told.

Kirilee's story was still on my mind a few hours later when we sat down for dinner. She and Lachlann had returned from gathering, and I watched her silently as she chatted and laughed with the other adults, seeming completely at ease. *Is it all a mask?* Halfway through the afternoon it had occurred to me that if Kirilee had no idea how to break the curse, then there was the possibility of her dying without warning after doing whatever was needed to fulfill its conditions. The thought unnerved me. I picked at my food, my stomach in knots, unable to relax and enjoy the feast that Willem had prepared.

"Everything all right, Saray?" Kirilee's voice jerked me out of my reverie, and I gaped at her for a moment.

"Everything's…fine," I mumbled, feeling my cheeks burn.

"Still thinking about the story I told you earlier?" Claudi asked.

I glanced at her, then at Kirilee, and nodded.

The two women exchanged a look. "Do you want to talk to me about what's bothering you?" Kirilee asked, a cautious note in her voice.

I looked at her warily. "I suppose so."

"All right. You and I can take a walk after dinner." I nodded again, feeling oddly embarrassed, and then turned my attention to the food.

After dinner was finished, I followed Kirilee outside. The sky was beginning to darken; the viletta by Willem's door was already glowing as we made our way down the familiar path. Kirilee seemed preoccupied at first, glancing around at the darkening forest as if in search of something. We'd been walking for a good five minutes before she spoke. "What's bothering you, Saray?"

I frowned. "Claudi told us your story today."

She nodded. "I know."

"And…the part about the curse. I don't understand it."

"You're not the only one." She chuckled. "I've spent almost fifty years trying to understand it, and I still don't."

"But if you don't understand it, then aren't you afraid you'll just drop dead one day?" I shuddered. "It must be terrifying, living like that."

She shook her head. "I don't think you need to worry about me just dropping dead," she told me. "I doubt the curse'll break anytime soon, if ever. I can't see how I'd fulfill it."

"Why's that?" I asked.

"Because the song seems to imply that for the curse to break, I need to undo the damage that I caused through Clarita's death. And I believe that's impossible." She sighed. "A lot more harm was done that day than one dead child, y'know. There'd been several magic crimes in the area at the time, and I learned later that my mistake was the final nail in the coffin that caused the Banishing of Magic." Her face turned grim. "In a way, I'm the reason you are fleeing your school."

I nodded slowly, pondering her words. "Well, at least I don't have to worry about you dropping dead," I said finally. "I'd miss you if that happened."

"You would, ai?" Kirilee raised an eyebrow. "I'm surprised; I thought you weren't too fond of me."

I stared at her, taken aback by her bluntness. "That's not true. I mean, I…I like you, but I think I'd like you more if I thought *you* liked *me*."

"You think I don't like you?" Kirilee frowned.

"It feels like you're always mad at me for something," I said. "Asking too many questions. Fighting with Kip. Eavesdropping on you and Lachlann."

Kirilee chuckled. "Well, you'd no business doing that last one."

I shook my head. "It's kind of funny that you're in love with Lachlann because you sort of remind me of his brother. He was always unhappy with me over something too." I let out a huff. "It always seems like adults are mad at me for one thing or another."

Kirilee stared at me for what felt like several minutes. "Y'know, Saray," she finally said, "I may remind you of Tomlin, but do you know who you remind me of?"

"Who?"

"Myself at your age." She grinned. "I was very much like you—full of questions, independent, a bit hot tempered. And I felt like most adults didn't like me much, either. Claudi was one of the first women who was kind to me, and it was quite a shock. When I was older, I realized that I'd really wanted adults to like me because I'd never known my parents. I wanted someone older to give me the approval that my mother and father should've."

I nodded, an unexpected lump rising in my throat.

"Maybe that's some of what you're feeling," she continued, eyeing me. "And I should've seen that." She sighed. "It seems I owe you an apology, Saray. I actually do quite like you. I'm not used to being around people your age, though, and I forget how dramatic teenagers can be."

I laughed. "Hey, we aren't the only dramatic ones. I mean, remember how Willem reacted when he found out Kip was scared of magic?"

"True enough." She chuckled, then sobered. "I'm also not used to people criticizing and questioning how I live."

I frowned. "I...I'm not trying to be rude," I told her. "It's just that everything out here is so *different.*"

"It certainly is. For many folks, these woods are a refuge from a world that wants them dead. It's the only place they can fully be themselves. Their ways may not be ones that you'd like to follow, but no one's asking you to act like us, only to let us be who we are." She glanced at me. "Does that make sense?"

I nodded. "It does."

"Good. And Tomlin may have been strict, but don't forget he was the one who got you out of the school before the Breoch Guard could get to you. Perhaps he didn't dislike you as much as you thought, either." She smiled. "Sometimes adults can be irritable for reasons that have nothing to do with you. Myself included."

My eyes narrowed. "When you're grumpy, is it because of the pain you're in?"

She frowned and then nodded. "That's one reason, ai."

I looked at her out of the corner of my eye. "I...I'm sorry you've had such a hard life. It must be awful to be in pain all the time."

Kirilee frowned and then let out a long sigh. For a moment, she seemed to show her true age, her face weary from many years of sadness. "My life's been difficult; I'd be a fool to deny that," she said slowly. "It's not been all bad, though, and it's getting better as of late. Lachlann is good for me, and it seems like you kids are good for me too." She grinned and clapped me on the shoulder. "Come on, let's head back to the house before it gets too dark."

Neither of us spoke on our way back to Willem's; the silence was only broken by the song of the night insects. I was glad that Kirilee's story was beginning to make some sense, but it bothered me that some parts were still so cryptic. As we reached the front door, I found myself running the song of the curse through my head, trying to decipher what exactly it was trying to say about Kirilee and how much longer she might have with us.

# Chapter Fourteen

**CLAUDI DECIDED TO** leave a few days later, bidding us farewell with hugs and smiles. When she went to say goodbye to Kirilee, she stood back and looked at her for a moment. "My dear," she said, "your friends will soon be embarking on what might be a difficult journey. I think it would be best if you accompany them to that journey's end." She smiled. "I dreamed the other night that you accompanied them, and you know that sometimes the fairies still speak to me in dreams."

Kirilee frowned. "You know I can't enter any of the cities in this land. And I don't think it's possible to find a ship to Dundere without doing that."

"Not necessarily," Lachlann spoke up.

Kirilee looked at him curiously.

"The ship I was planning on taking to Dundere is called the Lady Liara," he explained. "It leaves from Kirstein in the south, sails the west and north coasts of Breoch, and then heads to the open sea and in the direction of Dundere. It makes several stops along our coast, and one of them is in a fairly isolated area on the other side of the mountain pass. You'd hardly have to leave the Shrouded Woods to get to it; you certainly wouldn't need to venture into any cities."

Kirilee exchanged an uncertain glance with Claudi. "You think that would work?"

"Perhaps you should go speak to the priestess about that, given where I believe my dream came from," Claudi suggested. She reached into her pocket and extracted something. "And if you do accompany them, I think it's best you carry this."

Kirilee looked at the item in Claudi's hand, her eyes widening. "I can't take that," she whispered.

"You need to," Claudi replied firmly. "You don't have to use it, of course, but your journey thus far has been dangerous, and there's no telling what dangers you might still face. This is a matter of safety for both you and the children."

Kirilee hesitated and then slowly reached into Claudi's palm and took what I saw to be a glass pendant, its interior glowing with a fiery blue light. "What is it?" I asked.

Kirilee looked at me, her eyes bright with an emotion I didn't understand. "I hope you don't have to find out," she said softly, fastening the clasp behind her neck.

"As do I, though don't be afraid to use it if the need arises," said Claudi. "Now I'd best be off." She embraced Kirilee and then walked over to where her son was waiting on the couch. Willem took her hand and rubbed his amulet with his thumb, and Claudi slowly disappeared from our sight, returning to her home in Flavalan and leaving us all grateful for her visit.

Time passed quickly following Claudi's departure. I continued to spend most of my time with Willem, refining my magic skills. Now that I could better control the temperature and duration of my flame, he began to teach me how to "throw" my fire. We spent a day outdoors, setting distant trees on fire for moments at a time before extinguishing my flame. I found this to be even more challenging than the previous exercises, but Willem assured me it might become useful one day. When I wasn't training, I was usually curled up with a book in the library, often accompanied by Trina. Willem had recently introduced her to a reading system for blind people that used raised dots for letters, and she seemed to be learning it quickly. I found Willem's collection of novels to be fascinating enough, but the need to escape by reading wasn't as pressing as it had been back at Sylvenburgh Academy. My real life was interesting enough to be a story of its own now; perhaps one day, I mused, I would write it in a book so that other children trapped in boring schools with classmates who hated them could find a way to escape their lives.

At first, most of Lachlann's time was spent learning to use his new arm. Initially his arm was weak, and as Claudi had predicted, he had trouble with simple things like holding a fork, but as the weeks passed, he began to regain the strength and dexterity he'd once had. He began doing slow sword work with Willem and making a new suit of armour to replace the one he'd lost. He seemed to be working on something else as well; several times he mysteriously vanished from Willem's home, only to reappear by evening.

Kirilee came and went at random, sometimes heading into the forest for several days in a row, often accompanied by Kip, who didn't enjoy being sequestered inside for long periods of time. One day she returned carrying a few rolls of fabric. After that, she spent her spare time cutting and sewing in one of Willem's classrooms, and within three days she had produced tunics and breeches similar to hers for Trina and me. My tunic was an iridescent blue-green colour that Kirilee said would bring out my eyes; Trina's, of course, was purple. The breeches were made of a heavy black material and felt strange and constricting when I first put them on. "Wearing pants is strange when you've only ever worn dresses," Kirilee told us. "But once you're used to them, you'll find them marvellously easy to move about in. And they're a necessity for ship life; you can't work aboard a ship in a dress."

Kirilee disappeared again the day after that, and a few days later she returned, grinning. "I'd like to take you all on a trip tomorrow," she said. "I've a couple of friends I'd like you to meet."

"Do I know these friends?" Willem asked.

"I believe you've met Hilda and Carmine several times," she replied. Willem brightened, clearly also excited about the journey.

"This'll be a good test for you, to see how you do on a day's journey," Kirilee said to Lachlann. "If you can manage this trek without trouble, we can assume it's safe for you and the young ones to head to Dundere."

"I thought you were coming along now," Lachlann said.

"That'll depend on how tomorrow goes," Kirilee replied.

The following morning we set off, climbing a trail that led us through rocky terrain high in the mountains. Persius flew overhead, causing Bailey to howl comically. Willem had traded his customary black robes for a tunic and set of breeches that weren't too different from what the rest of us wore, and he wore a sword strapped to his belt, which surprised me. "Why do you need a sword?" I asked him.

"Because there are some situations where magic doesn't work well," he replied. "Perhaps you should learn how to use one too."

"What sorts of situations are those?" I asked.

"Well," Willem said, "there are certain people who are skilled in the use of anti-magic—that is, the ability to nullify the magical abilities of people like you and me. I've only met a few in the many years I've lived in these woods, but they do exist."

I frowned. "I wonder if that's what the Breoch Guard uses."

"It's possible, but I doubt it," Willem replied. "Anti-magic is considered by many in Breoch to be its own form of magic. Though I wouldn't be entirely surprised if there are a few elite Breoch Guards who know how to use it."

I nodded.

"I've heard that the guards on the Isle of Dundere use anti-magic," Lachlann put in. "It's their way of dealing with the problems that magic creates."

"Is that so?" Willem asked.

Lachlann nodded. "If I understand correctly, magic users are allowed to practice openly in Dundere, so long as they keep the laws. If one of them gets out of line, though, the guards won't hesitate to use anti-magic on them."

"Interesting," I mused.

"It's bloody brilliant," Lachlann said. "I wish that the government in Breoch had taken the same course of action."

Willem frowned. "The only trouble with that is it could be used to render the magikai completely powerless," he countered. "If anti-magic got into the wrong hands, it could be just as deadly as magic."

"Same as any tool," Lachlann answered. "It's not a perfect solution, but it beats the government maiming and enslaving people they feel threatened by."

At noon we sat down, and Kirilee passed around our lunch—various types of meat and vegetable pies that Willem had handmade that morning. We were in the middle of devouring them when Bailey jumped up suddenly and growled, his fur standing on end. Trina cocked her head. "Men nearby," she whispered. "Bailey thinks they're a threat."

"Get behind Willem and me, everyone," Lachlann hissed, jumping to his feet. "Stay close, all right?" We all obeyed, Kip nocking an arrow and moving so that he was just behind Lachlann and off to his right. On Willem's other side, Kirilee pulled out one of her skunkflower bombs, while I hovered just behind Kip, ready to use my magic if need be. Trina huddled behind me, and Bailey stood next to her, alert and ready. I didn't miss the flurry of action in the bushes behind us; clearly, Trina had animals ready to attack on command. My heart pounded in my chest; I wasn't certain if the men were truly a threat, but I knew we would take no chances.

"Come out," Willem demanded in a loud voice. "Whoever you are, whatever you want, come out and talk to us face to face." There was no movement for a moment, and then a pair of men stepped out of the brush. They wore uniforms, I saw—not the blue shirts of the city guards who had pursued us earlier but pressed black pants, flat white caps, and red sashes across their chests. One of them was broad, with skin similar in colour to Willem's and a head full of black curls; the other was tall, blond, and lean, with a greying beard and an eye patch over one eye. I didn't miss Willem's sharp intake of breath.

The blond one grinned at us. "Well, well," he said, "it's been a while, Willem. I don't think I've seen you since the day after I cut off your mother's hand."

"You mean the day I took your eye?" Willem shot back, his voice hard. "What do you want, Angus?"

Angus smirked at him. "I see you're traveling in the company of criminals and runaways."

"These folks are nothing of the sort; they are guests in my own home," Willem protested. "Which, by the way, you still haven't managed to find."

The other uniformed man chuckled. "I'm sure we'll be able to get that information out of the little witch and her friend, once we take them off your hands." My eyes widened at his words, and I put a protective arm around Trina.

"Only you're not taking anyone off our hands," Lachlann said, stepping forward.

"Though you're welcome to try," Willem added.

The two men looked at him with narrowed eyes. I frowned. *What are you doing, Willem?*

"You'll have to get past my magic, Lachlann's sword, Kip's bow, and Kirilee's skunkflower bombs first. And then, if you somehow manage to survive all that, you get to deal with *them.* And trust me, you don't want to be on the receiving end of Saray's fire." Willem glanced at me and raised an eyebrow, and I grinned and made fire dance on my hands.

The darker man snorted. "We have guns, you know." He gestured at a small weapon with a round barrel that sat on his hip, and my eyes widened as I recalled Lachlann mentioning them.

"Which aren't much good if they've been flung out of your reach," Willem replied. "My telekinesis skills have improved since the day I put that pen in your eye, Angus." He smirked. "Do you wish to play our game?"

I watched Angus glare at Willem. He stared at me with one hungry blue eye and then huffed. "You haven't seen the last of us, elfieblood," he muttered before clapping his companion on the shoulder and motioning at the way they'd come with his head.

Willem let out a long sigh as the two men retreated into the bush. "By the Fae," he muttered. "This changes things."

"How so?" I asked

He turned to look at me. "You have Breoch Guard pursuing you into the deepest parts of the Shrouded Woods, that's how. I can't believe they're this far in; they normally stick close to the cities."

A thrill of fear went through me. "Those men were Breoch Guard?"

Willem nodded. "And as you can tell, I have a history with one of them." He grimaced. "I encountered Angus when Father and I were helping Mother escape the guard compound all those years back."

"Did he really cut off your mother's hand?"

"I'm not sure, I wasn't there," Willem replied. "I really did take his eye out, though."

"With a pen?" I said. "Just like…"

"Yes, just like *that.*" He threw a cautious glance at Kip. "I'm fairly certain it was the story of Kirilee's mistake that prompted me to do what I did. It's a long story, I'll tell you a different day." He sighed. "But you folks are going to need to be very careful on your journey to the coast. If the Breoch Guard are hunting you this deep in the Shrouded Woods, then they must really, really want you. In fact, I think I'll be teleporting us all home tonight."

Kip's eyes widened. "You can teleport six people that far?"

Willem gave him a wry grin and glanced at me. "Have you figured out my innate talent yet, Saray?"

"I suppose I should have," I chuckled. "If that's the case, then why don't you just teleport us all the way to Dundere?"

He snorted. "I'm not *that* powerful. Dundere is two weeks away by ship, you know. I might be able to send myself there, but certainly not five other people." He frowned. "Though I'll speak with Hilda about borrowing some of her magic and teleporting you all to the coast, at least. That would get you out of the area where you're being hunted."

We were quiet after that, and I found myself unable to rid myself of the knot in my stomach or the anxious thoughts that played about in my head. *Why are the Breoch Guard so intent on capturing Trina and me? And how did they know where we were?*

The woods began to thicken around us, and after another few hours of walking, we came across what looked to be an impenetrable tangle of bushes. Kip looked at Kirilee. "Where to from here, ai?"

"This way." Kirilee turned left and led us alongside the brambles for what felt like a good half hour. Then we turned a corner, and I stared at the scene before me. Nestled up against the bushes was a tiny cottage that appeared to be built from white stone. It had a thatched roof and a flower garden out front, and smoke curled lazily upward from the chimney. Kirilee strode towards the door and knocked, and a moment later, it creaked open.

The woman who stared up at us was nearly as short as Trina. White-blond hair curled on her shoulders, and she was clad in a gaudy purple dress that was decorated with lace and gemstones, and a black top hat that reminded me of Mr. Jeffries', save for the fact that it had a large pink feather tucked into its band. "Kirilee!" the woman exclaimed.

"It's good to see you, Hilda," she replied, leaning forward to embrace the other woman. "I brought friends."

"I see that." Hilda looked past Kirilee. Her face lit up when she saw Willem, and he stepped forward and hugged her as well. Then she eyed each of us as Kirilee made introductions. Her eyes, I noticed, were nearly the same colour as her dress, and, like Kirilee, it was hard to determine her age by looking at her. She was very pretty, I decided. "I take it you've brought your friends to see the garden?" she asked, to which Kirilee gave her a nod.

"Your garden is lovely," I said, gesturing at the flowers around us.

Hilda laughed at my words. "Not this garden, child, the other one." She looked me over. "The girl isn't from around here, ai?"

"Both girls are from the cities," Kirilee told her. "They know very little about your house. You needn't worry about them causing trouble, though. They're becoming used to our ways."

Hilda nodded. "Even so, you know what I'll have to cast on them in order for them to come in."

"Of course," Kirilee replied.

"What's that?" Kip asked cautiously.

Hilda turned to him. "The garden around the back of this house is a sacred place, and its location is a well-kept secret," she explained. "For the protection of those who call it home, I can't let many people know where it is. There are fewer than a dozen people within Firenholme who know how to get to this hut, and two of them are in your company." She gestured at Willem and Kirilee. "To keep those numbers as low as possible, I cast a spell on all who enter the garden that'll keep them from remembering the exact location of my home or how they got here. It's not that I don't trust you folks, but I need to keep my friends safe."

I cast an anxious glance at Kip, remembering how he'd reacted to Willem's threat to wipe his memory of his home's location. To my surprise, Kip was nodding slowly.

"Why don't you all come in?" Hilda said, gesturing at her door. "Carmine's in the garden, I'll go fetch her. I have a pot of soup on the stove, so you might as well have dinner with us. You can stay the night too, so long as you don't mind all being crowded into our living room."

Willem shook his head. "Thank you, but I think we'll take the quick route home. We ran into some trouble on the way here, and I'd like to avoid encountering it again."

"Is that so, ai? You'll need to fill me in later on." She paused and eyed Bailey. "Here we have a small problem," she said. "I myself quite like dogs, but my cats aren't fond of them, and the inhabitants of the garden are rather afraid of animals they're not used to." She looked at Trina, who was holding onto Bailey. "Do you mind if I put a spell on your dog that will make him sleep for the duration of your stay? It won't hurt him, I promise."

Trina shrugged. "He's not my dog," she said. "Ask Kip."

Hilda looked to Kip, who hesitated briefly before nodding.

Hilda smiled at him and then crouched down and spoke softly to Bailey. Trina let go of him, and the dog walked off to the corner of the lawn, curled up, and promptly closed his eyes.

"Well, that was dealt with easily enough," Hilda said. "Now come on inside, and let's have some food."

The inside of Hilda's house was nearly all one room. A section was cordoned off by a bead curtain—I assumed that to be a bedroom—but the kitchen, dining room and living room were all part of the same space. The walls were decorated by bright, bizarre pieces of art, and one wall housed several clocks, some with cuckoos and others with black-and-white faces and long elegant chimes, and others still with flowers painted where the numbers should have been. A cheery fire burned in the fireplace, and the mantle above held several clear glass vases containing vibrant rocks and pearlescent shells and multicoloured sprays of flowers. On one side of the fireplace was a floor-to-ceiling bookshelf crammed with books; on the other side was another set of shelves containing a large collection of teapots and teacups. The couches and chairs that occupied the centre of the room were mismatched, and several cats of varying colours and sizes lounged about on most of the furniture. A rectangular dining table sat off to one side, its surface uncovered. A kitchen area lay beyond that, and on the stove sat a large black pot. Hilda went over and stirred its contents. I breathed in deep; I could smell the aroma of her soup from where I was standing. "Just about ready," she said in a satisfied tone.

"What are you doing, Trina?" Kip asked. Glancing at her, I saw that Trina was hunched over; her hand moving back and forth across what appeared to be nothing but air.

"I'm saying hello to the kitty, what does it look like?" Trina replied.

Hilda let out a laugh. "I see you've found Ghost." She looked at Kip, her grin widening. "One of my cats is invisible, though I suppose Trina didn't realize this. Ghost is a lovely cat, and on occasion he's been known to serve as a spy for me, just like Persius does for Kirilee." She glanced at me. "He actually told me about you, Saray."

"Really?" I frowned. "Did he see me?"

"No. But the woods are buzzing with rumours about a firebrand who can cast with her mind. You've gained a reputation."

I frowned at her words. *I suppose Ambrose has been talking about me.*

"I'll be back in a moment," she told us. "I have someone to introduce you to."

She disappeared out the back door and returned a couple of minutes later followed by another woman. This woman was the opposite of Hilda in many ways; she was tall and curvy, with skin a shade darker than Trina's and greying black curls piled on her head. She wore breeches and a tunic that was made from a soft fabric with a floral pattern. "This is Carmine," Hilda told us. "My wife."

Kirilee and Willem stepped forward to embrace Carmine, and Hilda introduced the rest of us, remembering our names with surprising ease. Carmine greeted us all with a small bow. I studied her, a little surprised at the apparent age gap between the women. Hilda didn't look much older than thirty, while Carmine had to be close to fifty.

I noticed something else about Carmine then, and my eyes widened. "You're a krossemage," I blurted out. Kirilee turned around and gave me a disapproving look.

"We don't use that word in this house." Hilda's voice was firm. "Carmine is mute and is missing her right hand. But she is *not* shattered." Carmine nodded in agreement but gave me a wry smile, seeming amused by my outburst.

Trina cocked her head. "You know, we're going to Dundere so I can get my eyes healed. You could come with us if you wanted."

"Or at the very least, Willem and I could make you one of these," Lachlann offered, showing her his metal hand.

Carmine shook her head and turned to Hilda. She began signing rapidly with her left hand, and Hilda nodded. "Carmine wants you to know that she's learned to be happy the way she is. Not all folk who are different wish to change themselves, you know. However, she's well aware that she's in a better position than many who've had the same treatment."

"Because you're here in the woods, you mean?" Lachlann asked Carmine.

"That, and she still has her magic," Hilda explained.

"How?" I asked. "Can you cast with your mind too, Carmine?"

She shook her hand and waved her left hand at me.

"Remember when you asked me what happens to left-handed magikai if they're caught, and I told you about the one woman I knew who used her magic to get away?" Willem asked me. "You're looking at her."

"What's your talent, Carmine?" asked Trina.

Kirilee laughed. "Carmine's talent is one you might find interesting, Trina. You know how you can talk to animals? Carmine can talk to plants."

Kip frowned. "I didn't know plants were smart enough to talk back."

Hilda shrugged. "Depends on the plant. Carmine tells me that trees are very intelligent." Carmine grinned and nodded. "Let's eat dinner," Hilda continued, gesturing at the table, "and then we can go see Carmine's garden and meet my friends."

I couldn't tell exactly what sorts of vegetables and meats Hilda's soup contained, but I knew that it was delicious. As we ate, Hilda told us the story of how she and Carmine had met. She told us nothing about what Carmine had escaped from, only that, while on the run, Carmine had become one of the only people to stumble upon Hilda's cottage by chance. Upon learning about the purpose of Hilda's backyard, Carmine had told her about her talent with plants and offered her services as a gardener in exchange for a place to stay. Their relationship had progressed from a professional one to friends, then lovers, and then wives. "I certainly wasn't expecting to find love out here," Hilda concluded. "But I think the fairies knew what I needed."

"What exactly is so special about your garden?" Kip asked.

"You mean Kirilee didn't tell you?" Hilda chuckled. "Well, in that case, I'm going to let it be a surprise. We should head out there soon so you can see Carmine's handiwork before the sun sets."

We finished dinner, and Carmine cleared our dishes, piled them in the sink, and motioned that we should put on our shoes and coats again. Then she and Hilda led us through the house to the back door.

Carmine's garden was as bright and haphazard as her and Hilda's home, I saw. It was backed on all three sides by brush-covered hills, forming a small glen of sorts. A rock structure that looked like a small castle sat at one end, slightly elevated above the rest, and rocks were arranged in patterns throughout the area. Patches of flowers, seemingly without any defined pattern, were interspersed with the rocks, and fruit trees and large mushrooms grew here and there. A small stream trickled through the yard, winding its way around the rocks. The entire place looked magical in the fading light. "This is beautiful," I breathed.

Carmine nodded and gestured that we should follow her. She walked over to a patch of wildflowers and flicked her wrist, and I gasped as several buds burst open, and a few flowers grew taller. Then she took Trina by the hand and led her to a flowering vine that was climbing up a tree. She put Trina's hand on a flower and then flicked her wrist again. The vine grew rapidly, snaking over Trina's shoulders. Trina giggled and touched the flowers. "That's amazing."

"Quite the gift my wife has, isn't it?" Hilda said, putting an arm around Carmine. "I think it's getting dark enough for you all to meet our friends."

I looked around the garden uncertainly. Except for the occasional butterfly flitting from flower to flower, I saw no inhabitants. "Where are they?"

"Watch." Hilda stepped forward and began to hum a low, haunting melody that reminded me of Claudi's casting.

The lights began slowly, small flickers of pink and blue and yellow darting in and out of my vision. I squinted at first, wondering if I was seeing things. Then a small, bright purple ball of light emerged from behind a nearby rock. It floated up to Hilda and rested on her hand. I stared at it curiously.

And Trina let out a shriek.

"What?" Kip asked, turning to her. "You all right?"

Trina's eyes were wide, her face paler than normal. She raised a trembling hand and pointed directly at whatever was sitting on Hilda's hand. "That," she said, her voice a squeak. "There's something there, and I can...I can *see* it!"

I turned to her, my own eyes widening. "You...*can?*"

"Can you see anything else?" Kip asked her, his voice uncertain.

She shook her head. "Only...only the purple thing." Her voice trembled, and a tear rolled down her cheek.

Kirilee let out a chuckle. "I figured you might be able to see them," she said. "That's a large part of why I brought you here with me."

"What are they?" I asked.

"You haven't figured it out yet? Really, Saray, you and I had an entire conversation about these beings, once."

I thought for a moment, and then I gasped. "Fairies." Then I stared at Hilda, recalling Kirilee's earlier words. "You're the fairy priestess?"

"That I am." Hilda gave me a small bow.

"Wait a minute." Kip's eyes widened. "If you're the fairy priestess and your name's Hilda...does the word *hildakin* come from your name?"

She frowned. "I'd rather you not use that word, but yes. The Seekers were once known as 'Hilda's kin.'"

Kip nodded, and Hilda walked over to Trina. "Stretch out your hand." Trina obeyed, her hand shaking still, and the small purple fairy alighted on it. She stared at it in wonderment, tears streaming down her face. Kip put an arm around her and held her to himself, but I could tell that he too was fascinated by the fairy.

More of the creatures had begun to come out of hiding now. A yellow one circled Lachlann's head, causing him to look every which way in awe, laughing like a child. I felt a tug on my braid and looked down to find a green fairy holding onto the end. I carefully held the end of my braid up to my eyes, staring. The creature was tiny, but I could make out a ragged dress, long hair, and a mischievous face. Kirilee had seated herself on a nearby rock, and several fairies of varying colours had settled on her; they were obviously familiar with her.

"Fairies used to run all about Firenholme," Hilda told us. "They lived under every rock, in every patch of mushrooms, and they lit up the woods at night. About forty years back, though, word got into the cities of Breoch that these creatures still lived in the woods. And a group of rather stupid young folks who called themselves the Witch Slayers decided that fairies were evil and that it was their job to try to stamp them out. They came through hunting fairies and magikai and tried to burn the woods down."

"Is that the story that Kirilee told us about why you call this place Firenholme?" I asked.

Hilda nodded. "When they tried to burn Firenholme down, the magic in the trees not only kept most of them from burning, it also made them stronger. They grew taller and sturdier after that, and vilettas—which had never been seen in the woods before then—began to grow from the ashes of the trees that did burn. That's why calling these woods a *kingdom of fire* is more than appropriate. We were forged and strengthened by the thing that was meant to destroy us.

"But at the time, it was terrifying. We humans knew to hide whenever the Witch Slayers came through, but the fairies don't speak our language, so they had no idea what was happening. I lived in an area that was well populated by fairies, and so I took it upon myself to gather a bunch of them up and create a sanctuary. Since that time, fairies outside of this glen are rare. The Seekers hope to change that, though; they do what they can to make Firenholme a more welcoming place for the fairies, in hopes that one day they'll return."

Lachlann stared at her. "You were there forty years ago?" he asked. "You look quite a bit younger than me, and I'm still a few years shy of forty."

"The fairies were grateful for my help, so they extended my life in exchange for guarding this place," she explained. She glanced at Carmine.

"Carmine looks like the older one of the two of us, but really, I'm older by a lot."

Kirilee and Lachlann both chuckled at this information and exchanged a knowing glance.

"There are things that happen in this garden that don't happen elsewhere," Hilda continued, "like little Trina here being able to see."

"Can you do anything special when the fairies are around?" I asked Carmine. "Talk, for instance?"

Carmine shook her head and signed to Hilda. "She can't talk," Hilda translated. "But sometimes when she's harvesting fruit, the fairies will come join her, and they'll give her the ability to taste the fruit while they are present, despite her not having a tongue." I raised my eyebrows and nodded.

"How do the Seekers come visit this place if it's so hard to find?" Lachlann asked.

"They find a guide, one of the few people I've trusted with the location of my home. Kirilee's been one of these guides for decades." She smiled at Kirilee. "Speaking of which, she and I have some business to attend to. Feel free to stay out here as long as you'd like; the fairies are more than happy to entertain you. Or head inside if you'd prefer."

She turned and walked further into the garden, Kirilee following her. Lachlann wandered off on his own, and Carmine began tending to a patch of wilting strawberries. Trina was still entranced by the purple fairy that had yet to move from her hand, and Kip hadn't moved from his place next to her. A blue fairy had landed on his shoulder, though, and he was staring at it in fascination. A flash of light to my left caught my eye, and I noticed several fairies congregating near a ring of mushrooms. I crept over and watched while they arranged themselves in a circle inside the ring. Strange, ethereal music began to emanate from the area, and the fairies started to dance and move about in their ring. I looked up for a brief moment, then waved the others over and returned to watching the dance.

Kirilee and Hilda had returned now, and Kirilee walked up to Lachlann and took him by the hand. "Come with me," she said. I watched as she led him into a far corner of the garden, laughing, a string of colourful lights trailing her. Hilda smiled, watching them, and then headed into the house, followed by Carmine and Willem.

Kip and Trina had joined me at the fairy dance, and we all stared at the celebration that was taking place before us. "It's like that Moon Dance that Kirilee took us to the day you two met her, only much smaller," Kip commented. "I s'pose that's why the Seekers do it."

Several of the fairies were departing the dance now. They floated up towards Trina and began to move and flit wildly about her. Trina laughed and then began to cry again. "They know," she said in a choked voice. "They know I can't normally see, so…" Her voice broke, and she trailed off, staring at the dancing lights in wonderment.

I watched the dance for a few minutes longer and then felt a hand on my shoulder. Kip was motioning to the house with his head. I nodded, understanding, and followed him inside so that Trina could be alone with the fairies.

Inside there was more tea, as well as cookies and cakes. Kip wandered the room, studying Hilda's teacup collection and clocks and vases, and I settled on the couch with a book and listened as Willem and Hilda talked about very complex types of magic that I'd never before heard of. At one point I startled when something soft brushed against my legs, then I heard purring and realized that Ghost had come to say hello. My eyes began to droop after a while, and some time later Kirilee and Lachlann arrived inside, Lachlann carrying Trina, who was fast asleep. He set her down on the couch and smiled. "This was a special night for her."

"I'm glad," Hilda said. "And I hope that one day, when her vision has been restored, she can come back and see our garden in all its beauty."

Lachlann nodded. "It was a special night for the two of us too." He put his arm around Kirilee, and she raised her left hand. Only now did I see something glinting on her finger.

My hands flew up to my mouth. "You're…engaged?"

Kirilee nodded, grinning. "The fairies gave me permission to leave the woods and go to Dundere," she said. "And Lachlann's captain friend should be able to marry us on his ship, so we figured it was a good time to make it official."

"Can I see the ring?" Hilda asked.

Kirilee nodded and extended her hand. "Lachlann made it himself. He had Willem teleport him back home several times over the last few weeks so he could use his forge."

Lachlann grinned and glanced at me. "My brother says hello to you and Trina, by the way."

I moved closer to Hilda and stared at the ring. It appeared to be fashioned from three bands of gold that twisted together in a whirling, leafy pattern resembling a laurel crown. A few of the leaves were inlaid with tiny diamonds and emeralds. "It's gorgeous." I stared at Lachlann in admiration. "I can't believe you made that!"

He smiled proudly. "It's the most delicate thing I've ever made. It was definitely a challenge, especially with the new hand, but it seems to have turned out well."

"I'll say." Kirilee beamed. "My *fiancé* is incredibly talented." The two of them exchanged a smile, and Lachlann leaned down and kissed her. I grinned at them, ignoring the familiar twist of jealousy in my stomach. "We should head home," Kirilee said when she pulled away from him. Lachlann nodded and went to pick up Trina, who had not stirred.

We made our way into the front yard, and Kip walked over to wake up Bailey. Persius sat nearby, occasionally giving the sleeping dog a nudge with his beak. Kip returned with the dog trailing him a few minutes later, and Persius settled on Kirilee's shoulder. Then we all turned to face Hilda and Carmine, who both smiled at us. "It was a pleasure meeting all of you," Hilda said, giving us a curtsy. "If you wish to visit again, ask one of the guides to bring you here." Her gaze shifted to Willem. "Willem, let me know when you want me to come help you with that teleport spell. And congratulations, you two." She smiled at Lachlann and Kirilee. Then she waved her hand in front of our faces, muttering words I did not know.

"Everyone hold on to each other," Willem said once she was done casting. I nodded and took Kip's arm with one hand, holding onto Bailey's neck with the other. "*Arius ravenous momentus,*" Willem intoned, and a moment later, we were standing in the entryway to his home. "Well," Willem said, letting go of us. "That was an easy trip home."

"I'll say," Kip agreed.

"How was the journey for you, Lachlann?" Willem asked. "Were you tired by the end of it?"

"Perhaps a bit more than I would have been before," he answered. "But not by much." He nodded at Trina, who was still sleeping in his arms. "And I've been carrying her around just fine, so clearly I have my strength back."

"Do you feel ready to move on, ai?" asked Kirilee.

Lachlann nodded. "I think so, yes. In which case, we should begin preparations to leave. The Lady Liara leaves Kirstein every second new moon, and it reaches the port that we will be using by the fourth day. The moon was full tonight, so we have two weeks and four days to reach the port." He glanced at Willem. "If you can teleport us, then we should be able to leave the same day that the ship arrives there."

Willem nodded. "That can be arranged."

"Good." Kirilee smiled at him and then turned to Lachlann. "I'll take Trina to bed."

Lachlann passed Trina's sleeping form to Kirilee, and we all headed to our rooms. "You must be so excited," I whispered to Kirilee. "Though I'm a bit surprised that you want to get married."

"Why's that?" she asked.

I frowned. "It just seems like one of the traditions of the city folk, and I thought you didn't care for those."

She nodded. "I doubt I would've suggested it for us, and I'm not one who believes that if two people love each other, they have to get married. But what Lachlann said a few weeks back about another person being home for me, that sounds wonderful. I quite like the idea of a bit of permanence in my life." She shifted Trina's weight in her arms. "Perhaps the ideas of the city folk aren't *all* nonsense."

"Well, I'm happy for you two," I said, opening the bedroom door so that Kirilee could carry Trina inside.

"And maybe a little jealous, ai?" Kirilee guessed, setting Trina down and giving me a wry grin.

"Maybe a little." I let out a nervous laugh. "You know, it's strange. Back at the Academy, most of the girls in my grade were obsessed with the boys.

They were always flirting with them and giggling and doing whatever they could to make the boys notice them, and I always thought it was so *silly*. But when I watch you and Lachlann, this love stuff…it actually makes some sense."

Kirilee nodded. "Falling in love is completely natural, y'know," she told me. "A crush is nothing to be ashamed of, so long as you're respectful of the other person's feelings." She gave me a wink, and I felt myself blush. *Has she noticed how awkward I can be around Kip?*

Kirilee left the room, and I crawled into bed. As I settled beneath the covers, I found myself trying to recall exactly how to get to Hilda's home, but that memory, as promised, had faded from my mind completely.

# Chapter Fifteen

WE SPENT THE next two weeks preparing for our departure from Willem's home. Lachlann began waxing his armour, readying it for the journey ahead, and Kip and Kirilee headed out to hunt and gather so that we would have food while we waited for our ship to arrive. Lachlann and Willem continued their sword practice, now fighting at full speed. Trina talked incessantly about the evening at Hilda and Carmine's, and, at her prompting, I began scouring Willem's library for books about the fairies to read to her so she could better understand the creatures. One evening, Kirilee and Lachlann sat down with Kip, Trina, and me and told us their plans for their wedding and how they wanted each of us to be involved.

When the time for departure came, we all stood outside Willem's home, facing the man who had been an incredibly gracious host to us for well over a month. "I can't thank you enough for all you've done for us, Willem," Kirilee said.

Willem waved away her words. "It's nothing, my dear," he assured her. "Your stay has made me realize that I've turned into a bit of a recluse over the years. I don't wish to stay that way, though." He paused and then cleared his throat. "I suppose you'd best be off. I'll fetch Hilda." He reached into his robe pocket and removed a small pink rock which he began to rub with his thumb.

I watched as Hilda materialized next to him. She smiled at Willem and then glanced down at the stone. "It worked!"

"Of course it worked. I do this with my mother all the time." Willem gave her a quick smile. Then he turned to the rest of us. "I have one for you folks, as well. And I think I'll give it to Trina."

Trina cocked her head as Willem walked towards her and pulled out a pendant made from a round, polished purple stone. "I figure you're the least likely to end up directly in the middle of a fight," he said. "If you're ever in need of me, you only have to rub the pendant, and I'll appear within a few minutes' time."

He placed the pendant in Trina's palm, and she grinned at him and fastened the chain behind her neck. "Thank you," she whispered.

"You're welcome. Use it well." He turned to the rest of us. "I'm going to warn you all, you need to keep your eye out for Breoch Guard. They are fast moving, and they could show up anywhere. Don't let your guard down, all right?"

We all nodded solemnly, and Willem turned to Hilda. "Let's get these folks to the coast."

Willem and Hilda joined hands, and Willem spoke a soft, now-familiar phrase to join their magic. "Come," Willem said when the spell was complete. "Everyone hold onto one another, just like last time." I took Trina's hand in my own and leaned into Kirilee, and Willem spoke the teleportation spell.

Unlike the last time we'd teleported, there was an instant where I could tell that we were not really *anywhere*. We were floating, in limbo, the world around us white and silent and still. Then, a moment after, we were standing under thin tree cover. Brightness was visible through the trees to our left, the sun glinted off water in the distance, and the air had a strange, salty tang to it. Willem and Hilda had not come with us, I noticed. Beside me, Kip groaned slightly. "That was *strange.*"

"It was," Lachlann agreed, nodding. "But we made it; we're right where we need to be." He grinned at us and then set off in the direction of the water, the rest of us following him.

When we cleared the trees, we found ourselves on a long sandy beach strewn with pebbles and sticks and shells. Large white birds circled overhead, letting out the occasional loud caw. Kirilee stopped walking for a moment and gazed at the water. "It's been so long," she whispered.

I, meanwhile, was transfixed by the ocean's sheer vastness. It stretched out in front of me, silver-blue and massive. Endless waves of blue-green water tumbled toward the shore, each one dissolving in a mass of white foam as it hit the sand. "How big is it?" I asked.

Lachlann laughed. "It's huge, Saray. That's the nature of the ocean. You've never been this close to it, have you?"

I shook my head. "You can see the ocean from Sylvenburgh Academy if you're up in one of the towers. But I've never been right next to it."

Nearby, a long, crude dock stretched out into the water. Lachlann strode towards it and began to walk down its length; the rest of us followed. I shuddered as the wooden planks rolled underneath my feet but forced myself to keep walking. At the end, Kip reached down and tested the water with his hand. Trina and I both did the same; I flinched at its coldness, and Trina shivered. "Don't drink it," Lachlann warned us.

Kip snorted. "I know enough about the ocean to know that, ai."

"Good." Lachlann grinned and sat down on the wooden planks. "Now we wait."

Kip returned to staring intently into the water. Lachlann sat down on the deck, and Kirilee sank down next to him, Persius perched on her shoulder. Both Kirilee and Lachlann were throwing occasional glances around the area, no doubt scanning for the Breoch Guard we'd been warned about. Trina pulled out her pipe and began to play, and I lay back and closed my eyes, enjoying the sun on my face and the salty sea breeze.

Some time later a shadow fell across us, and I half opened my eyes. Then they flew open, and I gaped at the massive ship that loomed in the harbour. Three towering masts rose from the deck, and at least twenty open sails flapped in the wind. The figure of a woman was carved into its bow, and I could see crew members moving up and down the masts, going about their work. I gawked at the vessel as it moved towards us.

Lachlann was on his feet, waving at the people onboard. The ship pulled slowly up to the dock, and I watched as dozens of crew members worked to secure it. Then a gangplank was being lowered, and a tall man wearing a navy blue coat with long tails and a large hat descended. "Lachlann!" the man exclaimed, grinning broadly as he walked towards us. "I've not seen you in close to a year!"

"It's been too long," Lachlann agreed, shaking the other man's hand and clapping him on the back. "Gareth, I'd like you to meet my friends who I'm traveling with."

He named each of us off, and Gareth offered greetings and handshakes to all of us. He had to be in his fifties or sixties, I decided, looking the man over. His shoulder-length hair and beard were decidedly grey, his face weathered with age and many years at sea. His bright blue eyes sparkled when he smiled though, defying his years. "Gareth, as you may have guessed, is the captain of this ship," Lachlann informed us.

Gareth was staring at Lachlann's metal hand now. "Well, now, what happened to you?" he asked in an accent that I didn't recognize. "And what's that contraption?"

"Got in a fight with a cursed arrow," Lachlann replied. "I'll tell you the story later." He raised his left hand and wiggled his fingers. "I made this myself, with a little help and some magic."

Gareth shook his head. "My, how times have changed. When I was a lad, if you lost a hand, they'd give you a hook and expect you to make do." He chuckled, and then his gaze turned to the rest of us. "Am I correct to assume that you mean to bring all these folks aboard? Children too? And the animals?"

"No, I thought I'd leave the children and animals behind," Lachlann replied in a sarcastic tone. "Of course I'm bringing them along. We're hoping to contact the governor in Dundere; we hear that she can heal people, and the little one is blind."

"Ah, yes, I know the governor and her husband well." Gareth nodded. "She should be more than willing to help you out. Do your friends here know how things work on my ship?"

"They will once I've told them," Lachlann replied, turning to us. "Gareth has a rule that anyone can come aboard his ship and sail with him for free, provided they are willing to do their share of the work on the ship. He manages to find something that everyone can do."

"Even me?" Trina asked.

Lachlann laughed. "Perhaps you can talk to the rats at the bottom of the ship, keep them away from us." He looked at Gareth. "The girl can speak with animals," he explained.

"You're not supposed to tell people that," I protested.

Gareth chuckled. "You needn't worry about me, lass," he told me. "I'm not afraid of a little magic. I can guarantee you that I've seen stranger things in my life than you have. There's not much room for magic fearers on my ship."

I nodded slowly. "Well in that case," I informed him, "I'm a firebrand, so I know how to make fire."

"She knows how to make fire," Lachlann repeated, snorting. "You're too modest, Saray." He looked at Gareth. "The girl is a living furnace. I wouldn't have this without her." He wiggled his metal fingers.

Gareth eyed me. "Are you the girl who can cast with her mind, by chance?"

My eyes widened. "You've heard of me too?"

He nodded. "Rumours spread fast in the woods, and I've picked up a few woods-dwellers over the past months." He grinned. "I'm honoured to have someone with such a rare gift aboard my ship. Though I'd ask you to keep it in check while we're at sea."

I nodded and looked up at the sails. "Those look pretty flammable."

He nodded. "They are, but it's the ropes I'm more concerned about. Especially the shrouds and the standing ropes—those are coated with pitch, and they're flammable enough to catch fire in the middle of a rainstorm."

I nodded; I had no idea what he meant, but I made a mental note to be careful with my gift around the ropes.

"Are any of the rest of you magic users?" Gareth asked.

"I'm not exactly a magic user," Kirilee said, "but I can speak with my hawk. I'll make sure he does his business somewhere other than your decks." She grinned.

"Good to know," Gareth said, returning her smile. "And don't you worry, I have plenty of work for non-magical folk as well."

"Um," Lachlann interjected, clearing his throat, "about that. I was going to request a possible exception to your rule about everyone working."

Gareth's eyes narrowed, and he turned back to Lachlann. "And why's that?"

Lachlann smiled and took Kirilee's hand. "Well, you see, Kirilee and I were hoping to be married on your ship. We were, in fact, going to ask you to perform the ceremony. And we were hoping to be able to spend the first week of our journey not working, having a honeymoon of sorts." He eyed Gareth. "I can pay our way for that part of the journey, of course."

Gareth's eyes widened, and a wry grin formed on his face. Then he let out a loud laugh and clapped Lachlann on the shoulder. "Fool boy! You think I'm going to abide by those terms?"

Lachlann's eyebrows arched in protest.

"I will absolutely marry you," Gareth went on, "*and* allow you and your bride a week of rest—in my ship's best cabin, of course—and you will not pay me a cent, do you understand?"

Lachlann stared at Gareth for a moment. Then he grinned back at his friend. "You're a good man, Captain."

"Some of the time, yes." Gareth chuckled and gestured at the gangplank. "Come aboard, all of you, and I'll let the crew know what's happening. I say we wed you tonight and take to sea tomorrow. Is that too soon?"

Kirilee and Lachlann exchanged a glance. "Definitely not," they said, nearly in unison.

I stared at the figurehead on the ship's bow as I walked towards the gangplank. "Who is the Lady Liara?" I asked Gareth.

"Ah." Gareth glanced back at me. "This ship is named after my late wife. I lost her many, many years back."

"Oh." I frowned. "I…I'm sorry."

"Don't be," he said. "I'm just happy I got to be with her for the time that I did. That in itself was a miracle; she and I have quite the story."

"Will you tell us?" I asked

"Absolutely, but not today. We have a different love story to tell today." He grinned. "Come along."

We followed Gareth over to the wheel, where he rang the ship's bell. I watched as people began streaming from all areas of the ship, sliding down masts and coming up from below deck, and soon enough we found ourselves facing a good three dozen people. Both men and women were present in the crowd, and there was a good variance in ages, though Trina, Kip and I were undoubtedly the youngest people present. Gareth explained the situation to the crew, eliciting a few squeals from some of the younger women when he mentioned the impending wedding. "Now, I've officiated dozens of weddings," Gareth said to them, "but planning one is not my strong point." His gaze turned to a large woman with a mound of dark curls piled on her head. "Can I trust that you'll do a better job of it than I would, Kezia?"

"Absolutely, Captain." The woman beamed as she strode up the steps and stood next to him.

Gareth grinned at her, and then Kezia began barking out orders, directing people to set up the deck for a wedding, find the bride and groom suitable clothes, and begin preparing the food. "We don't have enough meat for a proper feast," she mentioned, a sad note in her voice.

"I can handle that," Kip said, motioning at his bow. "Send a few crew members with me, and I'll have you a good-sized beast in a couple of hours."

"Then go," she said, gesturing at a few other young men. "Talbot, Lucien, Dirk—you three go with him, help him bring back whatever he kills."

The four men made their way down the gangplank, and Kezia turned to me. "Do you know these woods well, girl?" she asked.

I frowned. "Not extremely well, but likely better than most people here."

"If I send you out to gather as many flowers as possible for decoration and for the bride's bouquet, would you be able to do that?"

I nodded. "That should be easy enough."

Kezia sent me off along with two other girls and a boy, all of them likely only a little older than Kip. Then she disappeared from the deck, leaving me staring after her. "Is she a vanisher?" I asked the tall, dark-haired girl standing next to me.

She shook her head. "Teleporter. Dirk is our only vanisher." She turned to me. "And I hear you're a firebrand, like me."

I nodded, and we made introductions. The girl's name was Janice, and the other girl was Anika, the boy—who appeared to be Anika's boyfriend—was Landon. I led them into the forest, trying to keep an eye out for any unfriendly visitors while also scanning for flowers. "There are some nice ones up there," I said, motioning at the bell-shaped blooms hanging from the branches above us. "Though we'd have to climb for them."

Landon grinned and shook his head. "*Incantus dominus intransae,*" he said, and I watched as the flowers detached themselves from the tree and floated down to his outstretched hands. "You're a telekinetic," I whispered. "Like Kirilee used to be."

"That I am," he said, presenting the flowers to me.

I smiled as I took them from him, and we continued moving forward. My job for the day, it seemed, had just gotten far easier.

We returned to the ship a few hours later, our arms overflowing with flowers. Nearly everything else was ready, Kezia told us, and so she sent me down into the cabin area with Janice to find a suitable dress for the occasion. Janice, who was only a bit taller than me, had me try on several of her dresses before settling on a flowing jade green one topped by a gold and green corset and a gold necklace and earrings to match. Once I was dressed, she directed me to a small mirror on the cabin wall. "Take a look at yourself."

I hadn't bothered to look in mirrors much since leaving Sylvenburgh, and now I stared at my reflection, more preoccupied by the changes in my appearance than at the clothes I currently wore. My skin had darkened to a deep tan, making my freckles stand out and contrasting sharply with the blue of my eyes. I saw new definition in my shoulders and arms, and my hair was wild as always, but not in a way I disliked. "I look *fierce*," I whispered, grinning at the mirror.

"Yes, you do." Janice laughed and worked a few white viletta blooms into my hair. "But you look pretty as well. And now you'll glow in the dark. Come on, let's head upstairs."

The sky was beginning to darken when I arrived above deck. My eyes widened at the scene; the plain wooden deck had been transformed. Coloured lanterns hung all around the ship's perimeter, and viletta blooms were worked into the rigging here and there, lighting up the entire area with an ethereal glow. Persius sat in the rigging, letting out an occasional screech as he looked down on the deck, where a long carpet had been laid out and several rows of chairs set up. Two torches lit the area at the front where the ceremony would be performed, their flames changing colour as they flickered; behind them sat a table where the parts of the ceremony that Trina, Kip and I would be involved in would take place. Gareth stood in front of the table, dressed in a slightly fancier dark blue coat than the one he'd been wearing earlier, and Lachlann stood next to him. I stared for a moment; I'd never seen Lachlann dressed up before, and he looked rather dashing. His hair was tied back, and he was dressed in a black jacket with golden patterns embroidered into it, crisp black trousers, and tall boots. He caught my eye and grinned at my expression, then inclined his head to the left. I followed his gaze and locked eyes with Kip.

If Lachlann in fancy clothes was shocking to me, then Kip was utterly astonishing. I'd only ever seen Kip wear green and brown; now he was clad in a light blue waistcoat with silver buttons that accented the colour of his eyes. His trousers and boots were nearly identical to Lachlann's, and his long hair was pulled back as always but somehow looked tidier than normal. I felt heat creep into my cheeks as I walked over to him. "You, uh, look quite nice," I said.

"As do you." He gave me a shy smile and looked me over.

"Do I look nice?" Trina piped up; I had hardly noticed her standing near Kip.

I took in her frilly purple dress and intricate braided updo and laughed. "You look perfect, Trina," I told her.

Gareth called us to order, and Kip, Trina and I took our places at the table behind Gareth. I watched Lachlann as the guests seated themselves, wondering if he was nervous. He certainly didn't look it; he was chatting animatedly with the captain, his posture relaxed. Then the captain stepped forward and cleared his throat, and a hush fell over the crowd.

I'd hardly noticed the group of musicians that stood to our far right; now I turned to watch the pipers and fiddlers as they began to play a soft, haunting melody. Then I heard a few gasps as Kirilee came out of one of the cabins and into view.

I'd never seen Kirilee dressed in city clothes before. She was not wearing a traditional wedding dress, but the gown she was garbed in was beautiful nonetheless. It was the colour of the sea in summertime, with white lace designs on the bodice and long bell sleeves. On her head she wore a crown made of fresh white vilettas. She was still barefoot and still wore her shell jewelry, but her makeup was more subtle than I was used to, and her hair hung loose, save for a few tiny braids here and there. She smiled broadly as she made her way down the aisle to Lachlann; looking at him, I saw that his eyes were wide.

Kirilee reached the stage, and the music slowly faded out as Lachlann stepped forward, took her hand, and led her to where Gareth stood. Gareth looked them over and then cleared his throat. "My friends," he said, looking out over the crowd, "today we are gathered to join Lachlann Jeffries and Kirilee Westwood together in marriage."

He had them join hands and then turned to the groom. "Lachlann, do you take this woman to be your wife?" he asked, to which Lachlann gave an enthusiastic yes. He asked the same question of Kirilee and received an equally eager response.

"At this point in the ceremony, I might normally give a speech," Gareth said, "but I don't think any of you are here to listen to an old man ramble. So I'm going to let Lachlann and Kirilee walk through the symbols they've requested and let those symbols speak for themselves."

Lachlann and Kirilee turned to face us. They walked over to Trina first; in front of her sat a goblet of wine. Trina began to play a simple melody on her pipe as Lachlann lifted the goblet, offered it to Kirilee, and then drank from it himself.

Next they came to me, where I stood with two vials of sand. I ran my fire underneath one vial, causing the sand to turn from pure white to coal black, and then offered the vials to them. They each took one, uncapped their vials, and simultaneously began to pour them into the small glass vase that sat in front of me. The result was a swirling black-and-white pattern within the vase.

They moved back so they were standing in front of Gareth and joined hands again. Kip walked out from behind the table holding a long white ribbon, and I watched as he carefully wrapped the ribbon around their hands. Kip rejoined us behind the table when he was finished, Trina ended her song, and Gareth spoke again. "As this binding of hands shows, today you choose to join yourself to another, to walk through life's storms hand in hand." He gestured at the goblet. "Today you choose to drink from the same cup, to share your life and future with another." Then he pointed at the vase. "And over time, your lives will become like this, layered together to create a beautiful pattern. In some ways you will still be distinct from one another," here he pointed at the patches of black and white in the vase, "and in some ways you will meld together," his hand moved to the places where black and white had turned to grey. "And if a person were to try to separate the two of you again, there would almost certainly be a little bit of the other left in you." He smiled at them. "Now I will lead you in your vows."

I listened as Kirilee and Lachlann spoke their vows to one another, each of them promising to love and be faithful to the other regardless of circumstance. Then Gareth unwrapped their hands, stood back and smiled. "Lachlann and Kirilee, I now pronounce you husband and wife," he said triumphantly. "You may kiss."

Lachlann smiled at Kirilee, then took a step towards her, cupped her chin in his hand, and leaned forward so his forehead was touching hers. They paused for a moment, then he moved in, and their lips met. I grinned. For once, I felt only happiness for them, not jealousy.

Lachlann pulled away a few seconds later, and the entire ship erupted in cheers. Fireworks exploded above us, and at Trina's command a swarm of butterflies flew from behind the table and surrounded Kirilee and Lachlann. The music began to play again, this time a merry, fast-paced tune, and a throng of well-wishers enveloped the newly married couple. I grinned and impulsively grabbed Trina's hand on one side and Kip's on the other. "Come on," I said to them, "let's go congratulate our friends."

The party that followed the wedding was one of the merriest I'd ever attended. Kip had managed to hunt down a large boar, and so there was plenty of meat, as well as potatoes and vegetables and salt fish, and pastries made up by Kezia herself. The adults drank freely from the barrels of rum that Gareth had brought up from the ship's supply. Once most people had eaten their fill, Gareth took the stage and quieted the crowd. "I'd like to play a song now," he said, pulling a pipe out of his pocket that looked like a larger version of Trina's. "This dance will be for the bride and the groom only." People began to move towards the sides of the ship, opening up a dance floor for Kirilee and Lachlann. When they had made their way to the center of the floor, Gareth closed his eyes, raised the pipe to his lips, and began to play.

I understood a few seconds into the song why Kirilee claimed to only be decent at playing the pipe. Kirilee was good by my standards, but Gareth was outstanding. His fingers flew over the slender instrument as a slow, lilting tune emanated from it. On the dance floor, Kirilee and Lachlann smiled at one another and began to sway together in a slow dance. A shower of bright, multicoloured sparks swirled around them as they moved. I looked around, trying to identify who was working the magic, but was unable to pinpoint them. One of the fiddle players joined in with Gareth from where he stood, his harmonies perfectly complimenting Gareth's melody. When the music stopped several minutes later, I couldn't help but burst into applause.

The band began to play after that; this time their melody was a fast-paced jig. Kirilee and Lachlann split up to dance with other people, and the floor began to fill with couples. I glanced over at Kip, remembering how he'd stayed rooted to one spot the last time we'd been at a dance. *Though he's changed a lot since then,* I reminded myself. I took a deep breath and turned to him. "Want to dance?"

Kip let out a nervous laugh. "I'm no good at this type of dancing," he said slowly, "but all right."

"Neither am I," I admitted and took his arm, giving him a reassuring grin.

What followed was an awkward, laughter-filled few minutes of Kip and I trying not to bump into one another as we made fools of ourselves on the dance floor. Eventually, we resorted to spinning in circles while holding hands. By the time the song was over, we were both blushing and hoping that no one had noticed our endeavours. The band began to play a slow dance after that, and to my surprise, Kip offered me a hand. "Another? This sort of dancing I know how to do."

I hesitated and then took his hand. Kip pulled me into the proper position, and we began to move together slowly. He wasn't as heavy as Ambrose, so it was a bit more difficult to let him lead, but after a few minutes I started to pick up the rhythm. I was acutely aware of his touch, of the warmth of his hand in mine and his other hand against the small of my back, the muscles of his left arm tense under my palm, and I bit my lip and willed myself not to revert to the awkward, blushing girl that I'd been around him when we first met. "Where'd you learn how to do this?" I asked, forcing myself to make conversation with him.

"A girl in the woods," he replied.

"Really?" I looked up at him. "You had a girlfriend?"

He laughed and looked away. "No. I've never had a girlfriend. She was just a friend who wanted to trade dance lessons for food. I agreed." He returned his gaze to me. "I'm surprised they didn't teach you how to slow dance in that fancy school of yours."

I chuckled. "We had dances, but Trina and I never went. We didn't think anyone would want to dance with the blind girl or the clumsy orphan. The boys at my school never paid much attention to me."

"Well, their loss. I quite like dancing with the clumsy orphan, y'know." He grinned at me.

I was about to reply when Persius let out a loud screech above us. I frowned and glanced up. "Huh," Kip said. "I wonder what…"

A loud *boom* echoed throughout the party then, and everything stopped.

The musicians ceased their playing, the dancers stilled, and all eyes turned to the man who was standing on the forecastle, his weapon raised in the air. *A gun.* I looked at his gun, the uniform under his now-opened black tailcoat, and the patch over his eye, and felt my heartbeat pick up. *Angus.*

# Chapter Sixteen

**THE CROWD WAS** mumbling now, looking every which way and trying to discern what was happening. I heard several whispers about the Breoch Guard; it seemed that I wasn't the only one who recognized the uniform. More Breoch Guard seemed to be materializing in the crowd; several of the men on deck had opened their coats to reveal their uniforms and guns. *They must have snuck on board while we were partying,* I realized. *Don't let your guard down,* Willem had warned us just hours earlier.

We had done exactly that.

"Quick." Kip was grabbing at my hand, pulling me towards an upside-down dinghy. He pointed at it, and I slithered underneath into semi-darkness. A few moments later, I felt Trina crawl in beside me; Kip remained crouched behind the rowboats.

"Quiet everyone!" I heard Angus's voice boom across the ship, causing the crowd to fall silent again. I slid forward on my stomach, peering out of the narrow gap, my heart pounding in my ears. "Nobody move, or we'll start shooting."

"By the gods, what is this?" Gareth demanded from somewhere out of my vantage point.

"*They* know what this is." I was at exactly the right angle to see Angus stride down the forecastle stairs and onto the deck, his gun pointed in the direction of Kirilee. I felt the blood drain from my face; only now did I see that her dance partner was also clad in an open black tailcoat, and he had a gun pressed to her temple. Her eyes were wide, and I noticed that her hand was closed around the pendant that Willem had given her. Lachlann stood a few feet away; I couldn't see his face from my hiding spot, but I imagined his expression mirrored my own.

Angus walked up to Lachlann and clapped him on the shoulder. "Tell us where the fire-witch is, or say goodbye to your bride."

For a moment, time seemed to stop. I stared at Lachlann, realizing that this was one of the few times outside of Willem's that I'd seen him completely unarmed. *None of us are armed,* I realized. *What a time for them to attack.* Then my eyes swept over the crowd; just hours earlier I'd seen the talents of teleporters and telekinetics and fellow firebrands in action. They, of course, didn't need weapons. *Why aren't they fighting back?*

My thoughts were interrupted by a crunching sound. My head snapped up. Then there was a flash of eerie light, and all heads turned towards Kirilee.

Kirilee had crushed her glass pendant in her palm, and the blue light that had been contained in the pendant now enveloped her. Hazy blue smoke swirled around her for a few seconds, and when it cleared, her eyes glowed bright blue. Her dance partner stared at her, seemingly frozen.

I thought I heard her mumble something, and then I watched as both Angus's gun and the one belonging to her dance partner suddenly flew from their grasp, pulled away by an invisible force, and disappeared into the ocean. They both gaped at Kirilee. Then Kirilee's dance partner keeled forward as her elbow met his stomach. A second after that, Lachlann whirled around and punched Angus in the face with his metal hand, sending him tumbling back onto the deck.

Lachlann closed the gap between himself and Kirilee in a few quick strides and pulled her close. I noticed that all the Breoch Guards' guns were pointed at the couple now, and I stared at Kirilee. *Did she make those guns move?*

"*Incantus dominus intransae.*" Kirilee spoke the words clearly, and I watched in awe as every single one of the weapons flew from the hands of the men and disappeared into the ocean. Less than a second later, each man's sword moved seamlessly from its scabbard and floated to the level of their throats, the blades inches from their skin. My jaw dropped. *How is she doing that?*

Nearly everyone on deck gaped at her for a few long seconds. Then one of the guards, an older man, inhaled sharply. "I…I remember you." His voice shook, and he pointed a bony finger at Kirilee. "I saw you die; my father was your hangman. How in the king's name are you ali—"

He stopped talking abruptly as the knife surged forward, opening his throat. I gawked as he tumbled to the deck, blood gushing from his neck. Kirilee glared at the men. "Do you wish to continue this?" Her voice was hard.

The men stared at her for a few long, dumbfounded seconds. Then Angus struggled to his feet, his hand to his nose and blood oozing between his fingers. "Fall back," he gasped.

I watched as the entire crew of the Lady Liara parted to allow the guards to make their way down the gangplank, off the ship. The moment the last of them had disembarked, the loud din of questions and murmurs returned. I shimmied out from under the boat and helped Trina do the same. She was shaking, I noticed. "What just happened?" she whispered when she was standing up.

I began to fill her in on what I'd just seen. Halfway through, I spotted Kirilee and Lachlann walking over to us, their faces concerned. "Are you all right?" Kirilee asked when they'd reached us. Her eyes, I noticed, had returned to their normal colour.

"We're fine," I told her. "Are *you* okay?"

"I'm a little shaken up, but I'll be all right." She gave us a wry smile. "You know he couldn't have actually killed me, ai?"

*Right.* In the moment, I'd completely forgotten about the curse. "What would have happened if he'd shot you?"

"I'm not sure," Kirilee replied. "I didn't want to find out, though."

"You're bleeding," Kip said, staring at the hand that she'd used to break the pendant. "You want me to find the ship's doctor?"

She glanced down at the blood that was trickling down her arm, pushed her sleeve back with her other hand, and shook her head. "It's not as bad as it looks; I'll bandage it myself. I just don't want to ruin this dress." She chuckled.

I stared at her. "So you…you got your powers back then?"

She nodded. "It was my magic that was contained in that pendant. I…"

Kirilee was cut off by a whistle. All heads turned to see Gareth standing at the wheel. He gave the crowd a sad smile and looked us over. "My friends," he said, "we're going to have to cut this party short. We are in danger right now, and we'll need to take to sea immediately. Those of you who have stations, head to them. The rest of you, let's get this party cleaned up. And also, get *that* cleaned up." He gestured at the fallen man. He was met with a few groans, but people began to drift to their stations regardless.

"What do we do now?" I asked, glancing from Kip to Kirilee.

"You do nothing," Gareth replied, walking over to us. He turned to Kirilee and Lachlann. "You two, go. Enjoy your wedding night. We'll take care of everything. I'm sorry your party had to be cut short; we'll have more dancing again tomorrow night, I promise."

Kirilee shook her head. "It's all right, Captain. We're married now, that's what matters. Thank you for marrying us."

I watched as they turned and walked towards their cabin. "Is there anything we can do?" I heard Kip ask.

He looked over the ship. "Not much, in all honesty. It's getting late; it'd probably be best if you all headed to bed. You'll have a long day of learning tomorrow."

I turned to Gareth, and my eyes narrowed. "I have a question."

"What's that?"

"Why didn't anyone help Kirilee?" I frowned. "I mean, I know that lots of people on this ship are magikai. Why didn't they fight the Breoch Guard?"

"Because most of them are terrified of the Breoch Guard knowing what they are," Gareth replied. "The Lady Liara is a safe haven for many of them, just like the Shrouded Woods is for some of you. And if they used their powers in front of the Breoch Guard, it'd compromise all that—the ship would likely be hunted. My core crew would have fought if I'd ordered it, and I was about to do so when Kirilee broke that pendant."

"Won't the ship be hunted anyway, now that they know we're on it?" Kip asked.

Gareth shrugged. "Hard to say. I'm going to have your group stay below deck whenever we reach a port, until we leave Breoch. Once we're away from land, I doubt they'll follow. I don't imagine they'll care much about Saray and Trina once they're in another country. Also, they don't know where we're headed." He gave us a tight smile. "Anyway, you kids better get to bed."

Kip caught my eye before I turned to leave. "We'll dance again tomorrow?"

"Definitely." I felt some of the earlier excitement return to my chest. Then I turned and headed to our cabin, Trina in tow, hoping that I'd be able to dance with Kip several more times before this voyage was over.

The following morning I was awakened by footsteps on the deck above me and voices calling out orders. I dressed quickly and stumbled out of the cabin, and to my surprise I discovered the sun was already high in the sky. I scanned the ship hastily for a familiar face and located Gareth at the wheel. "Am I supposed to be doing something?" I asked him uncertainly.

"Soon enough, yes," he replied, glancing down at me with a smile. "Go have breakfast, and afterward I'll have Dirk show you and the boy around."

I retreated to the galley, where Kezia was standing over a steaming pot of porridge. Kip was sitting at a table eating, and once I had my own food, I joined him. "Ready to learn how to be a sailor?" he asked me, grinning.

"It should be fun," I replied. "I'm sure you'll be splendid at it—you're so used to climbing trees that navigating the sails should be easy for you."

He shrugged. "You might find that you're good at it too, y'know. You were decent at slow dancing last night, and you said you were no good at that." He blushed when he spoke and looked away.

The young man named Dirk met us when we were done eating and took us on a quick tour of the ship. The names of all the masts and sails and various pieces of equipment went over my head, but I was able to remember port and starboard easily, and so Dirk decided to put us on bow watch for our first shift. It was easy enough; we were meant to scan the horizon for any approaching objects and report them to whoever was at the wheel. Kip was quiet for most of the morning, concentrating, but when we broke for lunch, he talked excitedly to Dirk and me about the task and about how he was eager to learn to navigate the ropes. Dirk laughed at his enthusiasm. "In that case,

I'll show you the ropes after we eat," he said. "I have a feeling that being a sailor is going to come easily to both of you."

Late that afternoon, we reached the port of a small town called Amberline. At dinner that night, Kip, Trina and I sat at a table with Gareth's first mate Harvey, a tall man with a long, dark ponytail. Kirilee and Lachlann joined us as well, and Kip introduced us to a young man who was perhaps a couple years older than him, with blond hair and a sparse goatee. "This is Jasper. He's my new cabin-mate; he just came aboard today."

Jasper smiled and shook hands with everyone. "How long have you been aboard?" he asked us.

"Just for a day," I told him. "Ship life is certainly interesting."

"You kids are enjoying yourselves, then?" Harvey asked us.

We nodded eagerly, and Kip told him about the things that he and I had learned that day. Harvey smiled in approval. "I'm not used to having folks quite as young as you on board," he admitted. "I'm glad you're having fun."

"You're right, it is a little odd to see children on a ship," Jasper said. "May I ask why you're on this journey?"

"I was in danger back in my home city," I told him. "And Trina's hoping to have her eyes healed by the governor of Dundere. Kirilee and Lachlann are escorting us there, and Kip, well, he came along a bit unexpectedly."

"I'm sure the governor will be glad to assist Trina," Harvey told us. "And you'll be safe in Dundere, magic is quite accepted there."

"Can I ask why ships can sail so freely to Dundere from Breoch if the two countries view magic so differently?" Kirilee asked. "If the governor is a magikai, you'd think she'd have issue with a nation that treats magic users the way Breoch does."

Harvey nodded. "The governor certainly doesn't like Breoch's policies," he said. "But Dundere is only a small colony of the larger nation of Candesh, similar to how Breoch was once a colony of Cherin. That's why Dundere only has a governor, not a king. And the king of Candesh sees it to be in the nation's best interests to trade with Breoch, despite their policies on magic."

"Ah." Kirilee nodded.

"Of course, that doesn't change the fact that most in Dundere don't trust the people of Breoch," Harvey continued. "They look at you folks with a mix of suspicion and pity. But they do have a soft spot for magic user refugees. And the governor's not one to turn away any in need." He glanced at me. "If Saray's magic was what had the Breoch Guard chasing her, then you may want to speak with the governor about seeking asylum."

"We'll keep that in mind," Kirilee said.

"So, you folks are magic users, then?" Jasper asked.

"Some of us are," I told him.

"What do you do?"

I explained my gift, and he smiled. "I don't use magic myself, but I find it fascinating. Feel free to show me what you can do, if you want."

I heard music begin to play above deck then, and I brightened. "You still owe me that dance," I said to Kip.

He laughed. "I was just thinking the same thing."

"My husband and I might have to join you two," Kirilee put in.

"Gareth said I can play my pipe with the musicians," Trina added. "So I'm coming too."

"I'll show you my gifts another time," I promised Jasper. Then I grabbed Kip's hand and pulled him to his feet. "Let's go."

"Well, I might as well join all of you," Jasper said. "This sounds like fun."

We headed above deck to music and whirling couples. Trina made her way over to where the musicians were congregated, Kirilee and Lachlann joined the dancers right away, and Kip offered me a hand. Our dancing was very much like last night's, awkward and uncertain, but this time, Kip seemed more relaxed. I was surprised when, halfway through the song, I felt a hand on my shoulder. "May I cut in?"

I glanced back to see Jasper giving us a cocky smile. I threw a nervous glance at Kip and then looked back at him. "Uh, sure, I suppose so." I smiled apologetically at Kip and then turned and took Jasper's hands.

Dancing with Jasper was similar to dancing with Ambrose; he was more muscular than Kip, more assured. I found myself laughing as we whirled around the dance floor, and I had no trouble keeping up with him. When the song ended, it was followed by another fast one, and Jasper pulled me into the dance without invitation. I threw a glance at Kip halfway through; he was standing by the edge of the ship, talking with Trina. He caught my eye for a moment, and then I thought I saw him glaring at Jasper. *Maybe I shouldn't have left him.*

"So let me get this straight," Jasper said to me. "You're from Sylvenburgh, and you're travelling with your best friend and…a bunch of strangers you just met along the way?"

I shrugged. "I suppose so. I mean, I was directed to Kirilee by someone else, but I didn't know her or Lachlann or Kip before all this started."

"Running around the forest with strangers." He chuckled. "Your parents must love that. Let me guess, you ran away from home?"

I shook my head, ignoring the familiar twinge. "I ran away from boarding school," I told him. "I don't know my parents; I'm an orphan."

"Ah. Lucky you, not having to deal with parents."

"Lucky?" I repeated. "I hardly think so. Why, what's wrong with your parents?"

Jasper frowned. "My parents are very…critical. My older brother is the shining star in the family, and my kid sister is a little princess, but everything I do is done wrong, according to my father." His mouth turned up in a half-smile. "I'm quite enjoying this little vacation from him."

I nodded slowly. "Well, you know how to dance," I said, wanting to make him feel better. "You seem to be able to do that much right."

He smiled, his melancholy seeming to fade. "I'm glad you think so."

When the next song was a slow one, I pulled away from Jasper before he could begin to move. "That was fun," I assured him, "but I think I'm going to go dance with Kip now."

He gave me an amused look. "Suit yourself, my dear. I'll be around if you'd like another dance, though."

Jasper walked off in search of a new partner, and I made my way over to Kip. "Sorry about that," I mumbled, suddenly self-conscious. "Would you like to dance with me now?"

Kip hesitated for a moment and then nodded. "I know I'm not as good as he is, but…"

"Don't worry about it," I assured him. "There's only one way to get better, right? Come on."

I offered him my hand, and he smiled shyly as he took it, and we headed to the dance floor together.

# Chapter Seventeen

**THE DAYS MELDED** together after that, each one holding new sights and lessons as we skirted the coast of Breoch, stopping often at various ports to pick up passengers and goods. Kip managed to navigate the ropes without much trouble; I took a bit longer to gain my "sea legs," as Gareth called them, but soon I was opening and closing sails and walking across the yards without too much difficulty. It wasn't all fun; Trina was seasick for a few days, and I found most of the food to be bland and dry, and we had to hide below deck whenever we were in port. Nevertheless, I found that I was enjoying myself by the end of the first week when the ship turned north toward the open sea and, hopefully, away from the threat of the Breoch Guard.

By that point, I had become very aware of the many magic users on the ship who were making use of their abilities. The telekinetics would open and close sails with a few words, and there was one woman with extraordinary sight who could spot a nearby ship miles away. Harvey, I learned, was a stormbrewer—a magikai with weather-controlling abilities—and Gareth claimed that he was the sole reason that our sailing was so smooth on this voyage.

Gareth had taken a liking to Trina when she'd asked if she could join the musicians the day after the wedding; now she followed him around, Bailey and occasionally Persius in tow, doing whatever small things he found for her to do. Thanks to that, and to Lachlann and Kirilee keeping mostly to themselves, Kip and I were left on our own much of the time. Jasper worked with us in the afternoons, constantly peppering me with questions about my magic, and the adults usually joined us at dinner, but after dinner, everyone went their separate ways. Most nights Kip and I would settle on deck with some of the others who weren't on duty, and Gareth would entertain us with music and tales from the sea. After the stories, there was always dancing, which I found myself looking forward to more than I would have expected. Some nights Jasper showed up as well, always asking me for at least one dance, but despite his prowess on the dance floor, I found myself much preferring to dance with Kip.

"I'll miss this," Kip admitted to me on what we were told would be our last night at sea. We had moved to the stern of the ship after the music stopped, and now we leaned against the ship's railing, watching as the band began putting away their instruments.

I nodded. "Me too. But we can always dance more on the way back."

He frowned. "You're coming back with us? I thought you and Trina were staying in Dundere."

My shoulders hunched in a shrug. "I don't know. I mean, Mr. Jeffries seemed to think that the governor would be able to find us somewhere to stay, but I'm not sure if it'll be that easy. I'd be happy to live in the Shrouded Woods, though."

He nodded, smiling shyly. "I could help you and Trina make a home in the woods somewhere, y'know. Maybe we could…"

Kip stopped talking as Jasper sauntered up to us. "Do you know where Kirilee and Lachlann are?" he asked.

Kip frowned. "I've not seen them since dinner."

"Ah. So they're probably in their cabin, not wishing to be disturbed." Jasper smirked. "In that case, I'll ask the two of you. Am I correct that you're heading to the governor's house when we land tomorrow?"

I nodded.

"Mind if I tag along?" he asked. "I have some business with the governor myself. And I'm friends with a fellow in Dundere who rents out carriages, so I should be able to secure us a free ride to the place."

Kip and I exchanged glances. "I don't see why not," Kip said.

"Excellent." Jasper nodded. "I'll leave you two lovebirds alone—have a good evening." He winked at us and strode off, whistling.

I felt my cheeks begin to burn. "Lovebirds?" I repeated, staring at my hands. "Do you think he's trying to set us up?"

Kip laughed nervously. "I don't know what he's trying to do. He probably noticed me getting jealous whenever he danced with you and..." He trailed off.

"Jealous?" I raised an eyebrow. "So you...uh...you do like me then?"

"Oh, c'mon, isn't it obvious?" He looked away from me for a moment and then glanced back. "I'm sorry," he muttered. "I...that's probably not how you're s'posed to tell a girl that you like her."

"Probably not," I agreed, giggling.

Kip shook his head. "This is all so new to me, y'know? I haven't had much time to pay attention to girls; I've been too busy trying to survive." He paused and took a deep breath. "But ever since I got back to Willem's after Lachlann and I got attacked, I've felt...*different* around you. I feel awkward and silly, but I also want to be around you as much as I can." He glanced at me, his ice-blue eyes meeting my own, and gave me a shy smile. "I never thought I'd fall for someone who set me on fire once, but here we are."

I chuckled and nodded. "And I never thought I'd fall for someone who punched me in the face. But as you say, here we are."

"So you feel the same way?"

I gave him another nod, trying to ignore my pounding heart and sweaty palms. "I've had those same kinds of feelings around you since the day we met, in honesty. I remember feeling all embarrassed the night we stayed at your house; I'd never slept in the same room as a cute boy." I chuckled and looked away, my cheeks burning. "I used to think all this romance stuff was so silly, but it doesn't feel that way now, especially since the wedding."

"I know what you mean." He grinned. "I'm glad you asked me to dance that night. I've really enjoyed our dances. There've been times when we were dancing that I've wanted to kiss you," he admitted, ducking his head.

I felt my heart begin to hammer at his words. "And...why didn't you?"

He let out a short laugh and met my eyes again. "First, you don't just go kissing people without asking them, y'know. And second, I don't really know how."

"I don't know how either," I admitted. "But I would think that kissing is kind of like magic. The only way you're going to learn how to do it well is to try."

"Only you're not likely to kill the other person if you do it wrong," Kip said, grinning. He paused and cleared his throat. "Well then. You…want to give it a try, ai?"

I stared at him for a moment, trying to calm my racing heart. "All right, sure."

He grinned nervously in response, then reached up and put a hand under my chin, tilting my face upwards. His icy eyes gazed into mine for a long, tense moment, and then he leaned towards me.

Kip's lips were warm and soft on mine, hesitant at first, then more decisive. He pulled me to himself with his free arm, and his other hand moved from under my chin and into my hair, his fingers winding into my curls. I could feel his heartbeat through his shirt, intense and frantic like my own. I leaned into him, kissing him harder, savouring the strange novelty, the intimacy, of the kiss. For a moment it felt like the world dropped away; the ship around us and our voyage to Dundere and all the times that I'd been hunted since fleeing my school, none of these things were important anymore.

Right now, the only thing that mattered was *him*.

When Kip finally pulled away, he was gasping for breath. He stared down at me for a moment and then turned towards the sea, put an arm around my shoulders, and laughed. "Y'know," he said, "I think we'll have to do that again sometime."

I nodded my agreement and rested my head against his collarbone, then reached up and wound my fingers into his. We were quiet after that, enjoying each other's presence as we stared out at the sea spread out beneath us and the stars above.

Tonight was magical, in every sense of the word.

\*　　　　\*

The next morning, I awoke to a hand shaking me. "Time to wake up, Saray," I heard Kirilee saying. "We've made it to Dundere."

I blinked and then shook my head. "Already?"

She nodded. "We had a stronger wind than we expected last night, and it blew us right into Dundere Harbour. Most of the crew have been up since four this morning, bringing us into port. You and Trina should dress and meet the rest of us outside." She smiled and then slipped from the cabin.

Trina and I dressed silently, but I didn't miss the small smile that played on her lips. *We've made it.* Finally, we were safe in Dundere, and it was only a matter of time before Trina's sight was restored. I was fairly certain I was grinning too as I recalled all that had happened with Kip the night before.

Outside, we were greeted by blinding sun and loud white birds cawing overhead. The sailors on our ship scurried about, doing the final preparations for disembarkment, and beyond them the docks teemed with sailors and travellers and merchants. Men in blue uniforms moved through the crowds; one of them had made his way onto our ship and was speaking with Gareth.

I spotted Lachlann on deck and headed over to him. He was standing with Kirilee, Jasper, and Kip, who gave me a drowsy smile when he saw me. "Morning, Saray." Kip stepped forward and pulled me into an embrace, burying his face in my hair as he hugged me. When he pulled back, everyone was staring at us.

Lachlann was the first to speak. "Did I miss something?"

Kip blushed. "Don't tell me you didn't see this coming," he mumbled.

"Oh, he didn't." Kirilee was smirking at us. "I, on the other hand, saw this coming weeks ago." She turned to Lachlann. "I believe an 'I told you so' is in order, ai?"

"Wait, what just happened?" Trina asked.

"Saray and Kip are acting all lovey-dovey," Kirilee informed her.

"Oh." Trina's face broke into a knowing grin, and she laughed. "I saw that coming too. And I can't even see."

"You had the animals spying on us, didn't you?" Kip said.

"Maybe." She smirked

Jasper was grinning as well. "Well, congratulations, you two." He turned to Kip. "I'll make a point of not dancing with your girlfriend quite as much on the trip home."

Kip and I exchanged a glance; we hadn't discussed yet whether I was officially his girlfriend now. But Gareth called everyone to order before we had a chance to talk further, explaining to us that the guard who was with him would need to come around and take each of our names and reasons for visiting before we were allowed to enter Dundere. My stomach knotted slightly as the guard began making his rounds; I couldn't help but remember Harvey's words about how the Dundere folk viewed us.

When the guard reached our group, Lachlann stepped forward, clearly intending to be our spokesperson. He told the guard our names and that we had come to do business in Dundere and to seek healing for Trina. The guard wrote everything that Lachlann said in a book, a bored expression on his face. I noticed that he had a small gun on his belt and that he wore a strange stone necklace. "Lots of folks from Breoch arriving here these last few weeks," he drawled in an accent I'd never heard before.

"Why's that?" Kip asked, his voice tinged with concern.

But the guard had moved on to talking to Jasper, so Kip's question went unanswered. Once the guard was done with him, Lachlann turned to us. "Well, I think we're free to go," he said. "Jasper, why don't you lead the way, since you know where these carriages are?"

Jasper nodded, and we followed him off the ship, giving Gareth and Harvey a wave as we departed. We made our way onto the docks and began weaving our way through the throngs of people, Trina holding tightly to my arm. I noticed that some of them were garbed in shiny fabrics that I'd never seen before, others had skin darker than Willem's, and a few shouted back and forth in languages I did not understand. I grinned in excitement; I'd never been somewhere with so many different types of people before.

We made it off the docks and onto the edge of a busy cobbled road, and it was here that I got my first true glance of Dundere. Dundere City was not quite as large as Sylvenburgh, but it looked to be just as stately. Tall towers and spires rose up here and there; the buildings, unlike the soot-covered ones of downtown Sylvenburgh, were white and glistened in the afternoon sun, and steep hills rose beyond the city. I whispered to Trina about what I was seeing and then turned to Kip and grabbed his hand. "Isn't this exciting?"

Kip nodded and gave me a small smile, but I saw that his face looked paler than normal, and his jaw was slightly clenched. *What's gotten into him?*

"Wait here," Jasper told us. "I'll be back in a few minutes."

Jasper returned less than ten minutes later in a small carriage with glass windows that was being driven by a uniformed man. "Everyone climb in. It'll be a little crowded."

We all piled into the small space. Trina had to sit on Kirilee's lap for us all to successfully fit into the carriage. I was wedged into a corner next to Kip, with Jasper on his other side, and Bailey sat on my feet, while Persius perched on the roof of the carriage. "They use closed carriages in Dundere because it rains a lot here," Jasper told us. "Don't mind it, though, we'll be at the governor's in no time."

We began moving along the wide cobbled road, and I pressed my face against the cloudy glass and tried to see what was outside. Kirilee leaned against Lachlann, and Trina reached down and stroked Bailey. Beside me, Kip was still silent, rigid.

I was surprised when, a few minutes later, the carriage made a sharp left-hand turn, and the road beneath us turned bumpy. I glanced out the window to see not houses and shops and carriages, but trees. A second after that, I felt a strange ripple go through me, followed by an odd feeling of exhaustion. I frowned and looked around the carriage; both Kirilee and Trina also seemed uneasy. "What was that?" I asked.

"That," Jasper replied, "was anti-magic." Then he moved, lightning fast, pulling a gun from inside his jacket and jamming its barrel into Kip's temple. "And you are all going to do exactly as I say, or Kip dies."

# Chapter Eighteen

I STARED AT him in horror. *What is he doing?*

"What is this, Jasper?" Lachlann demanded. He leaned forward, attempting to shield Kirilee and Trina with his left arm. I could see that his metal hand hung limp, useless.

Jasper smirked at him. "Allow me to re-introduce myself," he said, reaching into his jacket with his free hand. He pulled out a badge and flashed it at us. "Officer Jameson of the Breoch Guard, at your service."

We all gaped at him.

"We've been hunting you folks for months, you know," he continued. "We got word that you were headed to Dundere, so the Guard planted men on as many Dundere bound ships as we could. It took us longer than we'd hoped to find you, but it seems we've succeeded, after that little wedding party of yours."

"What do you want with us, ai?" Kirilee asked, her voice hard.

"I want nothing with you or your husband," Jasper replied. "It's the fire-witch that we're after." His gaze landed on me, and I stared back at him, my heart pounding violently.

The carriage rumbled to a stop, and he glanced outside. "I think we've come far enough." He gestured at the door and then at the other bench. "You three, out. Take the dog with you. Saray, you stay here."

Lachlann and Kirilee both glared at Jasper, neither moving. "You know," Lachlan said, "when your commander tried this, he got a bloody nose."

"But only after your witch of a wife took away his gun." Jasper motioned at Kirilee. "But go ahead, Lachlann, punch me." His voice had turned soft, menacing, and he lifted his chin. "Do your worst. I don't exactly *want* to kill my old bunkmate, you know. If you punch me, maybe I'll feel like I was provoked."

"If you don't want to kill him, then don't." Kirilee's tone was exasperated. "You don't have to do any of this, Jasper. You've just spent two weeks on a ship full of magic users. You've worked with people like Saray and me, you've *danced* with Saray. Y'know we're not monsters." Her voice was both firm and pleading. "I know you have your orders, but you can walk away from them. We'll help you, if you'd like."

Jasper stared at her, frowning, and for a moment I wondered if he'd actually listen to her. Then he shook his head. "You don't understand," he said, his voice tight. "Saray isn't just another elfieblood. This needs to happen." His eyes narrowed, and I heard the gun make a clicking sound. "Now get out, or the boy dies."

The carriage door opened at that moment, and we all stared at the driver. He was smirking and brandishing a gun of his own, and I now noticed he wore a necklace similar to that of the Dundere guards. It seemed to be stuck to his skin, and I thought I saw it glowing slightly. I wondered if it was the source of the anti-magic. "Do your friends need a little persuasion?" he asked, pointing the gun at Trina. "Because I can always shoot the little one."

Panic rose in my chest at his words. "Go," I urged. "Just keep Trina safe."

Kirilee and Lachlann exchanged a glance and began to climb out of the carriage into the green beyond. They helped Trina out and then called for Bailey, who gave Kip a worried look before following the others. Once they were outside, the driver leaned in. "Want me to kill them as we drive off?"

Jasper shook his head. "They're no use to us. Let's go."

The driver slammed the door, and we were moving again. I could feel the carriage turning on the narrow road, leaving our friends alone in the wilderness. Instinctively, I tried to summon fire and found that I could not. "I'm glad you came so willingly," Jasper said to me as we started moving. His voice was cocky again; clearly, Kirilee's words had little effect on him.

"I was going to use Trina to persuade you, but Kip was easier to get to and clearly the next best option, especially after last night." He smirked.

"Why me?" I asked, my voice shaking. "What did you mean when you said that I'm not just another elfieblood? I'm only a kid who ran away from school, why go to such lengths to hunt me down? I'm not in Breoch anymore; I'm no longer a threat."

Jasper eyed me. "Do you know who the Breoch Guard is, Saray?"

"They're...the people who turn magic users into krossemages," I replied.

"We're a lot more than that," was his reply. "We're an organization that was established by King Patrick himself, and our highest officers answer to whoever is on the throne. We hunt magic." He stared at me, his blue eyes hard. "We seek to control it and eliminate it where necessary—and for the most part, we succeed. We create krossemages, as you say, and we keep magic users who haven't offended in check using things like Banishing Day." His eyebrows pulled together. "Every now and then, though, something abnormal catches our attention. Like when a few city guards from Sylvenburgh came to us, claiming that a girl they'd been pursuing in the Shrouded Woods had set one of their men on fire with only her mind." He shook his head at me. "That's not only a rare talent, but an extremely dangerous one."

My eyes narrowed. "Why?"

"Because witches who can cast with their minds are a threat to our system, to everything we've built to keep magic in check," he replied. "There's no point in making you into a krossemage if you can cast with your mind. And we know the fools in the Shrouded Woods are talking about you; we can't let them think that your kind can get away from us. You'll be executed back home, publicly, as a warning."

His last words hit me like a punch in the gut; my breath came in gasps, and I began to shake. "No," I whispered, tears pricking at my eyes. "I...I don't want to die."

"You won't." Kip turned to me and took my hand. "Listen to me, Saray. We'll find a way out of this, between you and me. You're strong and smart, and you've already overcome so much. And I swear I'll do whatever I can to get you away from this filthy traitor and his people." His voice was confident, reassuring even, but I noticed that his hand was ice cold.

"Filthy traitor?" Jasper snorted. "First of all, I'm no traitor. I'm just doing my job. My orders were to capture Saray and bring her home, and that's what I'm doing. And second, you of all people are calling *me* a traitor? After what *you* did?"

Kip turned to him. "What do you mean, ai?" The confidence, I noticed, had gone out of his voice.

Jasper laughed. "You think I don't know? My superiors told me exactly where they got some of their information. It's been quite entertaining watching the two of you fall for one another, knowing what sort of person you really are."

My eyes flickered toward Kip, and I saw that his face had gone pale. "Kip? What is he talking about?"

Kip stared back at me. "Saray, I..." He took a breath and looked away. "Remember how I ran off the night that I first learned about your powers and about what Kirilee did to my family? I was furious about it all, y'know? I felt like everyone in the group had betrayed me, and I was more convinced than ever that magic was evil. So I tracked down the guards who'd attacked us and told them that you were headed into the mountains and to Dundere from there. The Breoch Guard knew you were coming here because of me." His eyes flickered to me briefly. "I felt bad about it later, of course, but I figured we'd be safe once we left Breoch. Seems I was wrong."

I gaped at Kip, my head spinning. "Why...why didn't you tell us a long time ago?" I managed to say.

"Because I was scared." Kip's eyes were full of regret and fear. "I am so, so sorry, Saray."

"You're *sorry?*" My words came out angrier than I expected. "You think an apology will fix this? You acted like you cared about me, Kip. I mean, you even *kissed* me. And now I find out that you're just like *him?*"

"I know." Kip closed his eyes. "Forget me, Saray. Just get yourself out of here, ai? Make a run for it once we get to the docks. If I die, so be it."

Jasper chuckled. "You assume Saray will have that chance. Trust me, she won't." The carriage pulled to a stop as Jasper was speaking. Then the door was swinging open, and the driver was pulling me outside. "Stay close to us," I heard Jasper mumble to him. We were at the docks yet again, I saw; the large white birds flew above us, and the salt air stung my eyes. But we were in a different section of the docks, one that was isolated, away from the crowds. I glanced to my left; sure enough, I was able to make out the sails of the Lady Liara among the many ships that were moored here. The driver was prodding me in the opposite direction of the Lady Liara, towards a single ship docked far away from the others. I glanced back at the familiar sails, wishing I knew how to break away from the driver's anti-magic, from Jasper's facades, from *Kip.*

Two men were approaching us now, the one in front clad in what I recognized as the Breoch Guard uniform but with a large captain's hat instead of the typical guard's cap. Behind him walked a familiar blond man with an eye patch. *Angus.*

The captain clapped Jasper on the shoulder. "Good job, Officer." He glanced at the other man. "Don't you think your son did well, Angus?" My eyes flew open. *Angus is Jasper's father?*

"Mmm," Angus replied, his voice indifferent. "Yes, good work, son."

"We'll celebrate tonight, once we're at sea," the captain went on, taking a step towards me. He pulled out a gun of his own and then grabbed me from the driver and pressed it to the back of my head. He began pulling me towards the ship, away from the others. When we were almost at the gangplank, he looked back at Jasper and nodded at Kip. "Kill him."

The world froze.

Time seemed to stop, my vision blurred, and the noise of the docks went fuzzy in my ears. Jasper's head snapped up, and he stared at the captain; clearly, he wasn't expecting the order. Beside him, I saw Kip go white. His icy eyes met mine, and I stared back at him, my heart pounding in my ears.

"You have your orders, son." Angus's voice had a menacing edge. "The boy is no use to us now, and clearly he's sided with *them.* Do as you're told."

Jasper gaped at his father. For a moment, his eyes flickered to me, and I saw a storm of emotions churning in their depths. I shook my head at him weakly, unable to protest any further.

Then Jasper averted his eyes, and his fingers tightened around his weapon. I squeezed my eyes shut.

The gun went off.

I heard myself screaming. My eyes flew open to see an unexpected cone of fire flying from my hands towards Jasper. Then he was screaming too as his clothing ignited, his arms flailing as he clawed at his shirt. Something hard came down on the back of my skull. The last thing I saw before I blacked out was Kip's lifeless form tumbling forward onto the docks, blood beginning to ooze from a gaping hole in his temple.

# Chapter Nineteen

**WHEN I AWOKE**, I was lying on my stomach. My face was pressed into rough wooden planks, and my hands were bound beneath me by metal shackles. The room that I was in moved in a slow rocking motion, and my head pounded for reasons I didn't understand. *I'm on a ship,* I realized. *And my head hurts because I got knocked out by a Breoch Guard captain right after…*I sat upright as everything came flooding back. *Kip.* My vision began to blur with tears, my breath came in gasps. Out of nowhere, a flame appeared in front of me.

I stared at the flame, unbidden as it was, and felt a small flicker of hope. *At least I can still cast. But I need control.* I gritted my teeth against the grief and panic that churned in my stomach. *Forget Kip,* I told myself. *It's too late to save him. Focus on saving yourself.*

I took a few deep breaths and then tried to assess my surroundings. Given its rhythm, the ship had likely left port already, I decided. My cuffs were attached to a larger chain that was anchored to the floor of the small cell. Three of the cell's walls were comprised of a grid of metal bars. *Metal everywhere,* I noted. *To keep me from burning my way out of my prison. They sure know what they're doing.* I slumped against the wall of the ship and sighed, my panic turning into discouragement. *How do I get out of here?* I recalled how close I'd been to the Lady Liara and wondered if by chance they'd seen the guards take me. *But even if they did, would they help?* They'd been reluctant to intervene for Kirilee at the wedding; why would they do differently now? *Nobody is actually on my side, not Jasper or Kip or anyone. So why should I expect help?*

I wracked my brain for a few minutes, and when I was unable to come up with an immediate solution, I rested my head on my knees, blinking back tears. The slender metal links that joined the two cuffs pressed into my cheek, biting slightly. I winced at the pain and then sat straight up. *Wait a minute.* I stared at the cuffs, an idea beginning to form in my mind.

I summoned the flame again, concentrating to make it into a tiny, searing point of heat. Then I held my arms out in front of me and inched the flame towards the links. I applied the fire to the link that was attached to the large chain, focusing hard to make it as hot as I could. When the link began to glow, I pulled against the heavy chain, attempting to use it like an anvil. I grimaced; the heat was spreading, and the cuffs themselves were becoming uncomfortably hot, but I could see the link weakening, the metal becoming malleable. *Just a few more minutes.*

I kept pulling, squeezing my eyes shut and trying to focus. The pain worsened as the cuffs got hotter and hotter; I thought I could smell meat cooking, and I gagged when I realized it was my own flesh. I turned my head and bit into the fabric of my shirt to stifle a cry of agony. *I have to keep going.*

The link broke suddenly, and I went tumbling backwards, the chain that held the cuffs together snapping completely in two. I yelped as I hit the ground. Then I lay on the floor for a few moments, gasping, trying to ignore the searing pain of my burns.

A loud rumbling from outside the ship interrupted my thoughts, and I looked up, startled. *Was that thunder?* The ship listed to one side, throwing me against a wall. I shook my head; it had been sunny and calm at the docks. But a storm would be useful to me; it would force the crew above deck, which would give me a greater chance of escaping my cell unnoticed. *I need to move.*

The metal gridwork of my cell was too thick to burn through easily, but the floor and ceiling were both wooden. After a moment's deliberation, I chose the floor. I recalled that the brig on the Lady Liara had sat directly above the ship's cargo hold and hoped this ship was laid out similarly. I carefully burned a hole into the wood, ignoring the screaming pain in my wrists. When the hole was large enough for me to fit through, I extinguished the flame and let myself drop into the darkness.

The fall was longer than I expected, and I landed with a thud and a gasp, bashing my knee hard on the floor of a room that was completely dark. Summoning fire revealed me to be correct about the layout; I was in the ship's massive cargo hold, surrounded by wooden crates. I heard the scuffling of tiny feet in the darkness and shuddered. The ship rocked under my feet as I began to creep forward. I moved my fireball around, and I gasped when I saw a cluster of large barrels propped against a wall. *Water barrels.* I stumbled towards them and pulled a cover off one, grunting at its weight. Then I sniffed its contents and, satisfied that it contained water, plunged my hands into the barrel. I let out a groan as the water cooled the metal cuffs and the seared flesh below them.

After allowing myself a few minutes of relief, I moved away from the water and resumed looking around the hold with my fireball. Finding a hatch took me several minutes; once I'd successfully located one, I made my way towards it and then crept up three floors' worth of ladders as quietly as I was able.

I emerged on deck to find low, fearsome clouds rumbling above the ship. The decks were slick with rain, and the sails whipped in the wind. There were about a dozen Breoch Guard on deck, all of them scurrying about as they tried to escape the storm. "We're being followed," I heard the captain say from behind the wheel.

Angus, who was standing with the captain, nodded. "Ready the cannons."

"Yes, sir." One of the guards ducked down a hatch. I climbed the rest of the way onto deck, and hid myself behind one of the water barrels, and then glanced toward the stern. The other ship was just a smudge on the horizon, but I could see that the sky above it was blue and clear; it was obvious that the storm brewing above us was not natural. *Harvey.* I heard a familiar screech above me and looked up to see Persius perched on a yard. Despite everything, I couldn't help but smile; it appeared that I was being rescued after all.

A moment later, there was a faint shimmering in the corner of the quarterdeck, and I stared as six people appeared, an iridescent bubble surrounding them. Gareth stood in the center; he was flanked by Harvey, Landon, Kezia, Dirk, and Janice. A nearby guard let out a yelp of surprise, and every man on deck turned towards them, guns drawn. "Who are you, and what do you want?" the captain demanded.

"My name is Gareth. I'm the captain of the Lady Liara, and I believe you've taken one of my crew prisoner," Gareth replied, his tone even. "We'd like her back."

"The fire-witch?" Angus spat. "She's not your crew, old man. She's a runaway from Breoch, a lawbreaker, and a threat to us all."

"She served on my crew during this last voyage," Gareth replied. "Which means she matters to me. So again, we'd like her back, and if you don't cooperate, we'll be forced to fight you."

"Oh, you and your five friends?" the captain scoffed. "I'm terrified."

"You should be, seeing as we arrived here by magic, and you have no idea what my friends can do," Gareth shot back.

Angus crossed his arms. "I've studied the tactics of my enemies, and I know enough about witchery to know that the shield you're currently hiding behind won't hold if your friends start casting spells."

"And I know enough about guns to know that flintlocks don't fire well in the rain." Gareth drew his sword and grinned, the shield around him dissipating. "Looks like we'll have to settle this the old-fashioned way. Unless, of course, you're willing to hand Saray over."

Thunder rumbled ominously at that moment, and a fork of lightning snaked across the sky, narrowly missing the ship's sails. I saw Gareth glance up and recalled our conversation about ropes being flammable.

Then I had an idea.

This ship was rigged differently than Gareth's; I had to study the sails for a couple of minutes before finding the ropes I was looking for. I stared at my target, wishing for a moment that I'd had Willem teach me how to teleport before leaving his home. *I'll have to wait until I'm sure they can't see me.*

The sound of gunfire brought me back to reality. A second later I saw Janice's body fly backwards. She broke through the railing and plummeted into the ocean with a loud splash, her blood staining the deck where she'd once stood. For a moment, all eyes fell on the forecastle, where a lone guard stood hunched inside a window, his gun unaffected by the rain. I covered my mouth with my hand to stifle a cry. *No.*

Then mayhem broke loose.

Nearly every Breoch guard attempted to shoot at Gareth; only a handful of the guns actually fired, and Landon sent all the bullets into the ocean with a flick of his wrist. Then guns clattered to the deck, and I heard swords being drawn from scabbards. Dirk mumbled a phrase and then disappeared, and a moment later, I heard cries of pain coming from inside the forecastle. Gareth dove at the other captain, swords ready, and the two men began to hack mercilessly at each other. Kezia blinked in and out of teleportation, attempting to slit throats as she moved, and Persius dove at Angus, screeching as he tore at him with his beak. The rain stopped, but clouds still rumbled overhead, and a large fork of lightning snaked down from the sky, electrocuting one of the guards where he stood. I stared at the chaos, uncertain whether I should jump into the fighting or enact my original plan.

And then I felt a pair of strong arms wrap around my waist, pulling me back from my hiding spot. A knife hovered at my throat, its blade pressing into my skin. "Set me on fire again," a familiar voice whispered in my ear, "and I'll open your throat as I burn."

My heart dropped into my stomach. I caught a glimpse of Jasper out of the corner of my eye; he'd changed his clothes, but the left half of his face was blistered and red, and his left eyebrow and eyelashes had been singed off. His hand holding the knife was trembling slightly, I noticed. Despite everything, I couldn't help but feel a moment of satisfaction at my handiwork. "You're lying," I scoffed. "You won't kill me. You said earlier that I was meant to be publicly executed back home."

"You're *meant* to be executed back home," he shot back. "But if I have to kill you now, I'm not afraid to."

I snorted, glancing down at his shaking hand. "That's a lie too. You're terrified of me." I looked at him out of the corner of my eye. "I know what this is about, Jasper. You're trying to make your father proud. You've already shot one of us in the head, isn't that enough?" My voice wavered.

"Shut up," he snapped, his grip on me tightening as he dragged me up to the forecastle deck, knife still to my throat. When he'd positioned himself in full view of the fight on the other deck, he let out a shrill whistle.

I watched as the fighting stopped, and all eyes fell on me. "I believe this is what you are after," Jasper called out to the other deck. "Only she's not yours for the taking, she's a prisoner of the Breoch Guard now. And if you feel the need to come get her, you'll be taking a dead body back with you. Make one move, cast one spell, and she dies." The familiar cockiness had returned to his voice. "Now, how about we stop that storm?"

Everyone stared at me, frozen. The storm above us ceased, and the sun shone down again, its heat drying my soggy clothes. Angus smirked. "It's time to go back to your ship, folks."

I glanced at the ropes once again, remembering my original plan. *There's another way,* I realized.

I took a deep breath and then squeezed my eyes shut and concentrated, channeling everything I'd learned at Willem's into a silent, searing hot spell. Then I let it fly towards the center of the ship.

When I opened my eyes, the outermost rope of the mainsail's shrouds was on fire. I didn't miss the concerned murmur that spread through the Breoch Guard.

I grinned to myself and then looked at Jasper out of the corner of my eye. "Only Jasper won't kill me, not now," I said, raising my voice so the others could hear me. "Because I'm what's keeping that fire under control, and if he kills me, that fire will take the shrouds, and when they snap, it'll set more ropes on fire and maybe the deck too, and chances are you'll lose your ship. And where will you go then?"

"You'll have no choice but to head back to Dundere," Gareth finished for me, "where you'll be arrested by the governor—who, by the way, is a friend of mine. I'm sure she wouldn't mind locking up the lot of you." He turned to the other captain and grinned. "So you'd best let us take the girl and be on our way back to our ship."

The captain stared at Gareth, then at me. I eyed my fire and made it begin to slowly burn through the rope, until it snapped in two. Then I allowed the fire to move upwards and inwards to the next section of the shrouds.

"Well, let her go, you idiot," the captain finally said to Jasper. "And all of you, off my ship, or I'll loose my cannons on yours!"

Gareth gave the other man a mock salute. "Yes, sir." Then he turned to me and motioned me over.

"You haven't seen the last of me, witch," Jasper hissed in my ear and shoved me forward.

I ran across the deck to the others, gasping. Gareth put an arm around me when I reached him, and Persius perched triumphantly on my shoulder. Gareth glanced at Kezia. "Are you ready?"

She nodded.

"Then put out the fire, Saray."

I extinguished the flame with my mind; the rope I'd currently been burning was singed badly but still hung together by a few stubborn threads. Then I nodded at Kezia, who spoke the teleportation spell, and a moment later, I was standing on the deck of the Lady Liara, surrounded by several crew members.

A collective cheer went up at our return, followed by a wave of confusion. "Where's Janice?" someone asked.

"We lost her," Gareth said, his tone solemn. "One of the Breoch Guard shot her, and she fell into the sea. We'll have a service to honour her in the morning." He sighed, and the crew murmured amongst themselves, the collective mood on the ship darkening. Then Gareth glanced at Kezia's arm, which I now noticed was bloody. "Can someone fetch the doctor? There's a few of us who need patching up."

I glanced down at my wrists, still encased in their shackles. I'd all but forgotten about my pain in the excitement of the fight, but it was beginning to return. "I'm going to need tending to as well."

"What happened?"

I explained to Gareth how I'd escaped my prison, and he eyed my wrists and nodded. "You did well, Saray. I didn't know you could throw fire that far with your mind."

"Me neither," I admitted, holding onto the side of the Lady Liara as I watched the retreating ship. Then I turned to Gareth. "What happened here? How did you find me?"

"One of my men up in the sails saw two men leading you and Kip across the docks; he recognized you by your hair. He alerted me that the ship you'd been put on was leaving, and we decided to give chase. I had Harvey create the storm to slow them down. It took the talents of nearly everyone on board to pull off your rescue." He frowned. "Where are the rest of your friends? And what happened to all of you?"

I told him about what Jasper and his driver had done. Gareth's eyes widened at the story of Jasper's betrayal. "I should've known that boy was trouble; he seemed a little too interested in magic." He shook his head. "I'm not too worried about the others, though. Lachlann knows Dundere, Kirilee knows how to survive in the wild, and Trina can take care of any animals that might cause them trouble. I'm sure they'll be fine until we find them."

I stared at him; my one unspoken question caught in the back of my throat. "Kip," I finally managed to say.

"We picked him up before we left. My ship's doctor pronounced him dead on the way out here," he told me. "I have his body in the hold. But don't give up hope just yet. If there's anyone who might be able to help him, it's the governor. One of my men put a preserving spell on him, so he should be fairly intact when we get to her home."

My eyes narrowed. *We're going to try to bring him back?* I hadn't realized that was a possibility.

Gareth glanced down at my hands. "You'd best go see if Kezia can get those cuffs off you, and then see the doctor about your burns. We'll get them fully healed once we're at the governor's, of course." He turned towards the wheel. "It seems it's time to head back to Dundere," he said in a decided tone. "We have friends in need of our help."

Half an hour later we were back at the docks, and Gareth was giving orders to tie up the ship. I hadn't left his side since the doctor had finished bandaging my wrists; now he turned to me and gave me a tense smile. "You and I will go visit the governor right away, get Kip looked at and our friends found," he told me. "I'll rent us a carriage—a real one this time."

I followed Gareth off the ship and through the masses of people, to a stall situated near the docks. Several white carriages—these ones open air and

213

drawn by chestnut horses—sat nearby. Gareth paid for one and led me over to it. "Wait here," he said. "I need to go fetch something."

I nodded and climbed into the carriage while Gareth headed back to the ship. When I saw him next, he was accompanied by Harvey, and they were carrying a long, large bundle wrapped in rough burlap. It took me a moment to realize what the bundle contained. Arriving at the carriage, the two men lifted Kip's body and laid it across the backseat. Persius landed next to it and nudged at it with his beak.

Gareth got into the front seat, and we began our drive to the governor's house, which was located high on a hill in the heart of Dundere City. I looked around as the carriage moved slowly up the hill, taking in the clean white towers, the intricate golden metalwork laced into the tops of the city's many spires, and the broad, green-leafed trees.

The governor's mansion itself was tall and elegant, with golden columns and a fountain in the centre of the circular driveway. Gareth parked the carriage and made his way up to the front doors confidently, as if he were going to visit an old friend.

The door was not answered by a servant, as I'd expected, but by a man who was dressed formally in a waistcoat and boots. He was quite tall, and his hair was remarkably red, with a few grey streaks running through it. "Gareth!" he exclaimed, clapping the captain on the shoulder. "I haven't seen you in ages!"

Gareth grinned and nodded. "It's good to see you, my friend. Listen, is your wife in? You may wish to invite us in, we have quite the…"

"Gareth?" A familiar female voice spoke from behind the man. "Is that you?"

My eyes widened at the voice. "Trina?"

Trina appeared in the doorway, her eyes wide. "Saray!" she screeched. She launched herself in my direction, and I gasped as she collided with me. "I can't believe you're here!" she exclaimed. "I thought for sure that they were going to take you and…" Her voice broke, and I pulled her into an embrace, tears pricking at my own eyes.

"Glad to see you're safe, Saray." I looked up to see Kirilee grinning at me. Lachlann stood next to her, and, to my surprise, Willem was on her other side. She walked up to the man who'd answered the door and put her arm around him, her eyes wide with emotion. "Gareth, Saray," she said, "I'd like you to meet my son, Marcus Westwood."

I pulled back from Trina and gaped at her. "Your...son?" I repeated. "Your son is married to the governor of Dundere?"

"That's exactly what I thought when he opened the door," Kirilee said, her smile widening. "I was hoping to run into him while I was in Dundere, but I didn't expect to find him here, of all places. We've been welcomed to stay with him and his wife for as long as we need."

"Why does he have your last name?" I asked. "I would have thought he'd have Jacien's."

"My father wanted to honour Kirilee's memory—he believed her dead, of course—so he gave me her last name," Marcus answered, giving me a smile.

Gareth was staring at Kirilee. "Now, how'd you manage to have a son who looks twenty years older than you?"

She chuckled. "I'll have to tell you my story later tonight." She glanced past me and frowned. "Where's Kip?"

# Chapter Twenty

MY VISION BLURRED with unexpected tears at Kirilee's question. "He…" I began to speak, but the words caught in my throat.

Gareth put a hand on my shoulder. "As I was saying, you may wish to invite us in, Marcus," he said. "We have quite the tale to tell."

"Yes, come in." Marcus stood back, and I followed Gareth inside.

Marcus led us through the high-ceilinged entryway and into the parlour, a massive room papered in white and gold that held a grand piano, a stone fireplace, and several fat couches that sat atop a thick, intricately patterned rug. A woman was sitting on one of the couches; she rose when we entered. "Good to see you, Gareth," she said to the captain, giving him a smile.

"Good to see you as well, Governor." Gareth walked up to the woman and embraced her. Then he turned to me. "Noelle, this is Saray. Saray, meet the governor of Dundere."

"Pleasure to meet you," I said, looking her over. Noelle had long black hair which hadn't yet begun to grey, an olive complexion, and large brown eyes. She was nearly as tall as her husband, I noticed, and her height was accentuated by her perfect posture. *She looks like a governor,* I decided.

"You as well," she said. "I'm glad to see you're safe; I hear you've had quite an ordeal. Please, sit."

We all sank down into the plush couches, and Noelle turned to me. "I've already heard most of their story." She glanced at Kirilee, Lachlann, and Trina. "Now I'd like to hear yours. What happened after you were separated from your friends?"

I took a deep breath and began to speak. I told Noelle what Jasper had said in the carriage about the Breoch Guard's reasons for pursuing me so relentlessly. I stole a sad glance at my friends as I told them about Kip's admission of betrayal. And I had to squeeze my eyes shut when I spoke of how Jasper had shot him. My words here were met with gasps; I opened my eyes to see that Trina had buried her face in Kirilee's coat and was beginning to cry, while the adults all stared at me with shocked expressions. "So I suppose he and Jasper were both traitors," I concluded, ignoring the lump in my throat.

Trina shook her head, her face still buried in Kirilee's coat. "That's not true," she said, her words muffled. "Kip cared about you, Saray."

Kirilee put an arm around Trina. "I *hope* it's not true," she said. "What happened after that?"

Gareth took over, telling Noelle about the battle that had taken place on the Breoch Guard ship. Then he turned to Lachlann. "Saray and I weren't here for your part of the story," he said. "Tell us how you and the others managed to arrive here before us."

Lachlann nodded and took a deep breath, clearly trying to recover from the news about Kip. "Well, after Jasper dumped us, we decided it was best to head back into town. We'd been walking for about half an hour when Trina remembered that Willem had given her a means of summoning him." He gestured at Trina's pendant. "So we did that, and when Willem showed up, we got him to teleport us straight here, since we had no idea where Saray and Kip had been taken."

"I suppose I should tell all of you my story as well," Noelle put in. "The Breoch Guard have been lurking around here for the past month. Their ship showed up several weeks ago, and their captain came to me with talk of a group of criminals on the run, some children who were dangerous and adults who were supposedly their kidnappers."

Gareth snorted in response. "Really, Noelle? You listened to those magic-hating bastards? You should've known they were full of lies."

"I don't like the Breoch Guard," Noelle replied evenly, "but since we're technically their allies, I have to at least hear them out. And they had all the proper paperwork, so I had to let them stay for a time, at least, to see if they could find who they were after." She frowned. "I thought they were done here a couple weeks back when some of them headed home, but then another shipload showed up three days ago. I'm guessing that they figured out your timeline after their encounter with you at the wedding and decided to intercept you here, where they'd have access to our anti-magic to rein you in."

"How did the driver know how to use that?" Lachlann asked. "I thought only your guards could use anti-magic."

"Chances are he *was* one of our guards, and the Breoch Guard bought him," Noelle replied. "I could have him arrested if I knew who he was. And I think I can officially discredit the Breoch Guard's story, now that they've committed both kidnapping and murder within my jurisdiction."

Gareth nodded grimly. "Well, we made a point of bringing Kip's body with us, so perhaps that last crime can be undone. You think you can bring him back?"

Noelle gave him a sad smile. "In honesty, I doubt it. If the boy has been dead for several hours, then I likely can't help him. I can take a look, though."

"I know medicine," Kirilee was saying to Noelle. "I'll take a look at him along with you."

"His body is in the carriage, but perhaps Willem can teleport it elsewhere, if that would be best," Gareth put in.

"Put him in the backyard for now," Noelle responded. Willem nodded and followed Gareth out of the room. Noelle turned to me. "Saray, let me deal with your burns, before they become infected."

I nodded and walked over to her, and Noelle carefully removed the bandages. I grimaced at the sight of my own flesh; my wrists were seared red, blistering. The worst of the pain had abated after the ship's doctor treated them, but they looked terrible. Noelle didn't seem fazed, though. She gently closed a hand around each of my wrists, closed her eyes, and began to hum. My skin beneath her hands began to tingle, and I felt the last of the pain subsiding. When she removed her hands a minute later, I was staring down at perfectly normal, healthy skin. I shook my head. "I can't believe you can do that."

"I'm glad I could help you," Noelle said, smiling. "Now let's go see if I can do anything for Kip."

The governor's backyard was full of colourful flowers, winding paths, and leafy trees; it reminded me of Hilda's garden, but more organized. Willem and Gareth were hunched over the burlap bundle in a bare patch of grass, and Persius was standing near them, occasionally tugging at the fabric with his beak. "I'll warn you, this isn't pretty," Gareth told us. "Some of you may not want to look." His eyes flickered in my direction; clearly, his comment was intended for me. Then he nodded at Willem, who pulled back the blankets.

I clapped my hand over my mouth when I saw Kip; the entire right side of his head was caked in blood. His eyes were closed—obviously someone had thought to close them—but his mouth hung partly open, and his face was nearly white. "Does he look bad?" Trina asked.

"Yes," I whispered, unable to find words beyond that. Bailey bolted towards Kip, whimpering and sniffing the body, and I watched Trina cringe as the dog undoubtedly relayed to her what he was sensing. He lay down next to Kip, and Persius flew over and settled on Bailey's back, seeming to want to comfort him.

Kirilee and Noelle knelt next to Kip's still form, looking him over. Then Noelle looked up at us and sighed. "Poor boy. I fear this is at least somewhat my fault. If I'd kicked the guards out of Dundere like I wanted to, he'd still be with us."

"Can you bring him back?" Trina asked.

"I'm afraid not," Noelle replied. "Sometimes, if a lifebringer gets to a person in the first few minutes after their death, we can bring them back. But he's been gone for hours. There's not much I can do."

Trina frowned. "But Kirilee came back from the dead, and she'd been dead for longer than Kip. Could you use soul magic, like Claudi did?"

Noelle shook her head and got to her feet. "You have to be a very powerful, knowledgeable lifebringer and have access to fairies to use that. And even if I knew how, I'm not willing to try it. I'm the only lifebringer on this island, and soul magic sometimes results in lost abilities. I'm needed by my people; I can't risk it."

"That, and we don't know what soul magic might do to him," Kirilee put in. "I don't want Kip living the rest of his life in pain." She grimaced.

"But…there has to be a way," Trina's voice had gone up a few octaves, and her lip was beginning to tremble. "What about a…a life transfer?"

A good number of the adults turned and stared at her. "Do you know what a life transfer is, Trina?" asked Willem.

She shook her head. "I just know you can bring people back with them."

"A life transfer is exactly what it sounds like," Willem informed Trina. "It's a spell that takes the life of one person in order to bring back another. It's highly unethical, and I suspect it's illegal in Dundere." He glanced at Noelle, who nodded. "So no, we will not be doing a life transfer."

Noelle walked over to Trina, her eyes sad. "I can't bring him back," she said, putting a hand on her shoulder. "I think you need to accept that. But I can do something else for you." She gave her shoulder a squeeze. "You said earlier that you want your sight restored?"

Trina brightened slightly. "Yes, please," she said, her voice trembling.

"Do you want to wait until later or do it now?"

"I suppose we can do it now. That's why I came here, right?" She gave Noelle a watery smile.

"Of course. Let's head inside, then."

Trina swiped at her eyes once more and then squared her shoulders and let Noelle lead her into the house.

Inside, we all settled on the couches in the parlour, minus Trina and Noelle, who stood in the center of the room. Trina's hands twisted together nervously. "Will it hurt?"

"You might feel a slight burning," Noelle answered, "but nothing very painful. And it'll only take a few minutes. I'm going to warn you, though, I may not be able to make your eyes perfect. Eyes are very complex, and restoring them completely is nearly impossible. I should be able to make them near-perfect, though. Are you ready?"

Trina nodded.

"All right then, close your eyes."

She obeyed, and the governor gently placed her fingertips on Trina's eyes. She began to sing softly, a haunting tune in a language I didn't know. I held my breath as I watched Trina. Her shoulders were hunched, and she clenched and unclenched her hand against her dress as Noelle worked. Noelle paused for a moment, cocked her head, and then moved her hands to Trina's head. Her song became louder, more mournful. Trina gasped and balled the fabric of her dress in her hand, and I shivered involuntarily. For a moment, I understood why the people of Breoch feared people like us. The magic in the room felt ancient, palpable, and almost frightening.

Then Noelle's song ceased, and all was quiet, save for Trina's ragged breathing. Noelle stepped back and took a few deep breaths of her own. "How do you feel?" she asked Trina.

"That was strange," Trina replied, gasping for breath. "You're right, though, it didn't really hurt."

"Are you ready to find out if it worked?"

Trina nodded and smiled.

"All right then. I'm going to put my hand in your field of vision, and when you open your eyes, I want you to stare at that. Seeing everything at once will probably be very overwhelming for you, so I want you to have just one thing to focus on."

Trina frowned. "Does it have to be your hand, or can it be something else?"

"It can be something else if you want," Noelle said, "but nothing too complex or unfamiliar."

Trina hesitated and then spoke with her eyes still closed. "Saray," she said. "Come stand in front of me. You're my best friend, and I want your face to be the first thing I see."

"Really?" I squeaked. "Trina, I'm…I'm honoured."

"You should be." Trina grinned. "Get over here."

Noelle motioned that I should stand, and I rose from the couch and stood in front of Trina, stared down at her face and put a hand on her shoulder. "Now?" Trina asked.

"Now," Noelle said.

I watched as Trina's eyes fluttered open. She blinked several times, and then, for the first time in all our years together, I saw her large dark eyes truly focus on me. Her lips parted, and a tear rolled down her cheek. "Can you see me?" I asked.

She nodded, her eyes wide in awe. "You look just how I imagined," she whispered. She stared at me for a few seconds longer, then looked beyond me for a moment, shook her head and closed her eyes. "Noelle's right," she said. "Too overwhelming."

I laughed and pulled her to myself. "We did it, Trina."

"We did," she replied in a choked voice, returning my embrace. She pulled away and stared at me again, shaking her head. "This feels like a dream."

"Trina?" Noelle was moving into her field of vision now. "I'm Noelle. I want to do some tests on your eyes, and then you can meet the rest of your friends, all right?"

Trina nodded.

"How many fingers am I holding up?" Noelle asked Trina.

"Three."

"Good. All right, now I want you to follow my hand with your eyes." Noelle watched as Trina did as she was asked and then smiled, satisfied, and beckoned to the others. "All right, everyone. Take turns standing in front of Trina so she can see you—we don't want to overwhelm her."

I stepped away from Trina and let each of the others move in. Kirilee, Lachlann, Willem and Marcus each took their turn reintroducing themselves. Gareth had disappeared from the room, and a moment later, he returned with Bailey in tow. Trina grinned at them both. Then she looked at Bailey, and her expression sobered. "I want to see Kip."

A somber silence fell over the room. "Let me go outside and clean him up a bit," Kirilee offered. "Then you can see him." She glanced over at Lachlann. "Are you going to get healed while we're here?"

Lachlann frowned for a moment, then shook his head and patted his metal arm. "You know, I'm rather proud that I managed to oversee the crafting of a working arm and hand for myself. And Kip did a large part of the forging, so it's a good tribute to him. I think I'll keep it, for now at least."

Kirilee nodded and then filled a basin with water, picked up her pack, and disappeared into the backyard. Noelle looked at Trina and smiled. "Let's get you walking around slowly. It'll take you a bit of time to process seeing things while moving."

We led Trina around a section of the main floor of the house. She and I both gaped as we took in the rich mahogany furniture that sat in the dining room, the massive crystal chandelier and curved, sweeping staircase of the home's entryway, the library that rivalled Willem's for size and grandeur, and the intricate tapestries that hung in every hallway. Never before had I been in such an opulent home. After several minutes we heard Lachlann calling us, saying that Kirilee was ready for us. I led Trina outside into the garden; she let out a small shriek at the abundance of flowers surrounding us and stared at Persius, who was perched on Kirilee's shoulder. Then she walked slowly towards Kip.

Kirilee had done a good job of cleaning Kip up. His face was still ghostly white, but it was peaceful now and free of blood, minus a bit that was caked into his hair. Trina stared down at him and shook her head. "I think I remember him," she mused. "It's hard to tell with his eyes closed."

"He looks a lot better now," I said, glancing at Kirilee. "You did a good job."

"He doesn't look how I imagine dead people to look," Trina said. "He looks like he could wake up any minute and..." Her voice caught, and I watched as she covered her face and began to cry again. Kirilee moved over and pulled her into an embrace. "This isn't right," Trina wept, leaning into her shoulder. "I...I'd gladly be blind again if we could have him back, I..." Her words were lost in her sobs.

I watched as Kirilee's arms tightened around Trina, the familiar hot ball of anger roiling in my stomach again. "You shouldn't wish for things like that, Trina," I said. "He betrayed us. Who knows if he even cared about us at all?"

Trina's head snapped up, and she glared at me. "Stop saying things like that, Saray!" she protested. "It's not true, and you know it!" Her voice broke again, and she buried her face in Kirilee's shoulder. Kirilee raised her eyebrows and shook her head at me.

I turned away from her and Trina and stared at Kip's body, trying to ignore the lump rising in my own throat. *Trina's right about one thing,* I found myself thinking. *This doesn't feel like it's supposed to.*

Finally, we'd done what we set out to do. We were safely in Dundere, and Trina's eyes were healed. But nothing felt right or complete, not after all that had happened.

Dinner that night was one of the fanciest meals I could ever remember eating. Fish was a staple in Dundere, Noelle told us, and several of the courses contained fish cooked and flavoured in all sorts of exotic ways—a seafood bisque, grilled prawns with spices I'd never tasted before, a white fish cooked in some sort of red sauce. I barely tasted the meal, though; I had to force myself to eat. My head ached, my body felt like lead, and my stomach was twisted into a series of knots. The adults made polite conversation, but I didn't miss the concerned glances that both Kirilee and Lachlann kept shooting in my direction. Trina, on the other hand, seemed to be avoiding looking at me altogether while she picked nervously at her food.

During dessert, Willem cleared his throat. "We have a rather delicate matter to discuss," he said. "What exactly do we wish to do with the body in the backyard?"

I felt the mood at the table darken. "I can take him back to Breoch, so long as that preserving spell that's on him holds," Gareth offered. "But I'm not sure where'd be best to bury him. It sounds like he has very little family there."

"I'm sure Saray and I could find a good place for him," offered Trina, eying me.

Gareth turned to her. "Only you're not going back to Breoch," he said. "Well, perhaps you could. But certainly not Saray."

My eyes narrowed. "Why's that?"

"After what nearly happened to you with the Breoch Guard?" Gareth shook his head. "It won't be safe for you to set foot in Breoch for several years, if ever again, my dear. I wouldn't be surprised if the Guard sends more men out this way looking for you, but here you'd be under Noelle's jurisdiction, so they'd have more trouble taking you than they would back in

Breoch." He shook his head. "You're going to have to stay here. I'm sure we can find a place for you."

I nodded slowly. *Now where will I end up?*

"And Lachlann and I need to return to Breoch," Kirilee put in. She glanced at her son. "We'll visit, but I can't live here. I belong in Firenholme." She turned to Lachlann. "You and I could bury Kip somewhere, though I'm not sure where. Trina's his only family that we know of; it might be best to bury him here if she hopes to stay. Either way, I've an idea for how to bury him."

Trina nodded. "I...I think I want to stay with Saray," she said, giving me another cautious glance. "So maybe we should bury him here."

"What's your idea?" Marcus asked Kirilee.

"Do you have any trees native to Firenholme here in Dundere, ai? I feel like it'd be fitting to use one for this."

Marcus frowned. "We have one, yes, on the other side of the island. It's the sort that lights up at night."

"A viletta," Kirilee said. "Perfect."

She told us her plan, and everyone seemed to think that it would be a good memorial for Kip. "If we're going to do this, we won't be able to lay him to rest until the day after tomorrow," cautioned Marcus. "Noelle is working tomorrow, and I have a guild meeting, so we can't make the trip until the day after." He glanced at Willem. "Do you think the preservation spell will hold until then?"

Willem nodded. "I'll go put a new spell on him tonight and then again tomorrow night, just in case it doesn't."

"Then he should be safe in the garden. I'll wrap him back up after you're done." He looked around the table. "Are all of you in need of a place to stay for the next couple of nights? I've spoken to Kirilee about herself and Lachlann and the children, but what about the rest of you?" He looked at Willem and Gareth.

Willem nodded. "That'd be lovely, thank you. I have friends at the school of magic I'd like to visit in the morning."

Noelle smiled. "That can be arranged; I'll drop you off on my way to work. Gareth?"

Gareth chuckled. "I'll be returning to my ship tonight—I need to hold a memorial for Janice tomorrow morning. I can return the evening after next to help with Kip's burial if you'd like, though."

"Please do," Noelle said. She looked around the table. "I'll have someone show you to your rooms. You should retire soon; you've all had a very long day, and tomorrow will be busy as well."

# Chapter Twenty-One

**I WAS AWOKEN** the following morning by a shriek. I sat bolt upright, uncertain where I was for a brief moment, taking in the massive four-poster bed, the sunlight streaming onto the fluffy white bedspread, the colourful, daisy-themed wallpaper. *Who's screaming?*

Then I heard a door open into the room next to me, and then I heard voices. Kirilee's and Trina's. *Right. I'm at the governor's mansion in Dundere.* I flopped back on the bed and groaned as everything that had happened the day before crashed into my mind like a wave.

I lay there for a couple of minutes, listening to Kirilee's and Trina's muffled voices through the wall, my head spinning as I recalled the horrors of yesterday. Then I dragged myself off of my bed and to the window and stared out at the garden spread out below me, just to make sure I was remembering everything correctly. The long, wrapped bundle was still there. I sighed, swallowing the lump that rose in my throat, and made my way out into the hallway. I peeked my head into Trina's room. "Everything all right in here?"

Trina looked up at me and nodded sheepishly. "I woke up and forgot I could see now. It gave me a good scare!" She laughed, but it was a halting, uncertain laugh.

"Are you girls all right if Lachlann and I take the day to ourselves?" asked Kirilee. "We're both fairly tired today."

I nodded. "That's fine. I'm sure Trina and I can keep ourselves occupied."

As it turned out, keeping ourselves occupied wasn't that difficult, especially with Trina's desire to take in as many sights as possible. We spent a good chunk of the morning wandering the garden, both of us intentionally avoiding going near or talking about the ominous bundle on the lawn. Trina gaped at the vast array of colours in the garden, the stately roses and fragrant lilacs and playful multicoloured pansies, and the climbing flowers woven into trellises that arched overhead. Occasional butterflies and hummingbirds darted from flower to flower, much to her delight. I smiled as I watched her, wishing that I could be as happy for her as I knew I should be.

After lunch, we retreated to the library. Trina had learned to read at Willem's using raised dots, and I knew that one of her first tasks as a newly sighted person would be learning to read the alphabet of sighted folks. We went over letters several times; Trina knew the names of them all and seemed to remember the shapes of a few of them from before she lost her vision. Stringing them together into words proved difficult, though, as did writing them out. We stopped after about an hour of practice, deciding to come back to it another day.

Then we wandered the halls of the mansion, curious as to what we might find. We were thrilled to discover a door leading to an unused attic space inside a round tower, which, I told Trina, I would definitely claim for my own bedroom if I lived here. On the main floor, we discovered a massive ballroom in a wing we hadn't been in yet, with glittering chandeliers and maroon velvet curtains and a ceiling that was painted to look like the night sky. In another room we found dozens of musical instruments, including several pipes that were similar to Trina's and a large harp; another room was glassed in and held all sorts of exotic-looking plants. When we reached the room at the end of the hallway, my eyes widened.

In some ways, the room reminded me of Willem's library but more eccentric. There were bookshelves lining the walls, yes, but the room was also crammed with all sorts of things that were not books. An old-looking upright piano sat against one wall; another wall featured a massive grandfather clock. One table held dozens of vials of colourful liquids; another featured all sorts of oddities—a taken-apart watch, an odd-looking globe surrounded by concentric metal circles with writing on them, several rolled-up maps, and a small glass sphere that had what looked like lightning dancing inside of it. The tops of the bookshelves appeared to have a set of miniature train tracks running along them, and a toy train circled the room, seemingly of its own volition. Several large plants hung in the window. I stared at it all. *I could spend days in here.*

I was so enthralled by the contents of the room that I didn't see Marcus sitting in the corner at a worktable, facing away from us. Trina spotted him first. "Marcus? I thought you were at a guild meeting."

Marcus turned and greeted us with a grin. "Oh, hello girls. I got home about half an hour ago. I looked for you, but I couldn't find you."

"What is this place?" I asked him. "And what is all of *this?*" I gestured at the vials, the table full of oddities, the train circling the room.

"This is my hobby room, I suppose you'd call it. And these are my hobbies." His smile widened. "You know how your friend Willem enjoys learning various spells and new types of magic? Well, I enjoy learning how magic intersects with the natural world. Things like alchemy, and astronomy, and botany." He gestured at the vials, the odd-looking globe, and the plants. Then he pointed at the ball full of lightning. "And one of my favourites, electricity."

"Electricity?" I repeated the unfamiliar word. "What's that?"

"I don't know, exactly, but it's fascinating. Watch." He put his hands on the globe. I gaped as his hair began to stand on end. Trina laughed. "It has more applications than just entertainment, though," he explained. "Rumour has it that you can make lanterns that turn on and off with a push of a button using this. Though I haven't learned how to do that quite yet." He took his hands off the glass ball. "Want to try?"

Trina and I took turns putting our hands on the ball and giggling at the effect on one another's hair, and then I turned to him. "What do you do in your guild meetings?"

"Ah. Well, here in Dundere, all magikai are part of a guild, depending on what type of magic they practice. There's a guild for firebrands, and for vanishers, and telekinetics, like me." He glanced at Trina. "From what I hear, talking to animals is a pretty rare talent, so I don't think there's a guild for that."

"What's the rarest talent?" I asked

"That would be my wife's," he replied. "Healing magic is exceptionally rare, which is why it's so valued. Anyway, we have guild meetings once a month. And magikai here are only expected to work their regular job four days of the week. On the fifth day, they work for the guild, doing magic work using their talent. So, once a week I go to building sites and lift heavy things with my mind. Though some magikai choose to work full-time using their talent."

"That seems like a really good system," Trina observed.

"Oh, it is. This place has the use of magic very well figured out." He glanced up at the clock. "I'll tell you girls more about it another time, though. Dinner should be ready right about now."

I felt considerably better at tonight's dinner than I had at last night's. The pall of losing Kip still hung over us all, but my mood had been lightened at least a bit by Trina's and my adventures today and Marcus's room of magical curiosities. It seemed that one of the adults had let Marcus and Noelle know about Trina's preferences; tonight there were several grilled vegetable dishes accompanying the fish. Marcus had decided that this was the time to tell us all his own story, and I attempted to distract myself from the situation with Kip by focusing on his tale.

"They took me when I was fifteen," he told us, his voice solemn. "I tried to hide my gift, like most magic users, but I wasn't careful enough. And once they'd caught me, well, some unpleasant things happened." He gave Lachlann a sly grin. "You should be happy that you were unconscious when they started cutting parts off of you." Lachlann raised his eyebrows and nodded.

"After that, I was a slave to an older couple for nearly twenty years. Eventually, they both died, and I was inherited by their son. And it took me less than two years to do something that made him very angry. I knew I'd need to flee or face death."

"What'd you do?" asked Trina.

He laughed. "Well, I'm not sure if this is a story for young ears, but what I did is fall madly in love with his wife. And it didn't take long for her to return the sentiment."

Trina's eyes widened. "I can see why that would upset him."

"Well, he wasn't a kind man, so I can't quite blame his wife for falling for someone else," Marcus said. "Anyway, things progressed as they do, and one day she came to me and told me she was with child. She hadn't been with her husband in years; she insisted that he'd know I was the father and, therefore, I had to flee. So I did." He glanced at Kirilee. "I met you after that, of course, and once you'd gotten me to Flavalan, I headed for the docks and walked around, waiting for talk of a ship heading to Dundere. When I got wind of one, I hid on it. The captain found me once we'd been at sea for a day and found it mighty funny that I'd stowed away on a ship where people can sail for free so long as they work." He grinned.

"Do you know what happened to the child?" asked Kirilee.

Marcus shook his head, his smile fading. "I wish I did, but I can't exactly go back there and ask. I still wonder, though. I just hope they're safe and healthy."

Kirilee nodded. "It's hard not knowing where your kid is, isn't it?"

He gave her a sad smile. "Yes, yes it is." He sighed and then straightened up. "So, I made it to Dundere, and within about a month I'd located my father. I found out that he'd gotten married here, and now he had two stepsons who are a little younger than me. Once we were reunited, he told me he'd take me to the governor for healing. So I showed up here and was greeted by the most beautiful, strong, and accomplished woman I'd ever met." He smiled at Noelle. "I was so overwhelmed by her, and so grateful to have my hand and tongue back, that I asked her to dinner the next day. Perhaps that wasn't too smart; I'd forgotten how to eat the way most people do, and I probably looked like a fool. But she was kind to me, and that evening she told me that she hadn't been on a date in years. Most men were too intimidated by her to court her, she said. I said that was their loss."

"We were married a year later," Noelle put in, "and I've never looked back. I married a bit too late in life to have children, but beyond that I have no regrets."

"Is your father still alive?" asked Trina.

Marcus shook his head. "If he was, I would have invited him over," he said. "He passed two years back, and his wife soon after. I'm still good friends with my stepbrothers, though."

"Were your hand and tongue completely restored?" Lachlann asked Marcus.

"It took me about a year to be able to speak without slurring," Marcus replied. "As for my hand, it works just fine, but my left hand is the dominant one now. It's the one I cast with now too." He gestured with his left hand, and his water glass floated up towards him. Trina giggled. "Sometimes I wish Old Man McAllister could see me now. Completely whole, freely using my magic, and married to Dundere royalty." He grinned.

"Dear, I'm a governor, not a queen," Noelle replied, but she was smiling.

"Who's Old Man McAllister?" I asked.

"My old owner," he replied. "I suppose his son would have been Young Man McAllister, though he's not so young anymore, and...what is it?"

I stared at Marcus, my heart thudding in my chest as longings I'd pushed down for years surfaced in my mind. "Marcus," I said, my voice coming out oddly high-pitched, "you said you got that man's wife pregnant, and their last name is McAllister, and you don't know what happened to the kid, right?"

"That's right."

"Well, *my* last name is McAllister too. And I'm an orphan. And...you have red hair."

The table went silent, and I watched as everyone turned to look at either Marcus or myself. He stared back at me, his eyes wide. Then he took a deep breath. "All right," he said, "let's see if the details line up. How old are you, Saray?"

"Sixteen."

"What month were you born in?"

"August," I told him. "My birthday is coming up."

He paused, counting on his fingers, and then nodded. "And where were you raised?"

"Sylvenburgh Academy," I told him. "It's a boarding school."

"A boarding school? How does an orphan end up at a boarding school?"

I frowned, uncertain how to explain, and Lachlann cut in. "Sylvenburgh Academy mostly operates as a typical boarding school. But they also accept young children whose parents need to abandon them for various reasons but have the means to ensure their child gets a good education," he explained. "My brother works there."

Marcus nodded and then turned back to me. "That does make some sense. Lillian told me she might give the child up. She was worried about how her husband might treat them, but I wonder if she was also afraid the child would be a magikai and wasn't sure how to protect them from meeting a similar fate to mine."

I nodded, my heart still thumping in my chest. "Lillian," I said. "Is that…"

"That's the child's mother," he said. "Or, very likely, *your* mother."

"You…you think I'm right, then?"

"Well, I can't be completely certain. I don't know if there's any magical sort of way to test for these things. But the details all fit together. I think there is a very good chance, Saray, that you are my daughter." He gave me a smile, but it was hesitant; clearly, he was waiting to see what my reaction would be.

"My friend Hilda might be able to use magic to determine if you're both of the same bloodline," Willem put in, but I barely heard him. I was staring at Marcus, my head swimming. *I can't believe this is happening.*

I'd imagined this moment more times than I could count. I'd rehearsed, over and over, the things I'd say if I ever happened to come across my parents; I'd memorized the questions I would ask them. Now my words rushed out of me in a confused jumble. "I…I can't believe this. I've spent so long wondering why I was left at the school, and who my parents were, and I have so many questions, and I…" My voice broke, and a rogue tear escaped my eye. Kirilee, who was sitting next to me, put a hand on my shoulder.

"Well, perhaps you and I need to take a walk so you can ask me those questions," Marcus suggested.

I nodded weakly, and then my head snapped up. "Wait." I turned to Kirilee. "So if we're right, this means that you're…my grandmother?"

"So it would seem." She grinned. "I'd no idea I *was* a grandmother. No wonder you remind me of myself at your age."

"Do you want to go for our walk now or wait until after dessert?" Marcus asked me.

My shoulders hunched. "Now. I'm not hungry anymore."

He nodded, pushed back his chair and stood. "Let's head outside then."

The sun had just dipped below the horizon when we got outside, and the garden was bathed in the fading light. The scent of night-blooming flowers filled the air, and I could hear crickets playing their nighttime song. Marcus led me along twisting cobbled paths to the back of the garden, giving Kip's body a wide berth. He was silent at first, perhaps waiting for me to speak. When we reached a simple wooden bench in the far corner of the garden, he took a seat and then gestured that I should do the same. He turned to me. "All right, Saray. Ask me all your questions."

The initial shock of tonight's revelation was wearing off, and I cringed at the familiar bitter feeling in my stomach. I'd always read stories of joyous, tearful reunions between long-lost parents and children, but this didn't feel joyful to me. When I spoke, I could only get one word out. *"Why?"*

"Why?" he repeated. "Why were you given up as a child?" He sighed. "I can't answer that for Lillian. But I think you understand why I ran."

I nodded, tears pricking at my eyes. "But why didn't you come back for me? When I was older?"

"I didn't know where you were," he said. "Though I admit, I did entertain the thought. I thought about going back to Sylvenburgh and looking for you several times, but…"

"You *should* have!" I turned to face him. The tears had begun to escape, and now they trickled down my face as I stared at him. "Being raised as an orphan in Sylvenburgh Academy was awful! The other kids, they were terrible to me just because I didn't know who my parents were. And here you were, in your cushy governor's mansion, and you *didn't come back!*" My voice broke, and I buried my head in my arms and sobbed.

I felt a tentative hand on my shoulder, and part of me wanted to shrug him off, but there was another part of me, small but stubborn, that resisted that urge. "I wanted to come back for you," I heard him say, his voice gentle. I looked up at him through my tears. His eyebrows were knitted in concern, but he didn't seem angered by my outburst. He sighed. "Saray, I wanted to come back, but I had no idea where to even start looking for you. I didn't want to go anywhere near Lillian or her family, for fear of what they might do to me. I didn't know if they'd kept you, or given you up to another family, or put you in an orphanage. I had no idea that Sylvenburgh Academy even took in orphans. Even if I had searched for you, I likely wouldn't have found you." He sat back. "But none of that changes the fact that you spent all those years wondering why you were given up. And I'm so incredibly sorry for being a part of that."

I blinked back fresh tears and stared at him. "Why aren't you mad at me?"

"Mad at you?"

"For...lashing out at you like this. Don't you want me to fall into your arms, weeping and saying how much I've missed you? Isn't this supposed to be a happy occasion?"

A smile played on his lips. "If you want to fall into my arms, weeping and saying how much you missed me, I will gladly return your embrace. But I understand your position better than you realize. Or have you forgotten that I was abandoned as a child too?"

"By...Kirilee?"

He nodded. "I grew up believing my mother had died in childbirth. When I found out she was still alive, let me tell you, I had questions. The main one being exactly what you just asked me." He met my eyes. "Why didn't you come back? And she answered my questions, and her answers made sense, but it didn't change the fact that I grew up with a hole in my life where my mother should have been. Nothing can fix that. So I understand why you're angry. And you're allowed to be angry."

I sighed, rubbing my eyes as my anger began to fade. "I might not be so angry if this had happened differently."

"What do you mean?"

"It's just...the last couple of days have been awful. Having Jasper turn on us, finding out Kip betrayed me, seeing him get shot..." My voice broke again, and I swallowed hard. "And then everything that happened on the ship. I'm happy that Trina got her eyes healed and that you and your mother got to be reunited, but everything else has been terrible."

"And now this, to top it all off," he said.

I nodded and looked at him out of the corner of my eye. "Sorry for taking it out on you. Nothing that happened yesterday was your fault. There are other people who deserve my anger more than you." I glanced across the garden at the bundle on the lawn, now barely visible in the fading light.

Marcus followed my gaze. "You're still pretty angry at Kip, huh?"

"Do you blame me? I thought he was on my side, that he was looking out for me, that he *cared*. And then I find out that he went behind our backs like he did."

Marcus nodded. "He made a bad choice, and then he fled from it," he said softly. "Sounds familiar."

I turned to him. "So what, you think I should just forgive him for what he did?"

He shook his head. "Whether or not I am your father, it's not my job to tell you who to forgive. You're allowed to be angry at Kip. Do you mind if I offer some insight, though, as someone on the outside of this situation?"

I shrugged. "If you want to."

Marcus sat back. "I think you might want to look at the timeline of Kip's betrayal."

"What do you mean?"

"Well, if I understand the story correctly, Kip didn't betray you after he'd gotten close to you. He betrayed you immediately after finding out that you'd been hiding the fact that you're a magikai and then learning that my mother killed his aunt. He probably felt like *he'd* been betrayed by both of you. Then he was forced into travelling with you all, and the way things unfolded from there helped change his mind about you."

I nodded slowly. *Kip felt betrayed by* us. He'd said those exact words to me right before we'd arrived at the docks. Then I sighed. "But if he really cared, why didn't he warn us earlier about what he'd done?"

"Probably because he was falling for you, and he was afraid you'd react exactly how you're reacting," Marcus said. "Remember the part in the story where you hid your talent from everyone because *you* were afraid of how *they'd* react? People make bad decisions when they're scared, Saray. Kip's no exception."

I sighed. "I suppose that's true."

He was silent for a few moments and then glanced over at me. "Back to what we were talking about before, do you have any more questions for me?"

I frowned and then nodded. "Can you tell me about…Lillian?"

"Lillian," he repeated, nodding. "Lillian was a lovely woman. She was smart and fiery and incredibly kind. She never once treated me wrongly, and this was in a day when many folks who owned krossemages abused them. But she was stuck. She and her husband, Caspa, had been forced into an arranged marriage, and as far as I could tell, neither of them was happy. They had two little boys, and when I first came into the home, they all seemed miserable. The boys grew to like me, though, and once Lillian and I had fallen for each other, well, it was like she was lit up from the inside. She changed, she became happy and funny and…it was almost like she was floating." He smiled slightly. "In a way, I regret messing their family up the way that I did. I hope Caspa didn't mistreat her once he found out what had happened between her and me. But I'm glad I got to give her those few months of happiness." He sighed. "I'm quite content here in Dundere, with Noelle. But I do wonder about Lillian from time to time."

"Do you think she'd want to meet me one day?"

He frowned. "Perhaps. I don't think it would be safe for you to look for her yet. But in a few years maybe, once you're an adult and aren't in as much danger."

"Do I look like her at all?"

He studied my face in the fading light. "It's been over seventeen years since I last saw her, so it's hard to recall exactly. But yes, I do think I see some of her face in yours. And the curly hair you got from her. Your height and your colouring, though, are very much from me."

I nodded and tugged at a curl, wondering exactly what my mother looked like.

"Any other questions?"

"Just one." I looked at him out of the corner of my eye. "Did you…miss me? Did you think about me much?"

"Oh, Saray." He sighed. "I never stopped thinking about you. For years I've wondered what sort of person you grew to be. And now, finally getting to meet that person…" He looked away. "It's an honour," he whispered, his voice husky. He took a deep breath and looked back at me, tears glinting in his eyes. "I'm not going to force myself into your life, Saray. I haven't been a father to you all these years, so I'm not going to demand that you treat me like one now. But even if you decide to walk away after tonight and not have me in your life in any way, it will have been an honour just to have had a glimpse of the young woman you've become."

I stared at him, blinking back fresh tears of my own, uncertain how to respond to his words.

After a moment, he glanced up at the darkening sky. "It's getting late. As you said yourself, you've had quite the last couple of days. It's likely best that you get some sleep."

We walked back through the garden in silence, and when we were on the porch, I turned to him and gave him a small, tense smile. "Thank you."

"For what?"

"For…letting me vent at you like that. I feel a bit better now."

"Good." He reached out and put a hand on my shoulder again. "I know I haven't been there for you, Saray, but I'm here now. Whatever you need, let me know."

I nodded, and part of me wanted to step towards him and hug him, but things still felt too odd, too tense. I reached up, put my hand on his and gave it a quick squeeze. "Goodnight," I whispered and then turned and walked into the house.

# Chapter Twenty-Two

MY SLEEP THAT night was uneasy. I dozed on and off, my dreams troubled and confusing, only to find myself wide awake after some time. It was still quite early, I surmised; the birds were silent, and there was no light making its way through the curtains. I sighed and sat up. *I'm not getting back to sleep.*

I dressed quietly and padded across the hallway and down the stairs. I found myself walking towards the back of the house without thinking, my mind set on the backyard and what lay within it. I'd avoided the bundle yesterday, but now I felt oddly drawn to it. Last night's conversation with Marcus had helped me clarify some of what I was feeling about Kip, to find words for my pain.

Now it was time to talk to him about it.

I pushed open the back door and was greeted by the cool morning air. I shivered and wrapped my arms around myself. The sky was beginning to lighten; I could just see the paths of the garden and the outlines of the trees and the ominous bundle that lay in the bare patch in the center of the yard. I walked over to the bundle and stood over it for a few long moments, and then slowly, I reached down. My fingers brushed Kip's face as I drew the burlap back, and I shuddered. His skin was cold, as cold as the early morning air that bit at my cheeks. *Cold as death.* My mind wandered back to the moment, only three days before, when he'd pressed his lips against mine and held me to himself, his skin warm and inviting against my own. Then I pushed the memory away, the familiar knot tightening in my stomach.

"I don't know what to do with you," I muttered to the corpse in front of me. "Nothing's like it should be. We're supposed to be happy right now. I mean, Trina should be thrilled about getting her sight back. But she's not as happy as she should be because you're not here. And Kirilee and Lachlann are acting all worried about me and Trina. And Janice from Gareth's ship is *dead*, and it's all because of *you!*" The anger in my stomach flared, hot and raw, and my hands began to burn. I shoved them in my pockets and sighed. "But Marcus...Father...whoever he is...he said some things last night that made sense. It did seem like you cared about me. About us." I shook my head. "I'm going to miss you, but I'm still so *angry* at you..." The tears came unexpectedly, and I turned away, as if a corpse could see me cry. Then I turned back. "*This*," I said, gesturing at the body in front of me, "didn't have to happen. You could still be with us, and we could still be together, if you hadn't been so *stupid*." The tears were coming hard now, and I turned away from Kip and walked further into the garden, trying to rein them in. Unable to do so, I sank to the ground, buried my face in my arms, and wept quietly.

After some time, my weeping was interrupted by a sob, this one louder than mine. My eyes narrowed, and I stood and turned towards Kip's body. Kirilee had come outside and was kneeling over Kip, her form barely illuminated by the pre-dawn sky, her shoulders shaking as she wept. I swiped at my own eyes and stared at her. *I've never seen Kirilee cry like this.* Part of me wanted to walk over and comfort her, or perhaps cry with her, but my feet wouldn't move. *I don't think she knows I'm here. And she probably wouldn't want me to see her like this.*

I stood rooted to my spot in the garden for what felt like a good hour, watching Kirilee cry. Then the door behind her opened, and Lachlann walked outside, his hair dishevelled. I watched as he walked towards his wife, knelt down next to her and put an arm around her. Kirilee's sobs turned to gasps, and she leaned into him. "This...this isn't right..."

"I know." Lachlann's voice was barely a whisper. "It's hard."

"It's more than that." She pulled away from Lachlann and stared at him. "I've lost plenty of people in my lifetime, Lachlann. And usually I can accept it. But this just feels *wrong*, y'know?" She dabbed at her eyes. "There has to be a way to bring him back. I spent all of yesterday and all of last night trying to come up with something, and I just can't..." Her voice broke.

Lachlann pulled her against himself again. "If there is a way, I'm sure you'll find it." He sighed, and his eyes wandered around the garden. Then they settled on me. "Hello, Saray."

Kirilee's head snapped up, and she stared at me. I raised my hands. "I wasn't trying to eavesdrop," I said, walking towards them. "I was out here before you, wandering around, and I didn't want to disturb you."

Kirilee nodded, and I thought I saw her blush. "I...I'm sorry you had to see me like this," she said, her voice shaking slightly. She put her hand on her chest and winced. "The pain is worse than normal right now, and I s'pose you heard how I'm feeling about Kip."

I nodded.

"How are *you* feeling?" Lachlann asked me. "Still angry? You've been crying too."

"Marcus and I had a good talk last night, and I'm feeling a bit better about Kip now," I told him. "It's strange. I'm still mad at him, but I'm sad as well." I sighed, blinking back fresh tears. "I'm going to miss him."

Lachlann nodded. "It's perfectly fine to be sad and angry at the same time."

"How was your conversation with Marcus, anyway?" Kirilee asked.

"It was...emotional," I replied. "In honesty, I was pretty angry at him for not coming back for me. But we talked it out, and he didn't get upset with me for being angry, so that helped. I think. I'm glad I found him." I grinned at Kirilee. "I still can't believe you're my grandmother!"

She gave me a watery smile. "I can't believe it either. I knew the fairies brought us together for a reason."

I nodded in agreement. "I should leave you two alone to talk. Thanks for checking on me." I gave Kip's body a parting glance and then headed back into the house.

My emotions had settled down somewhat by the time Trina, Kirilee, Lachlann, Willem and I set out on our trip across the Isle of Dundere with

Marcus an hour later. Dundere City, as it turned out, was the only settlement on the island; the rest of it was a wild mix of rocky crags, hills covered in brush, forested valleys and ferocious rivers. Trina all but ignored the rest of us, letting out the occasional squeal at the magnificent displays of nature that the isle held. What had passed between Marcus and me last night hadn't come up yet this morning; he'd given me a warm smile at breakfast but was obviously waiting for me to approach him next. As we drove, he told the others about the guild system and educated us on the tasks various guilds undertook in Dundere. Firebrands, I learned, created most of the fires in the factories here and put out house fires when needed, while telekinetics used their powers to help build large structures. As the city's only lifebringer, Noelle healed the wounded, and there were stormbrewers whose entire job was to watch for storms approaching the city and divert them. And the city guard, of course, kept all these people in check with their anti-magic. In the center of town, Marcus said, was a school of magic that sounded similar to Willem's, where both children and adults could take classes to refine their magic skills. He taught classes there regularly, and Noelle was known to make appearances too.

"Does the school have dorms?" I asked him.

"Not yet," Marcus replied. "But it's in the works. One day we'd like to be able to welcome magic users from beyond our island to the school."

"Perhaps we can help," Kirilee suggested. "Once your dorms are ready, maybe Lachlann and I can bring more young magikai from Breoch to Dundere, get them out of danger." She glanced at Lachlann.

Lachlann brightened at her suggestion. "That's a wonderful idea. Though I'd hope that those trips wouldn't be quite as...*eventful* as this one was."

She chuckled and nodded. "You think Tomlin would be willing to help from inside the city?"

"Probably," he replied. "And we'd have to see if Gareth is up for being involved too."

"Or we could build another way," Willem put in. "If Noelle is willing to let us do this, I might be able to build a portal from my home to somewhere here in Dundere, so we could save time and hassle."

"A portal?" I eyed him. "You can do that?"

"Indeed you can," Willem replied. "Though I've never tried it myself. I can look into it, though."

"Noelle will have the final say, but I'm certainly willing to help from this side," Marcus put in. "At the very least, we can try to put more resources into the building of those dorms."

We chatted animatedly about the idea of bringing more young magikai to Dundere until the carriage reached a tall cliff overlooking the ocean far below. Marcus led us up to the cliff's edge, where a lone viletta tree sat, its blossoms swaying in the wind. "One of the first magic users from Breoch who sought refuge here brought a viletta branch with him," Marcus explained. "This tree is one of my favourite places on the island." He took out a knife and carefully cut off a small branch. He handed it to Kirilee, and we piled back into the carriage.

It was beginning to get dark by the time we arrived back at the mansion. Noelle was waiting for us with dinner, and Gareth had returned, as promised. He was holding a small package; when he saw me, he held it out to me. I opened it to find a familiar jade green dress and gold corset. "You looked lovely in them at the wedding," Gareth said, his face solemn. "I'm sure Janice would like you to have them."

I nodded, a lump rising in my throat. "Thank you," I whispered.

We sat down to dinner and dug into our food eagerly but silently; as enjoyable as our day had been, it was hard not to be somber at the thought of what would take place after dinner. "Before we head outside," Marcus said to us as the servants cleared our plates, "perhaps we should move to the parlour. We have some other business to attend to before we lay Kip to rest."

We all nodded and followed Marcus to the parlour. I exchanged a curious glance with Trina. *What is Marcus up to?*

Marcus and Noelle remained standing as the rest of us seated ourselves. Then Marcus cleared his throat and looked at me. "Noelle and I spoke about this matter this morning, and we have an offer for Saray and Trina." He smiled. "You may recall Noelle saying yesterday that we married at too old an age to have children of our own. We talked about adopting, but it never happened. And now I find that a girl who is very likely my own daughter is here, in need of a home. The solution seems obvious." His smile widened.

"Saray, Trina, how would the two of you like to stay with us for the next few years, until you're ready to strike out on your own?"

My mouth fell open.

Trina spoke before I did. "You'd...take me as well?"

"Of course," Noelle said.

She took a deep breath and then nodded enthusiastically. "Yes," she said to them. "Absolutely, yes. I mean, I'll stay anyway. Thank you so much." I watched as Trina stood up and walked towards them. She stared at Noelle and then shyly opened her arms. "I should've given this to you the other day when you fixed my eyes."

Noelle laughed and embraced her, and Marcus put his arms around both of them. Then Trina turned back to me. "Saray?"

I stared at them, my heart in my throat. "I..." My voice broke.

"You don't have to say yes," Marcus assured me. "As I said yesterday, you get to decide if you want me in your life. But you need a home, and I have one, and that home is yours if you want it."

I blinked back tears as I stared at the three of them already acting like a family. *This is what I've always wanted, isn't it? A family.* I took a deep breath and then stood up. "A home would be wonderful."

Marcus and Noelle's faces both broke out in smiles, and Marcus held an arm out tentatively. I cleared the space between myself and them and walked into his embrace. "Thank you," I mumbled, burying my face in his shoulder. "Thank you...Father."

Marcus pulled back and looked at me. I saw tears in his eyes. "Don't feel rushed to call me that," he said. "If you want to, of course, you're welcome to, but I won't be offended if you don't."

I shrugged. "I think I like it. I..."

I was cut off by a strange buzzing sound behind me, followed by several gasps. I turned, and my eyes narrowed. Kirilee was enveloped in yellow light, her limbs shaking and a look of shock on her face. I thought I heard a faint strain of music; after a moment, I recognized it as the melody of the curse's song. Then the strange light faded, and she keeled forward, nearly hitting her head on a table.

"Kirilee!" Lachlann was on his feet, staring down at his wife. He dropped to his knees in front of her and lifted her chin. "What just happened? Are you all right?"

Kirilee met his gaze, and I saw that she was still shaking. "The...the curse," she said in a hoarse whisper. "It just broke. I...I'm not in any pain." She stared down at her body for a moment and then began to laugh softly.

Lachlann's eyebrows knitted together, and he exchanged a glance with Willem. "How did it break?" he whispered.

"I have no idea," Willem said softly. "I'll call in my mother, and we can sort this out."

Lachlann and Willem helped Kirilee back onto the couch. A large knot was developing in my stomach, my excitement over my newfound family replaced with sudden fear. *What's happening?*

I watched as Claudi began to materialize next to Willem. When she was fully present, she took one look at Kirilee and shook her head. "Well, now. It's finally happened."

Willem nodded, frowning. "And we have no idea why."

"Why don't you tell me what's happened since I last saw you, my dear," Claudi said, sitting down next to Kirilee.

Kirilee and Lachlann filled Claudi in on the events of the past month or so. When Trina's eyes were mentioned, Claudi turned to her and smiled. She sobered when she was told about Kip. When the story was over, Claudi shook her head slowly. "I think I know what happened."

"Tell me," Kirilee said.

"It's the children." Claudi turned to us. "You know already that your story is tied into some of theirs. I think that one verse in your song, the one you never understood, was about them." She turned to Kirilee and began to sing.

*Restless and wild, you'll live out your days*
*'Til the one that you've maimed is made whole*
*'Til the one you've made hate learns instead how to love*
*'Til the orphan you've left finds true home*

"Now, the line about the one that you've maimed being made whole—that's clearly about Trina," Claudi explained. "Kip's mother was the one who attacked her, and we know that was because Clarita's death damaged her mind. And I would suspect that the one you've made hate learning how to love—that was about Kip. He may no longer be with us, but this journey certainly changed him, helped him let go of a lot of his anger."

"And the orphan I've left finding true home?" Kirilee asked.

"Well, the spell broke when Saray accepted Marcus and Noelle's offer," she said. "I suppose that answers the question of whether Marcus is really Saray's father. If he is, this would very much be her true home."

I nodded and exchanged a glance with Marcus.

"So the spell, it all makes sense now," Claudi went on. "You weren't meant to completely undo the effects of your crime after all. You were only meant to stop the pain that it caused to the three children, the ripple effect down the generations."

She nodded. "I s'pose it makes sense that the fairies brought the children to me, then. And why they let me leave Breoch for this place."

Claudi nodded. "I told you there's always a reason behind their ways. It was to bring you all here so all that happened to the children could be made right."

Trina glanced at Kirilee anxiously. "So now what will happen to you?"

Claudi answered for Kirilee, her expression sobering. "*And then, on the day that all of this has passed, you'll age, and then sleep, and then die,*" she quoted. She gave Kirilee a sad smile. "I'm afraid it's time, my dear. You're already beginning to age; I don't know if you've noticed."

Kirilee nodded, and looking at her, I could see that Claudi was right. She still appeared fairly young, but the hollows around her eyes were deeper, her face was more gaunt, and I thought I saw a few glints of silver in her hair. "I thought it might be time," she said softly. She turned to Lachlann and took his hand. "I just wish I didn't have to leave you so soon."

I blinked against the fresh round of tears that threatened to spill over. "How long do you have?"

Kirilee frowned. "It's nearly eight o'clock. If I understand the spell, less than four hours."

"No!" Trina exclaimed, her voice breaking. She began to cry. "We...we've just lost Kip...we can't lose you too...it's too much..." Her words were lost in her sobs, and Noelle put an arm around her.

Kirilee looked at Trina with sad eyes. "I'm sorry, Trina, it can't be helped. I know it's a lot, losing two people you love so close together, but..." She stopped suddenly, her eyes growing wide. "Wait."

"What?" Lachlann asked.

She took his hands and stood up. "Come with me," she said to him. "We need to speak privately. I have an idea." She pulled him to his feet and led him out of the room, leaving us all staring after them in confusion.

Kirilee returned from her conversation with Lachlann less than fifteen minutes later, but I could tell she'd aged in that time. The beginnings of laugh lines were starting to form around her eyes, and there were definite streaks of grey in her hair. Lachlann looked older too, I noticed. His shoulders were hunched, his face drawn and tired. Kirilee's expression was triumphant, though, her eyes wide with excitement as she looked at Trina. "What you said earlier doesn't have to happen," she exclaimed. "You don't have to lose two people you love. There's a way to get Kip back now." She glanced at Lachlann and gave his hand a squeeze. Then she turned to Willem and spoke with the authority of a woman who'd lived over seven decades. "I want to do a life transfer."

# Chapter Twenty-Three

**WE ALL STARED** at Kirilee as if she'd gone mad. "A…a *life transfer?*" Willem was the first to speak. "Using who?"

"Me, obviously," Kirilee replied. "I've only got a few hours left, Willem. If I'm to die tonight, I might as well accomplish something doing it." She frowned. "You know how they're done?"

Willem's eyebrows knitted. "I…uh…well, I'm not sure if it's a good idea. But yes, I do have a book with the spell's casting words in it at home. And if we were going to actually go through with it, we'd need a large amount of magical energy—likely the combined magic of everyone here and also a lifebringer who's willing to say the casting words." He looked beyond Kirilee to Noelle.

"No." Noelle shook her head emphatically. "We can't do this."

"And why not, ai?" Kirilee protested. "It makes no sense *not* to do it. If you don't, by the end of the night both Kip and I will be dead. If you do, then I'll die a few hours earlier than I would've otherwise, but you'll have Kip with you again."

"Even so, it's extremely illegal, not to mention unethical," Noelle argued. "If you start casting spells like that, it sets a precedent. Pretty soon you'll find folks all over the island trying to kill people off in order to resurrect their friends."

"Which they won't be able to do, given that you're the only lifebringer on the island," Willem countered.

Noelle frowned. "You're supporting her in this? I'm surprised—you seem like the type who would have some understanding of the ethics of magic."

"Normally, I'd be very against the idea of a life transfer," Willem replied. "And I didn't like it at first, either. But if Kirilee's right about only having a few hours left, then it's the sensible thing to do in this situation."

Noelle's gaze fell on Lachlann. "And you? You're fine with us doing this to your wife?"

Lachlann grimaced visibly, but when he spoke his voice was firm. "We've talked it through. And obviously I don't like the idea much. But, as Willem said, it makes sense if she's about to leave us anyway. It's her life; she can do with it what she wants. And she wants this." He sighed. "My only request is that you give the two of us some time alone before you start so we can say goodbye properly."

"Of course," Willem said. "It would take us some time to get set up for something of this magnitude, anyway."

"Would you feel better about this if you weren't the one to cast the spell?" Kirilee asked Noelle.

"Why? Can Willem do it?"

"No, but I know someone else who likely could," she replied. "It's our friend Hilda, back in Breoch. Willem would have to go fetch her, but that's easy enough for him. And I'm sure the two of them have enough magic between them to make it back here without trouble." She glanced at Willem, who nodded.

"Why would Hilda be able to cast a spell like this?" I asked.

"Because she has access to the fairy magic, and there are plenty of tales of them performing rituals like this. They were involved in the soul magic that brought me back, so I figure they could also facilitate a life transfer and that Hilda could be the conduit for all your magic." Kirilee turned to Noelle. "If you'll allow it, that is."

Noelle flinched. "I still don't like it."

"None of us *like* it, but it seems like the best thing to do," Gareth spoke up. "And you yourself said yesterday that you're partly to blame for the boy's death. It's the least you can do for us, Noelle."

Noelle eyed Gareth and then sighed. "Fine. But no word of it leaves this house, do you all understand?"

"Of course." Willem nodded. "This will work best if all the magikai participate, but I'm not going to force anyone into it," he said. "Is everyone here all right with helping?"

I watched as heads slowly began to bob. Trina nodded more quickly than I expected, followed by Claudi, then Father. Noelle gave a reluctant sigh before nodding her assent. Then all eyes turned to me. "Please, Saray?" Trina's voice quavered.

I bit my lip. "I...suppose Kirilee's curse wouldn't have broken if Kip hadn't cared about us, now would it?"

"That's right." Kirilee nodded. "The one you've made hate learns instead how to love," she quoted softly, winding a strand of silver hair around her finger. "He cared about you, Saray. Me being like this is proof."

I nodded slowly. "Right. But I don't want to do this to you..."

"Saray." Kirilee's voice was firm. "This is *my* choice. I'm the one asking for this; it's not for you to carry. I don't want you feeling guilty about this, ai?" She glanced around the room. "That goes for all of you."

I nodded and let out a long sigh. "All right."

"So you're in?" Willem asked.

I glanced at Kirilee and then gave Willem a shaky nod. "I'm in."

"Well, I suppose it's settled then." Noelle turned to Kirilee. "Where do you want to do this? Is the garden all right?"

"The garden would be lovely," Kirilee replied. "And once it's done, will you lay me to rest in the fashion we intended for Kip? If Carmine accompanies Hilda, then the spell should be quite easy to cast."

"Of course." Noelle nodded.

"I'll go fetch them and get the book," Willem said. "I shouldn't be longer than fifteen minutes." He looked Kirilee over, his face turning sad. "I suppose I'll say my goodbyes now. In fact, we all should say our goodbyes and then head out to the garden so that Kirilee and Lachlann can have their time alone. We should need about an hour to set up." He walked over to Kirilee and pulled her into an embrace, and the two exchanged a few soft words. Then he mumbled a phrase and disappeared from sight.

We took turns saying our farewells, all of us but Lachlann keeping a respectful distance when it was not our turn. When my turn came, I approached Kirilee slowly, a lump rising in my throat. She looked at me steadily, her blue-green eyes sincere. "Saray," she said when I reached her, "it's been an honour getting to know you."

I responded by bursting into tears.

Kirilee pulled me towards herself, wrapping her arms around me while I cried into her shoulder. "I wish I'd had more time with you," she whispered. "Me too," I sniffled. "I'll miss you, Kirilee."

She nodded. "I know. But I suspect you'll be pleased about getting Kip back." She pulled away and gave me a wry smile. "And I'll be on to new adventures."

I gave her a shaky nod. "Aren't you...afraid?"

"Of death?" She shook her head. "Not at all. I'm quite curious to see the world beyond this one. There are some Seekers who believe that we who care for the fairies become one of them after death. Maybe I'll still be with you, but in another form."

I blinked. "You...you think so?"

"It's possible." She smiled, then sobered. "Promise me something, Saray."

"What's that?"

"Be careful with your gifts. Don't ever be afraid to ask for help. Don't make the mistakes I did. Promise me that."

I swiped at my eyes. "I promise."

She responded by pulling me to herself once more and then kissed me on the forehead. "Be strong, my little firebrand," she whispered, releasing me.

I gave Kirilee one last look, then stumbled towards the back door and into the night.

Willem had rejoined us outside, accompanied by Hilda, Carmine and about half a dozen fairies. He was all business, casting a spell over each magikai to allow our magical energy to flow from one person to another. Kip's lifeless form lay in the patch of grass, the blanket pulled back to reveal his face. Bailey and Persius both hovered nearby, and the fairies were beginning to

251

congregate around him as well; it seemed that they all knew something significant was about to happen. Hilda was studying one of her books, but she looked up and met my eyes as I approached. "Good to see you again, Saray." She looked beyond me. "And you too, Trina." Carmine, who was standing next to Hilda, gave us a wave of greeting.

"It's good to see both of you for the first time," Trina said, her voice catching slightly as if she, like I, had recently been crying. "Though it's hard to see you in this light."

I responded by making a ball of fire, and Trina looked the two women over. One of the fairies floated over to Trina and landed in her hair. "I think we found the flaw in your eyesight that Noelle promised," I said. "I can see just fine in this light."

"I can see well enough with your fire," Trina told me. Then she looked at Hilda anxiously. "What's going to happen? Will it hurt for Kirilee?"

Hilda smiled and shook her head. "Not at all. For her, it will feel like falling asleep. She might enjoy that, given how long it's been since she last slept. And Willem will explain the spell to you soon enough."

Noelle was walking towards Kip's body, I saw; Marcus—*Father,* I corrected myself—was trailing her. I watched as they both knelt by Kip's head. "What are you doing...Father?" The word still felt strange on my tongue.

He met my eyes, smiling at my choice of words. "We need to heal his brain before we bring him back. And Noelle and I realized a while ago that our combined skills are useful for healing bullet wounds. Watch." Noelle pulled Kip's hair back to reveal the bullet hole, still ugly and encrusted with blood. Then the two of them joined hands, each placing their free hand on Kip's head, and Noelle began to hum while Father spoke the telekinesis spell. I watched, fascinated, as something shiny appeared in the center of the wound. Then the bullet fell out of the hole and onto the ground. Father picked it up, cleaned it off, and pocketed it, while Noelle sang a spell to close up the wound and repair the internal damage.

I saw Carmine watching us as Father and Noelle stood up, and I waved her over. "I should make some introductions." She walked over to us, and I smiled at her. "Carmine, this is my father, Marcus, and my adopted mother,

Noelle." The words felt surreal. "Father, Noelle, this is Hilda's wife, Carmine."

"Pleasure to meet you," Noelle said, obviously noting Carmine's condition and greeting her with a bow rather than a handshake.

Father, however, extended his left hand to her. "Good to meet you, Carmine," he said as she shook his hand. "I see you and I have undergone the same, uh, surgery." He smiled wryly. "Do you know how to sign?" he asked, signing the words as he spoke.

Carmine brightened and began rapidly signing back to him. He nodded and laughed. "My old master insisted that I learn so he could communicate with me," he told her, continuing to sign while he talked. "Tell me, Carmine, are you happy the way you are? Noelle is a healer and the reason I have my hand and tongue back. She can restore yours later tonight, if you'd like."

Carmine shook her head and began signing, no doubt telling Father what she'd told us earlier about being happy the way she is.

"Ah." Father nodded. "Well, if you ever change your mind, you know where we live. Tell me, how did you escape?"

The two of them moved into a rapidly signed conversation, and I drifted over to Trina just as Willem called everyone to order. He began to explain the mechanics of the spell to us. He had us arrange ourselves in a circle, close enough to the person next to us to join hands when the time came. I exchanged a nervous glance with Trina; despite Kirilee's assurances, the thought of what we were about to do still felt strange to me.

Kirilee and Lachlann walked into the garden then, and everyone fell silent. Looking at her, I could see that she'd aged further in the time that we'd given the two of them alone. Her hair was more grey than brown now, and the lines around her eyes had deepened. She held her head high, though. Lachlann looked a little worse for wear; it was obvious he was trying to put on a brave face, but his eyes were red, his expression grim. Kirilee let go of his hand and walked towards Hilda to embrace her, Persius landing on her shoulder when she pulled away. Willem, meanwhile, moved towards Lachlann and touched his shoulder while mumbling a spell. I saw an iridescent bubble envelop him, barely visible in the near darkness. "You'll be shielded from the effects of the spell now," he said. "You can sit with her and hold onto her while it's happening, if you wish."

Lachlann nodded. "Thank you." His voice was ragged.

Kirilee and Hilda exchanged a few words, and then Hilda gestured at a spot on the grass near Kip. Kirilee nodded and stepped forward into the grassy patch, Lachlann following her. Kirilee reached up and removed Persius from his perch, stared at him for a moment and gave his feathers a stroke, then placed him onto Lachlann's shoulder. "Make yourselves comfortable," Hilda said to them. "The rest of you, get into position."

We all joined hands, and I suddenly became aware of the magic of each person involved in the spell. There was the familiar storminess of Willem, and Hilda's magic, which felt just as ancient and powerful, but was tinged with music and fairy laughter. Trina's magic was full of birdsong, Carmine's was bursting with flowers and fruit, and Father's was raw and powerful yet smooth, like silk. Noelle and Claudi both possessed white, pure healing magic that tasted oddly like pineapple. Our circle broke where Hilda stood; instead of holding her hands, Willem and Claudi each placed a hand on her shoulder. Hilda knelt in the grass next to Kip, placing her open book in front of her, and then reached out and put her left hand on his forehead. On her other side, Lachlann sat down cross-legged, while Kirilee lay down, her head in his lap. She grasped one of his hands and looked up at him. "I love you," she whispered.

"I love you," he responded, leaning down to kiss her gently.

Kirilee gave him a sad smile and then turned to Hilda. "It's time."

Willem nodded and muttered a few words under his breath. I gasped, feeling energy begin to flow out of me. "The conduit is open," Willem said. "Say the words when you're ready, Hilda."

I watched as Hilda took Kirilee's free hand and then looked down at the book in front of her. She spoke the words slowly and deliberately, and I watched as a soft yellow light enveloped Hilda, crackling on her skin like lightning. The fairies flew frantically around her; I thought I could hear them singing.

The light was enveloping Kirilee now too. She didn't appear uncomfortable, though; her eyes had drifted closed, and she wore a peaceful expression. I watched as a brighter, white light began to travel up Hilda's arm. She gasped, seeming to convulse for a moment when the light reached her chest. Then it travelled all the way around the circle, and suddenly I could feel Kirilee's magic. It was like a song, cool and smooth and green, bursting with flowers and herbs and smelling of pine and rainstorms. It filled my head, and for a brief second, I could see pieces of her life. I could feel the horror of waking to see a child killed by her own hand; I could feel the sharp stabbing in my chest that Kirilee had carried with her for most of her life. I saw her years spent wandering in the woods, her wedding to Lachlann, the moment when she first held her son. It was in my mind, bright and clear, and then it was gone, and the white light was surging down Hilda's left arm and into Kip. The same light enveloped him now, bathing his features in pure, iridescent white.

Then the magic stopped, as quickly as it started. Hilda's hands dropped, and she slumped forward, and the garden fell silent. The quiet was broken a moment later as Bailey, who'd been watching anxiously from outside the circle, bolted towards Kip and began whimpering and licking his face.

Hilda lifted her head and stared at Kip. "Did…did it work?"

Willem walked over and placed a hand on Kip's head, then inclined his ear to his face. "He's breathing," he said. "It worked!" A collective cheer went up in the garden and then died just as quickly as all heads turned to Kirilee and Lachlann. Kirilee's eyes were closed, her silver hair splayed out around her, her form completely still. Lachlann was hunched over her, also unmoving. He did not look up at any of us.

"Leave him," Gareth, who had been silently observing our ritual, spoke up. "Willem can move Kip into the living room so he can wake up there, with friends. I'll stay with Lachlann; I understand this sort of loss."

Willem touched Kip's head, and they disappeared from view, and we all began to file inside silently. Before I left the garden, I glanced back at Kirilee's unmoving body. "Thank you for everything," I whispered and then turned and walked into the house.

Inside, Kip was stretched out on a couch in the parlour, Bailey by his side. His eyes were still closed, but I could see that the colour had returned to his skin. I watched Hilda walk towards him and loosen the burlap blanket. Then she turned to me. "I think you should be the one to wake him up, Saray."

My eyes widened. "Me?" I repeated. "W...why?"

"Because you're the last person Kip saw before he died, and when he wakes up, the first thing he'll want to know is that you're alive and safe."

"She's right, Saray," Trina put in. "Do it."

"All right." I perched on the edge of the couch, my heart pounding with nervous excitement, and then reached out and took Kip's hands in mine. They were warm. *He really is alive.* An unexpected thrill shot through me. *I've missed him.* A few hours ago, I'd struggled to admit it, but now it was undeniable.

I took a deep breath and then gave his hands a squeeze. "Kip," I said softly. "Wake up, Kip."

He didn't respond for a second. Then he coughed, and I watched as his eyelids fluttered. "Saray?" he mumbled. Then he sat bolt upright, staring at me, his ice-blue eyes wide and full of confusion. "You're...you're safe?"

I nodded and squeezed his hands again, blinking back tears. "I'm safe," I assured him. My voice was ragged as I spoke the next words. "Welcome back, Kip."

# Epilogue

*One month later*

**THE SOUNDS OF** laughter and music wafted up the staircase and down the long hallway to the bedroom that I shared with Trina. I stood in front of the mirror as she tightened my gold corset, trying to remember how to breathe correctly. Women in Dundere didn't wear impossibly tight corsets like they supposedly did in other places, but it was still taking some getting used to.

"There." Trina's tone was satisfied. "You look lovely."

I stared at the familiar jade green dress and the intricate braid that Noelle had done in my hair earlier and smiled. Then my gaze shifted to Trina's reflection; her dark hair had been done up into ringlets, and she wore a soft, shell-pink dress with bell sleeves that contrasted beautifully with her skin tone. I grinned at us in the mirror. "*We* look lovely."

"Is everyone ready?" Father and Noelle were standing in our doorway. They looked rather lovely too, I thought; Father was dressed in a fine, long-tailed black coat over a blue and gold waistcoat, and Noelle was resplendent in a floor-length golden dress, her hair piled on top of her head and secured with a long, elegant pin.

I glanced at the hallway beyond the door and gave them a tight smile. "I'm a bit nervous."

"Don't be. You're home, and you're safe; you have nothing to fear." Noelle tucked a stray lock of hair back into my braid. "I can prove it to you if you want to see the papers."

I laughed. "I'm pretty sure I signed those papers just a few hours ago."

"As did we all," Father said. "And now it's time for the people of Dundere to meet the Westwood daughters." He stepped towards me and offered his arm. "Let's go."

I gave him a quick grin and took his arm. We all headed out the door and down the hall and then began our slow, deliberate walk down the winding staircase.

The applause began as soon as we came into view of the foyer. I stared down at the room full of dignitaries and common Dundere folk, and a few familiar faces from other lands, all of whom had come to welcome Trina and me into this family, this society. Noelle paused and raised a hand when we were halfway down the stairs, and the room fell silent.

"My friends," she said to everyone assembled, "today we are here to celebrate family and new beginnings. A month ago, a pair of teenage girls came to me seeking help and healing, with no idea that they would find a home here. This afternoon, Marcus and I signed the adoption papers, and it is our deepest pleasure to introduce to you our daughters, Saray and Trina Westwood!"

The room burst into applause, and I smiled and waved. The new surname would take some getting used to; it had been easier for me to take on than Trina, but she'd decided it was for the best. One day, she said, she might return to Breoch and look for her mother, if her mother didn't find her here first. But for now, this was her home. *Our* home.

Noelle informed the crowd that there would be dancing in the ballroom, followed by dinner in the garden, and then we resumed our walk down the stairs, into the crowd of well-dressed men and women. They flocked around us, offering smiles and handshakes and exclamations about how much I looked like Marcus. I leaned into him, my nerves returning, and he glanced down at me. "If you folks will excuse us," he said to them, "I'd like the chance to dance with my daughter."

The guests stepped away obligingly, and we made our way across the foyer. Trina and Noelle followed, and I didn't miss Trina's gasp of delight when we walked through the ballroom doors. The room was lit up with dozens of coloured hanging lanterns, their lights casting vibrant, flickering hues all about the room. I saw several familiar faces among the crowds here; Willem was chatting with a group of intellectual-looking men and women, and Gareth and several crew members occupied a sitting area in the corner of the room. Noelle had timed the party so that it would take place when the Lady Liara was in port; tomorrow the ship would leave for Breoch with Willem, Lachlann and Kip aboard.

I saw Kip making his way through the crowd as the musicians began to play, his eyes set on me. He was wearing a red waistcoat tonight, and his long hair was loose, as was a common fashion among the men of Dundere. He met my eyes, and my heart skipped a beat; sometimes it was hard to believe that he was *here,* in the flesh, alive once again.

"You're going to have to wait your turn, you know." Father's voice held a teasing note.

Kip chuckled. "I'll go dance with your other daughter, then." He moved past us towards Trina, touching my shoulder lightly as he did so.

Father took my hands and pulled me into position as the music began. "Are you still feeling nervous?"

"Not quite so much now." I frowned. "You know, I used to hate things like this. I mean, last Banishing Day we had a huge ball at my school, and I skipped it completely."

Father laughed. "Well, I'm happy to tell you that you will never again have to celebrate Banishing Day. Though you will be expected to attend a few balls." His expression sobered. "Being part of the governor's family isn't all easy. There are responsibilities, expectations. I'm sure you'll adjust, though."

I shrugged. "I'm allowed to be myself here. I've never had that before. If I need to look pretty and attend a few fancy events so that I can live in a place where I don't have to hide, I'll do it."

Father smiled, and we were quiet after that, moving together to the music. When the song ended, Kip made his way over to us, Trina in tow. "She's just figuring out how to do this," he said to me. "I'm going to give her a few more dances, and then I'll come find you."

I nodded and glanced at Father. "Go dance with Noelle. I'll be all right on my own."

I scanned the room as I walked off the dance floor and began my way around its perimeter. I gave Gareth and his crew a grin and then headed towards Willem when I saw him waving me over. When I reached the couch where he was sitting, he gestured at his newfound friends. "Saray, these folks are all teachers at the school of magic here in Dundere City."

I nodded and smiled at the group. "It's a pleasure to meet you."

"As I said earlier, Saray is not only a powerful firebrand, she's also one of the only mental casters I've ever met," Willem said to the group. He beamed at me, and the others all looked me over with interest. "I expect Saray to be one of your best students and perhaps one day a teacher at your school."

I eyed him. "You think I could teach magic?"

"One day, absolutely," he replied. "It's just a matter of time."

I answered a few questions from the gathered teachers about my abilities while glancing around the room for the one person I hadn't yet seen. When I could not find him, I excused myself from the group and headed for the back doors.

The backyard was decorated much like the ballroom; lanterns were strung throughout the trees, sparkling like stars and illuminating the scene below. Several dozen tables were set in the yard, each one flanked by chairs and topped by silver and china place settings. One tree dominated the center of the yard, providing the majority of the light for the upcoming feast, its blossoms glowing pink and violet. I felt my mood shift; the many reasons for celebration tonight did not change the fact that we'd all lost someone dear to us just a month before.

The past month had been one of mixed emotions. There was the joy of having a family, of watching Trina rediscover her world and marvel at the colours and life around her. There was the strange, unexpected pleasure of having Kip back and the excitement about my enrollment in the school of magic. Mingled with all of that, though, was the deep pain of losing Kirilee. It was easy to push away the pain of the loss tonight, but there had been several moments in the past month where it had been crushing, all-consuming. There'd been many tears cried by all of us, many stories told about Kirilee's life, and several songs and paintings and other works of art made in her honour—the most incredible, of course, being the tree in front of me.

We had buried Kirilee in the manner we'd promised, funnelling all of our magic into the spell that Carmine had cast on the viletta branch that we'd picked earlier that day. Now a small but sturdy tree stood in the spot where we'd performed the life transfer, its roots encasing what remained of our friend and its blooms a constant, luminescent reminder of the wild and colourful force that Kirilee had been in our lives. A long table was placed in front of the tree; behind it, a solitary figure sat on a blanket, leaning up against the tree. He'd spent every evening here since Kirilee's death, with or without the company of others. Now I glanced down at him. "There you are."

Lachlann looked up and offered me a small smile. Bailey was lying at his feet, I saw, and Persius was perched in the branches above. A few fairies flitted about Lachlann and the animals; Hilda, Carmine and Claudi had all returned home after the life transfer, but Hilda had left the fairies here, as a gift.

"Your last night with us," I scolded him, "and you're spending it out here?"

"If people wish to see me, they know where to find me." He patted the blanket next to himself. "Sit, if you'd like."

I sank down gingerly, trying not to rumple my dress. Silence reigned for a few awkward seconds; I often found it hard to know what to say to Lachlann now. *What do you say to someone who's lost so much?* "I'll miss you," I finally said, giving him a smile.

He nodded. "I'll miss you too. But you know I'll be back soon enough, hopefully with a few more young magic users in tow."

My smile widened. "I'm glad you're still planning to do that, even without Kirilee."

"It's the best way I can think to honour her memory," he replied solemnly.

"I wish I could help," I told him. "I mean, I know *my* life is going to get better from here. But what about all those other folks in Breoch? All those kids who are like me, who hide their talents and need a way to escape? All those people like Walter who've had their magic taken away from them? I want to help them."

Lachlann nodded. "I think for now it's best you stay here. But you can certainly help from this side. There'll be young folk coming in with me who will be new to this place and in need of someone to show them around and make them feel welcome."

"True," I replied.

"And perhaps one day when you're a bit older and the Breoch Guard have given up on hunting you, you and Trina can come back and help me with what I'll be doing."

"Do you think they'll try to come back here for me? The Breoch Guard? Before he let me go, Jasper said I hadn't seen the last of him." I shuddered at the memory.

"If Jasper—or any of them—do come back, they'll be trying to take away the adopted daughter of the Governor herself and a full Dundere citizen," Lachlann replied. "You don't think they'd get away with that very easily, now do you?"

I shrugged. "They might still try."

"They might, it's true. But I highly doubt they'll succeed. And I think one day you'll get your chance to go back and help the magic folks in Breoch. You'd make your grandmother proud, you know, with your desire to help others like you." He reached back and ran his fingers along the tree's bark. Then he smiled wryly. "You think I'm going crazy, don't you?"

"I hope not." I trailed my own fingers over the tree's bark. "You really think she's in there? She seemed to think she'd become a fairy after she died."

Lachlann shrugged. "Six months ago I would have thought both ideas were madness. But a lot has happened since then." He sighed and glanced up at the glowing blooms. "I'm just glad that she's at peace now, wherever she is. I'm glad she's not in pain anymore."

I nodded, the awkward feeling returning to my stomach. "I...I'm sorry it hasn't turned out so well for you, though," I offered.

Lachlann's shoulders hunched, and he looked away for a moment. "I married Kirilee knowing about the curse and knowing I might lose her like this one day. Though I certainly didn't expect it to happen so soon."

I nodded.

"You know," he went on, "there's a part of me that thinks that if I hadn't agreed to accompany you kids here to Dundere, none of this would have happened. But then, if I hadn't agreed to come along, I wouldn't have lost my arm, and Kirilee and I might have never had that conversation that you girls eavesdropped on." He shook his head. "I'm not sure if you know this, Saray, but I was in love with Kirilee for years."

I nodded again. "Your brother said something about that before I'd met either of you."

"So Tom knew, huh?" He smiled wryly.

I nodded.

"Figures. He did always know how to read me like a book." He shook his head. "Anyway, Kirilee made it clear early on that she didn't feel the same about me. I decided that I'd rather have her in my life as a friend than not at all, and I stuck around. But my attraction never completely went away. And so the fact that I got to marry her, to love her in the way I'd wanted to for so long, I'm still in awe that it happened at all."

"Doesn't that make all this harder?" I asked. "Having that love in your life for such a short time?"

"In a way, yes. But the point is, I *had* it, short time or not." He met my eyes. "You don't need to worry about me, Saray. Yes, this is hard for me. Very hard. But I'll get through." He gave me an obviously forced smile. "I'll have plenty to distract me on my journey home, at least; Kip's finally going to let me teach him the sword."

"It's true." We both looked up to see Kip walking towards us. He eyed Lachlann. "Gareth is planning on playing a few songs in about ten minutes' time. He's wondering if you'll accompany him on your drum." His gaze shifted to me. "And I was hoping to dance with you before that."

Lachlann chuckled. "You folks are really determined to get me inside, aren't you?" He let out a mock sigh. "Well, I suppose if I'm needed…" He got to his feet, and Kip offered me a hand and pulled me up.

We had taken a few steps towards the house when Kip paused. "You forgot your coat, Lachlann." He pointed at Lachlann's jacket, which was slung over a low-hanging tree branch, and then grinned and flicked his wrist.

I watched as the jacket rose from its place and sailed towards Kip's outstretched hand.

Lachlann gave Kip a wry smile as he took the coat from him. "Trying to impress your girlfriend?"

Kip laughed. "I think it'd take more than that to impress Saray. She's much more powerful than I am."

Lachlann shook his head. "Clearly, you don't know just how strong your magic is, Kip."

"I know it killed my aunt once, a long time ago. I think I've some idea how deadly it can be." Kip's voice had an edge to it, and I put a hand on his arm. He glanced at me, and I gave him a reassuring smile; I was well aware of how terrified he was of his new abilities.

It was a side effect of the life transfer, Willem had explained to us. Sometimes when a life transfer is done, he said, the recipient will inherit something that belonged to the person whose life was used. And it seemed that Kip had inherited Kirilee's magic. "Saray's better trained than me, though," Kip was saying to Lachlann now. "I don't doubt she could best me in a magic duel."

"And I don't doubt that you'll catch up quickly, with Willem's training," I replied as we followed Lachlann through the back door, into the house. "Soon you'll be just as well trained as me."

We were approaching the ballroom now; the musicians were just beginning to play a slow dance. Kip offered me his arm, and together we made our way through the doors and into the throng of dancing couples.

"I wish I didn't have to leave," Kip admitted, pulling me into position.

"Me too." I smiled up at him. "But it's not forever. You'll be back soon enough."

He looked down at me, shaking his head. "I still can't believe this is real," he whispered. "You and I together, after everything. I don't deserve you; I don't deserve to be alive…" His voice faltered, and his shoulders slumped. "Kirilee shouldn't have done what she did for me."

I nodded; we'd had this conversation several times already. Our first talk after the life transfer had been awkward, full of mumbled apologies from him and remnants of my own anger, but both our emotions had begun to settle down as the weeks progressed. I knew, though, that he still felt some amount of guilt over the sacrifices made to bring him back.

"But she did," I said, giving his hand a squeeze. "And here we are. You're back, and you have another chance at life, and you have me. You'd better do some good with all of this."

"I will. I promise you that much." He let go of my hand and pushed a stray lock of hair out of my face and then leaned down and kissed me on the forehead.

I giggled and threw a glance at the large double doors that sat at the far end of the ballroom. "Want to go to the balcony?"

He grinned and nodded, his earlier melancholy fading for now, and we began making our way through the dancers, hand in hand, towards the balcony doors.

This particular balcony did not look out over the backyard; everything beyond the railing was dark, save for the stars. I let out a soft laugh as Kip closed the door behind us with a mumbled spell. He stared at me for a few long moments and then leaned down.

Kissing Kip was different now. Most things were the same as before— the feel of his lips on my own, the way he always worked his hands into my hair, the hammering of my heart in my chest. As always, time fell away when I kissed him; the music in the background and the cool night air were an afterthought, hardly noticeable next to the intensity of *us*. Now, though, I could sense his magic whenever he kissed me. Kip's magic felt nearly the same as it had on Kirilee, cool and green and smelling like pine, but on him, it felt less playful, more restless, like a storm waiting to be unleashed. It made my skin tingle. My magic, Kip had told me, was just as fierce, full of fire, and tasted like cinnamon. I wondered what the two of us might be able to accomplish together with this much fury and fierceness under our skin.

The sound of a throat clearing jerked me back to reality. I pulled away from Kip and looked over to see the ballroom door cracked open and Father staring at us, an amused smile playing on his lips. "You know, I'm still new at having teenage daughters," he said, "but I think I'm supposed to yell at you for this."

I stared at him, my cheeks burning. "We were…just kissing," I protested. "Nothing wrong with that."

He frowned. "I suppose not," he conceded. "Just don't do anything stupid, all right? I'm still getting used to being a father; I have no desire to be a grandfather quite yet." He smirked and wagged his finger at us before shutting the door.

I burst out laughing as soon as the door closed. Kip shook his head as I buried my face in his shoulder and chortled. "Y'know, I think he has the 'embarrassing his children' part of fatherhood figured out just fine," he grumbled.

"You've got that right." I laid my head against his collarbone, giggling. Kip let out a huff, and then he began to laugh too and wrapped his arms around me.

Inside, I heard a familiar tune begin on the pipe. I pulled away from Kip and turned to him. "Speaking of embarrassment," I said, "how about we go inside and make fools of ourselves on the dance floor, just like old times?"

Kip glanced at the doors and then grinned. "I'd like that," he said. "Let's go."

One hour and several dances later, Kip, Trina and I followed Father and Noelle outside to the garden. The guests had begun to trickle outside some time ago; a good number of the tables were already occupied, the guests sipping from crystal goblets of wine and cider. The long table sitting directly under Kirilee's tree was vacant, though. Father and Noelle took the center two seats and directed Trina and me to sit on either side of them. The smell of cooking meat had begun to permeate the garden, and I felt my stomach rumble.

"Who are the last two seats for?" Trina asked, gesturing at the vacant seats on either side of her and me.

"I suspect one of them is for my boyfriend," I said.

"You mean *my* cousin?" Trina replied, grinning.

"All right you two, stop fighting over Kip," Noelle admonished us. "And you're right, one of them is for him." She glanced over at Kip and motioned that he should join us.

"And the last seat?" Trina asked.

"The last seat is for the man who was married to my mother, of course," Father said.

"Really?" Lachlann had been sitting with Gareth and his crew; now he stood up and looked uncertainly at our table.

"Absolutely." Father grinned at him. "You're part of this family now too, Lachlann, and you're welcome here any time. I hope you know that."

"I…I do now," Lachlann said, both surprise and emotion evident in his voice. "Thank you." He walked over to where Kip was standing, and the two of them looked dubiously at the empty seats. "You sit with your girlfriend," Lachlann said to Kip.

I laughed as Kip slid into the seat next to me. "Is it strange that I'm your sister now, but I'm dating your cousin?" I asked Trina.

She shrugged. "We have a strange family. I mean, Lachlann is sort of our grandfather now…"

"Don't you ever say that again," Lachlann protested, but he was smiling.

Father got to his feet then, and with a flick of his wrist, the bottles of wine and cider on our table uncorked themselves and rose to fill our glasses. When he was finished casting, Father cleared his throat and tapped his wine glass, and the noise in the garden died down. "Before we eat," he said to the crowd, "I'd like to make a toast." He smiled and raised his glass. "To family."

"To family," we all echoed, clinking our glasses together.

A wind caught the leaves of the viletta tree as we toasted, and I glanced up. For a moment, the pink and purple blossoms seemed to glow more intensely, as if Kirilee was joining in on our toast. I let out a laugh, raised my glass toward the branches of the tree, and then tilted my head back and took a drink.

There were still many uncertainties in the future, this much I knew. We all had our losses to grieve, I wasn't sure if the Breoch Guard were still a threat to me, and I had no idea what would happen when more young folks showed up here in a few months to seek safe haven.

But for now, I was home. And it was time to celebrate.

## THE END

# About the Author

Mary Walz was born and raised on the west coast of British Columbia. She's been writing stories since she was a child and wrote her first novel-length story at sixteen (spoiler: it wasn't very good). She's participated in several writing communities over the years and has won a few prizes for her short stories. When she is not writing, she can be found tending her garden, feeding the neighbourhood crows, baking delicious goodies, or running around in the woods dressed as a fairy or a wizard. She lives in Sidney, BC, a sleepy seaside town with one main street and about a dozen bookstores, with her husband Dave and her plant babies.

# Acknowledgements

THERE ARE MANY people without whom this book would not exist, and I am deeply grateful to each one of you.

TO MY HUSBAND, Dave- thank you for being the person who got me reading fantasy in the first place, and for sharing your love of swords and armour and LARP and fantastical worlds with me. Also thank you for letting me ignore you when I'm on writing binges, and for being an incredibly wonderful and supportive husband in general.

TO COLTON NELSON - thank you for allowing me to live the dream of becoming a published author. Thank you for the many hours of work put into formatting, giving feedback, cover design, promotion, and ultimately publishing Firebrand. Thank you for endless phone calls, silly memes, random cat videos, and general banter that has made this entire process much more entertaining than I anticipated. Ultimately, thank you for believing in me and being willing to take a chance on a newbie author.

TO ETHEL NEWBERRY - thank you for the many hours you put into polishing my work. Thank you for noticing the tiny inconsistencies and missed semicolons and grammar errors that I did not see. Thank you for the excellent communication, and the attention to detail that you put into all your work.

TO MY INCREDIBLE team of beta readers- Brianna Nichols, Gen Moore, Rowan Smith, Christie-Anne Dear, Joanna Hickman, Jessie Lampton, Christine Lavallee, Nathaniel Doherty, Nicholas Brossard, Meghan Walker, Patrick Lee, Helena Bown, Kelly Port, Bonnie Unwin, Zoe Baker, and Alissa Schactman- thank you so much for being willing to read through my manuscript and point out things that could be improved. My book is better because of all of you!

TO CHRISTINE LAVALLEE, Holly Maley and Maia Rocklin- thank you so much for your many hours of work on the earlier versions of the novel. You helped get Firebrand to a place where it could actually get picked up by a publisher, and I'm incredibly grateful for that.

TO ROWAN SMITH - thank you for your work on the cover art and the map. You helped make my book extra pretty, and I'm grateful for that.

**TO JAZ LAVERICK** - thank you for being the one to introduce me to RCN Media.

**TO MERCIE FALCONBERG** - thank you for being my first teen reader, and to Mercie's mother Dot Masingale- thank you for telling me that "Mercie's still talking about your book!" years after I let her read my (very rough) draft of it. Both of your encouragement has helped me get to where I am.

**TO ROBIN STEVENSON** and everyone in the Continuing Studies writing class that I took through UVic back in 2016- thank you for helping improve my early iterations of Firebrand and for providing excellent feedback on the first few chapters.

**TO JARED QWUSTENUXUN** Williams and Medieval Chaos Productions- thank you for giving me permission to adapt the spellcasting words from the Medieval Chaos magic system in order to create my own.

**TO LAURA AVERY** Brown- thank you for sharing your knowledge of all things nautical to make my ship scenes more believable.

**TO STEVIE BARNES,** my Bookrix buddy and international bestie- thank you for being one of the people who has read many of my works and encouraged me to keep writing as the years have passed. Your friendship and support mean the world to me.

**TO MY FAMILY** - my parents John and Penny, my siblings Alice and Ash, and my grandma Enid- thank you all listening to the crazy stories I made up as a child, reading and sharing my writing as I got older, and encouraging me to keep going. To my nieces, Ebi and Mae, I look forward to the day when you are old enough to read my stories. Love you all.

**AND LASTLY, TO** everyone who went out of their way to pick this book up and read it- thank you for giving me and my book a chance. I hope you enjoyed Firebrand, and I look forward to giving you more to read in the future.